George Thorn-Drury, Edmund Waller

The Poems of Edmund Waller;

George Thorn-Drury, Edmund Waller

The Poems of Edmund Waller;

ISBN/EAN: 9783744771771

Printed in Europe, USA, Canada, Australia, Japan

Cover: Foto ©Andreas Hilbeck / pixelio.de

More available books at **www.hansebooks.com**

THE POEMS

OF

EDMUND WALLER

EDITED BY

G. THORN DRURY.

LONDON:

LAWRENCE & BULLEN,
16 HENRIETTA STREET, W.C.

1893.

NEW YORK:

CHARLES SCRIBNER'S SONS,
743 & 745 BROADWAY.

1893.

London :
Printed by Henderson & Spalding, Limited,
Marylebone Lane, W.

PREFACE.

IF any justification be needed for the publication of a new edition of Waller's Poems, it will surely be found in the fact that they had for some time ceased to be accessible, except in the shape of second-hand copies.

I have adopted, as far as practicable, the text of the edition of 1686, the last published during the poet's life. I have noted the sources of such verses as are here printed for the first time, and I have omitted one poem, hitherto ascribed to Waller, the lines on "The British Princes," the MS. of which Thyer discovered among Butler's papers, in his autograph. I desire to express my sense of the great kindness I have received from Edmund Waller, Esq., the present representative of the poet, who has placed at my disposal everything in his possession relating to his ancestor, and has also allowed the two portraits which accompany this book to be reproduced from pictures in his possession—that of Edmund Waller from the picture by

Cornelis Janssens, and that of Lady Dorothy Sidney from a picture which was certainly in the poet's possession, and is believed to have been presented to him by Sacharissa herself. My thanks are also due to H. Buxton Forman, Esq., who very kindly allowed me to collate two rarities in his library, the folio edition of the " Panegyric," and the " Divine Poems " of 1685.

G. THORN DRURY.

THIS EDITION

OF

THE POEMS OF HIS ANCESTOR IS DEDICATED

TO

EDMUND WALLER, Esq.,

OF

FARMINGTON LODGE, NORTHLEACH.

INTRODUCTION.

INTRODUCTION.

A GREAT novelist has justified the mention of his hero's ancestors by the suggestion that he might, if they were omitted, be in danger of being supposed to have had none. In no sense is such an imputation true of Edmund Waller : the name which he has rendered familiar to so many (albeit they mispronounce it), was known long before his time as that of a family of great wealth and antiquity, originally settled in the county of Kent. From Groombridge, his seat, near Speldhurst, Richard Waller, afterwards sheriff of the county, set out to join Henry V. in France, and thither he returned from Agincourt, bringing with him Charles, Duke of Orleans, whom he had taken prisoner in the battle. For four-and-twenty years he kept the the Prince "in honourable confinement," and it is recorded of him, that during that time he rebuilt his own house and beautified the parish church, in the porch of which were carved his arms with the addition, the royal shield of France, and the motto " Hæc fructus virtutis," granted to him in memory of his exploit. His eldest son, another Richard Waller, married the daughter and heiress of Edmund Brudenell, lord of the manor of Coleshill, and this union no doubt led to the migration from Kent of that part of the family from which the poet was immediately descended. The exact date when the Wallers of Beaconsfield branched off from the main stock cannot now be ascertained, but it is certain that well back into the sixteenth century they were in possession of lands in Hertford-shire and Buckinghamshire, all of which appear to have eventually devolved upon Robert Waller, the father of the poet. Robert Waller had been bred to the study of the law, and for some time practised as a barrister, but his circumstances rendering this occupation un-necessary, he retired into the country and devoted himself to the improvement of his estates. He took for his wife, Anne, daughter of Griffith Hampden.[1] Edmund, their eldest son, was born on the 3rd of March, 1606, at the manor-house, Coleshill, a hamlet which then formed part of the county of Hertford, but which, since 1832, has been absorbed into Buckinghamshire. All traces of the mansion have disappeared, and the site upon which it is said to have stood is now occupied by a dilapidated farm-house, little better than a cottage, known as "Stocks Place," or "Old

1.—Her brother, William, was the father of the celebrated John Hampden by his marriage with Elizabeth, daughter of Sir Henry Cromwell and aunt of the Protector.

Stocks." From his birth-place, the future poet
was taken, on the 9th of March, to the parish
church at Amersham, or, as it was then called,
Agmondesham, to be baptized.[1] His father is
said to have sold his property at Coleshill and
to have betaken himself to another house of his
at Beaconsfield, which sadly weakens the
pleasant tradition that clings to a huge old oak
still standing in a little meadow at the back of
"Stocks Place." A niche cut in this tree has
been pointed out as Waller's favourite seat,
where he was wont to sit and write his verses ;
and if there are not now to be found in the
bark any initials which recall my Lady Carlisle
or Sacharissa, the swains of the neighbourhood
have done their best to make up for it by carving
almost every other conceivable combination of
letters. What little we know of his early
education is derived from Aubrey, who was
told by Waller himself that "he was bred under
severall ill, dull, and ignorant schoolmasters,
till he went to Mr. Dobson at Wickham, who
was a good schoolmaster and had been an

---

[1] The register containing the entry of his baptism is still to
be seen, and although one at least of his editors knew of the
existence of the " writ of oustre," reciting that on Oct. 4, 1616,
Edmund Waller was ten years —— months old (a word is
obliterated), it never seems to have occurred to him or any one
else to examine the register and make the obvious discovery that
the birth and baptism of the poet have been wrongly assigned
to 1605, in consequence of the practice of beginning the New
Year on March 25.

Eaton schollar," while one Mr. Thomas Bigge, who was in the same form with him at Mr. Dobson's school, and "was wont to make his exercise for him," confessed to the same authority, that "he little thought then he would have been so rare a poet."

Robert Waller died Aug. 26, 1616, lamenting the idle life he had led, and leaving a paper of advice to his son which, though it continued for several generations in the possession of the family, has now unfortunately disappeared. The care of the poet's education then devolved upon his mother, a lady of unusual capacity for business, and, if we may trust Aubrey, not without a sense of humour of a somewhat robust order. She sent him to Eton, and thence to Cambridge, where he was admitted a Fellow-Commoner of King's College, March 22, 1620. He had for his tutor a relative, who is said to have been a very learned man, and under him probably acquired some of that familiarity with the Latin language which he retained to the end of his life. His stay at the University can hardly have been a long one, and there is no record of his having taken a degree. He was, says Clarendon, "nursed in parliaments," but though the returns show that he was a member at an unusually early age, there is some difficulty in determining the date of his first entrance. According to the inscription on his monument, "nondum octodecennalis inter ardua regni tractantes sedem habuit a burgo de Agmondesham missus." **Now the** right of Amersham to return members was in abeyance till the last Parliament **of James I.** (Feb. **12, 1624),** when the **town was** represented **by** Hakeville **and Crew,** but it has **been suggested that** Waller was allowed **to** sit for **Amersham in the** previous Parliament, which met **Jan. 16, 1621,** *sub silentio,* without the privilege of taking **part in** the debates. **This view** is confirmed **by his own** statement **in the** House, that he **was but** sixteen when he **first sat,** which would **point rather to 1621 than 1624,** and **by the fact that,** according **to the** writer of his "Life" (ed. **1711), who had** it from **Dr. Birch, the** poet's son-in-law, **he** always assigned **to** the day **of the** *dissolution* **of a Parliament of which he was a member, a remarkable story,** without which **no biography of** him appears to be complete. **"He went, out of curiosity or respect, to see the King** at **dinner, with whom were Dr.** Andrews, **Bishop of Winchester, and Dr. Neal,** Bishop of Durham, **standing behind** his Majesty's chair; . . . **His Majesty asked the** Bishops, 'My **Lords, cannot I take my** subjects' money when **I** want **it without all this** formality **in Parliament?'** **The Bishop of Durham** readily answered, **'God forbid, Sir, but** you **should, you are the** breath of our nostrils:' Whereupon the **King turned, and said to** the Bishop **of** Winchester, **'Well, my Lord,** what **say you?'**

'Sir,' replied the Bishop, 'I have no skill to judge of Parliamentary cases :' The King answered, 'No puts-off, my Lord, answer me presently :' 'Then, Sir,' said he, 'I think it's lawful for you to take my Brother Neal's money, for he offers it.'" It is unnecessary to relate how James, with his customary coarseness, repaid this with a jest at the expense of the Bishop : the only point of the story in this connection is its date, the next Parliament, which met Feb. 12, 1624, being only dissolved by the King's death. In that assembly Waller's name appears as member for Ilchester, a seat which he obtained by favour of Nathaniel Tomkins, his brother-in-law, whose connection with the poet was afterwards to bring him to such a tragic fate. Tomkins appears to have been elected for Ilchester and Christchurch Twynham, and to have preferred to sit for the latter. Waller was member for Chipping Wycombe in the first Parliament of Charles I : he appears to have had no seat in the second, but represented Amersham in the third and fourth. His parliamentary career up to this time appears to have been uneventful : as he told the House in after years, there was then no great competition for seats, "the neighbourhood desired him to serve : there was a dinner, and so an end." Whatever may have been his poetical reputation up to the year 1631, Clarendon is probably right in saying that the first sensation Waller created was by his marriage.

John[1] Bankes, citizen and mercer, having amassed a considerable fortune, which he is credited with having worthily used, died Sept. 9, 1630, leaving an only daughter, Anne. A contest for the hand of the heiress at once arose, and even the Court condescended to interfere and to support with its influence the suit of Mr. William Crofts, afterwards Baron Crofts of Saxham, but another aspirant had influences nearer at hand, and through the agency of a relative, Capt. Henry Waller (a citizen), and his wife, Mistress Bankes was conveyed out of the jurisdiction of the Court of Aldermen, of which she was a ward, into the country, and there contracted in marriage to the poet. The marriage was celebrated July 5, 1631, at St. Margaret's Westmister.

This was too much for the Court of Aldermen —they brought the matter before the Lords of the Council, instituted proceedings in the Star Chamber against Waller, and all who had aided and abetted him, and sent a sergeant-at-arms in search of the bride. Mrs. Edmund Waller, having been brought back, was lodged in the custody of the Lord Mayor, Sir Robert Ducie,

---

[1] The inscription on Waller's monument says, "Edward," but the "Repertories" and Maitland's London (3rd edition) ii. 1151, unite in giving "John" as the Christian name.

and duly appeared with her husband before the
outraged City Fathers. The poet was told that
as the lady had chosen to marry him without
the consent of her guardians, she had forfeited
her portion, but that having regard to the fact
that he had, as they were informed, settled upon
her a jointure of £1,000 a year, and had also
given her power to dispose of £2,000 of her
fortune at her own pleasure, the Court was
inclined, notwithstanding the custom of the City
and the expenses incurred in prosecuting the
suit against him and his accomplices before the
Lords of the Council and the Star Chamber, to
take a lenient view of the case, and to accept
a fine of five hundred marks, to be deducted out
of so much of his wife's portion as remained in
the hands of the Chamberlain, after which
the balance would be handed to him. This
generosity on the part of the Aldermen does
not appear to have been altogether spontaneous,
and Court influence, however unsuccessful in
support of Mr. Crofts' suit, prevailed on behalf
of Waller. On Dec. 15, 1631, Mrs. Waller's
ex-guardians were informed by letter from the
King, that, as he had pardoned Edmund Waller
and the rest of the defendants to the information
before the Star Chamber, he expected like
clemency on their part, and the payment of
Mrs. Waller's portion to her husband. The
fortune which Waller inherited from his father,
which must have been largely increased during

his long minority, has been variously estimated
at from £2,000 to £3,500 a year ; adding to this
the amount which he received with Miss Bankes,
said to have been about £8,000, and allowing for
the difference in the **value of** money, it appears
probable that, with the exception of Rogers, the
history of English literature can show **no** richer
poet. " Waller himself," says Oldham, meaning
no disrespect to his powers,

> " Waller himself may thank inheritance
> For what **he** else, had never got by sense."

The few years **during** which the poet was to
enjoy the society **of his first wife were** spent at
Beaconsfield: **there, on May 18, 1**633, his eldest
son was born, **and there, but a few** months later,
his wife **died in giving** birth **to a** daughter,
baptized **on** Oct. **23,** 1634, **the day** of her
mother's funeral, by the significant **names of**
Anne Marah. **Waller's first marriage has**
generally been **regarded as** a mercenary one, and
even **those of his** biographers **who have not**
been **most** eager **to turn everything to** his
disadvantage **have treated his** capture **of the**
heiress as something in **the nature of an exploit ;**
whatever **his relations with** her before **and**
during his married **life, the poet,** writing nearly
fifty years **later to his niece,** Lady Speke, to
console her for the death of her son, reminds
her of the grief he himself suffered in the loss of
an **excellent** wife, **of** which she was then his
witness **and his** comforter.

We have no certain information as to the course of Waller's life during the next year or two, but it is probable that it was about this time that he obtained an entrance into the society which gathered round Lucius Carey, Lord Falkland, which was known as his "club." This, according to Clarendon, the poet owed to the good offices of George Morley, afterwards Bishop of Winchester. The writer of the "Life" prefixed to the edition of 1711, transfers the obligation, and says that the members of the "club," among whom was Waller, being one day disturbed by a noise in the street, sent to ascertain the cause of it, and were informed that a "son" of Ben Jonson was being arrested for debt ; this member of the tribe of Benjamin proved to be the future Bishop, with whose appearance and conversation the poet was so delighted that he immediately paid his debt, £100, and took him home to live with him. George Morley's pecuniary difficulties were no doubt serious enough to justify one part of this story, but as Clarendon was himself a member of the society in question, his account of Waller's introduction to it is obviously to be preferred. It seems to be agreed that, for some time at least, Morley was an inhabitant of Waller's house and directed his studies, but it is difficult to reconcile any lengthened stay with the position of domestic chaplain which he occupied,

for many years previous to 1640, in the family
of the Earl of Carnarvon.

By Lord Falkland and his friends, among
whom were Sir Francis Wenman, Chillingworth,
and Sidney Godolphin, Waller **was** "received
and esteemed with great applause." **His semi-**
public recognition as a poet, which Clarendon
assigns to his thirtieth year, **can hardly have**
been separated **by** any long interval from his
introduction to this society. About this time
too, in all probability, began his connection with
the lady whom, as Aubrey **says, "he has**
eternized in his poems." The subject is involved
in uncertainty, and **one** is surprised to find,
upon examination, how very slender are the
links which bind together the names of Waller
and Sacharissa. Sacharissa (a name which **the**
poet formed, **"as** he used **to say** pleasantly,"
from *sacharum*, sugar), **or** Lady Dorothy
Sidney, was the eldest daughter of Robert,
second Earl **of** Leicester, and Dorothy, daughter
of Henry, ninth Earl **of** Northumberland. She
was born at Sion House, and baptized Oct. 5,
1617, at Isleworth.[1]

It is impossible **to** say exactly when she first
attracted the attention of Waller : " a very good
friend" of the **poet's told the** writer of his " Life"

---

[1] This information, which Mrs. Ady ("Sacharissa," by Julia
Cartwright, 1893) appears to announce as a discovery, **we**
owe **to Peter** Cunningham, who inserted it in a note to his
edition of Johnson's " Lives."

(1711) that he "believed his first wife was dead before he became enamoured of my Lady Dorothy Sidney"; but it seems to me that the key to the situation, so far as there is one, is supplied by the poem, "To my Lord of Leicester" (p. 47). The Earl of Leicester is in France, and Waller begs him to return to England to determine by his prudent choice the contention which has arisen among them for "one bright nymph," his daughter, and goes on to speak of—

> "That beam of beauty, *which begun*
> *To warm us so when thou wert here.*"

The Earl left for France, May 17, 1636, and though he is said, presumably before his departure, to have loved the poet, and to have been willing to give him one of his younger daughters (he had a large family), I think it is hardly likely that Waller can have begun to pay his addresses, in any form, to Lady Dorothy till towards the end of the year 1635. Aubrey says that he was passionately in love with the lady, and even goes so far as to suggest that his rejection by her was probably the cause of a fit of madness, from which village-gossip told him the poet had suffered. Later critics have been by no means inclined to accept this view of the situation. Nothing in the verses which Waller addressed to Sacharissa has been more re-marked than the absence of anything like the appearance of passion; it does not, however, it seems to me, follow that the poet's love was not real, or that it was, as has been suggested, merely the outcome of ambition. He was no doubt vain, and, in a sense, shallow, and if his love did not express itself with that fervency which burns in some of the earlier verses of Donne, for instance, it was because his nature was essentially different, and he gave of that he had. Waller is the last man in the world in whose published writings one would expect to find anything of self-revelation, and without materials it is worse than useless to attempt to follow the course of his suit. It is perfectly true that almost all the poems which we can directly assign to the inspiration of Sacharissa, appear to have been written upon " occasions," but to conclude, on that account, that the poet only addressed her when he was "sure to make a direct social sensation," is to misunderstand the nature of Waller's poetical endowments.

He was practically without " invention," and if he now and then succeeded in giving to his verse the appearance of being " inevitable," it was only because those happy moments which occasionally visited so many of the lyrists of the seventeeth century were not wholly absent from his literary life. There is not, as far as I know, any authority for connecting the name of Sacharissa with the famous lines " On a Girdle" (p. 95), or with the still more famous song, " Go, lovely rose " (p. 128) : they may, or may not, have been addressed to her ; in any case our appreciation of them is hardly likely to be increased by certain knowledge on the subject.

The exact date at which Waller abandoned his suit is no more attainable than that of its beginning : he was still offering his poetical homage in the latter half of the year 1638, and one cannot help thinking that " haughty Sacharissa's scorn " must have been manifested, not so much by any peremptory rejection of him, as by a more humiliating but good-tempered refusal to regard his pretensions in any serious light at all. The following letter[1] has been dated May, 1639, by the compilers of the " Calendars of State Papers," but there is nothing in the document itself to favour that or any other ascription.

" Madam

" The handkercher I receaved frō Mi^{ts} Vane having so neer resemblance to a dream, wch presents us wth a mixture of things that have no affinitye one wth another, I have (as the Assirian kings did wth their dreams) consulted wth all the magicians & cunning woemen in our countrie, & though it be easie to see through it, I finde none that can enterpret it ; I am sending it to Oxford to the Astrologers to know yf ther be any constellations or fygures

---

[1] The original is to be found among the State Papers, Dom. Ch. 1. ccccxxii. 122 ; it has been imperfectly and incorrectly printed by Mrs. Ady, " Sacharissa," pp. 44-5.

in the upper Globe to wch those in the 4 corners
may allude, for on Earth the Herball tells us of
nothing like them : I did first apprehend it was
as a potent **charme,** having power like the
wande of Cyrce, to transforme mee into some
strange shape[1] but the **crosses in** the middle
perswading **mee it was a good** Christian
handkercher I ventured to wipe my face wth it,
when the golden fringe wth a rough salute told
me it was **for** some nobler use : Madam **I**
beseech your **La**ᵖ **use your interest** in hir to
unriddle this handkercher **wch** so perplexes us.
I am sorrie that a **Ladie of** so various a phansye
hath not the power of framing living things too,
that wee might behold some **new** compositions
and kindes **of** things **wch dull nature never**
thought **of :** seriously (Madam) **I humbly kiss**
hir hands for **this fauor,** wch **not** being **to be**
wasted **by** use, **I shall** æternally keepe for **hir**
sake, and **doe** presume shee will pardon this
rambling acknowled**gement** made in imitation
of the style of hir handkercher ; **by (Madam)**
Yʳ **L**ᵖˢ most humble servant

"**Edm.** Waller."

On the outside, "for my Ladye Dorothye
Sidney."

Whether "**Mistress Vane**" was a name **by**
which **Lady Dorothy chose to** be known to her
admirer, or whether **the gift** simply reached the

---

1 After this some words have been written and obliterated,
apparently, " yf I but touched my nose wth it."

2

poet by the hand of one Mistress Vane, one cannot now tell, but it can hardly be that he was writing his "acknowledgement" to Sacharissa, and promising her "æternally to keep" the handkerchief of "another Kentish young lady, a member of the Vane family," as Mrs. Ady supposes him to have been. Though Mr. Waller is never mentioned, there were other possible suitors for the hand of her daughter, upon whose eligibility Lady Leicester had to report to her husband in Paris : now it is Lord Russell, now Lord Devonshire, and now Lord Lovelace who is to be the happy man, but all these gentleman, one after another, disappointed expectations, either by fixing their affections elsewhere or by failing to come up to the requisite moral standard. At last, on July 20, 1639, Sacharissa was married at Penshurst to Lord Spencer of Wormleighton, afterwards created Earl of Sunderland, and for years passed completely out of Waller's life. The following letter, (first printed in 1711) the poet addressed to Lady Lucy, the sister of the bride, upon the occasion of the wedding.

"Madam,

"In this common joy at Penshurst I know none to whom complaints may come less unseasonable than to your Ladyship, the loss of a bed-fellow being almost equal to that of a mistress ; and therefore you ought, at least to pardon, if you consent not **to the** imprecations of the deserted, which just Heaven no doubt will hear. May my **Lady** Dorothy, if we may yet call her so, suffer as much **and** have the **like** passion for this young Lord, whom she has preferred **to the rest of** mankind, **as** others have had for her ; and may this **love,** before the year **go** about, make h**er taste of the first** curse imposed on womankind, the **pains of** becoming a mother. May her first born be none **of her own** sex, nor so like her, **but that he may** resemble her Lord as much **as** herself. May she that always affected silence and retiredness, have the house filled with the noise **and** number of **her** children, and hereafter of **her** grand-children, and then may **she arrive at that great curse so** much declined **by fair ladies, old age :** may she live to be very **old, and** yet seem young, be told so by her glass, **and have no aches to** inform her of the truth : **and when she** shall appear to be mortal, may her Lord not mourn **for** her, but go hand in hand **with her to that place where we** are told **there is** neither marrying nor giving in marriage, **that** being there **divorced** we may all have **an equal interest in her** again. My revenge being **immortal, I** wish **all** this may also befall **their posterity to the world's** end, and afterwards.

To you, Madam, I wish all good things, and **that this loss may in** good time be happily supplied with **a** more constant bed-fellow of the

opposite sex.   Madam, I humbly kiss your
hand, and beg pardon for this trouble, from
    " Your Ladyship's most humble Servant,
                    "E. Waller."

Thus ends the Sacharissa episode in Waller's
life, and if one is disposed to take offence at
the manner in which he applied to himself the
story of Phœbus and Daphne, and the conceit
of his declaration that

    " what he sung in his immortal strain,
    Though unsuccessful was not sung in vain,"

it can only be said that so far at least his
remarkable confidence has been justified. However genuine his passion for Lady Dorothy, we
may be sure that his vanity would prevent him
from suffering to any serious extent for her loss,
and the story of his voyage and shipwreck on
the Bermudas may be dismissed, resting as it
does on nothing but the vaguest tradition. There
is on p. 75 a poem headed " When he was at
sea," but it is probable that Waller was no more
responsible for the title of this, than he was for
those of many other sets of verses which
appeared among his poems after his death.

The year 1640 saw Waller again returned to
Parliament as member for Amersham : an
account of the circumstances under which the
House met on April 13 belongs rather to the
history of England than to a brief review of the
life of any individual. Though it fully deserved
its title of " Short," during the few weeks that

this Parliament **sat** Waller gave unmistakable
signs of the nature **of** his political creed. He
was at heart **a** courtier, and if his relationship
to John Hampden caused him, **for a time, to**
throw **in** his lot with the popular party, **he never**
forgot **to** speak **of the** King in terms of exaggerated respect : **of** innovations of any sort he
had a natural horror, and **the** immediate **prospect of a** serious change **in** the constitution **of**
Church or State was enough to throw him **into
the** arms of those who opposed **it.**

On April 22 he made **his first** great speech
in the House, upon **the** question of Supply,
characterized by Johnson as " one of those noisy
speeches which disaffection and discontent
regularly dictate **; a** speec**h filled** with **hyper-**
bolical complaints **of imaginary** grievances."
The reality **of the** grievances **of** which Waller
complained is hardly open to discussion, **and**
upon the tone of his speech **one** may well differ
even with **Dr.** Johnson. Their presence **in that**
House, says the **poet, after such a** long inter-
mission of parliaments, is sufficient evidence of
his Majesty's occasions for **money :** let them
give the lie to **those who would have** dissuaded
him from **calling** them together, and let them
prove to him that **no new** way of government is
so ready **or so** safe for the advancement **of** his
affairs as that ancient and constitutional **way,**
by Parliaments. They must do their best even
at that **stage to** comply with his Majesty's

desires, in the face of the dangers that threaten
them, but they have a duty to those whom they
represent—the rights of liberty and of property
are sacred—if these be not restored to the
people, no evils that threaten can have any
terrors for them, they are undone already. The
King will surely restore these rights, for what
they have suffered they have suffered at the
hands of his ministers, else how comes it that
there was never king better beloved and never
people more dissatisfied with the ways of levy-
ing money ? The King must be told the truth,
more particularly concerning those ecclesiastics
who would persuade him that his monarchy is
absolute, a form of government unheard of in
this nation. They all know the dangers of
innovations, though to the better,—why should
so good a king be exposed to the trouble and
hazard of them, no, let him restore to his people
their fundamental liberties and the property of
their goods, and he will see that the House will
make more than ordinary haste to satisfy his
demands.—Further evidence of Waller's con-
ciliatory attitude is afforded by the story which
the writer of his "Life" (1711) tells in connection
with this Parliament. The King, it appears,
had sent to Waller to ask him to second in the
House his demand for supplies, and though the
poet was unable to do this, he strongly remon-
strated with Sir Thomas Jermyn, the Comptroller of the Household, for allowing to pass

uncontradicted a statement **of Sir Henry** Vane,
that the King would accept no vote that did not
come up **to** his demand : **" I "** **said** the poet, "am
but a country gentleman, and cannot pretend **to**
know the King's mind." **Sir Thomas, however,**
was silent, and years afterwards, his **son,** the
Earl **of St.** Albans, told Waller that his father's
cowardice had ruined the King. This Parliament was dissolved **May 5, and** with that
which followed **we** enter upon **the most**
momentous period **of** Waller's life. In the
Long Parliament, which met **Nov. 3,** 1640,
Waller **was** returned for **St.** Ives. He obtained
this seat through **the** resignation of **Lord** Lisle,
who preferred **to sit for Yarmouth, in the Isle**
of Wight, for which **he had also been** elected.
In the attack on the **Earl of** Strafford which
followed **the meeting of** Parliament, **Waller**
abandoned the **party of Pym** and his adherents.
It being alleged **that the** Earl had attempted **to**
subvert **"the** fundamental **laws of the** realm,"
Waller characteristically **asked in the** House,
what **these "**fundamental laws **"** were, and was
told **by** Maynard, **for** his pains, that if he did
not know, he had **no** business to sit there.

According **to his own** account **of the Earl of**
Strafford's **case, given many** years afterwards,
a state **of** terror prevailed among the members,
"a **fellow upon a barrell** in Westminster Hall
proclaimed **all traitors that** gave votes for him "
—**he** himself was one that did, and he **was in**

consequence **obliged to** pass himself off **on the mob** as Sir Arthur Hazelrigg.

In the debate upon the Ecclesiastical **Petitions, Feb.** 1641, Waller drew tighter the bonds which **united** him to such men **as Falkland and Hyde.**

His speech upon the Abolition of Episcopacy **has been praised by** Johnson as cool, firm, and **reasonable, though in** reality the spirit of it is **absolutely** consistent **with that which** imbued **his previous speech upon the question of Supply. He was not an** opponent **of ship- money because he wished to substitute the power of the people for the** prerogative **of the King, but because it was an** irregular **method of raising money, an innovation :** similarly, **he did not oppose the abolition of episcopacy** because **he thought his action would be** agreeable **either to Bishops or to King, but because** he saw **in the blow aimed at the** former **an** attempt to alter **the** constitution of the **Church, in fine, another innovation.** Doubtless, **he** said, this and that **poor man has suffered at** the hands of the **Bishops, but may** you **not soon** be presented **with thousands of instances of poor** men who **have received hard measure** from their **land- lords ? Scripture, it is** said, points out another **form of church-government : I will not** dispute **it in this place, but I am confident that** when- **ever an equal division of** lands **and** goods shall **be desired, there will be as many places in**

Scripture found out, which seem to favour that, as there are now alleged against the Prelacy or preferment in the Church. We have already curbed the power of the Bishops, let us not by acceding to this petition for the abolition of their office lead the people to think that if they but ask in troops we must deny them nothing. Let our answer be *nolumus mutare.*—Neither his action in the matter of the impeachment of Strafford, nor his speech on behalf of episcopacy, deprived Waller of the confidence of the popular leaders, and he was chosen to carry up to the House of Lords the articles of impeachment against Sir Francis Crawley, whose judgment and extra-judicial opinions upon the question of ship-money had rendered him particularly obnoxious to the Commons. It was probably thought that his relationship to Hampden would add a bitterness to his natural eloquence, and he appears to have realized the expectations of the most exacting. His speech, in presenting the charge, was delivered at a conference of both Houses in the Painted Chamber, July 6, 1641. It is unnecessary even to summarize it; Waller had joined in the groans which greeted the judgment in the Exchequer, and the position he took up with regard to ship-money was that of every opponent of the tax since its institution. His oration had evidently been most carefully prepared, but the scriptural and classical quotations and illustrations, numerous even for Waller, give it a tone altogether too academic for the occasion, and deprive it of any appearance of natural indignation in the speaker : it was, however, immensely popular among the poet's contemporaries, and twenty thousand copies of it are said to have been sold in one day. Waller's speeches in the House during the months that immediately followed his attack upon Crawley have not been preserved, but the following extract from a letter (dated Oct. 29, 1641) from Sir Edward Nicholas to the King leaves no doubt as to their tendency. "I may not forbeare," the Secretary writes, "to let yor Matie know, that the Lo^r : Falkland, S^r Jo. Strangwishe, M Waller, M^r Ed. Hide and Mr Holborne and diverse others stood as Champions in maynten'nce of yo Prerogative, and shewed for it unaunswerable reason and undenyable p^esidents, whereof yo Matie shall doe well to take some notice (as yo Matie shall thinke best) for their encouragem't." Upon the letter Charles has written, "I comande you to doe it in my name telling them that I will doe it myselfe at my return."

Before the end of the year Waller was involved in a direct conflict with Pym. The incident took place on the 5th of November, upon the occasion of settling the instructions for the committee on the subject of requesting the assistance of Scotland in suppressing the Irish Rebellion. Pym proposed to add a declaration that "howsoever we had engaged ourselves for the assistance of Ireland, yet unless the King would remove his evil counsellors and take such counsellors as might be approved of by Parliament, we should account ourselves absolved from this engagement." This, Waller said, was but little removed from the advice that the Earl of Strafford had given the King, that if Parliament did not relieve him, he was absolved from all rules of government. Pym took exception to the comparison. Waller was ordered to withdraw, and the matter having been debated in his absence, he was called in and told by the Speaker that "the House holds it fit that in his place he should acknowledge his offence given by his words both to the House in general and to Mr. Pym in particular : which he did ingenuously and expressed his sorrow for it."

It is apparently to this period that Clarendon's first mention of Waller relates. The Chancellor, for whatever reason, was no friend to the poet, and his testimony has coloured the accounts of later biographers. "When," he says, "the ruptures grew so great between the King and the two Houses, that very many of the members withdrew from those Councils, he, among the rest, with equal dislike absented himself ; but at the time the Standard was set up, (*Aug. 25, 1642*) having intimacy and friendship with some persons now of nearness about the King, with the King's approbation he returned again to London." This is distinctly contradicted by Waller's own statement, communicated by his son-in-law, Dr. Birch, to the writer of his "Life" (1711), and in any case it cannot be correct as to date, for he was certainly in his place in the House on July 9th, opposing the proposition that Parliament should raise an army of 10,000 men. He is said to have sent the King a thousand broad pieces when he raised his Standard at Nottingham. Clarendon gives him credit for subsequently speaking in the House "upon all occasions with great sharpness and freedom;" indeed, when some of the members declared that they were not allowed to express their sentiments freely, they were told that that was an idle allegation, "when all men knew what liberty Mr. Waller took, and spoke every day with impunity against the sense and proceedings of the House." In spite of his open declaration of his sentiments, it has been charged against Waller that he chose to sit and act the dishonourable part of a spy on behalf of the King, instead of taking active service in the field. The fact is, Waller had no real aptitude for politics, and no very deep political convictions : he found in the House of Commons a convenient theatre for the display of his remarkable eloquence, and his advocacy of the King's interests was well in accord with the selfish promptings of a rich man who has everything to lose and nothing to gain by innovation : he was "impatient," as he afterwards said " of the inconvenience of the war," he looked upon things with "a carnal eye " ; and he considered that nothing would so surely conduce to his personal comfort as an arrangement between the parties. When, therefore, on Oct. 29, the Lords proposed to negotiate with the King, one is not surprised to find his voice raised two days later in urgent appeal to the Commons to join them. The year 1643 opened with every prospect of the realization of his hopes. In January the desire of the City for peace had been manifested by petitions and clamorous assemblies, and on Feb. 1 Charles accorded a gracious reception to the Commissioners appointed by the House to treat with him.

When Waller, who was one of them, came, last of all in order of precedence, to kiss his hand, the King said to him, " Mr. Waller, though you are the last, yet you are not the worst, nor the least in our favour." Deep significance has been attached to these words : it has been suggested, on the one hand, that they betrayed a knowledge on the part of the King that Waller was already plotting some secret design on his behalf; on the other, that this " affectionate reproof " so wrought upon the poet that he was thereupon led to engage himself. Injudicious as it was, upon any view of it, I see no reason to suppose that this speech was any more than an acknowledgment, possibly that promised in the indorsement on Nicholas's letter, of open services in the House of Commons. It is impossible now to ascertain the date of the inception of "Waller's Plot," but it is significant that the Commission of Array, of which so much was afterwards made, is dated March 16, nearly a month before the recall of the Commissioners from Oxford, and that both Tomkins and Chaloner, in their dying speeches, declared that they had taken part in the conspiracy at the instigation of Waller.

An attempt has been made to distinguish the enterprise which bears the poet's name from another design, said to have been set on foot about the same time by Sir Nicholas Crispe. Waller's object, it has been said, was to render the continuance of the war impossible by raising up in the City a peace-party strong enough to defy the House and to refuse to pay the weekly assessments, while Crispe intended nothing less than the capture of London by force of arms. No doubt, the dissatisfaction which many felt at the failure of the petition for peace and the continuance of the weekly impositions, afforded favourable ground to build upon (it was said that the King's friends had fomented the discontent by urging the citizens to carry their grievances to the Committee at Haberdashers' Hall, well knowing they would get no relief), and perhaps some of the conspirators, Waller among them, expected, or rather hoped, that their object would be attained without bloodshed ; but however **varied** their hopes and expectations **as to the** issue, there can be no doubt that there **was but one** design, **the securing of** the **City of London, and that that received its** inspiration from the **advisers of** the King **at Oxford ;** even Waller himself, **at the** Bar **of the** House, **did not attempt to deny that he knew of** the proposal to resort **to arms, he only said he** "**disallowed** and rejected it." **Though he was** probably speaking **the truth when he** said he "made **not this** business **but found it"—he was not** a man **of sufficiently determined and independent** character **to have originated** such an enterprise— he was **undoubtedly at** the head of operations in **London. He** procured Nathaniel Tomkins, **Clerk of the Queen's Counsel, who had married his sister Cecilia, and Richard** Chaloner, **a wealthy linen-draper, to take the** necessary **steps among the citizens,** while he himself **undertook to forward the project** among **the** members **of the two Houses.** Hassell, **one of the King's** messengers, **and** Alexander **Hampden were to take advantage of** those occasions **when they came up from** Oxford **with "gracious** messages" **from** Charles to the **Parliament, to carry back with** them to Lord **Falkland news of the progress of** the enterprise.

Hassell appears to have been "horsed" by

Waller, and in the intervals of his service to have lain at the poet's house at Beaconsfield. It fell to the lot of Chaloner, Tomkins, and others whom they had engaged, to make lists of the inhabitants of the various parishes, marking them according to their dispositions, as Right-men, Roundheads, and Neuters. Tomkins appears to have ascertained the feeling in his own parish, St. Andrew's, Holborn, by introducing an Irish bishop as lecturer, and then calling meetings at his house for the pretended purpose of gathering subscriptions to reward him.

These lists, when completed, were taken to Waller, who was then living in the neighbourhood of his brother-in-law, at the lower end of Holborn, near Hatton House. It was obvious that nothing could be done without the sinews of war, and accordingly Hassell was despatched to Oxford, and returned with an authority, dated May 2, addressed to Chaloner, to receive subscriptions of money and plate on behalf of the King, who bound himself to repay them, On May 19, Alexander Hampden arrived, ostensibly to demand from the Parliament an answer to the King's message of April 12, and in his company came Lady Daubigny, bringing with her the Commission of Array, dated March 16, and having attached to it the Great Seal. It is said to have been handed to her by Charles himself, with the intimation that it was something that greatly concerned his service, of which she would be relieved upon her arrival in London. According to one account, she concealed it, during the journey, in her hair, according to another, in the crown of a beaver hat. It was directed to Sir Nicholas Crispe, among others, and a former servant of his, one Blinkhorne, a clerk in the Custom House, fetched it from Lady Daubigny, and delivered it to Chaloner. At various times during the progress of the plot Waller had assured the citizens that they would have the co-operation of many members of both Houses, but he excused himself from giving their names on the plea of an oath he had taken, not to reveal them till the time of action. The conspirators proposed to rise, if possible, when the outworks were guarded by such of the trained bands as contained the greatest proportion of men friendly to themselves, to seize upon the defences of the City, the magazines, and the Tower, from which they intended to liberate the Earl of Bath, and make him their general. The King, having been warned of the day, and, if possible, of the hour of the rising, was to be within fifteen miles with a force of three thousand men, which was to be admitted as soon as any part of the defences was in the hands of his friends. His two children were to be secured, and also the Lord Mayor, Lord Saye, Lord Wharton, Pym,

Strode, and other members of the House of Commons.

On Friday, May 26, there was a meeting of the conspirators at Waller's house, when Chaloner flatly told him that the citizens had done their part, and that until they were assured of the co-operation of the Lords, of whom he had spoken, either by a meeting with them or by writing under their hands, they would proceed no farther in the business. Waller hastened to reassure him, and submitted to him a series of questions, which he had, so he said, just received from one of those very Lords—he afterwards said he had them from Conway, and they are just such as his military instincts would have been likely to dictate. The citizens went off with the list of questions and returned to Waller, the next morning, with their answers.

It appears from these that the conspirators calculated upon having a majority of three to one against them within the walls, but a similar majority in their favour outside : but one third of their whole force would be fully armed, the remainder with halberds and such weapons as they could lay their hands on : they had ascertained the situations of the magazines, but doubted of their ability to capture the Tower : they intended to distinguish themselves by wearing pieces of white tape or ribbon, and the watch-word was to be " The India ship is in the Downs " : the time at which the attempt should be made, and the rendezvous, they left to be determined by the Lords, who were also to fix upon a place, Blackheath and Banstead were suggested, to which they could retreat if necessary. Waller drew up a declaration, which began, " We, the Knights, Gentlemen, Citizens, Burgesses and Commons of England," and went on to assert that "the cause of their taking up arms was to maintain the true reformed Protestant Religion against all Papists and Sectaries, the Laws of the Land, Privilege of Parliament, and Liberty of the Subject, and to oppose all illegal Taxations, Assessments, and the like." This was to be printed and posted, or otherwise distributed upon the night of the rising. Matters were considered to be in such a satisfactory state, that Hassell was again despatched in the afternoon of May 29 with a message to Falkland, who returned a verbal answer, begging them to hasten the execution of their enterprise. Hassell appears to have rarely carried any written communications, but on this occasion he had a few lines of instruction in Latin, which are said to have been sewn in his saddle by Mrs. Tomkins's maid. On the night of Tuesday, May 30, Waller, after speaking with great confidence in the House, returned home with his brother-in-law in high glee—"By God !" he cried, "if we can bring to pass this business, we will have anything !" Before morning, he and the other conspirators were under arrest.

Various causes seem to have combined to arouse the suspicions of the popular leaders. An imprudent letter, possibly brought by Hampden, from the Earl of Dover to his wife, warning her to leave London, had fallen into the hands of the Committee, and several days before the actual discovery of the plot Lord Denbigh had told them of hints which he had received that it would be better for him to retire to the country. On May 23, Hampden had asked for a pass to return to Oxford, but this, after a conference between the two Houses on the following day, had been refused, and he was detained, how, it is not said, to be examined upon some informations they had received. It had also been predicted by one, who had it from Hassell, that in ten days London would be in flames : the fact that Hassell was known to be on terms of familiarity with Waller and Tomkins directed attention to them, and finally the Earl of Manchester and Lord Saye succeeeded in bribing one Roe, Tomkins's clerk, and it was upon his information that the poet and his friends were arrested. The Earl of Dover's letter had been publicly read at a committee of examination, and the substance of it reported to the House, and this, with the arrest of Hampden, D'Ewes thinks, ought to have put Waller on his guard, more particularly as he had fallen under suspicion some months previously, when some saddles, which he had bought, were found at his house and confiscated. It was obviously the cue of the popular party, once they had the conspirators under lock and key, to make as much as possible of their discovery, and one cannot help suspecting that the manner of its announcement was arranged with an eye to effect. Wednesday, May 31, being a Fast Day, the members were assembled, as usual, in St. Margaret's Church, Westminster, when the service was interrupted by the sudden entrance of the Speaker's mace-bearer, who summoned Pym and some of the others to follow him at once to the House. The wildest rumours were circulated, and the general belief was that the Danes had landed in Kent, and, before night, might be expected in London. Gradually the truth leaked out, and it became known that a plot had been discovered, that the prisons and Laud's chamber in the Tower had been searched, and that Waller, Tomkins, Chaloner, Hampden, Hassell, Blinkhorne, Abbot, a scrivener, and White, a merchant, had been arrested. A committee of the House, consisting of Pym, Sir Gilbert Gerard, young Sir Harry Vane, the Solicitor General, and Glyn, the Recorder of London, was at once appointed to take such measures as they might think best for the public safety. The greatest reticence was maintained, and it was not until June 6 that Pym brought up to the House of Commons the report of the Committee, and their recommendations, which included the "Solemn League and Covenant." He repeated his account of the plot to the Lords on the following day, and again on the afternoon of Thursday the 8th, at a Common Hall, summoned by the Lord Mayor.

It is impossible to maintain that Waller played any but an ignoble part in the transactions which followed, but his conduct has lost none of its meanness in the hands of Lord Clarendon. Confounded, he says, with fear and apprehension, Mr. Waller "confessed whatever he had said, heard, thought, or seen, all that he knew of himself, and all that he suspected of others, without concealing any person of what degree or quality soever, or any discourse that he had ever upon any occasion entertained with them : what such and such ladies of great honour, to whom, upon the credit of his great wit, and very good reputation, he had been admitted, had spoke to him in their chambers of the proceedings in the Houses ; and how they had encouraged him to oppose them : what correspondence and intercourse they had with some ministers of State at Oxford ; and how they derived all intelligence thither." He informed them, "that the Earl of Portland and Lord Conway had been particular in all the agitations which had been with the citizens, and had given frequent advice, and directions how they should demean themselves ; and that the Earl of Northumberland, had expressed very good wishes to any attempt, that might give a stop to the violent actions and proceedings of the Houses, and produce a good understanding with the King." He goes on to say, "When the Committee were thus furnished, they took the examination of Mr. Tomkins," &c. Now, there is no evidence whatever, except this statement, that the *first* confession came from Waller ; on the contrary, the accounts of those who were on the spot rather go to show that Clarendon is as inaccurate in the main charge as he most certainly is in its details. D'Ewes says that Waller was " drawn after much tergiversation and shuffling to confess his own guilt," and he records, quoting Glyn's speech in the House, that "Mrs. Challenor said that a little after Mr. Waller was taken there was come to her a Lady in a hired coach and given herself a fained name and told her she was like to come in great danger about a writing in parchment to which there hung a great seale, and desired her if she had it in her custody shee would deliver it to her, and when the said Mrs. Challenor told her that it had been lately fetcht away in a blacke box, shee then desired her if she could use any possible meanes to come to her husband, shee should go to him and tell him that *Mr. Waller had confessed nothing*, and that there-

fore shee should persuade him to doe the like.
That the said Mrs. Challenor was since brought
to see the Lady Aubigny and affirmed that it
was the same Lady who came to her in the
hackney coach." The suggestion that some
members of the Upper House were privy to the
design must have come originally from some
person other than Waller, for when it was put
to him, he denied upon oath that he had communicated with any of the Lords upon the
subject. Some sort of inducement was no
doubt held out to him to tell all he knew, and
it is even possible that he *was* " troubled in
Conscience for his solemn professing in the
presence of God that he had not spoke with
any of the Lords concerning this designe, when
he was examined, and yet had done it," but in
any case, it was not till June 12 that he mentioned the names of Portland and Conway,
and, a fortnight later, that of the Earl of Northumberland, and in his speech at the Bar of
the House he confessed that at first he had
concealed some truth, not for his own sake, but
that of others. The only ladies who were called
to account, for their share in the plot, were
Lady Daubigny and Lady Sophia Murray, and
the evidence Waller gave against them was
incidental to his charge against the Lords.
Lady Daubigny, he said, had fallen out with
him, when she heard from Portland that he
(Waller) had told him that she had brought the

Commission of Array; and he had helped Lady Sophia Murray to decipher a letter from Falkland, in which Northumberland was said to be "right" in the business. Lady Daubigny remained under arrest for some time, but she was eventually allowed to cross to Holland without having been further proceeded against, while Lady Sophia Murry died before the end of September : she had refused to take an oath and be examined by the Committee, saying she "did not mean to give an account to such fellows as they were." On June 12, Portland and Conway were committed to the charge of some of the City officials, but the House of Lords appears, from the first, to have made light of the charge against them. On the next day their servants were allowed to attend on them, and before they were confronted with Waller, on June 29, the Lords had taken the precaution to discount his evidence by having them both examined upon oath. They denied the truth of all his allegations, and Portland declared that at an interview, on June 21, at the house where he was confined, Waller had urged him to save them both, by casting the blame upon Conway and Northumberland. No one who has read the intercepted letter[1] which the poet wrote to Portland can have any reasonable doubt of the truth of his accusation, but it was simply oath against oath, and there

[1] Sandford's " Illustrations," p. 563.

the Committee were obliged to leave the matter. During the succeeding weeks both the accused were continually petitioning for their release, and the Commons, having no further evidence to offer, were at last, on July 29, obliged to leave it to the Lords to free them or not, as they deemed advisable. They were both admitted to bail on July 31, and in August of the following year all restrictions upon their movements were at an end. Waller's allegation against Northumberland amounted to no more than this— that he had told him of the existence of the plot, which he said "he disliked as a thing not feasible or like to succeed:" a speech so characteristic of the Earl as to leave little doubt of its truth. He, however, scoffed at the charge, and desired to be examined immediately, that "his innocence may the sooner appear and he not lie under a jealousy." He was confronted with Waller, who failed to make good his deposition, "soe as," D'Ewes writes, "this noble Earle, descended by the Dukes of Lorraine in the male line from Charlemaign the Emperour, was noe further questioned in this folish busines." It is easy to be righteously indignant over Waller's conduct, and impossible to present any adequate defence of it. This much at least should be remembered in condemning him—it has never, so far as I know, been asserted, except, of course, by the persons immediately concerned, that the information he gave was untrue, he was not endeavouring to "swear away" the lives of others to save his own, nor had he the abject's craving for company at the gallows : he struggled to deliver himself from the jaws of death, by involving in his guilt, men, in his opinion, as guilty as himself, who, as they were too exalted to fall beneath the attack of the Commons, so, might in his desperate hope, be the means of preserving his life together with their own.

Whatever may be the opinions entertained as to the "incredible dissimulation" with which Waller "acted a remorse of conscience," a mere recital of events is sufficient to prove that Clarendon is in error, in saying that his trial was "put off out of Christian compassion that he might recover his understanding."

The commission, from the Earl of Essex, for the trial of the prisoners by Martial Law, reached London on June 26, but so unwilling were the members of the House of Commons to take part in the proceedings of the Council of War that it was necessary for Glyn, upon the authority of Dr. Dorislaus, the Judge Advocate General, to assure them of its regularity. On June 29, it was resolved that Waller should first be brought to the Bar, though the other conspirators were to be tried on the following Monday. The Court, under the presidency of the Earl of Manchester, assembled on Friday, June 30, when all the prisoners, with the excep-

tion of Waller, were paraded. On Monday,
July 3, Tomkins and Chaloner were brought up,
and though the former begged for some delay,
that he might prepare his defence, having only
had notice of his trial on Friday, "which was
too short a time as he conceived," the Court
"conceived the, contrary," and they were both
tried and sentenced to be hanged.

Blinkhorne, White, and Abbot were also tried
and condemned within the week—they appear
to have been afterwards pardoned—and Hassell
and Hampden both died in prison. On July 5,
Tomkins and Chaloner were hanged before
their own doors, the former at the Holborn end
of Fetter Lane, the latter in Cornhill. It would
be doing less than justice to a brave man, however poor a figure the poet makes by contrast,
to omit to tell how Tomkins died. His demeanour before the Court had been defiant, and
such he maintained it to the end. With the
rope about his neck, he said that affection to a
brother-in-law and gratitude to a king, whose
bread he had eaten now above twenty-two years,
had drawn him into this foolish business ; he
was glad it had been discovered, for the ill con-
sequences it might have had : he begged them
not to trouble him, who would have pressed him
to declare anything further he knew of that or
any other plot, and then, "with much boldness
descended three steps lower on the ladder, and
so bid adieu to this world." About this time

Waller wrote a letter[1] to Arthur Goodwyn, his neighbour and fellow-member, which showed that he was fully alive to the dangers of his position, and on July 4, at the Bar of the House, he gave further proof of being in possession of his understanding. Two of the members were commissioned to repair to the house where he was confined, and to see him safely conveyed into the custody of the Serjeant, who brought him to the Bar. "He was all clothed," writes D'Ewes, "in mourning as if he had been going to execution itself, his demeanour was also composed to a despairing dejectedness, and when he came to the Bar, he kneeled down, and so continued kneeling, until myself and some others who stood near the Bar bade him stand up. . . . . divers of the House seeing his sad and dejected condition whom they had formerly heard speak in public with so much applause, could not forbear shedding of tears." His depositions having been presented to him, and their contents acknowledged to be true, he was called upon to say what he could for himself before they proceeded to expel him the House, "whereupon, after a low reverence made, he spake—expressing in his very tone and gesture the lowest degree of a dejected spirit." Of Waller's sincerity I cannot presume to judge—he knew his audience, probably to a man, and for his speech, considered as a piece of

[1] Nugent's "Hampden," ii. 419.

advocacy, no praise is too high ; indeed, even Clarendon does not hesitate to say that it saved his life. He is reported to have expended as much as £30,000 in bribery, but I can only say that no traces of any dealing to this extent with his estate remain among the papers in the possession of his family, though there are to be found draft conveyances and mortgages which tell of the means employed to pay his fine some months later. He was taken back to imprisonment, and on July 14 it was resolved that " Mr. Edm. Waller shall be forthwith disabled for (*sic*) ever sitting or serving as a member in this House." Discussion upon the manner of his trial was postponed from day to day, and on Sept. 6 he was ordered to be removed to the Tower, an order which was repeated, in more stringent terms, on Sept. 14. On May 15 of the following year, " the humble petition of Edm. Waller late a member of this House " was read in the House of Commons—this was probably a petition to be allowed to put his affairs in order—and on Aug. 29 preparations were apparently being made for his trial by Court Martial, but they were not proceeded with, and on Sept. 23 comes another petition from " Edm. Waller, prisoner in the Tower." The poet had apparently by that time received an intimation that his life would be spared, and that he would be punished by a fine. He " thanks the House for enabling him to put his estate into such a position that he may be able to pay the fine imposed on him ; and is the more hopeful that, in regard of the free and ingenuous confession and discoveries made upon promised favour, the House will hold his life precious : that £10,000 may be accepted out of his estate ; and if he be not worthy to serve the House and spend his life in their glorious cause, that they would be pleased to banish him to some other part of the world." It was agreed, without a division, that his petition should be granted, and it was ordered that the vote of the House should be communicated to the Commissioners for Martial Law. On Nov. 4, "An Ordinance of Lords and Commons assembled in Parliament for the Fining and Banishment of Edmond Waller Esquire," was read and agreed to in the House of Lords. This instrument declares that it was formerly intended that the said Edmond Waller should be tried by Court Martial, but that, "upon further consideration and mature deliberation," it has been "thought convenient" that he should be fined £10,000 and banished the realm : twenty-eight days, from the 6th of November, are given him to remove elsewhere : no further proceedings will be taken against him, but he is not to return to this country upon pain of incurring such punishment as both Houses of Parliament shall think fit."

Thus closed this incident in Waller's life : his

conduct does not seem to have made him less welcome among the exiles in France, and in after years he himself did not hesitate to treat the part he had played, as that of a martyr. The date of his departure is uncertain, but it seems likely that he stayed in England long enough to marry his second wife, Mary Bracey, of the family of that name, of Thame in Oxfordshire : he was still a widower when he appeared at the Bar of the House, and his eldest daughter by his second marriage, Margaret, afterwards his amanuensis, is known to have been born at Rouen. His son Robert, who died young, for some time had Hobbes for his tutor, while his daughter was left in charge of her grandmother at Beaconsfield, whence, no doubt, supplies were sent to maintain the poet and his family in France. Of the details of his life on the continent we can only catch a glimpse here and there in the letters of himself and his friends. In August, 1645, Hobbes is writing to him at Calais : the philosopher is staying at Rouen with Lord Devonshire, and after telling the poet how he has been spending his time in arguing for the amusement of the company, he goes on to say, " I beleeve you passe much of yours in meditating how you may to your contentment and without blame passe the seas." He ends by thanking him for having expressed a wish to translate the " De Cive " into English, a project which Waller is said to have abandoned

on seeing a portion of the work translated by
the author himself.

Next year he is touring with Evelyn in Italy
and Switzerland, and in 1647 we hear of him at
St. Valery. In 1648 he writes to Evelyn from
Pont de l'Arche, whither he had removed from
Rouen on account of the plague, announcing
the birth of a daughter, and in April of the following year he and his wife are at Rouen once
more. Towards the end of the year they appear
to have removed to Paris, and to have resided
there until their return to England. Waller
and Lord Jermyn, amid the general poverty of
the exiles, are said to have been the only people
able "to keep a table," though the former gave
out that he was living upon the proceeds of the
sale of his wife's jewels. He was in constant
communication with the members of the English
colony, and particularly with Evelyn:—now he
consults him as to what is to be done with a
child of his whom the Popish midwife had
baptized, and now he begs him to send a coach
from Paris to St. Germains to fetch a child, to
whom Mrs. Evelyn had been godmother, "to be
buried by the Common Prayer." All this time
his mother, often in the company of Cromwell,
was watching and working on his behalf in
England. Only one of her letters to him has
survived. Addressing him as "deer ned," she
tells him his daughter is grown so handsome,
that there are already several suitors for her

4

hand, two of whom had been to see her (Mrs. Waller) that week, one a knight of very good fortune, the other Alderman Avery's eldest son. She tells the poet what she has learned of the " prospects " of these gentlemen, and only waits for his reply,—what will he give his daughter? The Alderman's son might be had, she thinks, for £2,000, if he intends to give so much. " I am not in hast," she writes, " to mary hir, she is yong enough to stay, but the danger is if she should catch the small poxe or hir beauty should change, it would be a great lose to hir." Then follow details about the estate, this lease, and that bond, and she ends, " I pray faile not to writ a full answer to all in this letter, so praying god to bles y^u & y^r wife, I rest y^r louing mother Anne Waller. as ever I shall intreat anything of y^u writ me an answer as soon as y^u can of this letter for I have past my credit they shall haue a speedy answer." What Miss Waller's dowery was we have no means of knowing, but she eventually married Mr. Donner of Oxfordshire, and was living, his widow, in 1711.

The manner of the poet's return to England appears to be uncertain. It has hitherto been said that he obtained permission from Cromwell, through the intercession of Col. Scrope, who was his brother-in-law, but on Nov. 27, 1651, the House of Commons, after having heard read " the humble petition of Edmond Waller," passed

a resolution revoking his sentence of banishment, and ordered a pardon under the Great Seal
to be prepared for him. Evelyn took leave of
him at Paris, on Jan. 13, 1652, and in August of
the same year he is writing to the diarist from
Beaconsfield, to congratulate him on the birth
of a son. We know even less of the course of
Waller's life between the date of his return to
England and the Restoration. He probably
occupied the early days in writing his Panegyric
to Cromwell, though it did not reach the Protector till 1655, as the following letter[1] proves.

"S^r, lett it not trouble you that by soe unhappy a mistake you are (as I heare) at Northampton, indaed I am passionately affected with
itt. I have noe guilt upon me unlesse it bee to bee
revenged, for your soe willinglye mistakinge
mee in your verses. This action will putt you to
redeeme mee from your selfe as you haue
already from the world. Ashamed I am, Y^r
freind and Seruant, Oliver P." "June 13th, 1655."

It is directed "For my very lovinge friend
Edward Waller, Esq. Northampton. hast, hast."
The mistake, no doubt, arising from his being
generally known as " Ned," of calling the poet,
" Edward," was by no means unfrequent among
his contemporaries, but of the subject-matter
of this letter I have no explanation to offer.
Waller appears to have lain under some sus-

[1] This letter is in Mr. Waller's possession—it was communicated by a relative of his to *Notes and Queries*, 2nd Series, v. 2.

picion after his return; for writing to Hobbes, some time between 1657 and the Protector's death, he says that he has been at his lodging to see him to give him his opinion of the political situation, which Lord Devonshire had requested, "because he could write nothing safely, wᶜʰ he (Lord Devonshire) might not find in print."

In April, 1653, he lost his mother; this, with the exception of his appointment as one of the Commissioners for Trade in Dec., 1655, is the only fact affecting him which I have been able to discover, down to the time of the death of Cromwell.

Nothing concerning Waller is better known than that he followed up an elegy on Cromwell with an address of welcome to Charles II., except, perhaps, the famous answer, "Sir, we poets never succeed so well in writing truth as in fiction," by means of which he extricated himself from the difficulty into which the King had put him by commenting on the inferiority of the latter poem to his Panegyric on the Protector. One obvious reason for this inferiority was long ago pointed out, and even in Charles's own time it was well summarized by the Dutch ambassador, who, when the King complained that his masters paid less respect to him than to the Protector, replied, "Ah! Sir, Oliver was quite another man." Waller appears to have at once entered fully into the new life of the Restoration, he was graciously received by the King, and he continued till the end of his days a favourite at Court. In May, 1661, having been elected for Hastings, he began a fresh Parliamentary career, and while he lived, "it was no House if Waller was not there." Burnet says of him that "he was only concerned to say that which should make him applauded, he never laid the business of the House to heart, being a vain and empty, though a witty, man ;" but, though it is true that he seldom spoke without delivering himself of an epigram or a more or less appropriate Latin quotation, his conduct in the House was in every way honourable to him. Day after day his voice was raised in appeals for toleration for Dissenters, more particularly for the Quakers, a body which his son Edmund afterwards joined. He had, he said, "a sense of kindness for any persons that suffer," and he would not have the "Church of England, like the elder brother of the Ottoman family, strangle all the younger brothers." He strenuously opposed the passing of the Act against Conventicles. "Revenge," said he, "makes the bee lose his sting, and so shall we if we pass this Bill. These people (the Quakers) are like children's tops, whip them and they stand up, let them alone and they fall." He spoke against the removal of the Duke of York from the Court, reminding the House, that Absalom

left the Court, and they knew what followed ;
but the only really important matter in which
he was directly engaged was the impeachment
of Clarendon, of which he was one of the
"managers." Then, and after Monmouth's
Rebellion, he spoke with the greatest horror
of the dangers of a military despotism and
" government by Janissaries," and Macaulay
has praised the course which his great age
and reputation emboldened him to take. He
was never weary of reminding the Members of
his long experience in the House, or of quoting
precedents to them—he even insisted upon
sitting on the steps, because " steps had been
seats and seats steps " in the Long Parliament—
and the attitude which he assumed was occasionally almost paternal : " Let us look to our
Government, Fleet, and Trade, 'tis the best
advice the oldest Parliament man among you
can give you, and so God bless you."

In spite of his age and eloquence, Waller
ever appears to have been in the inner circle
of politics after the Restoration, though he is
credited with having predicted that James II.
" would be left like a whale upon the strand."
His literary reputation, however, was at its
height, and he and Denham appear to have
occupied the position of unofficial dramatic
censors, for on March 22, 1663, Secretary Bennet
writes to Waller, directing him and Denham to
read, and give the King their opinions on " The

Cheats," a play which had been recently produced, and objected to as containing "many
things of a scandalous and offensive nature."
Nor was his fame confined to this country, La
Fontaine wrote of him with admiration, and
Corneille was flattered to hear that whenever
he published a play, Mr. Waller made a point
of translating some portion of it. But nothing
probably that Waller had written gave him
such a hold upon his contemporaries as the
charm of his manners and conversation, a
charm which Macaulay has compared to that
which must have been exercised by Bacon.
His transgressions were overlooked, and he
was again admitted to the conversation of great
ladies—the house of the Dowager Countess of
Devonshire is said to have been his "chief
theatre"—and so powerful were the attractions
of his wit, that Henry Savile declared that no
man in England should keep him company
without drinking, except Ned Waller. The
poet appears to have been a water-drinker, and
one wonders whether this abstemiousness
had any connection with a story which Mr.
Henshaw relates in a letter of July 16, 1670, to
Sir Robert Paston, which had also reached
Aubrey's ears. "On Thursday night," writes
Mr. Henshaw, "the Earl of St. Albans treated
the King and the Mareschal (de Bellefonde) at
supper, where Mr. Waller the poet made one,
who, when the King went away, waiting on him

down the stone steps towards the water, his feet slipping he fell and cracked his skull, which 'tis feared will put finis to his poetry." Some member of the company, Aubrey says, "made him damnable drunk at Somerset House, where at the water-stayres, he fell downe, and had a cruel fall. 'Twas pitty to use such a sweet swan so inhumanely." Another correspondent of Sir Robert Paston, Sir J. Clayton, throws some further light on the poet's conviviality : writing on June 8, 1669, he says, " I dined at Uxbridge, but never in all my life did I pass my day away with greater gusto, our company being his Grace (*the Duke of Buckingham*), Mr. Waller, Mr. Surveyor Wren, and myself, nothing but quintessence of wit and most excellent discourse." The Duke appears to have been on terms of great intimacy with Waller, for the latter used often to wander to Cliveden to wonder at his Grace's costly new buildings and magnificent gardens, and he writes to his wife from London (he lived in St. James's Street, "next doore to the sugar loafe"), "The Duke of Buckingham with the Lady Sh[rewsbury ?] came hither last night at this tyme & carried me to the usuall place to supper, from whence I returned home at four aclocke this morning, having ben earnestly entreated to supp wth them again to-night, but such howers can not be always kept, therfore I shall eat my 2 eggs alone & go to bedd." A prudent determination, which he re-echoes in a letter to the beautiful Mrs. Myddleton, who counted him and his friend St. Evremond among her devoted admirers : " Your ould Servant," he writes, " having found himself extreamely indisposed, & knowing the cause thereof to have ben the constant eating abroad for a whole week together, thought an immediate Abstinence & Retirement absolutely necessary if he meant to continue longer in the world."

Amid all these scenes of gaiety through which the poet moved, one naturally looks for Sacharissa. There was no romance lingering about their relations, she wrote of him as " Old Waller," and he, in her presence, forgot his wonted gallantry. They met at Lady Wharton's house, at Woburn ; " When Mr. Waller," said the Dowager Countess of Sunderland, " when, I wonder, will you write such beautiful verses to me again !" " When, Madam," replied the poet, " your Ladyship is as young and as handsome again."—"Something," says M. Taine, " to shock a Frenchman !"

On May 2, 1677, Waller buried his second wife, at Beaconsfield : she is said to have been a woman of great beauty, and he appears to have felt her loss deeply, for he retired to his house at Hall Barn, and wrote to Mrs. Myddleton, begging her to excuse him even to St. Evremond, who had expressed an intention of visiting him. Later he had the honour of entertaining there visitors more distinguished than the French exile. "Since you writ," (Mrs. Myddleton is again his correspondent), "I have had the honour to receive the Dutchess *(of York)* & Princess *(Anne)* with all their fair train, the Lady Sunderland *(probably Sacharissa's daughter-in-law)* was with them who sent me warning but a few hours before, and yett they eate heartily & seemed well content with what could so hastily be gotten for them."

Charles died, and James succeeded him, and Waller still continued a favourite at Court, but his visits to London became less frequent, and he was more often to be found roaming about in his woods at Beaconsfield, though, as he wrote to Lady Ranelagh, "he had not much joy in walking there, where he found ye trees as bare & withered as himselfe, but with this difference,

> That shortly they shall flourish and wax green,
> But I still old and withered must be seen,
> Yet if vain thoughts fall, like their leaves, away,
> The nobler part improves with that decay."

He bought a small house at Coleshill, hoping to die there, for he said, "A stagge, when he is hunted, and neer spent, always returns home." But this was not to be ; being alarmed at a swelling in his leg, he went to Windsor to consult Sir Charles Scarborough, the King's physician, as to the cause. " I am come, Sir," he said, "to you, as a friend as well as a physician, to ask you what this swelling means." "Why, Sir," answered the blunt doctor, "your blood will run no longer." Waller repeated a line of Virgil, and went home, to Hall Barn. He gathered his children about him, received the Sacrament with them, and died on Oct. 21, 1687. On Oct. 26 he was buried in Beaconsfield church-yard, by a curious piece of irony, "in woollen according to a late Act of Parliament." When the question of enforcing the penalties for not observing the Act which required persons to be buried in wool had come up in the House, Waller said, "Our Saviour was buried in linen. 'Tis a thing against the custom of nations, and I am against it."

No poetical reputation has suffered such vicissitudes as that of Edmund Waller: described, in the inscription upon his tomb, as "inter poetas sui temporis facile princeps," it was still possible, in 1766, to introduce him to the readers of the Biographia Britannica as "the most celebrated Lyric Poet that ever England produced," and when, in 1772, Percival Stockdale wrote his "Life," in which he declared that "his works gave a new era to English poetry," his performance was considered to be of such merit that he was on the point of receiving the commission to write "The Lives of the Poets," which was afterwards entrusted to Johnson.

The revolt against classicism extinguished

the reputation of Waller, as it impaired that
of men in every way greater than he, and
though in 1885 Mr. Gosse succeeded in throw-
ing a very strong light upon him, it was
scarcely a friendly office to assert that he
revolutionized English poetry. The history of
the classical couplet has yet to be written,
but the part that Waller took in its develop-
ment was ,certainly not that of an inventor.
Abundant evidence has been adduced by Mr.
Churton Collins and by Dr. Henry Wood, to
show that others (Dr. Wood insists specially
upon the claims of Sandys), before his time,
were in the habit of writing distichs, confining
the sense to the couplet, as smooth and correct
as any that ever came from the pen of Waller.
That "Waller was smooth" has been generally
admitted, and smoothness was the quality at
which he particularly aimed. "When he was
a briske young sparke, and first studyed
poetry, 'Me thought,' said he, 'I never
sawe a good copie of English verses; they
want smoothness; then I began to essay.'"
Such is Aubrey's account, but it is scarcely
in this direction that one must look for the
reason of Waller's extraordinary popularity
among his contemporaries. The volume of
his verse, having regard to the great age to
which he lived, is small, and one is half
inclined to believe the story of his having spent
a whole summer in elaborating the lines written

in the Tasso of the Duchess of York. He is credited with having polished his poetry like marble, but his execution is frequently careless, and his ear was by no means exceptionally acute. He uses the feeble expletive "so" upwards of twenty times as a rhyme, and occasionally he is satisfied with an assonance. Of the "essence of poetry, invention," he was practically destitute, but it would be difficult to find in the whole range of English Poetry any one more uniformly successful in improving an occasion. To many people his verses on this or that public occasion must have come as a relief, after the "conceited" obscurities of Donne. He makes no great demand on the understanding, he is singularly free from conceits, and his classical allusions are the most trite and ordinary. He took Edward Fairfax for his master, and traces of his indebtedness to the translator of Tasso are to be found scattered up and down his poems. His own poetical stock was exceedingly small, and probably no writer has repeated himself so often. He himself described his verses as "written only to please himself, and such particular persons to whom they were directed," and it was precisely this quality of appropriateness which gave him his tremendous vogue in his own time. The reputation of the Court and its surroundings clung to him, and, but for this, it would probably

have been left for some one in this century to
revive him, as the author of the lyrics by which
his reputation must stand or fall. He lived in
the most stirring period of our domestic history,
and to some of his poems, the outcome of his
relations with persons who played no unimportant
part in making it, a certain historical interest
must always attach. One would not wish to be
supposed to include in this category the famous
Panegyric. It has always been the custom to
brand Waller as the poet of a venal muse, but
it is difficult indeed to suppose that his two
poems on Cromwell were not inspired by
genuine admiration and regret. It is doubtful
if he owed to the Protector even the permission to return to England, and he can
have been but poorly recompensed by the
monstrous Latin eulogies of Payne Fisher for the
storm of invective which the Royalist poets,
headed by Charles Cotton, showered upon him.
From Charles II. Waller did indeed obtain
the only favour he is known to have asked for
himself, the grant of the Provostship of Eton
College, but this grant was rendered inoperative
by the refusal of Clarendon to admit him to
the office, on the ground that he was not in
Orders. Poetical panegyric has had its day,
and one is almost tempted to say that it needed
such a man as Cromwell praised by such a
poet as Waller to justify its existence.

It may well be doubted if the insertion of one

or two of his poems in anthologies does not do more harm than good to a man's general reputation, by a tendency to divert attention from anything else he has written. Waller lives as the author of "Go lovely rose," and the "Lines on a Girdle," and these lyrics might almost be chosen from English literature to serve as the examples of the charms of simplicity and directness. It would be almost stultifying what one has suggested to distinguish particularly other poems of his, but it may be said that the general level of Waller's lyrical work is distinctly high, and there is no such disparity between these famous pieces and the rest of his lyrics, as exists, in the case of some other poets of the seventeenth century, between the bulk of their writings and what Johnson has called their "lucky trifles."

Waller was sadly deficient in critical instinct as applied to the writings of others. Little attention need be paid to the commendatory verses which good-nature prompted him to address to such of his friends as were authors, but his opinion of "Paradise Lost" was that it was remarkable only for its length, and he laid unholy hands upon "The Maid's Tragedy," and constructed a last act in rhyme more in accordance with the requirements of the morals of the Court of Charles II. Little, from a literary point of view, can be said in praise of his "Divine Poems," and cynicism has not been slow to stamp them as the outcome of ill-health and old age. The poet used to say that "he would blot from his works any line that did not contain some motive to virtue," and if they are not didactic throughout, this at least should be remembered in his favour, that he lived through the period of the Restoration without suffering anything he wrote to be disfigured by the slightest trace of obscenity.

The date of Waller's earliest poem is uncertain, I am inclined to think it was written in his seventeenth year, though it was not printed till 1645, but it is certain that when he was over eighty years of age he composed the noble lines, "Of the last verses in the book," lines, surely, not unworthy of any poet in the meridian of his powers.

CONTENTS.

b

PAGE

CONTENTS.

TO THE QUEENE &c.

Madam,

If your Ma^{ty} had lived in those Tymes which sacrifiz'd to the Sun **and** Moone and of eatch glorious Creatoure made a new Dyety, as the admiration of your sacrad persone had supply'd them with **a** more excusable Idolatry, **So** could no incense have been more worthie **your** Altar then the **odore** of his **Maties** Heroyck deeds. **And** though the court **and** universities have no other mater **of** theer song, yet if your Matie please **to listen what Echo the** country returnes to so loud a praise, Wee shall likwayes teach the woods **to** sound your royall name, And tell **how great a** portion **of our** present hapines **is** owing **to** those **Divyne** Graces, whairin all **the** privat desires **of** our soueraine beeing accompleished, hee **is** wholie at Leasoure to confer fælicitie on others, for continence (soe greate a miracle in **the** vigour of youth and royalitie) Wee nomber amongst the Meanest of his Vertues, whose bed soe highly adornd with bloode and beauty presentes him with all that Antiquitie and youth cane

give ; Nor is our neighboure Kingdome Less
requited for the light it first shewed you in that
his Maties enjoying the fairest pairt, is so weell
content with a titill to the rest of France. But
we looke not on your Ma^tiee as the cause only
But as the pledg of our securitie, For as
Heaven threatens a Deluge of all calamities
uppone a land condemned to be the seat of
warr ; soe may our Natione well expect the
contrary blessings being chosen for the seat of
love. A love soe famous fruitfull and religiously
observed betwixt your most excelent Maties that
like the sacrad oil (whairwith the Roiall poet
soe perfum'd his song of fraternall Amity)
diffus'd from the head doune to the skirts, the
meanest of your people, it affects us all with the
joy of so noble a president. Nore doeth
Heaven seme less to acknowleadge this Pietie
still binding your Kingdomes together with soe
many hopfull knots that wee ar now confident
no other streame of bloode shall ever devyd the
poure of this hapie Iland ; for which Graces
your Matie is not named amongst us without
prayers, that when you shall have exceeded the
comoune fate of Humane conditioune no less in
tyme thane in glorie you may recaue that
welcome amongst the glad Angels To wich

the resemblance you have both of thare brightness and inocence Gives you alreadie so fair a
Titile.

Your Maties &c.

*Thus I intended long since to have presented
to hir Matie those things which I had writtin of
the King But besids that I held thame not
worthie of hir the Tymes alsoe hath made this
epistle unseasonable.*

TO MY LADY SOPHIA.[1]

MADAM,

Your commands for the gathering of
these sticks into a faggot had sooner been
obeyed, but, that intending to present you with
my whole vintage, I stayed till the latest grapes
were ripe ; for here your ladyship hath not only
all I have done, but all I ever mean to do of this
kind. Not but that I may defend the attempt
I have made upon poetry, by the examples (not
to trouble you with history) of many wise and
worthy persons of our own times ; as Sir Philip

1.—Ed. 1645, *To my Lady.*

Sidney, **Sir Fra** : Bacon, Cardinal Perron (the
ablest of his countrymen), and the former Pope,
who, they say, instead of the Triple Crown,
wore sometimes the poet's ivy, as an ornament,
perhaps, of less weight and trouble. But,
madam, these nightingales sung only in **the**
spring ; it was the diversion of their youth ; as
ladies learn to sing and play whilst[1] they are
children, what they forget when they are women.
The resemblance holds further ; for, as you quit
the lute the sooner because the posture is
suspected to draw the body awry, so this is not
always practised without some violence[2] to the
mind ; wresting it from present occasions, and
accustoming us to a style somewhat removed
from common use. But, that you may not think
his case deplorable who has made verses, we are
told that Tully (the greatest wit among the
Romans) was once sick of this disease ; and yet
recovered so well, that of almost as bad a poet
as your servant, he became the most perfect
orator in the world. So that, not so much to
have made verses, as not to give over in time,
leaves a man without excuse ; the former
presenting us at least with an opportunity of
doing wisely, that is, to conceal those we have

1.—Ed. 1645, *when.*   2.—Ed. 1645, *villany.*

made; which I shall yet **do, if** my humble
request may **be** of as much **force** with your
ladyship, as your commands have been with me.
Madam, I only whisper these in your ear; **if
you** publish them, they become [1] your own; **and
therefore, as you** apprehend **the reproach of a**
wit and **a poet,** cast them into the fire; **or, if
they** come **where green** boughs are in the
chimney, **with the** help of your fair friends (for
thus bound, **it will** be too stubborn [2] a task for
your hands alone), tear them in pieces, wherein
you shall [3] honour me with the fate of Orpheus;
for so his poems, whereof we **only hear the**
fame [4] (not **his** limbs, **as** the story would have
it), I suppose were scattered **by the Thracian**
dames. **Here, madam, I** might **take an oppor-**
tunity to celebrate **your** virtues, **and to** instruct
the **unhappy men that knew you not, who you
are,** [5] **how much you excel the most excellent of
your own, and how much you** amaze the least
inclined to wonder of **our sex.** But as they will
be apt **to take your ladyship's for a** Roman

1.—Ed. 1645, *are.*   2.—Ed. 1645, *hard.*   3.—Ed. 1645, *will.*
4.—Ed. 1645, *heare the forme;* **Park (ed.** 1806), substituted
tear, and Bell (ed. 1854,) *bear* for *heare,* without rendering
the sentence intelligible.
5.—Ed. 1645, *Instruct you how unhappie you are, in that
you know not who you are.*

name, so would they believe that I endeavoured the character of a perfect nymph, worshipped an image of my own making, and dedicated this to the lady of the brain, not of the heart, of

Your Ladyship's most humble servant,

E. W.

AN ADVERTISEMENT TO THE
READER.

Reader. This parcell of exquisit **poems, have**
pass'd up **and downe** through many hands
amongst persons of the best quallity, **in loose**
imperfect Manuscripts, **and** there **is lately**
obtruded **to** the world **an** adulterate **Copy,**
surruptitiously **and** illegally imprinted **to** the
derogation of the Author and the abuse of the
Buyer. **But in this booke** they apeare in their
pure originalls and true **genuine colours. In so**
much that they feare **not (as young** Eaglets use
to be tryed **whither they are spurious, or of** right
extraction) **to look** upon **the** *Sunne* in the
Meridian, **in regard** Apollo **himselfe,** the grand
Patron of **Poets seemd not only to cast** many
favourable **aspects, but by his more** then
ordinary **influence to** cooperate in their produc-
tion ; as will appeare **to** the intelligent **and**
cleare-sighted **Reader, by that** constant veine of
gold (**the minerall which** that planet ownes more
then any other) **which** runnes through every one
of them. Thus they go abroad unsophisticated
and like **the** present condition **of** the Author

himselfe they are expos'd to the wide world, to
travell, and try their fortunes ! And I beleeve
there is no gentle soule that pretends anything
to knowledge and the choycest sort of invention
but will give them entertainment and wellcome.

THE PRINTER TO THE READER.[1]

WHEN the author of these verses (written only
to please himself, and such particular persons
to whom they were directed) returned from
abroad some years since, he was troubled to find
his name in print ; but somewhat satisfied to see
his lines so ill rendered that he might justly
disown them, and say to a mistaking printer as
one did to an ill reciter,

> . . . . Male dum recitas, incipit esse tuum.[2]

Having been ever since pressed to correct the
many and gross faults (such as use to be in
impressions wholly neglected by the authors),
his answer was, that he made these when ill
verses had more favour, and escaped better,
than good ones do in this age ; the severity
whereof he thought not unhappily diverted by
those faults in the impression which hitherto
have hung upon his book, as the Turks hang old
rags, or such like ugly things, upon their fairest
horses, and other goodly creatures, to secure

1.—From the edition of 1664, the first printed after the
Restoration.

2.—Martial, lib. i. ep. 39.

them against fascination. And for those of a more confined understanding, who pretend not to censure, as they admire most what they least comprehend, so his verses (maimed to that degree that himself scarce knew what to make of many of them) might, that way at least, have a title to some admiration; which is no small matter, if what an old author observes be true, that the aim of orators is victory, of historians truth, and of poets admiration. He had reason, therefore, to indulge those faults in his book, whereby it might be reconciled to some, and commended to others.

The printer also, he thought, would fare the worse if those faults were amended; for we see maimed statues sell better than whole ones; and clipped and washed money go about, when the entire and weighty lies hoarded up.

These are the reasons which, for above twelve years past, he has opposed to our request; to which it was replied, that as it would be too late to recall that which had so long been made public, so might it find excuse from his youth, the season it was produced in; and for what had been done since, and now added, if it commend not his poetry, it might his philosophy, which teaches him so cheerfully to bear so great

a calamity as the loss of the best part of his
fortune, torn from him in prison (in which, and
in banishment, the best portion of his life hath
also been spent), that he can still sing under the
burthen, not unlike that Roman,

> . . . . Quem demisere Philippi
> **Decisis humilem pennis,** inopemque **paterni**
> Et laris et fundi.[1] . . . .

> **Whose** spreading wings, the civil war had clipped,
> And him of his old patrimony stripped.

Who yet not long after could say,

> Musis amicus, tristitiam et **metus**
> Tradam protervis in mare Creticum
> Portare ventis. [2] . . . .

> They that acquainted **with** the muses **be,**
> Send care and **sorrow by the winds to sea.**

Not so much moved with these reasons of
ours (or pleased with our rhymes), as wearied
with our importunity, he has at last given us
leave to assure the reader, that the Poems which
have been so long and so ill set forth under his
name, are here to be found as he first writ them;
as also to add some others which have since
been composed by him : and though his advice
to the contrary might have discouraged us, yet

1.—Varied from Horace, Epistles II. 2. 49-51.
2.—Horace, Odes I. 26. 1-3.

observing how often they have been reprinted, what price they have borne, and how earnestly they have been always inquired after, but especially of late (making good that of Horace,

    . . . . Meliora dies, ut vina, poemata reddit. [1]

"some verses being, like some wines, recommended to our taste by time and age") we have adventured upon this new and well-corrected edition, which, for our own sakes as well as thine, we hope will succeed better than he apprehended.

     Vivitur ingenio, cætera mortis erunt.

1.—Epistles II 1. 34.

POSTSCRIPT.[1]

NOT having the same Argument as at first to persuade the Author that I might print his *Verses* more Correctly, which he found so ill done at his Return ; I have now adventured, without giving him farther Trouble by importuning him for a new Permission, to Collect all that I can find, either left out of the former Edition or such as have been since made by him ; to which I am the more encouraged, because the first (tho' most of them were compos'd Fifty or Sixty years since) seem still New, which would be more strange in so changing a Language, had it not been by him improv'd, which may make one think it true that I have heard from some learned Criticks, that *Virgil* when he said—*Nova carmina pango* . . . meant not *Verses* that were never seen before (for in that sence all at first are New) but such as he thought might be ever New.   May these still appear to be so for the diversion of the Readers, and interest of

THEIR HUMBLE SERVANT.

1.—From the 1686 edition.

PREFACE TO THE SECOND PART OF MR. WALLER'S POEMS, PRINTED IN THE YEAR 1690.

THE reader needs be told no more in commendation of these Poems, than that they are Mr. Waller's; a name that carries everything in it that is either great or graceful in poetry. He was, indeed, the parent of English verse, and the first that showed us our tongue had beauty and numbers in it. Our language owes more to him than the French does to Cardinal Richelieu, and the whole Academy. A poet cannot think of him without being in the same rapture Lucretius is in when Epicurus comes in his way.

Tu pater, es rerum inventor; tu patria nobis
Suppeditas præcepta; tuisque ex, Inclute ' chartis,
Floriferis ut apes in saltibus omnia libant,
Omnia nos itidem depascimur aurea dicta,
Aurea! perpetua semper dignissima vita![1]

The tongue came into his hands like a rough diamond: he polished it first, and to that

1.—Lib. iii. ver. 9.

degree, that all artists since him have admired
the workmanship, without pretending to mend
it. Suckling and Carew, I must confess, wrote
some few things smoothly enough ; but as all
they did in this kind was not very considerable,
so it was a little later than the earliest pieces of
Mr. Waller. He undoubtedly stands first in the
list of refiners, and, for aught I know, last too ;
for I question whether in Charles II.'s reign
English did not come to its full perfection ; and
whether it has not had its Augustan age as well
as the Latin. It seems to be already mixed
with foreign languages as far as its purity will
bear ; and, as chemists say of their men-
struums, to be quite sated with the infusion.
But posterity will best judge of this. In the
meantime, it is a surprising reflection, that
between what Spenser wrote last, and Waller
first, there should not be much above twenty
years' distance ; and yet the one's language, like
the money of that time, is as current now as
ever ; whilst the other's words are like old coins,
one must go to an antiquary to understand
their true meaning and value. Such advances
may a great genius make, when it undertakes
anything in earnest !

Some painters will hit the chief lines and

masterstrokes of a face so truly, that through
all the differences of age the picture shall still
bear a resemblance. This art was Mr. Waller's :
he sought out, in this flowing tongue of ours,
what parts would last, and be of standing use
and ornament ; and this he did so successfully,
that his language is now as fresh as it was at
first setting out. Were we to judge barely by
the wording, we could not know what was
wrote at twenty, and what at fourscore. He
complains, indeed, of a tide of words that
comes in upon the English poet, and overflows
whatever he builds ; but this was less his case
than any man's that ever wrote ; and the
mischief of it is, this very complaint will last
long enough to confute itself ; for though
English be mouldering stone, as he tells us
there, yet he has certainly picked the best out
of a bad quarry.

  We are no less beholden to him for the new
turn of verse which he brought in, and the
improvement he made in our numbers. Before
his time men rhymed indeed, and that was all :
as for the harmony of measure, and that dance
of words which good ears are so much pleased
with, they knew nothing of it. Their poetry
then was made up almost entirely of mono-

syllables ; which, when they come together in any cluster, are certainly the most harsh, untuneable things in the world. If any man doubts of this, let him read ten lines in Donne, and he will be quickly convinced. Besides, their verses ran all into one another, and hung together, throughout a whole copy, like the hooked atoms that compose a body in Des Cartes. There was no distinction of parts, no regular stops, nothing for the ear to rest upon ; but as soon as the copy began, down it went like a larum, incessantly ; and the reader was sure to be out of breath before he got to the end of it : so that really verse, in those days, was but downright prose tagged with rhymes. Mr. Waller removed all these faults, brought in more polysyllables, and smoother measures, bound up his thoughts better, and in a cadence more agreeable to the nature of the verse he wrote in ; so that wherever the natural stops of that were, he contrived the little breakings of his sense so as to fall in with them ; and, for that reason, since the stress of our verse lies commonly upon the last syllable, you will hardly ever find him using a word of no force there. I would say, if I were not afraid the reader would think me too nice, that he commonly closes with verbs, in which we know the life of language consists.

Among other improvements we may reckon that of his rhymes, which are always good, and very often the better for being new. He had a fine ear, and knew how quickly that sense was cloyed by the same round of chiming words still returning upon it. It is a decided case by the great master of writing,[1] *Quæ sunt ampla, et pulchra, diu placere possunt; quæ lepida et concinna* (amongst which rhyme must, whether it will or no, take its place), *citò satietate afficiunt aurium sensum fastidiosissimum.* This he understood very well; and therefore, to take off the danger of a surfeit that way, strove to please by variety and new sounds. Had he carried this observation, among others, as far as it would go, it must, methinks, have shown him the incurable fault of this jingling kind of poetry, and have led his later judgment to blank verse; but he continued an obstinate lover of rhyme to the very last; it was a mistress that never appeared unhandsome in his eyes, and was courted by him long after Sacharissa was forsaken. He had raised it, and brought it to that perfection we now enjoy

---

1.—Cicero, *Ad Herennium*, lib. iv. 23, 32.

it in ; and the poet's temper (which has always
a little vanity in it) would not suffer him ever to
slight a thing he had taken so much pains
to adorn. My Lord Roscommon was more
impartial ; no man ever rhymed truer and
evener than he ; yet he is so just as to confess
that it is but a trifle, and to wish the tyrant
dethroned, and blank verse set up in its room.
There is a third person,[1] the living glory of our
English poetry, who has disclaimed the use of
it upon the stage, though no man ever employed
it there so happily as he. It was the strength
of his genius that first brought it into credit in
plays, and it is the force of his example that
has thrown it out again. In other kinds of
writing it continues still, and will do so till
some excellent spirit arises that has leisure
enough, and resolution, to break the charm, and
free us from the troublesome bondage of rhyming, as Mr. Milton very well calls it, and has
proved it as well by what he has wrote in
another way. But this is a thought for times
at some distance ; the present age is a little too
warlike ; it may perhaps furnish out matter for
a good poem in the next, but it will hardly
encourage one now. Without prophesying, a

1.—Mr. Dryden.

man may easily know what sort of laurels are like to be in request.

Whilst I am talking of verse, I find myself, I do not know how, betrayed into a great deal of prose. I intended no more than to put the reader in mind what respect was due to anything that fell from the pen of Mr. Waller. I have heard his last-printed copies, which are added in the several editions of his poems, very slightly spoken of, but certainly they do not deserve it. They do indeed discover themselves to be his last, and that is the worst we can say of them. He is there

Jam senior; sed cruda Deo viridisque senectus. [1]

The same censure, perhaps, will be passed on the pieces of this Second Part. I shall not so far engage for them, as to pretend they are all equal to whatever he wrote in the vigour of his youth; yet they are so much of a piece with the rest, that any man will at first sight know them to be Mr. Waller's. Some of them were wrote very early, but not put into former collections, for reasons obvious enough, but which are now ceased. The play was altered to please the court; it is not to be doubted who sat for the

1.—Virg. *Æn.* vi. 304.

Two Brothers' characters.   It was agreeable to
the sweetness of Mr. Waller's temper to soften
the rigour of the tragedy, as he expresses it :
but whether it be so agreeable to the nature of
tragedy itself to make everything come off
easily, I leave to the critics.   In the prologue
and epilogue there are a few verses that he has
made use of upon another occasion ; but the
reader may be pleased to allow that in him that
has been allowed so long in Homer and
Lucretius.   Exact writers dress up their thoughts
so very well always, that when they have need
of the same sense, they cannot put it into other
words but it must be to its prejudice.   Care has
been taken in this book to get together everything of Mr. Waller's that is not put into the
former collection ; so that between both the
reader may make the set complete.

It will, perhaps, be contended, after all, that
some of these ought not to have been published ;
and Mr. Cowley's [1] decision will be urged, that
a neat tomb of marble is a better monument
than a great pile of rubbish, &c.   It might be
answered to this, that the pictures and poems of
great masters have been always valued, though
the last hand were not put to them : and I

1.—In the preface to his works.

believe none of those gentlemen that will make the objection would refuse a sketch of Raphael's, or one of Titian's draughts of the first sitting. I might tell them, too, what care has been taken by the learned to preserve the fragments of the ancient Greek and Latin poets ; there has been thought to be a divinity in what they said ; and therefore the least pieces of it have been kept up and reverenced like religious relics ; and I am sure, take away the *mille anni*, [1] and impartial reasoning will tell us there is as much due to the memory of Mr. Waller, as to the most celebrated names of antiquity.

But, to waive the dispute now of what *ought* to have been done, I can assure the reader what *would* have been, had this edition been delayed. The following poems were got abroad, and in a great many hands ; it were vain to expect that, among so many admirers of Mr. Waller, they should not meet with one fond enough to publish

---

[1].— Alluding to that verse in Juvenal—

   . . . . Et uni cedit Homero
Propter mille annos. . . . —Sat. 7, 38-39.

And yields to Homer on no other score,
Than that he lived a thousand years before.

MR. C. DRYDEN.

them. They might have stayed, indeed, till by frequent transcriptions they had been corrupted extremely, and jumbled together with things of another kind ; but then they would have found their way into the world ; so it was thought a greater piece of kindness to the author to put them out whilst they continue genuine and unmixed and such as he himself, were he alive, might own.

POEMS.

OF THE DANGER HIS MAJESTY [BEING PRINCE] ESCAPED IN THE ROAD AT SAINT ANDREWS.[1]

Now had his Highness bid farewell to Spain,
And reached the sphere of his own power, the main;
With British bounty in his ship he feasts
The Hesperian princes, his amazed guests
To find that watery wilderness exceed   5
The entertainment of their great Madrid.
Healths to both kings, attended with the roar
Of cannons, echoed from the affrighted shore,
With loud resemblance of his thunder, prove
Bacchus the seed of cloud-compelling Jove;   10
While to his harp divine Arion sings
The loves and conquests of our Albion kings.

  Of the Fourth Edward was his noble song,
Fierce, goodly, valiant, beautiful, and young;

1.—1645, *St. Andere.* 1664, *Saint Anderes.*

He rent the crown from vanquished Henry's head, 15
Raised the White Rose, and trampled on the Red ;
Till love, triumphing o'er the victor's pride,
Brought Mars and Warwick to the conquered side ;
Neglected Warwick (whose bold hand, like Fate,
Gives and resumes the sceptre of our state)   20
Woos for his master ; and with double shame,
Himself deluded, mocks the princely dame,
The Lady Bona, whom just anger burns,
And foreign war with civil rage returns.
Ah ! spare your swords, where beauty is to blame; 25
Love gave the affront, and must repair the same ;
When France shall boast of her, whose conquering
     eyes
Have made the best of English hearts their prize ;
Have power to alter the decrees of Fate,
And change again the counsels of our state.   30
   What the prophetic Muse intends, alone
To him that feels the secret wound is known.
   With the sweet sound of this harmonious lay
About the keel delighted dolphins play,
Too sure a sign of sea's ensuing rage,   35
Which must anon this royal troop engage ;
To whom soft sleep seems more secure and sweet,
Within the town commanded by our fleet.
   These mighty peers placed in the gilded barge,
Proud with the burden of so brave a charge,   40
With painted oars the youths begin to sweep
Neptune's smooth face, and cleave the yielding deep ;

Which soon becomes the seat of sudden war
Between the wind and tide that fiercely jar.
As when a sort of lusty shepherds try   45
Their force at football, care of victory
Makes them salute so rudely breast to breast,
That their encounters seem too rough for jest ;
They ply their feet, and still the restless ball,
Tossed to and fro, is urged by them all :   50
So fares the doubtful barge 'twixt tide and winds,
And like effect of their contention finds.
Yet the bold Britons still securely rowed ;
Charles and his virtue was their sacred load ;
Than which a greater pledge Heaven could not give, 55
That the good boat this tempest should outlive.
  But storms increase, and now no hope of grace
Among them shines, save in the Prince's face ;
The rest resign their courage, skill, and sight,
To danger, horror, and unwelcome night.   60
The gentle vessel (wont with state and pride
On the smooth back of silver Thames to ride)
Wanders astonished in [1] the angry main,
As Titan's car did, while the golden rein
Filled the young hand of his adventurous son,   65
When the whole world an equal hazard run
To this of ours, the light of whose desire
Waves threaten now, as that was scared by fire.
The impatient sea grows impotent and raves,

1.—1645, *through.*

That, night assisting, his impetuous waves 70
Should find resistance from so light a thing ;
These surges ruin, those our safety bring.
The oppressed vessel doth the charge abide,
Only because assailed on every side ;
So men with rage and passion set on fire, 75
Trembling for haste, impeach their mad desire.
The pale Iberians had expired with fear,
But that their wonder did divert their care,
To see the Prince with danger moved no more
Than with the pleasures of their court before ; 80
Godlike his courage seemed, whom nor delight
Could soften, nor the face of death affright.
Next to the power of making tempests cease,
Was in that storm to have so calm a peace.
Great Maro could no greater tempest feign, 85
When the loud winds usurping on the main
For angry Juno, laboured to destroy
The hated relics of confounded Troy ;
His bold Æneas, on like billows tossed
In a tall ship, and all his country lost, 90
Dissolves with fear ; and both his hands upheld,
Proclaims them happy whom the Greeks had quelled
In honourable fight ; our hero, set
In a small shallop, Fortune in his debt,
So near a hope of crowns and sceptres, more 95
Than ever Priam, when he flourished, wore ;
His loins yet full of ungot princes, all
His glory in the bud, lets nothing fall

That argues fear ; if any thought annoys
The gallant youth, 'tis love's untasted joys,　　100
And dear remembrance of that fatal glance,
For which he lately pawned his heart in France ;
Where he had seen a brighter nymph than she
That sprung out of his present foe, the sea.
That noble ardour, more than mortal fire,　　105
The conquered ocean could not make expire ;
Nor angry Thetis raise her waves above
The heroic Prince's courage or his love ;
'Twas indignation, and not fear he felt,
The shrine should perish where that image dwelt.　110
Ah, Love forbid ! the noblest of thy train
Should not survive to let her know his pain ;
Who nor his peril minding nor his flame,
Is entertained with some less serious game,
Among the bright nymphs of the Gallic court,　　115
All highly born, obsequious to her sport ;
They roses seem, which in their early pride
But half reveal, and half their beauties hide ;
She the glad morning, which her beams does throw
Upon their smiling leaves, and gilds them so ;　　120
Like bright Aurora, whose refulgent ray
Foretells the fervour of ensuing day,
And warns the shepherd with his flocks retreat
To leafy shadows from the threatened heat.
　　From Cupid's string [1] of many shafts, that fled　125

1.—1645. *Strings* in 1664 and subsequent editions.

Winged with those plumes which noble Fame had
    shed,
As through the wondering world she flew, and told
Of his adventures, haughty, brave, and bold ;
Some had already touched the royal maid,
But Love's first summons seldom are obeyed ;   130
Light was the wound, the Prince's care unknown,
She might not, would not, yet reveal her own.
His glorious name had so possessed her ears,
That with delight those antique tales she hears
Of Jason, Theseus, and such worthies old,   135
As with his story best resemblance hold.
And now she views, as on the wall it hung,
What old Musæus so divinely sung ;
Which art with life and love did so inspire,
That she discerns and favours that desire,   140
Which there provokes the adventurous youth to swim,
And in Leander's danger pities him ;
Whose not new love alone, but fortune, seeks
To frame his story like that[1] amorous Greek's.
For from the stern of some good ship appears   145
A friendly light, which moderates their fears ;
New courage from reviving hope they take,
And climbing o'er the waves that taper make,
On which the hope of all their lives depends,
As his on that fair Hero's hand extends.   150
The ship at anchor, like a fixed rock,

1.—1664 and 1682, *the.*

Breaks the proud billows which her large sides knock ;
Whose rage restrained, foaming higher swells,
And from her port the weary barge repels,
Threatening to make her, forced out again,   155
Repeat the dangers of the troubled main.
Twice was the cable hurled in vain ; the Fates
Would not be moved for our sister states ;
For England is the third successful throw,
And then the genius of that land they know,   160
Whose prince must be (as their own books devise)
Lord of the scene where now his [1] danger lies.
   Well sung the Roman bard, "All human things
Of dearest value hang on slender strings."
O see the then sole hope, and, in design   165
Of Heaven, our joy, supported by a line !
Which for that instant was Heaven's care, above[2]
The chain that's fixed to the throne of Jove,
On which the fabric of our world depends ;
One link dissolved, the whole creation ends.   170

---

1 -1664, *the*.
2.—In the edition of 1636 at the end of this line there is a
comma, which is not found in the previous editions.

TO THE QUEEN,

OCCASIONED UPON SIGHT OF HER MAJESTY'S
PICTURE.

WELL fare the hand ! which to our humble sight
Presents that beauty, which the dazzling light
Of royal splendour hides from weaker eyes,
And all access, save by this art, denies.
Here only we have courage to behold   5
This beam of glory ; here we dare unfold
In numbers thus the wonders we conceive ;
The gracious image, seeming to give leave,
Propitious stands, vouchsafing to be seen,
And by our muse saluted, Mighty Queen,   10
In whom the extremes of power and beauty move,
The Queen of Britain, and the Queen of Love !
   As the bright sun (to which we owe no sight
Of equal glory to your beauty's light)
Is wisely placed in so sublime a seat,   15
To extend his light, and moderate his heat ;
So, happy 'tis you move in such a sphere,
As your high Majesty with awful fear
In human breasts might qualify that fire,
Which, kindled by those eyes, had flamed higher   20

Than when the scorched world like hazard run,
By the approach of the ill-guided sun.
  No other nymphs have title to men's hearts,
But as their meanness larger hope imparts ;
Your beauty more the fondest lover moves   25
With admiration than his private loves ;
With admiration ! for a pitch so high
(Save sacred Charles his) never love durst fly.
Heaven that preferred a sceptre to your hand,
Favoured our freedom more than your command ; 30
Beauty had crowned you, and you must have been
The whole world's mistress, other than a Queen.
All had been rivals, and you might have spared,
Or killed, and tyrannized, without a guard.
No power achieved, either by arms or birth,   35
Equals love's empire both in heaven and earth.
Such eyes as yours on Jove himself have thrown
As bright and fierce a lightning as his own ;
Witness our Jove, prevented by their flame
In his swift passage to the Hesperian dame ;   40
When, like a lion, finding, in his way
To some intended spoil, a fairer prey,
The royal youth pursuing the report
Of beauty, found it in the Gallic court ;
There public care with private passion fought   45
A doubtful combat in his noble thought :
Should he confess his greatness, and his love,
And the free faith of your great brother prove ;
With his Achates breaking through the cloud

Of that disguise which did their graces shroud ;   50
And mixing with those gallants at the ball,
Dance with the ladies, and outshine them all ?
Or on his journey o'er the mountains ride ?—
So when the fair Leucothoe he espied,
To check his steeds impatient Phœbus yearned,   55
Though all the world was in his course concerned.
What may hereafter her meridian do,
Whose dawning beauty warmed his bosom so ?
Not so divine a flame, since deathless gods
Forbore to visit the defiled abodes   60
Of men, in any mortal breast did burn ;
Nor shall, till piety and they return.

OF HIS MAJESTY'S RECEIVING THE NEWS OF THE DUKE OF BUCKINGHAM'S DEATH.

So earnest with thy God ! can no new care,
No sense of danger, interrupt thy prayer?
The sacred wrestler, till a blessing given,
Quits not his hold, but halting conquers Heaven ;
Nor was the stream of thy devotion stopped,   5
When from the body such a limb was lopped,
As to thy present state was no less maim,
Though thy wise choice has since repaired the same.
Bold Homer durst not so great virtue feign
In his best pattern : for Patroclus slain,[1]   10
With such amazement as weak mothers use,
And frantic gesture, he receives the news.
Yet fell his darling by the impartial chance
Of war, imposed by royal Hector's lance ;
Thine in full peace, and by a vulgar hand   15
Torn from thy bosom, left his high command.
   The famous painter could allow no place
For private sorrow in a prince's face :
Yet, that his piece might not exceed belief,
He cast a veil upon supposed grief.   20
'Twas want of such a precedent as this
Made the old heathen frame their gods amiss.

1.—1686, *In his best pattern, of Patroclus slain ; for* is the reading of the 1645 edition, but there the line ends with a full stop, which I have ventured to remove.

Their Phœbus should not act a fonder part
For their[1] fair boy,[2] than he did for his hart ;
Nor blame for Hyacinthus' fate his own,   25
That kept from him wished death, hadst thou been
    known.
He that with thine shall weigh[3] good David's deeds,
Shall find his passion, not his love, exceeds :
He cursed the mountains where his brave friend died,
But let[4] false Ziba with his heir divide ;   30
Where thy immortal love to thy best[5] friends,
Like that of Heaven, upon their seed descends.
Such huge extremes inhabit thy great mind,
Godlike, unmoved, and yet, like woman, kind !
Which of the ancient poets had not brought   35
Our Charles's pedigree from Heaven, and taught
How some bright dame, compressed by mighty Jove,
Produced this mixed Divinity and Love ?

TO THE KING,

ON HIS RETURN FROM SCOTLAND.

SEDIBUS emigrans solitis, comitatus inermi
    Rex turbâ, simplex et diadema gerens,
Ecce ! redit bino Carolus diademate cinctus :
    Hæc ubi nuda dedit pompa, quid arma dabunt.

1.—1645, 1664, 1668, *the.*   2.—Cyparissus.
3.—1645, *Yet he that weighs with thine.*
4.—1645, *lets.*   5.—1645, *blest.*

OF SALLE.

OF Jason, Theseus, and such worthies old,
Light seem the tales antiquity has told ;
Such beasts and monsters as their force oppressed,
Some places only, and some times, infest.
Salle, that scorned all power and laws of men,   5
Goods with their owners hurrying to their den,
And future ages threatening with a rude [1]
And savage race, successively renewed ;
Their king despising with rebellious pride,
And foes professed to all the world beside ;   10
This pest of mankind gives our hero fame,
And through the obliged world dilates his name.
    The Prophet once to cruel Agag said,
" As thy fierce sword has mothers childless made,
So shall the sword make thine ;" and with that word 15
He hewed the man in pieces with his sword.
Just Charles-like measure has returned to these
Whose Pagan hands had stained the troubled seas ;
With ships they made the spoiled merchant mourn ;
With ships their city and themselves are torn.   20

1.—1645, *crude.*

One squadron of our winged castles sent,
O'erthrew their fort, and all their navy rent ;
For not content the dangers to increase,
And act the part of tempests in the seas,
Like hungry wolves, these pirates from our shore   25
Whole flocks of sheep, and ravished cattle bore.
Safely they might [1] on other nations prey, —
Fools to provoke the sovereign of the sea !
Mad Cacus so, whom like ill fate persuades,
The herd of fair Alcmena's seed invades,   30
Who for revenge, and mortals' glad relief,
Sacked the dark cave, and crushed that horrid thief.
    Morocco's monarch, wondering at this fact,
Save that his presence his affairs exact,
Had come in person to have seen and known   35
The injured world's revenger and his own.
Hither he sends the chief among his peers,
Who in his bark proportioned [2] presents bears,
To the renowned for piety and force,
Poor captives manumised, and matchless horse.   40

1.—1645, *did.*   2.—1645, *well-chosen.*

TO THE KING, ON HIS NAVY.

Where'er thy navy spreads her canvas wings,
Homage to thee, and peace to all she brings;
The French and Spaniard, when thy flags appear,
Forget their hatred, and consent to fear.
So Jove from Ida did both hosts survey,   5
And when he pleased to thunder part the fray.
Ships heretofore in seas like fishes sped,
The mighty still upon the smaller [1] fed;
Thou on the deep imposest nobler [2] laws,
And by that justice hast removed the cause   10
Of those rude tempests, which for rapine sent,
Too oft, alas! involved the innocent.
Now shall the ocean, as thy Thames, be free
From both those fates, of storms and piracy.
But we most happy, who can fear no force   15
But winged troops, or Pegasean horse.
'Tis not so hard for greedy foes to spoil
Another nation, as to touch our soil.
Should nature's self invade the world again,
And o'er the centre spread the liquid main,   20
Thy power were safe, and her destructive hand
Would but enlarge the bounds of thy command;
Thy dreadful fleet would style thee lord of all,
And ride in triumph o'er the drowned ball;

1.—In all editions previous to 1686, *The mightiest still upon
the smallest fed.*
2.—1645, *stricter.*

Those towers of oak o'er fertile plains might go,   25
And visit mountains where they once did grow.
　The world's restorer never could[1] endure
That finished Babel should those men secure,
Whose pride designed that fabric to have stood
Above the reach of any second flood ;   30
To thee, his chosen, more indulgent, he
Dares trust such power with so much piety.

UPON HIS MAJESTY'S REPAIRING OF PAUL'S.

THAT shipwrecked vessel which the Apostle bore,
Scarce suffered more upon Melita's shore,
Than did his temple in the sea of time,
Our nation's glory, and our nation's crime.
When the first monarch of this happy isle,   5
Moved with the ruin of so brave a pile,
This work of cost and piety begun,
To be accomplished by his glorious son,
Who all that came within the ample thought
Of his wise sire has to perfection brought ;   10
He, like Amphion, makes those quarries leap
Into fair figures from a confused heap ;
For in his art of regiment is found
A power like that of harmony in sound.   [15
　Those antique minstrels sure were Charles-like kings,

1.—1645, *once could not.*

Cities their lutes, and subjects' hearts their strings,
On which with so divine a hand they strook,
Consent of motion from their breath they took :
So all our minds with his conspire to grace
The Gentiles' great apostle, and deface   20
Those state-obscuring sheds, that like a chain
Seemed to confine and fetter him again ;
Which the glad saint shakes off at his command,
As once the viper from his sacred hand :
So joys the aged oak, when we divide   25
The creeping ivy from his injured side.
    Ambition rather would affect the fame
Of some new structure, to have borne her name.
Two distant virtues in one act we find,
The modesty and greatness of his mind ;   30
Which not content to be above the rage,
And injury of all-impairing age,
In its own worth secure, doth higher climb,
And things half swallowed from the jaws of Time
Reduce ; an earnest of his grand design,   35
To frame no new church, but the old refine ;
Which, spouse-like, may with comely grace command,
More than by force of argument or hand.
For doubtful reason few can apprehend,
And war brings ruin where it should amend ;   40
But beauty, with a bloodless conquest, finds
A welcome sovereignty in rudest minds.
    Not aught which Sheba's wondering queen beheld
Amongst the works of Solomon, excelled

C

His ships, and building; emblems of a heart   45
Large both in magnanimity and art.
   While the propitious heavens this work attend,
Long-wanted showers they forget to send ;
As if they meant to make it understood
Of more importance than our vital food.   50
   The sun, which riseth to salute the quire
Already finished, setting shall admire
How private bounty could so far extend :
The King built all, but Charles the western end.
So proud a fabric to devotion given,   55
At once it threatens and obliges heaven !
   Laomedon, that had the gods in pay,
Neptune, with him that rules the sacred day,
Could no such structure raise : Troy walled so high,
The Atrides might as well have forced the sky.   60
   Glad, though amazed, are our neighbour kings.
To see such power employed in peaceful things ;
They list not urge it to the dreadful field ;
The task is easier to destroy than build.

>   . . . .Sic gratia regum
>   Pieriis tentata modis. . . . .—HORAT.[1]

1. –This quotation (Ars Poetica, 404-5) does not occur in the edition of 1645.

TO MR. HENRY LAWES,

WHO HAD THEN NEWLY SET A SONG OF MINE IN THE YEAR 1635.[1]

VERSE makes heroic virtue live ;
But you can life to verses give.
As when in open air we blow,
The breath, though strained, sounds flat and low ;
But if a trumpet take the blast,   5
It lifts it high, and makes it last :
So in your airs our numbers dressed,
Make a shrill sally from the breast
Of nymphs, who, singing what we penned,
Our passions to themselves commend ;   10
While love, victorious with thy art,
Governs at once their voice and heart.
   You by the help of tune and time,
Can make that song that was but rhyme.
Noy pleading, no man doubts the cause ;   15
Or questions verses set by Lawes.

1.—This poem was first printed in "Ayres and Dialogues, For one, two, and three voices." By Henry Lawes, London, 1653. Folio.

As a church window,[1] thick with paint,
Lets in a light but dim and faint ;
So others, with division, hide
The light of sense, the poet's pride :   20
But you alone may truly boast
That not a syllable is lost ;
The writer's, and the setter's skill
At once the ravished ears[2] do fill.
Let those which only warble long,   25
And gargle in their throats a song,
Content themselves with Ut, Re, Mi :
Let words, and sense, be set by thee.

1.—" Ayres and Dialogues," *For as a window.*
2.—" Ayres and Dialogues," *ear.*

THE COUNTRY TO MY LADY OF CARLISLE.

MADAM, of all the sacred Muse inspired,
Orpheus alone could with the woods comply;
Their rude inhabitants his song admired,
And Nature's self, in those that could not lie:
Your beauty next our solitude invades,   5
And warms us, shining through the thickest shades.

Nor ought the tribute which the wondering court
Pays your fair eyes, prevail with you to scorn
The answer and consent to that[1] report
Which, echo-like, the country does return: 10
Mirrors are taught to flatter, but our springs
Present the impartial images of things.

A rural judge disposed of beauty's prize;
A simple shepherd was preferred to Jove;
Down to the mountains from the partial skies,   15
Came Juno, Pallas, and the Queen of Love,
To plead for that which was so justly given
To the bright Carlisle of the court of heaven.

Carlisle! a name which all our woods are taught,
Loud as his Amaryllis, to resound;   20
Carlisle! a name which on the bark is wrought
Of every tree that's worthy of the wound.
From Phœbus' rage our shadows and our streams
May guard us better than from Carlisle's beams.

1.—1645, *the.*

THE COUNTESS OF CARLISLE IN MOURNING.

WHEN from black clouds no part of sky is clear,
But just so much as lets the sun appear,
Heaven then would seem thy image, and reflect
Those sable vestments, and that bright aspect.
A spark of virtue by the deepest shade   5
Of sad adversity is fairer made ;
Nor less advantage doth thy beauty get ;
A Venus rising from a sea of jet !
Such was the appearance of new formed light,
While yet it struggled with eternal night.   10
Then mourn no more, lest thou admit increase
Of glory by thy noble lord's decease.
We find not that the laughter-loving dame
Mourned for Anchises ; 'twas enough she came
To grace the mortal with her deathless bed,   15
And that his living eyes such beauty fed ;
Had she been there, untimely joy, through all
Men's hearts diffused, had marred the funeral.
Those eyes were made to banish grief : as well
Bright Phœbus might affect in shades to dwell,   20
As they to put on sorrow : nothing stands,
But power to grieve, exempt from thy commands.

If thou lament, thou must do so alone ;
Grief in thy presence can lay hold on none.
Yet still persist the memory to love   25
Of that great Mercury of our mighty Jove,
Who, by the power of his enchanting tongue,
Swords from the hands of threatening monarchs **wrung.**
War he prevented, or soon made it cease,
Instructing princes in the arts of peace ;   30
Such as made Sheba's curious queen resort
To the large-hearted Hebrew's famous court.
Had Homer sat amongst his wondering guests,
He might have learned at those stupendous feasts,
With greater bounty, and more sacred state,   35
The banquets of the gods to celebrate.
But oh ! what elocution might he use,
What potent charms, that could so soon infuse
His absent master's love into the heart
Of Henrietta ! forcing her to part   40
From her loved brother, country, and the sun,
And, like Camilla, o'er the waves to run
Into his arms ! while the Parisian dames
Mourn for their ravished glory ; at their[1] flames
No less amaz'd than the amazed stars,   45
When the bold charmer of Thessalia wars
With Heaven itself, and numbers does repeat,
Which call descending Cynthia from her seat.

1.—1645, *her.*

IN ANSWER TO ONE WHO WRIT
AGAINST A FAIR LADY.[1]

WHAT fury has provoked thy wit to dare,
With Diomede, to wound the Queen of Love ?
Thy mistress' envy, or thine own despair ?
Not the just Pallas in thy breast did move
So blind a rage, with such a different fate ;   5
He honour won where thou hast purchased hate.

She gave assistance to his Trojan foe ;
Thou, that without a rival thou mayst love,
Dost to the beauty of this lady owe,
While after her the gazing world does move.   10
Canst thou not be content to love alone ?
Or is thy mistress not content with one ?

Though Ceres' child could not avoid the rape
Of the grim god that hurried her to hell,
Yet there her beauty did from slander 'scape,   15
When thou art there, she shall not speed so well :
The spiteful owl, whose tale detains her there,
Is not so blind to say she is not fair.

1.—1645, *In Answer to a libell against her, &c.*, immediately
following the preceding poem, which is headed as in the text.

Hast thou not read of Fairy Arthur's shield,
Which, but disclosed, amazed the weaker eyes   20
Of proudest foes, and won the doubtful field?
So shall thy rebel wit become her prize.
Should thy iambics swell into a book,
All were confuted with one radiant look.

Heaven he obliged that placed her in the skies ;   25
Rewarding Phœbus, for inspiring so
His noble brain, by likening to those eyes
His joyful beams ; but Phœbus is thy foe,
And neither aids thy fancy nor thy sight,
So ill thou rhym'st against so fair a light.   30

OF HER CHAMBER.

THEY taste of death that do at heaven arrive ;
But we this paradise approach alive.
Instead of death, the dart of love does strike,
And renders all within these walls alike.
The high in titles, and the shepherd, here   5
Forgets his greatness, and forgets his fear.
All stand amazed, and gazing on the fair,
Lose thought of what themselves or others are ;
Ambition lose, and have no other scope,
Save Carlisle's favour, to employ their hope.   10
The Thracian could (though all those tales were true
The bold Greeks tell) no greater wonders do ;
Before his feet so sheep and lions lay,
Fearless and wrathless while they heard him play.
The gay, the wise, the gallant, and the grave,   15
Subdued alike, all but one passion have :
No worthy mind but finds in hers there is
Something proportioned to the rule of his ;
While she with cheerful, but impartial grace,
(Born for no one, but to delight the race   20
Of men) like Phœbus so divides her light,
And warms us, that she stoops not from her height.

TO PHYLLIS.

PHYLLIS! 'twas love that injured you,
And on that rock your Thyrsis threw ;
Who for proud Celia could have died,
Whilst you no less accused his pride.
 Fond Love his darts at random throws,   5
And nothing springs from what he sows ;
From foes discharged, as often meet
The shining points of arrows fleet,
In the wide air creating fire,
As souls that join in one desire.   10
 Love made the lovely Venus burn
In vain, and for the cold youth mourn,
Who the pursuit of churlish beasts
Preferred to sleeping on her breasts.
 Love makes so many hearts the prize   15
Of the bright Carlisle's conquering eyes
Which she regards no more than they
The tears of lesser beauties weigh.
So have I seen the lost clouds pour
Into the sea a useless shower ;   20
And the vexed sailors curse the rain
For which poor shepherds prayed in vain.
Then, Phyllis, since our passions are

Governed by chance ; and not the care,
But sport of Heaven, which takes delight   25
To look upon this Parthian fight[1]
Of love, still flying, or in chase,
Never encountering face to face
No more to love we'll sacrifice,
But to the best of deities ;   30
And let our hearts, which love disjoined,
By his kind mother be combined.

TO MR. GEORGE SANDYS,

ON HIS TRANSLATION OF SOME PARTS OF THE BIBLE.

How bold a work attempts that pen,
Which would enrich our vulgar tongue
With the high raptures of those men
Who, here, with the same spirit sung
Wherewith they now assist the choir   5
Of angels, who their songs admire !

Whatever those inspired souls
Were urged to express, did shake
The aged deep, and both the poles ;
Their numerous thunder could awake   10
Dull earth, which does with Heaven consent
To all they wrote, and all they meant.

1.—1686, *flight.*

Say, sacred bard ! what could bestow
Courage on thee to soar so high ?
Tell me, brave friend ! what helped thee so   15
To shake off all mortality ?
To light this torch, thou hast climbed higher
Than he who stole celestial fire.

UPON BEN JONSON.

MIRROR of poets ! mirror of our age !
Which her whole face beholding on thy stage,
Pleased, and displeased, with her own faults, endures
A remedy like those whom music cures.
Thou hast alone[1] those various inclinations   5
Which Nature gives to ages, sexes, nations,
So traced[2] with thy all-resembling pen,
That whate'er[3] custom has imposed on men,
Or ill-got habit (which deforms them so,
That scarce a brother can his brother know)[4]   10
Is represented to the wondering eyes
Of all that see, or read, thy comedies.

1.—*Thou not alone.*—" Jonsonus Virbius," 1638.
2.—*Hast traced*   *Ibid.*
3.—*But all that*   *Ibid.*
4.—*Or ill-got habits* (*which distort them so*
      That scarce the brother can the brother know).   *Ibid.*

Whoever in those glasses looks, may find
The spots returned, or graces, of his mind ;
And by the help of so divine an art,   15
At leisure view, and dress, his nobler part.
Narcissus, cozened by that flattering well,
Which nothing could but of his beauty tell,
Had here, discovering the deformed estate
Of his fond mind, preserved himself with hate.   20
But virtue too, as well as vice, is clad
In flesh and blood so well, that Plato had
Beheld, what his high fancy once embraced,
Virtue with colours, speech, and motion graced.
The sundry postures of thy copious Muse   25
Who would express, a thousand tongues must use ;
Whose fate's no less peculiar than thy art ;
For as thou couldst all characters impart,
So none could render thine, which still escapes,
Like Proteus, in variety of shapes ;   30
Who was nor this, nor that, but all we find,
And all we can imagine, in mankind.

TO MY LORD NORTHUMBERLAND,

UPON THE DEATH OF HIS LADY.

To this great loss a sea of tears is due ;
But the whole debt not to be paid by you.
Charge not yourself with all, nor render vain
Those showers the eyes of us your servants rain.
Shall grief contract the largeness of that heart,   5
In which nor fear, nor anger, has a part?
Virtue would blush if time should boast (which dries,
Her sole child dead, the tender mother's eyes)
Your mind's relief, where reason triumphs so
Over all passions, that they ne'er could grow   10
Beyond their limits in your noble breast,
To harm another, or impeach your rest.
This we observed, delighting to obey
One who did never from his great self stray ;
Whose mild example seemed to engage   15
The obsequious seas, and teach them not to rage.
   The brave Æmilius, his great[1] charge laid down,
(The force of Rome, and fate of Macedon)
In his lost sons did feel the cruel stroke
Of changing fortune, and thus highly spoke   20

1.—This word is omitted in the edition of 1645.

Before Rome's people : "We did oft implore,
That if the heavens had any bad[1] in store
For your Æmilius, they would pour that ill
On his own house, and let you[2] flourish still."
You on the barren seas, my lord, have spent   25
Whole springs and summers to the public lent ;
Suspended all the pleasures of your life,
And shortened the short joy of such a wife ;
For which your country's more obliged than
For many lives of old less happy men.   30
You, that have sacrificed so great a part
Of youth, and private bliss, ought to impart
Your sorrow too, and give your friends a right
As well in your affliction as delight.
Then with Æmilian courage bear this cross,   35
Since public persons only public loss
Ought to affect.   And though her form and youth,
Her application to your will and truth,
That noble sweetness, and that humble state,
(All snatched away by such a hasty fate !)   40
Might give excuse to any common breast,
With the huge weight of so just grief oppressed ;
Yet let no portion of your life be stained
With passion, but your character maintained
To the last act.   It is enough her stone   45
May honoured be with superscription
Of the sole lady who had power to move
The great Northumberland to grieve, and love.

1.—1645, *ill.*   2.—1664, *yours.*

TO MY LORD ADMIRAL,

OF HIS LATE SICKNESS AND RECOVERY.

WITH joy like ours, the Thracian youth invades
Orpheus, returning from the Elysian shades;
Embrace the hero, and his stay implore;
Make it their public suit he would no more
Desert them so, and for his spouse's sake,　　　5
His vanished love, tempt the Lethean lake.
The ladies, too, the brightest of that time,
(Ambitious all his lofty bed to climb)
Their doubtful hopes with expectation feed,
Who shall the fair Eurydice succeed:　　　10
Eurydice! for whom his numerous moan
Makes listening trees and savage mountains groan;
Through all the air his sounding strings dilate
Sorrow, like that which touched our hearts of late.
Your pining sickness, and your restless pain,　　　15
At once the land affecting, and the main,
When the glad news that you were admiral
Scarce through the nation spread, 'twas feared by all
That our great Charles, whose wisdom shines in you,
Would be perplexed how to choose a new.　　　20
So more than private was the joy and grief,

D

That at the worst it gave our souls relief,
That in our age such sense of virtue lived,
They joyed so justly, and so justly grieved.
Nature (her fairest lights eclipsed) seems   25
Herself to suffer in those sharp extremes ;
While not from thine alone thy blood retires,
But from those cheeks which all the world admires.
The stem thus threatened, and the sap in thee,
Droop all the branches of that noble tree !   30
Their beauty they, and we our love suspend ;
Nought can our wishes, save thy health, intend.
As lilies overcharged with rain, they bend
Their beauteous heads, and with high heaven contend ;
Fold thee within their snowy arms, and cry—   35
" He is too faultless, and too young, to die ! "
So like immortals round about thee they
Sit, that they fright approaching death away.
Who would not languish, by so fair a train
To be lamented, and restored again?   40
Or, thus withheld, what hasty soul would go,
Though to be[1] blest ?   O'er her[2] Adonis so
Fair Venus mourned, and with the precious shower
Of her warm tears cherished the springing flower.

   The next support, fair hope of your great name, 45
And second pillar of that noble frame,
By loss of thee would no advantage have,
But step by step pursue thee to the grave.

1.—1645, *the*.   2.—1645, *young*.

And now relentless Fate, about to end
The line which backward does so far extend   50
That antique stock, which still the world supplies
With bravest spirits, and with brightest eyes,
Kind Phœbus, interposing, bid me say,
Such storms no more shall shake that house ; but they,
Like Neptune, and his sea-born niece, shall be   55
The shining glories of the land and sea ;
With courage guard, and beauty warm, our age,
And lovers fill with like poetic rage.

TO THE QUEEN MOTHER OF FRANCE, UPON HER LANDING.

GREAT Queen of Europe ! where thy offspring wears
All the chief crowns ; where princes are thy heirs ;
As welcome thou to sea-girt Britain's shore,
As erst Latona (who fair Cynthia bore)
To Delos was ; here shines a nymph as bright,   5
By thee disclosed, with like increase of light.
Why was her joy in Belgia confined ?[1]
Or why did you so much regard the wind ?
Scarce could the ocean, though enraged, have tossed
Thy sovereign bark, but where the obsequious coast 10
Pays tribute to thy bed.   Rome's conquering hand

1.—1645, *so confined.*

D 2

More vanquished nations under her command
Never reduced.   Glad Berecynthia so
Among her deathless progeny did go ;
A wreath of towers[1] adorned her reverend head,   15
Mother of all that on ambrosia fed.
Thy godlike race must sway the age to come,
As she Olympus peopled with her womb.
　　Would those commanders of mankind obey
Their honoured parent, all pretences lay   20
Down at your royal feet, compose their jars,
And on the growing Turk discharge these wars,
The Christian knights that sacred tomb should wrest
From Pagan hands, and triumph o'er the East ;
Our England's Prince, and Gallia's Dauphin, might
Like young Rinaldo and Tancredo fight ;   [25
In single combat by their swords again
The proud Argantes and fierce Soldan slain ;
Again might we their valiant deeds recite,
And with your Tuscan Muse exalt the fight.   30

1.—This is the reading of the edition of 1645 ; the later editions
have *flowers*.

UPON THE DEATH OF MY LADY RICH.

MAY those already cursed Essexian plains,
Where hasty death and pining sickness reigns,
Prove all a desert ! and none there make stay,
But savage beasts, or men as wild as they !
There the fair light which all our island graced,   5
Like Hero's taper in the window placed,
Such fate from the malignant air did find,
As that exposed to the boisterous wind.
   Ah, cruel Heaven ! to snatch so soon away
Her for whose life, had we had time to pray,   10
With thousand vows and tears we should have
     sought
That sad decree's suspension to have wrought.
But we, alas, no whisper of her pain
Heard, till 'twas sin to wish her here again.
That horrid word, at once, like lightning spread,   15
Struck all our ears—The Lady Rich is dead !
Heartrending news ! and dreadful to those few
Who her resemble, and her steps pursue ;
That Death should license have to rage among
The fair, the wise, the virtuous, and the young !   20
   The Paphian queen from that fierce battle borne,
With gored hand, and veil so rudely torn,

Like terror did among the immortals breed,
Taught by her wound that goddesses may[1] bleed.
    All stand amazed ! but beyond the rest   25
The heroic dame whose happy womb she blessed,
Moved with just grief, expostulates with Heaven,
Urging the[2] promise to the obsequious given,
Of longer life ; for ne'er was pious soul
More apt to obey, more worthy to control.   30
A skilful eye at once might read the race
Of Caledonian monarchs in her face,
And sweet humility ; her look and mind
At once were lofty, and at once were kind.
There dwelt the scorn of vice, and pity too,   35
For those that did what she disdained to do ;
So gentle and severe, that what was bad,
At once her hatred and her pardon had.
Gracious to all ; but where her love was due,
So fast, so faithful, loyal, and so true,   40
That a bold hand as soon might hope to force
The rolling lights of Heaven as change her course.
    Some happy angel, that beholds her there,
Instruct us to record what she was here !
And when this cloud of sorrow's overblown,   45
Through the wide world we'll make her graces known.
So fresh the wound is, and the grief so vast,
That all our art and power of speech is waste.
Here passion sways, but there the Muse shall raise
Eternal monuments of louder praise.   .   50

1.—1645, *might.*   2.—1645, *that.*

There our delight, complying with her fame,
Shall have occasion to recite thy name,
Fair Sacharissa !—and now only fair !
To sacred friendship we'll an altar rear,
(Such as the Romans did erect of old)   55
Where, on a marble pillar, shall be told
The lovely passion each to other bare,
With the resemblance of that matchless pair.
Narcissus to the thing for which he pined,
Was not more like than yours to her fair mind,   60
Save that she graced the several parts of life,
A spotless virgin, and a faultless wife.
Such was the sweet converse 'twixt her and you,
As that she holds with her associates now.
How false is hope, and how regardless fate,   65
That such a love should have so short a date !
Lately I saw her sighing part from thee ;
(Alas that such[1] the last farewell should be !)
So looked Astræa, her remove designed,
On those distressed friends she left behind.   70
Consent in virtue knit your hearts so fast,
That still the knot, in spite of death, does last ;
For as your tears, and sorrow-wounded soul,
Prove well that on your part this bond is whole,
So all we know of what they do above,   75
Is that they happy are, and that they love.
Let dark oblivion, and the hollow grave,

1.—1645, *that.*

Content themselves our frailer thoughts to have ;
Well chosen love is never taught to die,
But with our nobler part invades the sky.   80
Then grieve no more that one so heavenly shaped
The crooked hand of trembling age escaped ;
Rather, since we beheld not her decay,
But that she vanished so entire away,
Her wondrous beauty, and her goodness, merit   85
We should suppose that some propitious spirit
In that celestial form frequented here,
And is not dead, but ceases to appear.

THYRSIS, GALATEA.

THYRSIS.

As lately I on silver Thames did ride,
Sad Galatea on the bank I spied ;
Such was her look as sorrow taught to shine,
And thus she graced me with a voice divine.

GALATEA.

You that can tune your sounding strings so well,   5
Of ladies' beauties, and of love to tell,
Once change your note, and let your lute report
The justest grief that ever touched the Court.

THYRSIS.

Fair nymph ! I have in your delights no share,
Nor ought to be concerned in your care ;   10
Yet would I sing if I your sorrows knew,
And to my aid invoke no muse but you.

GALATEA.

Hear then, and let your song augment our grief,
Which is so great as not to wish relief.
She that had all which Natures gives, or Chance,   15
Whom Fortune joined with Virtue to advance
To all the joys this island could afford,
The greatest mistress, and the kindest lord ;
Who with the royal mixed her noble blood,
And in high grace with Gloriana stood ;   20
Her bounty, sweetness, beauty, goodness, such,
That none e'er thought her happiness too much ;
So well-inclined her favours to confer,
And kind to all, as Heaven had been to her !
The virgin's part, the mother, and the wife,   25
So well she acted in this span of life,
That though few years (too few, alas !) she told,
She seemed in all things, but in beauty, old.
As unripe fruit, whose verdant stalks do¹ cleave
Close to the tree, which grieves no less to leave   30

1.—1645, *stalk does.*

The smiling pendant which adorns her so,
And until autumn on the bough should grow ;
So seemed her youthful soul not easily forced,
Or from so fair, so sweet, a seat divorced.
Her fate at once did hasty seem and slow ;   35
At once too cruel, and unwilling too.

THYRSIS.

Under how hard a law are mortals born !
Whom now we envy, we anon must mourn ;
What Heaven sets highest, and seems most to prize,
Is soon removed from our wondering eyes !   40
But since the Sisters did so soon untwine
So fair a thread, I'll strive to piece the line.
Vouchsafe, sad nymph ! to let me know the dame,
And to the muses I'll commend her name ;
Make the wide country echo to your moan,   45
The listening trees and savage mountains groan.
What rock's not moved when the death is sung
Of one so good, so lovely, and so young ?

GALATEA.

'Twas Hamilton !—whom I had named before,
But naming her, grief lets me say no more.   50

ON MY LADY DOROTHY SIDNEY'S PICTURE.

SUCH was Philoclea, such Musidorus' flame ![1]
The matchless Sidney, that immortal frame
Of perfect beauty on two pillars placed ;
Not his high fancy could one pattern, graced
With such extremes of excellence, compose ;   5
Wonders so distant in one face disclose !
Such cheerful modesty, such humble state,
Moves certain love, but with a[2] doubtful fate
As when, beyond our greedy reach, we see
Inviting fruit on too sublime a tree.   10
All the rich flowers through his Arcadia found,
Amazed we see in this one garland bound.
Had but this copy (which the artist took
From the fair picture of that noble book)
Stood at Calander's, the brave friends had jarred, 15
And, rivals made, the ensuing story marred.
Just nature, first instructed by his thought,
In his own house thus practised what he taught ;
This glorious piece transcends what he could think,
So much his blood is nobler than his ink !   20

1.—1645, *Such was Philocleas, such Dorus' flame.*
2.—1664 and 1682, *as.*

TO VANDYCK.

Rare Artisan, whose pencil moves
Not our delights alone, but loves !
From thy shop of beauty we
Slaves return, that entered free.
The heedless lover does not know   5
Whose eyes they are that wound him so ;
But, confounded with thy art,
Inquires her name that has his heart.
Another, who did long refrain,
Feels his old wound bleed fresh again   10
With dear remembrance of that face,
Where now he reads new hopes of grace :
Nor scorn nor cruelty does find,
But gladly suffers a false wind
To blow the ashes of despair   15
From the reviving brand of care.
Fool ! that forgets her stubborn look
This softness from thy finger took.
Strange ! that thy hand should not inspire
The beauty only, but the fire ;   20
Not the form alone, and grace,
But act and power of a face.
Mayst thou yet thyself as well,

As all the world besides, excel !
So you the unfeigned truth rehearse   25
(That I may make it live in verse)
Why thou couldst not at one assay,
That face to aftertimes convey,
Which this admires.   Was it thy wit
To make her oft before thee sit ?   30
Confess, and we'll forgive thee this ;
For who would not repeat that bliss ?
And frequent sight of such a dame
Buy with the hazard of his fame ?
Yet who can tax thy blameless skill,   35
Though thy good hand had failed still,
When nature's self so often errs ?
She for this many thousand years
Seems to have practised with much care,
To frame the race of women fair ;   40
Yet never could a perfect birth
Produce before to grace the earth,
Which waxed old ere it could see
Her that amazed thy art and thee.
  But now 'tis done, O let me know   45
Where those immortal colours grow,
That could this deathless piece compose !
In lilies ? or the fading rose ?
No ; for this theft thou hast climbed higher
Than did Prometheus for his fire.   50

AT PENSHURST.

HAD Sacharissa[1] lived when mortals made
Choice of their deities, this sacred shade
Had held an altar to her[2] power, that gave
The peace and glory which these alleys have ;
Embroidered so with flowers where she stood,   5
That it became a garden of a wood.
Her presence has such more than human grace,
That it can civilize the rudest place ;
And beauty too, and order, can impart,
Where nature ne'er intended it, nor art.   10
The plants acknowledge this, and her admire,
No less than those of old did Orpheus' lyre ;
If she sit down, with tops all towards her bowed,
They round about her into arbours crowd ;
Or if she walk, in even ranks they stand,   15
Like some well-marshalled and obsequious band.
Amphion so made stones and timber leap
Into fair figures from a confused heap ;
And in the symmetry of her parts is found
A power like that of harmony in sound.   20
   Ye lofty beeches, tell this matchless dame,
That if together ye fed all one flame,

1.—1645, *Dorothea.*   2.—1645, *the.*

It could not equalize the hundredth part
Of what her eyes have kindled in my heart !
Go, boy, and carve this passion on the bark   25
Of yonder tree, which stands the sacred mark
Of noble Sidney's birth ; when such benign,
Such more than mortal making stars did shine,
That there they cannot but for ever prove
The monument and pledge of humble love ;   30
His humble love whose hope shall ne'er rise higher,
Than for a pardon that he dares admire.

TO MY LORD OF LEICESTER.

NOT that thy trees at Penshurst groan,
Oppressed with their timely load,
And seem to make their silent moan,
That their great lord is now abroad :
They to delight his taste, or eye,   5
Would spend themselves in fruit, and die.

Not that thy harmless deer repine,
And think themselves unjustly slain
By any other hand than thine,
Whose arrows they would gladly stain ;   10
No, nor thy friends, which hold too dear
That peace with France which keeps thee there.

All these are less than that great cause
Which now exacts your presence here,
Wherein there meet the divers laws   15
Of public and domestic care.
For one bright nymph our youth contends,
And on your prudent choice depends.

Not the bright shield of Thetis' son,
(For which such stern debate did rise,   20
That the great Ajax Telamon
Refused to live without the prize)
Those Achive peers did more engage,
Than she the gallants of our age.

That beam of beauty, which begun   25
To warm us so when thou wert here,
Now scorches like the raging sun,
When Sirius does first appear.
O fix this flame! and let despair
Redeem the rest from endless care.   30

OF THE LADY WHO CAN SLEEP WHEN
SHE PLEASES.

No wonder sleep from careful lovers flies,
To bathe himself in Sacharissa's eyes.
As fair Astræa once from earth to heaven,
By strife and loud impiety was driven ;
So with our plaints offended, and our tears,   5
Wise Somnus to that paradise repairs ;
Waits on her will, and wretches does forsake,
To court the nymph for whom those wretches wake.
More proud than Phœbus of his throne of gold
Is the soft god those softer limbs to hold ;   10
Nor would exchange with Jove to hide the skies
In darkening clouds, the power to close her eyes ;
Eyes which so far all other lights control,
They warm our mortal parts, but these our soul !

   Let her free spirit, whose unconquered breast   15
Holds such deep quiet and untroubled rest,
Know that though Venus and her son should spare
Her rebel heart, and never teach her care,
Yet Hymen may enforce her[1] vigils keep,
And for another's joy suspend her sleep.   20

1.—Fenton altered this, admittedly without authority, but, as he hoped, for the better, to *Yet Hymen may in force his vigils keep.*

OF THE MISREPORT OF HER BEING PAINTED.

As when a sort of wolves infest the night
With their wild howlings at fair Cynthia's light,
The noise may chase sweet slumber from our eyes,
But never reach the mistress of the skies ;
So with the news of Sacharissa's wrongs   5
Her vexed servants blame those envious tongues ;
Call Love to witness that no painted fire
Can scorch men so, or kindle such desire ;
While, unconcerned, she seems moved no more
With this new malice than our loves before ;   10
But from the height of her great mind looks down
On both our passions without smile or frown.
So little care of what is done below
Hath the bright dame whom heaven affecteth so !
Paints her, 'tis true, with the same hand which
       spreads   15
Like glorious colours through the flowery meads,
When lavish Nature, with her best attire,
Clothes the gay spring, the season of desire ;
Paints her, 'tis true, and does her cheek adorn
With the same art wherewith she paints the morn ; 20
With the same art wherewith she gildeth so
Those painted clouds which form Thaumantias' bow.

OF HER PASSING THROUGH A CROWD OF PEOPLE.

As in old chaos (heaven with earth confused,
And stars with rocks together crushed and bruised)
The sun his light no further could extend
Than the next hill, which on his shoulders leaned ;
So in this throng bright Sacharissa fared,   5
Oppressed by those who strove to be her guard ;
As ships, though never so obsequious, fall
Foul in a tempest on their admiral.
A greater favour this disorder brought
Unto her servants than their awful thought   10
Durst entertain, when thus compelled they pressed
The yielding marble of her snowy breast.
While love insults, disguised in the cloud,
And welcome force, of that unruly crowd.
So the amorous tree, while yet the air is calm,   15
Just distance keeps from his desired palm ;
But when the wind her ravished branches throws
Into his arms, and mingles all their boughs,
Though loath he seems her tender leaves to press,
More loath he is that friendly storm should cease,   20
From whose rude bounty he the double use
At once receives, of pleasure and excuse.

E 2

THE STORY OF PHŒBUS AND DAPHNE, APPLIED.

THYRSIS, a youth of the inspired train,
Fair Sacharissa loved, but loved in vain.
Like Phœbus sung the no less amorous boy ;
Like Daphne she, as lovely, and as coy !
With numbers he the flying nymph pursues,   5
With numbers such as Phœbus' self might use !
Such is the chase when Love and Fancy leads,
O'er craggy mountains, and through flowery meads ;
Invoked to testify the lover's care,
Or form some image of his cruel fair.   10
Urged with his fury, like a wounded deer,
O'er these he. fled ; and now approaching near,
Had reached the nymph with his harmonious lay,
Whom all his charms could not incline to stay.
Yet what he sung in his immortal strain,   15
Though unsuccessful, was not sung in vain ;
All, but the nymph that should redress his wrong,
Attend his passion, and approve his song.
Like Phœbus thus, acquiring unsought praise,
He catched at love, and filled his arm with bays.   20

FABULA PHŒBI ET DAPHNES.

ARCADIÆ juvenis Thyrsis, Phœbique sacerdos,
Ingenti frustra Sacharissæ[1] ardebat amore.
Haud **Deus ipse** olim Daphni **majora canebat;**
Nec fuit **asperior Daphne, nec pulchrior illâ:**
Carminibus Phœbo dignis premit ille fugacem   5
Per rupes, per saxa, volans per florida vates
Pascua: formosam nunc his componere nympham,
Nunc illis crudelem insanâ mente solebat.
Audiit illa procul miserum, cytharamque sonantem;
Audiit, at nullis respexit mota querelis!   10
Ne tamen omnino caneret desertus, ad alta
Sidera perculsi referunt nova carmina montes.
Sic, non quæsitis cumulatus laudibus, olim
Elapsâ reperit Daphne sua laurea Phœbus.

SONG.

SAY, lovely dream! where couldst thou find
Shades[2] to counterfeit that face?
Colours of this glorious kind
Come not from any mortal place.

In heaven itself thou sure wert dressed   5
With that angel-like disguise:
Thus deluded am I blessed,
And see my joy with closed eyes.

1.—1645, *Galatea.*   2.—1686, *Shadows.*

But ah ! this image is too kind
To be other than a dream ;   10
Cruel Sacharissa's mind
Never put on that sweet extreme !

Fair dream ! if thou intend'st me grace,
Change that heavenly face[1] of thine ;
Paint despised love in thy face,   15
And make it to appear like mine.

Pale, wan, and meagre let it look,
With a pity-moving shape,
Such as wander by the brook
Of Lethe, or from graves escape.   20

Then to that matchless nymph appear,
In whose shape thou shinest so ;
Softly in her sleeping ear,
With humble words, express my woe.

Perhaps from greatness, state, and pride,   25
Thus surprised she may fall ;
Sleep does disproportion hide,
And, death resembling, equals all.

1.—1645, *this heavenly form.*

TO THE SERVANT OF A FAIR LADY.[1]

FAIR fellow-servant ! may your gentle ear
Prove more propitious to my slighted care
Than the bright dame's we serve : for her relief
(Vexed with the long expressions of my grief)
Receive these plaints ; nor will her high disdain   5
Forbid my humble muse to court her train.
  So, in those nations which the sun adore,
Some modest Persian, or some weak-eyed Moor,
No higher dares advance his dazzled sight,
Than to some gilded cloud, which near the light   10
Of their ascending god adorns the east,
And, graced with his beams, outshines the rest.
  Thy skilful hand contributes to our woe,
And whets those arrows which confound us so.
A thousand Cupids in those curls do sit,   15
Those curious nets thy slender fingers knit.
The Graces put not more exactly on
The attire of Venus, when the ball she won,
Than that young Beauty[2] by thy care is dressed,

1.—In the edition of 1645 these lines are headed, *To Mistris Braughton ;* they were omitted from the editions of 1664 and 1668, but reappeared in that of 1682 (with the above heading), with the exception of six lines, beginning at *So in those nations*, which Keck says were omitted by the author's direction.

2.—1645, *Sacharissa.*

When all our youth prefers her to the rest.   20
    You the soft season[1] know when best her mind
May be to pity, or to love, inclined :
In some well-chosen hour supply his fear,
Whose hopeless love durst never tempt the ear
Of that stern goddess.   You, her priest, declare   25
What offerings may propitiate the fair ;
Rich orient pearl, bright stones that ne'er decay,
Or polished lines, which longer last than they ;
For if I thought she took delight in those,
To where the cheerful morn does first disclose,   30
(The shady night removing with her beams)
Winged with bold love, I'd fly to fetch such gems.
But since her eyes, her teeth, her lip excels
All that is found in mines or fishes' shells,
Her nobler part as far exceeding these,   35
Nore but immortal gifts her mind should[2] please.
The shining jewels Greece and Troy bestowed
On Sparta's queen,[3] her lovely neck did load,
And snowy wrists ; but when the town was burned,
Those fading glories were to ashes turned ;   40
Her beauty, too, had perished, and her fame,
Had not the muse redeemed them from the flame.

1.—1645, *seasons.*   2.—1645, *can.*
3.—1645, *Those shining jewels Greece and Troy bestow'd,*
        The snowy wrists and lovely neck did lode
        Of Sparta's Queen.

TO A VERY YOUNG LADY.[1]

Why came I so untimely forth
Into a world which, wanting thee,
Could entertain us with no worth
Or shadow of felicity,
That time should me so far remove   5
From that which I was born to love?

Yet, fairest blossom! do not slight
That age which you may know so soon;
The rosy morn resigns her light,
And milder glory, to the noon;   10
And then what wonders shall you do,
Whose dawning beauty warms us so?

Hope waits upon the flowery prime;
And summer, though it be less gay,
Yet is not looked on as a time   15
Of declination or decay;
For with a full hand that does bring
All that was promised by the spring.

1.—1645, *To my young Lady Lucy Sidney.*

TO AMORET.

Fair ! that you may truly know
What you unto Thyrsis owe,
I will tell you how I do
Sacharissa love and you.

 Joy salutes me, when I set   5
My blessed eyes on Amoret ;
But with wonder I am strook,
When I on the other look.

 If sweet Amoret complains.
I have sense of all her pains ;   10
But for Sacharissa I
Do not only grieve, but die.

 All that of myself is mine,
Lovely Amoret ! is thine ;
Sacharissa's captive fain   15
Would untie his iron chain,
And, those scorching beams to shun,
To thy gentle shadow run.

 If the soul had free election
To dispose of her affection,   20
I would not thus long have borne
Haughty Sacharissa's scorn ;
But 'tis sure some power above,

Which controls our will in love !
   If not love, a strong desire   25
To create and spread that fire
In my breast, solicits me,
Beauteous Amoret! for thee
   'Tis amazement more than love,
Which her radiant eyes do move ;   30
If less splendour wait on thine,
Yet they so benignly shine,
I would turn my dazzled sight
To behold their milder light ;
But as hard 'tis to destroy   35
That high flame, as to enjoy ;
Which how easily I may do,
Heaven (as easily scaled) does know !
   Amoret ! as sweet and good
As the most delicious food,   40
Which, but tasted, does impart
Life and gladness to the heart.
   Sacharissa's beauty's wine,
Which to madness doth incline ;
Such a liquor as no brain   45
That is mortal can sustain.
   Scarce can I to heaven excuse
The devotion which I use
Unto that adored dame
For 'tis not unlike the same   50
Which I thither ought to send ;
So that if it could take end,

'Twould to heaven itself be due
To succeed her, and not you,
Who already have of me   55
All that's not idolatry ;
Which, though not so fierce a flame,
Is longer like to be the same.
    Then smile on me, and I will prove
Wonder is shorter-lived than love.   60

ON THE FRIENDSHIP BETWIXT TWO LADIES.[1]

TELL me, lovely, loving pair !
Why so kind, and so severe ?
Why so careless of our care,
Only to yourselves so dear ?

By this cunning change of hearts,   5
You the power of love control ;
While the boy's deluded darts
Can arrive at neither[2] soul.

1.—1645, *On the Friendship betwixt Sacharissa and Amoret.*
2.—1645, *neither's.*

For in vain to either breast
Still beguiled love does come,　　　　10
Where he finds a foreign guest,
Neither of your hearts at home.

Debtors thus with like design,
When they never mean to pay,
That they may the law decline,　　　15
To some friend make all away.

Not the silver doves that fly,
Yoked in Cytherea's car ;
Not the wings that lift so high,
And convey her son so far ;　　　　20

Are so lovely, sweet, and fair,
Or do more ennoble love ;
Are so choicely matched a pair,
Or with more consent do move.

ON HER COMING TO LONDON.

WHAT's she, so late from Penshurst come,
More gorgeous than the mid-day sun,
    That all the world amazes?
Sure 'tis some angel from above,
Or 'tis the Cyprian Queen of Love   5
    Attended by the Graces.

Or is't not Juno, Heaven's great dame,
Or Pallas armed, as on she came
    To assist the Greeks in fight,
Or Cynthia, that huntress bold,   10
Or from old Tithon's bed so cold,
    Aurora chasing night?

No, none of those, yet one that shall
Compare, perhaps exceed them all,
    For beauty, wit, and birth;   15
As good as great, as chaste as fair,
A brighter nymph none breathes the air,
    Or treads upon the earth.

'Tis Dorothèe, a maid high-born,
And lovely as the blushing morn,   20
    Of noble Sidney's race,
Oh ! could you see into [her] mind,
The beauties there locked-up outshine
    The beauties of her face.

Fair Dorothea, sent from heaven   25
To add more wonders to the seven,
    And glad each eye and ear,
Crown of her sex, the Muse's port,
The glory of our English court,
    The brightness of our sphere.   30

To welcome her the Spring breathes forth
Elysian sweets, March strews the earth
    With violets and posies,
The sun renews his [da]rting fires,
April puts on her best attires,   35
    And May her crown of roses.

Go, happy maid, increase the store
Of graces born with you, [and] more
    Add to their number still ;
So neither all-consuming age,
Nor envy's blast, nor fortune's rage   40
    Shall ever work you ill.

AT PENSHURST.

WHILE in the[1] park I sing, the listening deer
Attend my passion, and forget to fear.
When to the beeches I report my flame,
They bow their heads, as if they felt the same.
To gods appealing, when I reach their bowers   5
With loud complaints, they answer me in showers.
To thee a wild and cruel soul is given,
More deaf than trees, and prouder than the heaven !
Love's foe professed ! why dost thou falsely feign
Thyself a Sidney ? from which noble strain   10
He sprung, that could so far exalt the name
Of love, and warm our nation with his flame ;
That all we can of love, or high desire,
Seems but the smoke of amorous Sidney's fire.
Nor call her mother, who so well does prove   15
One breast may hold both chastity and love.
Never can she, that so exceeds the spring
In joy and bounty, be supposed to bring
One so destructive.   To no human stock
We owe this fierce unkindness, but the rock,   20
That cloven rock produced thee, by whose side
Nature, to recompense the fatal pride

1.—1645, *this.*

Of such stern beauty, placed those healing springs,
Which not more help, than that destruction, brings.
Thy heart no ruder than the rugged[1] stone,   25
I might, like Orpheus, with my numerous moan
Melt to compassion ; now, my traitorous song
With thee conspires to do the singer wrong ;
While thus I suffer not myself to lose
The memory of what augments my woes ;   30
But with my own breath still foment the fire,
With flames as high as fancy can aspire !
    This last complaint the indulgent ears did[2] pierce
Of just Apollo, president of verse ;
Highly concerned that the muse should bring   35
Damage to one whom he had taught to sing,
Thus he advised me : " On yon aged tree
Hang up thy lute, and hie thee to the sea,
That there with wonders thy diverted mind
Some truce, at least, may with this passion[3] find." 40
Ah, cruel nymph ! from whom her humble swain
Flies for relief unto the raging main,
And from the winds and tempests does expect
A milder fate than from her cold neglect !
Yet there he'll pray that the unkind may prove   45
Blessed in her choice ; and vows this endless love
Springs from no hope of what she can confer,
But from those gifts which heaven has heaped on her.

1.—1645, *that ragged.*   2.—1645, *does.*
3.—1645, *may with affection find.*

F

THE BATTLE OF THE SUMMER ISLANDS.

CANTO I.

What fruits they have, and how Heaven smiles
Upon those late-discovered isles.

AID me, Bellona ! while the dreadful fight
Betwixt a nation and two whales I write.
Seas stained with gore I sing, adventurous toil,
And how these monsters did disarm an isle.
    Bermudas, walled with rocks, who does not know ?
That happy island where huge lemons grow,   [5
And orange trees, which golden fruit do bear,
The Hesperian garden boasts of none so fair ;
Where shining pearl, coral, and many a pound,
On the rich shore, of ambergris is found.   10
The lofty cedar, which to heaven aspires,
The prince of trees ! is fuel for their fires ;
The smoke by which their loaded spits do turn,
For incense might on sacred altars burn ;
Their private roofs on odorous timber borne,   15
Such as might palaces for kings adorn.
The sweet palmettos a new Bacchus yield,
With leaves as ample as the broadest shield,
Under the shadow of whose friendly boughs
They sit, carousing where their liquor grows.   20

Figs there unplanted through the fields do grow,
Such as fierce Cato did the Romans show,
With the rare fruit inviting them to spoil
Carthage, the mistress of so rich a soil.
The naked rocks are not unfruitful there,   25
But, at some constant seasons, every year,
Their barren tops with luscious food abound,
And with the eggs of various fowls are crowned.
Tobacco is the worst of things, which they
To English landlords, as their tribute, pay.   30
Such is the mould, that the blessed tenant feeds
On precious fruits, and pays his rent in weeds.
With candied plantains, and the juicy pine,
On choicest melons, and sweet grapes, they dine,
And with potatoes fat their wanton swine.   35
Nature these cates with such a lavish hand
Pours out among them, that our coarser land
Tastes of that bounty, and does cloth return,
Which not for warmth, but ornament, is worn ;
For the kind spring, which but salutes us here,   40
Inhabits there, and courts them all the year.
Ripe fruits and blossoms on the same trees live ;
At once they promise what at once they give.
So sweet the air, so moderate the clime,
None sickly lives, or dies before his time.   45
Heaven sure has kept this spot of earth uncursed,
To show how all things were created first.
The tardy plants in our cold orchards placed,
Reserve their fruit for the next age's taste.

There a small grain in some few months will be   50
A firm, a lofty, and a spacious tree.
The palma-christi, and the fair papà,
Now but a seed, (preventing nature's law)
In half the circle of the hasty year
Project a shade, and lovely fruit do wear.   55
And as their trees, in our dull region set,
But faintly grow, and no perfection get ;
So, in this northern tract, our hoarser throats,
Utter unripe and ill-constrained notes,
Where the supporter of the poets' style,   60
Phœbus, on them eternally does smile.
Oh! how I long my careless limbs to lay
Under the[1] plantain's shade, and all the day
With amorous airs my fancy entertain,
Invoke the Muses, and improve my vein !   65
No passion there in my free breast should move,
None but the sweet and best of passions, love.
There while I sing, if gentle love be by,
That tunes my lute, and winds the strings so high,
With the sweet sound of Sacharissa's name   70
I'll make the listening savages grow tame.——
But while I do these pleasing dreams indite,
I am diverted from the promised fight.

1.—1645. a.

CANTO II.

Of their alarm,[1] and how their foes
Discovered were, this Canto shows.

THOUGH rocks so high about this island rise,
That well they may the numerous Turk despise,
Yet is no human fate exempt from fear,
Which shakes their hearts, while through the isle they
    hear
A lasting noise, as horrid and as loud   5
As thunder makes before it breaks the cloud.
Three days they dread this murmur, ere they know
From what blind cause the unwonted sound may grow.
At length two monsters of unequal size,
Hard by the shore, a fisherman espies;   10
Two mighty whales ! which swelling seas had tossed,
And left them prisoners on the rocky coast.
One as a mountain vast; and with her came
A cub, not much inferior to his dam.
Here in a pool, among the rocks engaged,   15
They roared, like lions caught in toils, and raged.
The man knew what they were, who heretofore
Had seen the like lie murdered on the shore;
By the wild fury of some tempest cast,
The fate of ships, and shipwrecked men, to taste. 20
As careless dames, whom wine and sleep betray
To frantic dreams, their infants overlay :

1.—1645, *affright.*

So there, sometimes, the raging ocean fails,
And her own brood exposes ; when the whales
Against sharp rocks, like reeling vessels quashed,   25
Though huge as mountains, are in pieces dashed ;
Along the shore their dreadful limbs lie scattered,
Like hills with earthquakes shaken. torn, and shattered.
Hearts sure of brass they had, who tempted first
Rude seas that spare not what themselves have nursed.
The welcome news through all the nation spread, [30
To sudden joy and hope converts their dread ;
What lately was their public terror, they
Behold with glad eyes as a certain prey ;
Dispose already of the untaken spoil,   35
And, as the purchase of their future toil,
These share the bones, and they divide the oil.
So was the huntsman by the bear oppressed,
Whose hide he sold—before he caught the beast !
  They man their boats, and all their young men arm
With whatsoever may the monsters harm ;   [40
Pikes, halberts, spits, and darts that wound so far,
The tools of peace, and instruments of war.
Now was the time for vigorous lads to show
What love, or honour, could invite them to ;   45
A goodly theatre ; where rocks are round
With reverend age, and lovely lasses, crowned.
Such was the lake which held this dreadful pair,
Within the bounds of noble Warwick's share ;
Warwick's bold Earl ! than which no title bears   50
A greater sound among our British peers ;

And worthy he the memory to renew,
The fate and honour to that title due,
Whose brave adventures have transferred his name, [55
And through the new world spread his growing fame.
   But how they fought, and what their valour gained,
Shall in another Canto be contained.

CANTO III.

The bloody fight, successless toil,
And how the fishes sacked the isle.

THE boat which on the first assault did go,
Struck with a harping-iron the younger foe ;
Who, when he felt his side so rudely gored,
Loud as the sea that nourished him he roared.
As a broad bream, to please some curious taste,   5
While yet alive, in boiling water cast,
Vexed with unwonted heat, bounds,[1] flings about
The scorching brass, and hurls the liquor out ;
So with the barbed javelin stung, he raves,
And scourges with his tail the suffering waves.   10
Like Spenser's[2] Talus with his iron flail,
He threatens ruin with his ponderous tail ;
Dissolving at one stroke the battered boat,
And down the men fall drenched in the moat ;
With every fierce encounter they are forced   15
To quit their boats, and fare like men unhorsed.

    1.—Editions after 1645, *boils*.   2.—1645, *Fairy*.

The bigger whale like some huge carrack lay,
Which wanteth sea-room with her foes to play ;
Slowly she swims ; and when, provoked she would
Advance her tail, her head salutes the mud ;   20
The shallow water doth her force infringe,
And renders vain her tail's impetuous swinge ;
The shining steel her tender sides receive,
And there, like bees, they all their weapons leave.

This sees the cub, and does himself oppose   25
Betwixt his cumbered mother and her foes ;
With desperate courage he receives her wounds,
And men and boats his active tail confounds.
Their forces joined, the seas with billows fill,
And make a tempest, though the winds be still.   30
Now would the men with half their hoped prey
Be well content, and wish[1] this cub away ;
Their wish they have : he (to direct his dam
Unto the gap through which they thither came)
Before her swims, and quits the hostile lake,   35
A prisoner there, but for his mother's sake.
She, by the rocks compelled to stay behind,
Is by the vastness of her bulk confined.
They shout for joy ! and now on her alone
Their fury falls, and all their darts are thrown.   40
Their lances spent, one bolder than the rest,
With his broad sword provoked[2] the sluggish beast ;
Her oily side devours both blade and haft,

1.—1645, *wish'd.*   2.—1645, *provokes.*

And there his steel the bold Bermudian left.
Courage the rest from his example take,   45
And now they change the colour of the lake ;
Blood flows in rivers from her wounded side,
As if they would prevent the tardy tide,
And raise the flood to that propitious height,
As might convey her from this fatal strait.   50
She swims in blood, and blood does spouting throw
To heaven, that heaven men's cruelties might know.
Their fixed javelins in her side she wears,
And on her back a grove of pikes appears ;
You would have thought, had you the monster seen
Thus dressed, she had another island been.   [55
Roaring she tears the air with such a noise,
As well resembled the conspiring voice
Of routed armies, when the field is won,
To reach the ears of her escaped son.   60
He, though a league removed from the foe,
Hastes to her aid ; the pious Trojan so,
Neglecting for Creusa's life his own,
Repeats the danger of the burning town.
The men, amazed, blush to see the seed   65
Of monsters human piety exceed.
Well proves this kindness, what the Grecians sung,
That Love's bright mother from the ocean sprung.
Their courage droops, and, hopeless now, they wish
For composition with the unconquered fish ;   70
So she their weapons would restore again.
Through rocks they'd hew her passage to the main.

But how instructed in each other's mind ?
Or what commerce can men with monsters find ?
Not daring to approach their wounded foe,   75
Whom her courageous son protected so,
They charge their muskets, and, with hot desire
Of fell revenge, renew the fight with fire ;
Standing aloof, with lead they bruise the scales,
And tear the flesh of the incensed whales.   80
But no success their fierce endeavours found,
Nor this way could they give one fatal wound.
Now to their fort they are about to send
For the loud engines which their isle defend ;
But what those pieces framed to batter walls,   85
Would have effected on those mighty whales,
Great Neptune will not have us know, who sends
A tide so high that it relieves his friends.
And thus they parted with exchange of harms ;   [90
Much blood the monsters lost, and they their arms.

WHEN HE WAS AT SEA.

WHILST I was free I wrote with high conceit,
And love and beauty raised above their height ;
Love, that bereaves us both of brain and heart,
Sorrow and silence doth at once impart.
What hand at once can wield a sword and write   5
Or battle paint, engaged in the fight ?
Who will describe a storm must not be there :
Passion writes well, neither in love nor fear.
Why on the naked boy have poets then
Feathers and wings bestowed, that wants a pen ?   10

TO MY LORD OF FALKLAND.

BRAVE Holland leads, and with him Falkland goes.
Who hears this told, and does not straight suppose
We send the Graces and the Muses forth,
To civilize and to instruct the north ?
Not that these ornaments make swords less sharp ;   5
Apollo bears as well his bow as harp ;
And though he be the patron of that spring,
Where, in calm peace, the sacred virgins sing,
He courage had to guard the invaded throne
Of Jove, and cast the ambitious giants down.   10
   Ah, noble friend ! with what impatience all
That know thy worth, and know how prodigal

Of thy great soul thou art, (longing to twist
Bays with that ivy which so early kissed
Thy youthful temples) with what horror we   15
Think on the blind events of war and thee !
To fate exposing that all-knowing breast
Among the throng, as cheaply as the rest ;
Where oaks and brambles (if the copse be burned)
Confounded lie, to the same ashes turned.   20
    Some happy wind over the ocean blow
This tempest yet, which frights our island so !
Guarded with ships, and all the sea our own,
From heaven this mischief on our heads is thrown.
    In a late dream, the Genius of this land,   25
Amazed, I saw, like the fair Hebrew stand,
When first she felt the twins begin to jar,
And found her womb the seat of civil war.
Inclined to whose relief, and with presage
Of better fortune for the present age,   30
Heaven sends, quoth I, this discord for our good,
To warm, perhaps, but not to waste our blood ;
To raise our drooping spirits, grown the scorn
Of our proud neighbours, who ere long shall mourn
(Though now they joy in our expected harms)   35
We had occasion to resume our arms.
    A lion so with self-provoking smart,
(His rebel tail scourging his noble part)
Calls up his courage ; then begins to roar
And charge his foes, who thought him mad before. 40

OF THE QUEEN.[1]

THE lark, that shuns on lofty boughs to build
Her humble nest, lies silent in the field ;
But if the promise of a cloudless day,
Aurora smiling, bids her rise and play,
Then straight she shows 'twas not for want of voice,   5
Or power to climb, she made so low a choice ;
Singing she mounts ; her airy wings are stretched
Towards heaven, as if from heaven her note she fetched.
   So we, retiring from the busy throng,
Use to restrain the ambition of our song ;   10
But since the light which now informs our age
Breaks from the court, indulgent to her rage,
Thither my muse, like bold Prometheus, flies,
To light her torch at Gloriana's eyes.
   Those sovereign beams which heal the wounded
     soul,   15
And all our cares, but once beheld, control ;
There the poor lover, that has long endured
Some proud nymph's scorn, of his fond passion cured,
Fares like the man who first upon the ground
A glow-worm spied, supposing he had found   20

1.—1645, *Of and to the Queene.*

A moving diamond, a breathing stone ;
For life it had, and like those jewels shone ;
He held it dear, till by the springing day
Informed, he threw the worthless worm away.

She saves the lover, as we gangrenes stay,   25
By cutting hope, like a lopped limb, away ;
This makes her bleeding patients to accuse
High Heaven, and these expostulations use :
" Could Nature then no private woman grace,
Whom we might dare to love, with such a face,   30
Such a complexion, and so radiant eyes,
Such lovely motion, and such sharp replies ?
Beyond our reach, and yet within our sight,
What envious power has placed this glorious light ? "

Thus, in a starry night, fond children cry   35
For the rich spangles that adorn the sky,
Which, though they shine for ever fixed there,
With light and influence relieve us here.
All her affections are to one inclined ;
Her bounty and compassion to mankind ;   40
To whom, while she so far extends her grace,
She makes but good the promise of her face ;
For Mercy has, could Mercy's self be seen,
No sweeter look than this propitious queen.
Such guard, and comfort, the distressed find   45
From her large power, and from her larger mind,
That whom ill Fate would ruin, it prefers,
For all the miserable are made hers.
So the fair tree whereon the eagle builds,

Poor sheep from tempests, and their shepherd
   shields ;   50
The royal bird possesses all the boughs,
But shade and shelter to the flock allows.
   Joy of our age, and safety of the next !
For which so oft thy fertile womb is vexed ;
Nobly contented, for the public good,   55
To waste thy spirits and diffuse thy blood,
What vast hopes may these islands entertain,
Where monarchs, thus descended, are to reign ?
Led by commanders of so fair a line,
Our seas no longer shall our power confine.   60
   A brave romance who would exactly frame,
First brings his knight from some immortal dame,
And then a weapon, and a flaming shield,
Bright as his mother's eyes, he makes him wield.
None might the mother of Achilles be,   65
But the fair pearl and glory of the sea ;
The man to whom great Maro gives such fame,
From the high bed of heavenly Venus came ;
And our next Charles, whom all the stars design
Like wonders to accomplish, springs from thine.   70

THE APOLOGY OF SLEEP,

FOR NOT APPROACHING THE LADY WHO CAN DO ANYTHING BUT SLEEP WHEN SHE PLEASETH.

My charge it is those breaches to repair
Which Nature takes from sorrow, toil, and care ;
Rest to the limbs, and quiet I confer
On troubled minds ; but nought can add to her
Whom Heaven and her transcendent thoughts have
    placed   5
Above those ills which wretched mortals taste.
  Bright as the deathless gods, and happy, she
From all that may infringe delight is free ;
Love at her royal feet his quiver lays,
And not his mother with more haste obeys.   10
Such real pleasures, such true joys suspense,
What dream can I present to recompense?
  Should I with lightning fill her awful hand,
And make the clouds seem all at her command ;
Or place her in Olympus' top, a guest   15
Among the immortals, who with nectar feast ;
That power would seem, that entertainment, short
Of the true splendour of her present court,
Where all the joys, and all the glories, are

Of three great kingdoms, severed from the care. 20
I, that of fumes and humid vapours made,
Ascending, do the seat of sense invade,
No cloud in so serene a mansion find,
To overcast her ever-shining mind,
Which holds resemblance with those spotless skies, 25
Where flowing Nilus want of rain supplies ;
That crystal heaven, where Phœbus never shrouds
His golden beams, nor wraps his face in clouds.
But what so hard which numbers cannot force?
So stoops the moon, and rivers change their course. 30
The bold Mæonian made me dare to steep
Jove's dreadful temples in the dew of sleep ;
And since the Muses do invoke my power,
I shall no more decline that sacred bower
Where Gloriana their great mistress lies ;   35
But, gently taming those victorious eyes,
Charm all her senses, till the joyful sun
Without a rival half his course has run ;
Who, while my hand that fairer light confines,
May boast himself the brightest thing that shines. 40

PUERPERIUM.

You gods that have the power
To trouble, and compose,
All that's beneath your bower,
Calm silence on the seas, on earth impose.

Fair Venus! in thy soft arms   5
The God of Rage confine ;
For thy whispers are the charms
Which only can divert his fierce design.

What though he frown, and to tumult do incline?
Thou the flame   10
Kindled in his breast canst tame
With that snow which unmelted lies on thine.

Great goddess! give this thy sacred island rest ;
Make heaven smile,
That no storm disturb us while   15
Thy chief care, our halcyon, builds her nest.

Great Gloriana ! fair Gloriana !
Bright as high heaven is, and fertile as earth,
Whose beauty relieves us,
Whose royal bed gives us   20
Both glory and peace,
Our present joy, and all our hopes' increase.[1]

1.—1645. *Our present joy, our hopes increase.*

TO AMORET.

AMORET ! the Milky Way
Framed of many nameless stars !
The smooth stream where none can say
He this drop to that prefers !

Amoret ! my lovely foe !   5
Tell me where thy strength does lie?
Where the power that charms us so?
In thy soul, or in thy eye?

By that snowy neck alone,
Or thy grace in motion seen,   10
No such wonders could be done ;
Yet thy waist is straight and clean
As Cupid's shaft, or Hermes' rod,
And powerful, too, as either god.

TO PHYLLIS.

PHYLLIS ! why should we delay
Pleasures shorter than the day
Could we (which we never can
Stretch our lives beyond their span,
Beauty like a shadow flies,　　　　　　　5
And our youth before us dies.
Or would youth and beauty stay,
Love hath wings, and will away.
Love hath swifter wings than Time ;
Change in love to heaven does climb.　　10
Gods, that never change their state,
Vary oft their love and hate.
　Phyllis ! to this truth we owe
All the love betwixt us two.
Let not you and I inquire　　　　　　　15
What has been our past desire ;
On what shepherds you have smiled,
Or what nymphs I have beguiled ;
Leave it to the planets too,
What we shall hereafter do ;　　　　　　20
For the joys we now may prove,
Take advice of present love.

À LA MALADE.

AH, lovely Amoret! the care
Of all that know what's good or fair!
Is heaven become our rival too?
Had the rich gifts, conferred on you
So amply thence, the common end   5
Of giving lovers—to pretend?
   Hence, to this pining sickness (meant
To weary thee to a consent
Of leaving us) no power is given
Thy beauties to impair; for heaven   10
Solicits thee with such a care,
As roses from their stalks we tear,
When we would still preserve them new
And fresh, as on the bush they grew.
   With such a grace you entertain,   15
And look with such contempt on pain,
That languishing you conquer more,
And wound us deeper than before.
So[1] lightnings which in storms appear,
Scorch more than when the skies are clear. **20**

1.—1645, *The.*

And as pale sickness does invade
Your frailer part, the breaches made
In that fair lodging, still more clear
Make the bright guest, your soul, appear.
So nymphs o'er pathless mountains borne,   25
Their light robes by the brambles torn
From their fair limbs, exposing new
And unknown beauties to the view
Of following gods, increase their flame,
And haste to catch the flying game.   30

OF LOVE.

ANGER, in hasty words or blows,
Itself discharges on our foes ;
And sorrow, too, finds some relief
In tears, which wait upon our grief ;
So every passion, but fond love,   5
Unto its own redress does move ;
But that alone the wretch inclines
To what prevents his own designs ;
Makes him lament, and sigh, and weep,
Disordered, tremble, fawn, and creep ;   10
Postures which render him despised,
Where he endeavours to be prized.
For women (born to be controlled)
Stoop to the forward and the bold ;
Affect the haughty and the proud,   15
The gay, the frolic, and the loud.
Who first the generous steed oppressed,
Not kneeling did salute the beast ;
But with high courage, life, and force,
Approaching, tamed the unruly horse.   20
  Unwisely we the wiser East
Pity, supposing them oppressed
With tyrants' force, whose law is will,
By which they govern, spoil, and kill :
Each nymph, but moderately fair,   25
Commands with no less rigour here.
Should some brave Turk, that walks among

His twenty lasses, bright and young,
And beckons to the willing dame,
Preferred to quench his present flame,   30
Behold as many gallants here,
With modest guise and silent fear,
All to one female idol bend,
While her high pride does scarce descend
To mark their follies, he would swear   35
That these her guard of eunuchs were,
And that a more majestic queen,
Or humbler slaves, he had not seen.

    All this with indignation spoke,
In vain I struggled with the yoke   40
Of mighty Love ; that conquering look,
When next beheld, like lightning strook
My blasted soul, and made me bow
Lower than those I pitied now.

    So the tall stag, upon the brink   45
Of some smooth stream about to drink,
Surveying there his armed head,
With shame remembers that he fled
The scorned dogs, resolves to try
The combat next ; but if their cry   50
Invades again his trembling ear,
He straight resumes his wonted care,[1]
Leaves the untasted spring behind,
And, winged with fear, outflies the wind.

1.—1645, *fear.*

FOR DRINKING OF HEALTHS.

AND is antiquity of no more force !
Whoe'er opposed that ancient friendly course,
And free expression of our absent love,
Against the custom of all nations strove
And lost his labour, it does still prevail,   5
And shall, while there is friendship, wine, or ale.
Let brutes and vegetals, that cannot think,
So far as drought and nature urges, drink ;
A more indulgent mistress guides our sprites,
Reason, that dares beyond our appetites,   10
(She would our care, as well as thirst, redress)
And with divinity rewards excess.
Deserted Ariadne, thus supplied,
Did perjured Theseus' cruelty deride ;
Bacchus embraced, from her exalted thought   15
Banished the man, her passion, and his fault.
Bacchus and Phœbus are by Jove allied,
And each by other's timely heat supplied ;
All that the grapes owe to his ripening fires
Is paid in numbers which their juice inspires.   20
Wine fills the veins, and healths are understood
To give our friends a title to our blood ;
Who, naming me, doth warm his courage so,
Shows for my sake what his bold hand would do.
'Twere slender kindness that would not dispense   25
With health itself, to breed a confidence
Of true love in a friend, and he that quits

Each custom which the rude plebeian gets,
For his reserv'dness will too dearly pay,
Employ the night and loose the cheerful day :   30
The burnished face oft decked with hoary hairs
Shows drinking brings no death, but to our cares.
Who with a full red countenance ends his days,
He sets like Phœbus and discerns his bays.

OF MY LADY ISABELLA,

PLAYING ON THE LUTE.

SUCH moving sounds from such a careless touch !
So unconcerned herself, and we so much !
What art is this, that with so little pains
Transports us thus, and o'er our[1] spirit reigns ?
The trembling strings about her fingers crowd,   5
And tell their joy for every kiss aloud.
Small force there needs to make them tremble so';
Touched by that hand, who would not tremble too ?
Here love takes stand, and while she charms the ear,
Empties his quiver on the listening deer.   10
Music so softens and disarms the mind,
That not an arrow does resistance find.
Thus the fair tyrant celebrates the prize,
And acts herself the triumph of her eyes :
So Nero once, with harp in hand, surveyed   15
His flaming Rome, and as it burned he played.

1.—1645, *the.*

OF MRS. ARDEN.

BEHOLD, and listen, while the **fair**
Breaks in sweet sounds the willing air,
And with her own breath fans the fire
Which her bright eyes do first inspire.
What reason can that love control, 5
Which more than one way courts the soul ?
  So when a flash of lightning falls
On our abodes, the danger calls
For human aid, which hopes the flame
To conquer, though from heaven it came ; 10
But if the winds with that conspire,
Men strive not, but deplore the fire.

OF THE MARRIAGE OF THE DWARFS.

DESIGN,[1] or chance, makes others wive :
But Nature did this match contrive ;
Eve might as well have Adam fled,
As she denied her little bed
To him, for whom Heaven seemed to frame,   5
And measure out, this only dame.
   Thrice happy is that humble pair,
Beneath the level of all care !
Over whose heads those arrows fly
Of sad distrust and jealousy ;   10
Secured in as high extreme,
As if the world held none but them.
   To him the fairest nymphs do show
Like moving mountains, topped with snow ;
And every man a Polypheme   15
Does to his Galatea seem ;
None may presume her faith to prove ;
He proffers death that proffers love.
   Ah, Chloris, that kind Nature thus
From all the world had severed us ;   20
Creating for ourselves us two,
As love has me for only you !

1.—1645, *The signe.*

LOVE'S FAREWELL.

TREADING the path to nobler ends,
A long farewell to love I gave,
Resolved my country, and my friends,
All that remained of me should have.

And this resolve no mortal dame,　　　　5
None but those eyes could have o'erthrown,
The nymph I dare not, need not name,
So high, so like herself alone.

Thus the tall oak, which now aspires
Above the fear of private fires,　　　　10
Grown and designed for nobler use,
Not to make warm, but build the house,
Though from our meaner flames secure,
Must that which falls from heaven endure.

FROM A CHILD.

MADAM, as in some climes the warmer sun
Makes it full summer ere the spring's begun,
And with ripe fruit the bending boughs can load,
Before our violets dare look abroad ;
So measure not by any common use   5
The early love your brighter eyes produce.
When lately your fair hand in woman's weed
Wrapped my glad head, I wished me so indeed,
That hasty time might never make me grow
Out of those favours you afford me now ;   10
That I might ever such indulgence find,
And you not blush, or think yourself too kind ;
Who now, I fear, while I these joys express,
Begin to think how you may make them less.
The sound of love makes your soft heart afraid,   15
And guard itself, though but a child invade,
And innocently at your white breast throw
A dart as white, a ball of new fall'n snow.

ON A GIRDLE.

THAT which her slender waist confined,
Shall now my joyful temples bind ;
No monarch but would give his crown,
His arms might do what this has done.

It was[1] my heaven's extremest sphere,   5
The pale which held that[2] lovely deer.
My joy, my grief, my hope, my love,
Did[3] all within this circle move !

A narrow compass ! and yet there
Dwelt[4] all that's good, and all that's fair ;   10
Give me but what this ribband bound,
Take all the rest the sun goes round.[5]

1.—1645, *is.*   2.—1645, *the.*
3.—1645, *Do.*   4.—1645, *Dwells.*
5.—1645, *Give me but what this Ribban ty'd,*
       Take all the sun goes round beside.

THE FALL.

See ! how the willing earth gave way,
To take the impression where she lay.
See ! how the mould, as loth to leave
So sweet a burden, still doth cleave
Close to the nymph's stained garment.   Here 5
The coming spring would first appear,
And all this place with roses strow,
If busy feet would let them grow.
Here Venus smiled to see blind chance
Itself before her son advance,   10
And a fair image to present,
Of what the boy so long had meant.
'Twas such a chance as this, made all
The world into this order fall ;
Thus the first lovers on the clay,   15
Of which they were composed, lay ;
So in their prime, with equal grace,
Met the first patterns of our race.
Then blush not, fair ! or on him frown,
Or wonder how you both came down ;   20
But touch him, and he'll tremble straight,
How could he then support your weight ?
How could the youth, alas ! but bend,
When his whole heaven upon him leaned ?
If aught by him amiss were done,   25
'Twas that he let you rise so soon.

OF SYLVIA.

Our sighs are heard ; just Heaven declares
The sense it has of lover's cares ;
She that so far the rest outshined,
Sylvia the fair, while she was kind,
As if her frowns impaired her brow,   5
Seems only not unhandsome now.
So when the sky makes us endure
A storm, itself becomes obscure.

Hence 'tis that I conceal my flame,
Hiding from Flavia's self her name,   10
Lest she, provoking Heaven, should prove
How it rewards neglected love.
Better a thousand such as I,
Their grief untold, should pine and die,
Than her bright morning, overcast   15
With sullen clouds, should be defaced.

H

THE BUD.

LATELY on yonder swelling bush,
Big with many a coming rose,
This early bud began to blush,
And did but half itself disclose ;
I plucked it, though no better grown,   5
And now you see how full 'tis blown.

Still as I did the leaves inspire,
With such a purple light they shone,
As if they had been made of fire,
And spreading so, would flame anon.   10
All that was meant by air or sun,
To the young flower, my breath has done.

If our loose breath so much can do,
What may the same in forms[1] of love,
Of purest love, and music too,   15
When Flavia it aspires to move?
When that, which lifeless buds persuades
To wax more soft, her youth invades?

1.—This is the reading of the edition of 1645, and I have preferred to retain it, although the other editions have *inform's*, and in that of 1682 *inform'd* in the text is corrected to *inform's* in the Errata.

ON THE DISCOVERY OF A LADY'S PAINTING.

PYGMALION'S fate reversed is mine;
His marble love took flesh and blood;
All that I worshipped as divine,
That beauty! now 'tis understood,
Appears to have no more of life   5
Than that whereof he framed his wife.

As women yet, who apprehend
Some sudden cause of causeless fear,
Although that seeming cause take end,
And they behold no danger near,   10
A shaking through their limbs they find,
Like leaves saluted by the wind:

So though the beauty do appear
No beauty, which amazed me so;
Yet from my breast I cannot tear   15
The passion which from thence did grow;
Nor yet out of my fancy raze
The print of that supposed face.

A real beauty, though too near,
The fond Narcissus did admire!   20
I dote on that which is nowhere;
The sign of beauty feeds my fire.
No mortal flame was e'er so cruel
As this, which thus survives the fuel!

OF LOVING AT FIRST SIGHT.

Not caring to observe the wind,
Or the new sea explore,
Snatched from myself, how far behind
Already I behold the shore !

May not a thousand dangers sleep   5
In the smooth bosom of this deep ?
No ; 'tis so rockless and so clear,
That the rich bottom does appear,
Paved all with precious things, not torn
From shipwrecked vessels, but there born.   10

Sweetness, truth, and every grace
Which time and use are wont to teach,
The eye may in a moment reach,
And read distinctly in her face.

Some other nymphs, with colours faint,   15
And pencil slow, may Cupid paint,
And a weak heart in time destroy ;
She has a stamp, and prints the boy ;
Can, with a single look, inflame
The coldest breast, the rudest tame.   20

THE SELF-BANISHED.

IT is not that I love you less,
Than when before your feet I lay ;
But to prevent the sad increase
Of hopeless love, I keep away.

In vain, alas ! for everything   5
Which I have known belong to you,
Your form does to my fancy bring,
And makes my old wounds bleed anew.

Who in the spring, from the new sun,
Already has a fever got,   10
Too late begins those shafts to shun,
Which Phœbus through his veins has shot ;

Too late he would the pain assuage,
And to thick shadows does retire ;
About with him he bears the rage,   15
And in his tainted blood the fire.

But vowed I have, and never must
Your banished servant trouble you ;
For if I break, you may mistrust
The vow I made—to love you too.   20

TO A FRIEND,

OF THE DIFFERENT SUCCESS OF THEIR LOVES.[1]

THRICE happy pair ! of whom we cannot know
Which first began to love, or loves most now ;
Fair course of passion ! where two lovers start,
And run together, heart still yoked with heart ;
Successful youth ! whom love has taught the way　　5
To be victorious in the first essay.
Sure love's an art best practised at first,
And where the experienced still prosper worst !
I, with a different fate, pursued in vain
The haughty Celia, till my just disdain　　　　　10
Of her neglect, above that passion borne,
Did pride to pride oppose, and scorn to scorn.
Now she relents ; but all too late to move
A heart directed to a nobler love.
The scales are turned, her kindness weighs no more
Now than my vows and service did before.　　　[15
So in some well-wrought hangings you may see
How Hector leads, and how the Grecians flee ;
Here, the fierce Mars his courage so inspires,
That with bold hands the Argive fleet he fires ;　　20
But there, from heaven the blue-eyed virgin falls,
And frighted Troy retires within her walls ;
They that are foremost in that bloody race,
Turn head anon, and give the conquerors chase.

1.—1645, *To A. H., of the different success of their Loves.*

So like the chances are of love and war,   25
That they alone in this distinguished are,
In love the victors from the vanquished fly ;
They fly that wound, and they pursue that die.

TO ZELINDA.

FAIREST piece of well-formed earth !
Urge not thus your haughty birth ;
The power which you have o'er us lies
Not in your race, but in your eyes.
"None but a prince !"—Alas ! that voice   5
Confines you to a narrow choice.
Should you no honey vow to taste,
But what the master-bees have placed
In compass of their cells, how small
A portion to your share would fall !   10
Nor all appear, among those few,
Worthy the stock from whence they grew.
The sap which at the root is bred
In trees, through all the boughs is spread ;
But virtues which in parents shine,   15
Make not like progress through the line.
'Tis not from whom, but where, we live ;
The place does oft those graces give.

Great Julius, on the mountains bred,
A flock perhaps, or herd, had led.   20
He that the world subdued had been
But the best wrestler on the green.
'Tis art and knowledge which draw forth
The hidden seeds of native worth ;
They blow those sparks, and make them rise 25
Into such flames as touch the skies.
To the old heroes hence was given
A pedigree which reached to heaven ;
Of mortal seed they were not held,
Which other mortals so excelled.   30
And beauty, too, in such excess
As yours, Zelinda ! claims no less.
Smile but on me, and you shall scorn,
Henceforth, to be of princes born.
I can describe the shady grove   35
Where your loved mother slept with Jove ;
And yet excuse the faultless dame,
Caught with her spouse's shape and name.
Thy matchless form will credit bring
To all the wonders I shall sing.   40

TO A LADY

SINGING A SONG OF HIS COMPOSING.

CHLORIS ! yourself you so excel,
When you vouchsafe to breathe my thought,
That, like a spirit, with this spell
Of my own teaching, I am caught.

That eagle's fate and mine are one,   5
Which, on the shaft that made him die,
Espied a feather of his own,
Wherewith he wont to soar so high.

Had Echo, with so sweet a grace,
Narcissus' loud complaints returned,   10
Not for reflection of his face,
But of his voice, the boy had burned.[1]

1.—1645, *mourned.*

TO THE MUTABLE FAIR.

HERE, Celia! for thy sake I part
With all that grew so near my heart;
The passion that I had for thee,
The faith, the love, the constancy!
And, that I may successful prove,   5
Transform myself to what you love.

   Fool that I was! so much to prize
Those simple virtues you despise;
Fool! that with such dull arrows strove,
Or hoped to reach a flying dove;   10
For you, that are in motion still,
Decline our force, and mock our skill;
Who, like Don Quixote, do advance
Against a windmill our vain lance.

   Now will I wander through the air,   15
Mount, make a stoop at every fair;
And, with a fancy unconfined,
(As lawless as the sea or wind)
Pursue you wheresoe'er you fly,
And with your various thoughts comply.   20

   The formal stars do travel so,
As we their names and courses know;

And he that on their changes looks,
Would think them governed by our books;
But never were the clouds reduced   25
To any art; the motions[1] used
By those free vapours are so light,
So frequent, that the conquered sight
Despairs to find the rules that guide
Those gilded shadows as they slide;   30
And therefore of the spacious air
Jove's royal consort had the care;
And by that power did once escape,
Declining bold Ixion's rape;
She, with her own resemblance, graced   35
A shining cloud, which he embraced.

   Such was that image, so it smiled
With seeming kindness, which beguiled
Your Thyrsis lately, when he thought
He had his fleeting Celia caught.   40
'Twas shaped like her, but, for the fair,
He filled his arms with yielding air.

   A fate for which he grieves the less,
Because the gods had like success;
For in their story, one, we see,   45
Pursues a nymph, and takes a tree;
A second, with a lover's haste,
Soon overtakes whom he had chased,

1.—In all the editions *motion*, but I have ventured to alter it
in accordance with Mr. Waller's MS.

But she that did a virgin seem,
Possessed, appears a wandering stream ;   50
For his supposed love, a third
Lays greedy hold upon a bird,
And stands amazed to find his dear
A wild inhabitant of the air.

   To these old tales such nymphs as you   55
Give credit, and still make them new ;
The amorous now like wonders find
In the swift changes of your mind.
   But, Celia, if you apprehend
The muse of your incensed friend,   60
Nor would that he record your blame,
And make it live, repeat the same ;
Again deceive him, and again,
And then he swears he'll not complain ;
For still to be deluded so,   65
Is all the pleasure lovers know ;
Who, like good falconers, take delight,
Not in the quarry, but the flight.

TO A LADY,

MADAM ! intending to have tried
The silver favour which you gave,
In ink the shining point I dyed,
And drenched it in the sable wave ;
When, grieved to be so foully stained,   5
On you it thus to me complained :

" Suppose you had deserved to take
From her fair hand so fair a boon,
Yet how deserved I to make
So ill a change, who ever won   10
Immortal praise for what I wrote,[1]
Instructed by her noble thought ?

" I, that expressed her commands
To mighty lords, and princely dames,
Always most welcome to their hands,   15
Proud that I would record their names,
Must now be taught an humble style,
Some meaner beauty to beguile ! "

So I, the wronged pen to please,
Make it my humble thanks express,   20
Unto your ladyship, in these :
And now 'tis forced to confess
That your great self did ne'er indite,
Nor that, to one more noble, write.

1.—1645, *wrought.*

ON THE HEAD OF A STAG.

So we some antique hero's strength
Learn by his lance's weight and length;
As these vast beams express the beast,
Whose shady brows alive they dressed.
Such game, while yet the world was new,   5
The mighty Nimrod did pursue.
What huntsman of our feeble race,
Or dogs, dare such a monster chase,
Resembling, with each blow he strikes,
The charge of a whole troop of pikes?   10
O fertile head! which every year
Could such a crop of wonder bear!
The teeming earth did never bring
So soon, so hard, so huge a thing;
Which might it never have been cast,   15
(Each year's growth added to the last)
These lofty branches had supplied
The earth's bold sons' prodigious pride;
Heaven with these engines had been scaled,
When mountains heaped on mountains failed.[1]   20

1.—In a MS. in the British Museum (from Bliss's sale):
    With Ladders Jove's high seat to scale,
    When Hills on Hills could not prevaile.

THE MISER'S SPEECH.

IN A MASQUE.

BALLS of this metal slacked At'lanta's pace,
And on the amorous youth[1] bestowed the race ;
Venus, (the nymph's mind measuring by her own)
Whom the rich spoils of cities overthrown
Had prostrated to Mars, could well advise　　5
The adventurous lover how to gain the prize.
Nor less may Jupiter to gold ascribe ;
For, when he turned himself into a bribe,
Who can blame Danae, or the brazen tower,
That they withstood not that[2] almighty shower ?　　10
Never till then did love make Jove put on
A form more bright, and nobler[3] than his own ;
Nor were it just, would he resume that shape,
That slack devotion should his thunder 'scape.
'Twas not revenge for grieved Apollo's wrong,　　15
Those ass's ears on Midas' temples hung,
But fond repentance of his happy wish,
Because his meat grew metal like his dish.
Would Bacchus bless me so, I'd constant hold
Unto my wish, and die creating gold.　　20

1.—Hippomenes.　　2.—1645, *the.*　　3.—1645, *noble.*

TO CHLORIS.

CHLORIS ! since first our calm of peace
Was frighted hence, this good we find,
Your favours with your fears increase,
And growing mischiefs make you kind.
So the fair tree, which still preserves
Her fruit and state while no wind blows,
In storms from that uprightness swerves,
And the glad earth about her strows
With treasure, from her yielding boughs.

TO A LADY IN A GARDEN.[1]

SEES not my love how time resumes
The glory which he lent these flowers?
Though none should taste of their[2] perfumes,
Yet must they live but some few hours;
Time what we forbear devours !   5

Had Helen, or the Egyptian Queen,
Been ne'er so thrifty of their graces,
Those beauties must at length have been
The spoil of age, which finds out faces
In the most retired places.   10

Should some malignant planet bring
A barren drought, or ceaseless shower,
Upon the autumn or the spring,
And spare us neither fruit nor flower;
Winter would not stay an hour.   15

Could the resolve of love's neglect
Preserve you[3] from the violation
Of coming years, then more respect
Were due to so divine a fashion,
Nor would I indulge my passion.   20

1.—1645, *To a Lady in retirement.*
2.—1645, *these sweet.*
3.—1645, *thee.*

I

CHLORIS AND HYLAS.

MADE TO A SARABAND.[1]

CHLORIS.

Hylas, oh Hylas ! why sit we mute,
Now that each bird saluteth[2] the spring
Wind up the slack'ned[3] strings of thy lute,
Never canst thou want matter to sing ;
For love thy breast does fill with such a fire,　　　5
That whatsoe'er is fair moves thy desire.

HYLAS.

Sweetest ! you know, the sweetest of things
Of various flowers the bees do compose ;
Yet no particular taste it brings
Of violet, woodbine, pink, or rose ;　　　10
So love the result[4] is of all the graces
Which flow from a thousand several faces.

1.—1645, headed simply *Chloris and Hilas.*
2.—1682, *salutes.*
3.—Thus 1645 ; 1686, *slackned.*
4.—1645, 1664, 1668, *resultance.*

CHLORIS.

Hylas ! the birds which chant in this grove,
Could we but know the language they use,
They would instruct us better in love,　　　　15
And reprehend thy inconstant Muse ;
For love their breasts does fill with such a fire,
That what they once do chose, bounds their desire.

HYLAS.

Chloris ! this change the birds do approve,
Which the warm season hither does bring ;　　　20
Time from yourself does further remove
You, than the winter from the gay spring ;
She that like lightning shined while her face lasted,
The oak now resembles which lightning hath blasted.

IN ANSWER OF SIR JOHN SUCKLING'S VERSES.

CON.

Stay here, fond youth! and ask no more ; be wise ;
Knowing too much, long since lost Paradise.

PRO.

And, by your knowledge, we should be bereft
Of all that paradise which yet is left.

CON.

The virtuous joys thou hast, thou wouldst should still
Last in their pride ; and wouldst not take it ill   [5
If rudely from sweet dreams, and for a toy,
Thou wert awaked ;[1] *he wakes himself that does enjoy.*

PRO.

How can the joy, or hope, which you allow
Be styled virtuous, and the end not so?   10
Talk in your sleep, and shadows still admire !
'Tis true, he wakes that feels this real fire ;
But to sleep better ; for whoe'er drinks deep
Of this Nepenthe, rocks himself asleep.

1.—1686, *Thou awaked.*   Suckling's " Fragmenta Aurea,"
1646, *Tho' wert wak't.*

CON.

Fruition adds no new wealth, but destroys,   15
And while it pleaseth much, yet still it cloys.[1]
Who thinks he should[2] be happier made for that,
As reasonably might hope he might grow fat
By eating to a surfeit ; this once passed,
What relishes ? even kisses lose their taste.   20

PRO.

Blessings may be repeated while they cloy ;
But shall we starve, 'cause surfeitings destroy ?
And if fruition did the taste impair
Of kisses, why should yonder happy pair,
Whose[3] joys just Hymen warrants all the night,   25
Consume the day, too, in this less delight ?

CON.

Urge not 'tis necessary ; alas ! we know
The homeliest thing that[4] mankind does is so.
The world is of a large[5] extent we see,
And must be peopled ; children there must be :—   30
So must bread too ; but since there are enough
Born to that[6] drudgery, what need we plough ?

1.—"Frag. Aur.," And while it pleaseth much the palate,
cloyes.

2 —1645, shall. "Frag. Aur.," Who thinks he shall be
happier for that.

3.—1645, Where.   4.—"Frag. Aur.." which.

5.—"Frag. Aur.," vast.   6.—"Frag. Aur.," the.

PRO.

I need not plough, since what the stooping hind [1]
Gets of my pregnant land, must all be mine ;
But in this nobler tillage 'tis not so ;   35
For when Anchises did fair Venus know,
What interest had poor Vulcan in the boy,
Famous Æneas, or the present joy ?

CON.

Women enjoyed, whate'er before [2] they've been,
Are like romances read, or scenes once seen ;   40
Fruition dulls or [3] spoils the play much more
Than if one read, or knew, the plot before.

PRO.

Plays and romances read and seen, do fall
In our opinions ; yet not seen at all,
Whom would they please ?   To an heroic tale   45
Would you not listen, lest it should grow stale ?

CON.

'Tis expectation makes a blessing dear ;
Heaven were not heaven if we knew what it were.

1.—1645, *hine.*
2.—The reading of " Frag. Aur."   All the editions of Waller
have *what e'retofore.*
3.—" Frag. Aur.," *Fruition's dull and spoils,* &c.

PRO.

If 'twere not heaven if we knew what it were,
'Twould not be heaven to those[1] that now are there.

[50

CON.

As[2] in prospects we are there pleased most,
Where something keeps the eye from being lost,
And leaves us room to guess ; so here, restraint
Holds up delight, that with excess would faint.

PRO.

Restraint preserves the pleasure we have got,   55
But he ne'er has it that enjoys it not.
In goodly prospects, who contracts the space,
Or takes not all the bounty of the place?
We wish removed what standeth in our light,
And nature blame for limiting our sight ;   60
Where you stand wisely winking, that the view
Of the fair prospect may be always new.

CON.

They, who know all the wealth they have, are poor ;
He's only rich that cannot tell his store.

PRO.

Not he that knows the wealth he has is poor,   65
But he that dares not touch, nor use, his store.

1.—1645, *them.*   ' 2.—" Frag. Aur. " *And as in,* &c.

AN APOLOGY FOR HAVING LOVED
BEFORE.

THEY that never had the use
Of the grape's surprising juice,
To the first delicious cup
All their reason render up ;
Neither do, nor care to know,   5
Whether it be best[1] or no.

So they that are to love inclined
Swayed by chance, not choice, or art,
To the first that's fair, or kind,
Make a present of their heart ;   10
'Tis not she that first we love,
But whom dying we approve.

To man, that was in the evening made,
Stars gave the first delight,
Admiring, in the gloomy shade,   15
Those little drops of light ;
Then at Aurora, whose fair hand
Removed them from the skies,
He gazing toward the east did stand,
She entertained his eyes.   20

1.—1645, *the best.*

But when the bright sun did appear,
All those he 'gan[1] despise ;
His wonder was determined there,
And[2] could no higher rise ;
He neither might, nor wished to know   25
A more refulgent light ;
For that (as mine your beauties now)
Employed his utmost sight.

ON A BREDE OF DIVERS COLOURS,

WOVEN BY FOUR LADIES.

TWICE twenty slender virgin-fingers twine
This curious web, where all their fancies shine.
As Nature them, so they this shade have wrought,
Soft as their hands, and various as their thought.
Not Juno's bird, when his fair train dispread,   5
He woos the female to his painted bed ;
No, not the bow, which so adorns the skies,
So glorious is, or boasts so many dyes.

1.—1686, *can.*   2.—1645, *Hee.*

TO CHLORIS.

CHLORIS ! what's eminent, we know
Must for some cause be valued so ;
Things without use, though they be good,
Are not by us so understood.
The early rose, made to display   5
Her blushes to the youthful May,
Doth yield her sweets, since he is fair,
And courts her with a gentle air.
Our stars do show their excellence
Not by their light, but influence ;   10
When brighter comets, since still known
Fatal to all, are liked by none.
So your admired beauty still
Is, by effects, made good or ill.

SONG.

STAY, Phœbus! stay;
The world to which you fly so fast,
Conveying day
From us to them, can pay your haste
With no such object, nor salute your rise,   5
With no such wonder as De Mornay's eyes.

Well does this prove
The error of those antique books,
Which made you move
About the world; her charming looks   10
Would fix your beams, and make it ever day,
Did not the rolling earth snatch her away.

SONG.[1]

Peace, babbling Muse !
I dare not sing what you indite ;
Her eyes refuse
To read the passion which they write.
She strikes my lute, but, if it sound,　　　　5
Threatens to hurl it on the ground ;
And I no less her anger dread,
Than the poor wretch that feigns him dead,
While some fierce lion does embrace
His breathless corpse, and licks his face ;　　10
Wrapped up in silent fear he lies,
Torn all in pieces if he cries.

1.—In Mr. Waller's MS. this piece is headed, *Banist if he made Loue.*

TO FLAVIA.

A SONG.

'TIS not your beauty can engage
My wary heart ;
The sun, in all his pride and rage,
Has not that art ;
And yet he shines as bright as you,   5
If brightness could our souls subdue.

'Tis not the pretty things you say,
Nor those you write,
Which can make Thyrsis' heart your prey ;
For that delight,   10
The graces of a well-taught mind,
In some of our own sex we find.

No, Flavia ! 'tis your love I fear ;
Love's surest darts,
Those which so seldom fail him, are   15
Headed with hearts ;
Their very shadows make [1] us yield ;
Dissemble well, and win the field.

1.—1645, *shadow makes.*

BEHOLD THE BRAND OF BEAUTY TOSSED !

A SONG.

BEHOLD the brand of beauty tossed !
See how the motion does dilate the flame !
Delighted love his spoils does boast,
And triumph in this game.
Fire, to no place confined,   5
Is both our wonder and our fear ;
Moving the mind,
As [1] lightning hurled through the air.

High heaven the glory does increase
Of all her shining lamps, this artful way ;   10
The sun in figures, such as these,
Joys with the moon to play ;
To the [2] sweet strains they advance,
Which do result from their own spheres,
As this nymph's dance   15
Moves with the numbers which she hears.

1.—1645, *Like.*   2.—1645, *these.*

WHILE I LISTEN TO THY VOICE.

WHILE I listen to thy voice,
Chloris ! I feel my life decay ;
That powerful noise
Calls my flitting [1] soul away.
Oh ! suppress that magic sound,   5
Which destroys without a wound.

Peace, Chloris ! peace ! or singing die,
That together you and I
To heaven may go ;
For all we know   10
Of what the blessed do above,
Is, that they sing, and that they love.

1.—1645, *fleeting.*

GO, LOVELY ROSE!

Go, lovely Rose !
Tell her that wastes her time and me
That now she knows,
When I resemble her to thee,
How sweet and fair she seems **to** be.   5

Tell her that's young,
And shuns to have her graces spied,
That hadst thou sprung
In deserts, where no men abide,
Thou must have uncommended died.   10

Small is the worth
Of beauty from the light retired ;
Bid her come forth,
Suffer herself to be desired,
And not blush so to be admired.   15

Then die ! that she
The common fate of all things rare
May read in thee ;
How small a part of time they share
That are so wondrous sweet and fair !   20

UNDER A LADY'S PICTURE.

SOME ages hence, for it must not decay,
The doubtful wonderers at this piece, will say
Such Helen was! and who can blame the boy
That in so bright a flame consumed his Troy?
But had like virtue shined in that fair Greek,   5
The amorous shepherd had not dared to seek
Or hope for pity; but with silent moan,
And better fate, had perished alone.

WRITTEN IN MY LADY SPEKE'S
SINGING-BOOK.

HER fair eyes, if they could see
What themselves have wrought in me,
Would at least with pardon look
On this scribbling in her book :
If that she the writer scorn,   5
This may from the rest be torn,
With the ruin of a part,
But the image of her graces
Fills my heart and leaves no spaces.

K

OF A LADY WHO WRIT IN PRAISE OF MIRA.

WHILE she pretends to make the graces known
Of matchless Mira, she reveals her own ;
And when she would another's praise indite,
Is by her glass instructed how to write.

TO ONE MARRIED TO AN OLD MAN.

SINCE thou wouldst needs (bewitched with some ill
    charms !)
Be buried in those monumental arms,
All we can wish is, may that earth lie light
Upon thy tender limbs ! and so good night.

AN EPIGRAM ON A PAINTED LADY WITH ILL TEETH.

WERE men so dull they could not see
That Lyce painted, should they flee,
Like simple birds, into a net
So grossly woven and ill set,
Her own teeth would undo the knot,   5
And let all go that she had got.
Those teeth fair Lyce must not show
If she would bite ; her lovers, though
Like birds they stoop at seeming grapes,
Are disabused when first she gapes ;   10
The rotten bones discovered there,
Show 'tis a painted sepulchre.

ON MR. JOHN FLETCHER'S PLAYS.

FLETCHER ! to thee we do not only owe
All these good plays, but those of others too ;[1]
Thy wit repeated does support the stage,
Credits the last, and entertains this age.
No worthies, formed by any Muse but thine,   5
Could purchase robes to make themselves so fine.

1.—This is the reading of the folio Beaumont and Fletcher, 1647. Waller's 1664, and subsequent editions, *All our good plays, and all those other too.* 1645, *All these good plays, but those others too.*

K 2

What brave commander is not proud to see
Thy brave Melantius in his gallantry?
Our greatest ladies love to see their scorn
Outdone by thine, in what themselves have worn; 10
The impatient widow, ere the year be done,
Sees thy Aspasia weeping in her gown.

 I never yet the tragic strain essayed,
Deterred by that inimitable Maid;
And when I venture at the comic style,   15
Thy Scornful Lady seems to mock my toil.

 Thus has thy Muse at once improved and marred
Our sport in plays, by rendering it too hard!
So when a sort of lusty shepherds throw
The bar by turns, and none the rest outgo   20
So far, but that the best are measuring casts,
Their emulation and their pastime lasts;
But if some brawny yeoman of the guard
Step in, and toss the axletree a yard,
Or more, beyond the furthest mark, the rest   25
Despairing stand, their sport is at the best.

VERSES TO DR. GEORGE ROGERS,

ON HIS TAKING THE DEGREE OF DOCTOR OF PHYSIC AT PADUA, IN THE YEAR 1646.

WHEN as of old the earth's bold children strove,
With hills on hills, to scale the throne of Jove,
Pallas and Mars stood by their sovereign's side,
And their bright arms in his defence employed ;
While the wise Phœbus, Hermes, and the rest,   5
Who joy in peace, and love the Muses best,
Descending from their so distempered seat,
Our groves and meadows chose for their retreat.
There first Apollo tried the various use
Of herbs, and learned the virtues of their juice,   10
And framed that art, to which who can pretend
A juster title than our noble friend?
Whom the like tempest drives from his abode,
And like employment entertains abroad.
This crowns him here, and in the bays so earned,   15
His country's honour is no less concerned,
Since it appears not all the English rave,
To ruin bent ; some study how to save ;
And as Hippocrates did once extend
His sacred art, whole cities to amend ;   20
So we, great friend ! suppose that thy great skill,
Thy gentle mind, and fair example, will,
At thy return, reclaim our frantic isle,
Their spirits calm, and peace again shall smile.

TO MY LADY MORTON, ON NEW-YEAR'S DAY, 1650.

AT THE LOUVRE IN PARIS.

MADAM ! new years may well expect to find
Welcome from you, to whom they are so kind ;
Still as they pass, they court and smile on you,
And make your beauty, as themselves, seem new.
To the fair Villiers we Dalkeith prefer,[1]   5
And fairest Morton now as much to her ;
So like the sun's advance your titles show,
Which as he rises does the warmer grow.

 But thus to style you fair, your sex's praise,
Gives you but myrtle, who may challenge bays ;   10
From armed foes to bring a royal prize,
Shows your brave heart victorious as your eyes.
If Judith, marching with the general's head,
Can give us passion when her story's read,
What may the living do, which brought away,   15
Though a less bloody, yet a nobler prey ;
Who from our flaming Troy, with a bold hand,
Snatched her fair charge, the Princess, like a brand ?
A brand ! preserved to warm some prince's heart,
And make whole kingdoms take her brother's part.
            [20

1.—1682, *did prefer.*

So Venus, from prevailing Greeks, did shroud
The hope of Rome, and save him in a cloud.
   This gallant act may cancel all our rage,
Begin a better, and absolve this age.
Dark shades become the portrait of our time ;   25
Here weeps Misfortune, and their triumphs Crime !
Let him that draws it hide the rest in night ;
This portion only may endure the light,
Where the kind nymph, changing her faultless shape,
Becomes unhandsome, handsomely to 'scape,   30
When through the guards, the river, and the sea,
Faith, beauty, wit, and courage, made their way.
As the brave eagle does with sorrow see
The forest wasted, and that lofty tree
Which holds her nest about to be o'erthrown,   35
Before the feathers of her young are grown,
She will not leave them, nor she cannot stay,
But bears them boldly on her wings away ;
So fled the dame, and o'er the ocean bore
Her princely burthen to the Gallic shore.   40
Born in the storms of war, this royal fair,
Produced like lightning in tempestuous air,
Though now she flies her native isle (less kind,
Less safe for her than either sea or wind !)
Shall, when the blossom of her beauty's blown,   45
See her great brother on the British throne ;
Where peace shall smile, and no dispute arise,
But which rules most, his sceptre, or her eyes.

TO SIR WILLIAM DAVENANT,

UPON HIS TWO FIRST BOOKS OF GONDIBERT.

Written in France.

THUS the wise nightingale that leaves her home,
Her native wood, when storms and winter come,
Pursuing constantly the cheerful spring,
To foreign groves does her old music bring.
 The drooping Hebrews' banished harps, unstrung
At Babylon upon the willows hung;   [5
Yours sounds aloud, and tells us you excel
No less in courage, than in singing well;
Whilst, unconcerned, you let your country know,
They have impoverished themselves, not you;   10
Who, with the Muses' help, can mock those fates
Which threaten kingdoms, and disorder states.
So Ovid, when from Cæsar's rage he fled,
The Roman Muse to Pontus with him led;
Where he so sung, that we, through pity's glass,   15
See Nero milder than Augustus was.
Hereafter such, in thy behalf, shall be
The indulgent censure of posterity.
To banish those who with such art can sing,
Is a rude crime, which its own curse does bring;   20

Ages to come shall ne'er know how they fought,
Nor how to love their present youth be taught.
This to thyself.—Now to thy matchless book,
Wherein those few that can with judgment look,
May find old love in pure fresh language told,   25
Like new-stamped coin made out of Angel gold ;
Such truth in love as the antique world did know,
In such a style as courts may boast of now ;
Which no bold tales of gods or monsters swell,
But human passions, such as with us dwell.   30
Man is thy theme ; his virtue, or his rage,
Drawn to the life in each elaborate page.
Mars, nor Bellona, are not named here,
But such a Gondibert as both might fear ;
Venus had here, and Hebe been outshined   35
By thy bright Birtha and thy Rodalind.
Such is thy happy skill, and such the odds
Betwixt thy worthies and the Grecian gods !
Whose deities in vain had here come down,
Where mortal beauty wears the sovereign crown ;   40
Such as of flesh composed, by flesh and blood,
Though not resisted, may be understood.

A PANEGYRIC TO MY LORD PROTECTOR,

OF THE PRESENT GREATNESS, AND JOINT INTEREST, OF HIS HIGHNESS, AND THIS NATION.

WHILE with a strong and yet a gentle hand,
You bridle faction, and our hearts command,
Protect us from ourselves, and from the foe,
Make us unite, and make us conquer too ;

Let partial spirits still aloud complain,   5
Think themselves injured that they cannot reign,
And own no liberty but where they may
Without control upon their fellows prey.

Above the waves as Neptune showed his face,
To chide the winds, and save the Trojan race, 10
So has your Highness, raised above the rest,
Storms of ambition, tossing us, repressed.

Your drooping country, torn with civil hate,
Restored by you, is made a glorious state ;
The seat of empire, where the Irish come, 15
And the unwilling Scotch, to fetch their doom.

The sea's our own ; and now all nations greet,
With bending sails, each vessel of our fleet ;
Your power extends as far as winds can blow,
Or swelling sails upon the globe may go. 20

Heaven, (that has placed this island to give law,
To balance Europe, and her states to awe)
In this conjunction does on Britain smile ;
The greatest leader, and the greatest isle !

Whether this portion of the world were rent,   25
By the rude ocean, from the continent ;
Or thus created ; it was sure designed
To be the sacred refuge of mankind.

Hither the oppressed shall henceforth resort,
Justice to crave, and succour, at your court ;   30
And then your Highness, not for ours alone,
But for the world's protector shall be known.

Fame, swifter than your winged navy, flies
Through every land that near the ocean lies,
Sounding your name, and telling dreadful news   35
To all that piracy and rapine use.

With such a chief the meanest nation blessed,
Might hope to lift her head above the rest ;
What may be thought impossible to do
For[1] us, embraced by the sea and you ?   40

Lords of the world's great waste, the ocean, we
Whole forests send to reign upon the sea,
And every coast may trouble, or relieve ;
But none can visit us without your leave.

1.—Quarto, *By.*

Angels and we have this prerogative,   45
That none can at our happy seat [1] arrive ;
While we descend at pleasure, to invade
The bad with vengeance, and the good to aid.

Our little world, the image of the great,
Like that, amidst the boundless ocean set,   50
Of her own growth has all that Nature craves ;
And all that's rare, as tribute from the waves.

As Egypt does not on the clouds rely,
But to her [2] Nile owes more than to the sky ;
So what our earth, and what our heaven, denies,   55
Our ever constant friend, the sea, supplies.

The taste of hot Arabia's spice we know,
Free from the scorching sun that makes it grow ;
Without the worm, in Persian silks we shine ;
And, without planting, drink of every vine.   60

To dig for wealth we weary not our limbs ;
Gold, though the heaviest metal, hither swims ;
Ours is the harvest where the Indians mow ;
We plough the deep, and reap what others sow.

Things of the noblest kind our own soil breeds ;   65
Stout are our men, and warlike are our steeds ;
Rome, though her eagle through the world had flown,
Could never make this island all her own.

1. -Quarto, *seas*.   2.—Quarto, *the*.

Here the Third Edward, and the Black Prince, too,
France-conquering Henry flourished, and now you ;
For whom we stayed, as did the Grecian [1] state, [70
Till Alexander came to urge their fate.

When for more worlds the Macedonian cried,
He wist not Thetis in her lap did hide
Another yet ; a world reserved for you,   75
To make more great than that he did subdue.

He safely might old troops to battle lead,
Against the unwarlike-Persian,[2] and the Mede,
Whose hasty flight did, from a bloodless field,
More spoil than honour to the victor yield.   80

A race unconquered, by their clime made bold,
The Caledonians, armed with want and cold,
Have, by a fate indulgent to your fame,[3]
Been from all ages kept for you to tame.

Whom the old Roman wall so ill confined,   85
With a new chain of garrisons you bind ;
Here foreign gold no more shall make them come ;
Our English iron holds them fast at home.

They, that henceforth must be content to know
No warmer region than their hills of snow,   90
May blame the sun, but must extol your grace,
Which in our senate has allowed them place.

1.—Quarto, *Trojan.*   2.—Quarto, *Persians.*
3.—Quarto, *name.*

Preferred by conquest, happily o'erthrown,[1]
Falling they[2] rise, to be with us made one ;
So kind dictators made, when they came home,   95
Their vanquished foes free citizens of Rome.

Like favour find the Irish, with like fate,
Advanced to be a portion of our state ;
While by your valour and your courteous[3] mind,
Nations, divided by the sea, are joined.   100

Holland, to gain your friendship, is content
To be our outguard on the continent ;
She from her fellow-provinces would go,
Rather than hazard to have you her foe.

In our late fight, when cannons did diffuse,   105
Preventing posts, the terror and the news,
Our neighbour princes trembled at their roar ;
But our conjunction makes them tremble more.

Your never-failing sword made war to cease ;
And now you heal us with the arts[4] of peace ;   110
Our minds with bounty and with awe engage,
Invite affection, and restrain our rage.

Less pleasure take brave minds in battles won,
Than in restoring such as are undone ;
Tigers have courage, and the rugged bear,   115
But man alone can, whom he conquers, spare.

1.—Quarto, *overthrown.*   2.—Quarto, *you.*
3.—Quarto, *bounteous.*   4.—Quarto, *acts.*

To pardon willing, and to punish loath,
You strike with one hand, but you heal with both ;
Lifting up all that prostrate lie, you grieve
You cannot make the dead again to live. 120

When fate, or error, had our age misled,
And o'er these nations[1] such confusion spread,
The only cure, which could from Heaven come down,
Was so much power and clemency[2] in one !

One ! whose extraction from an ancient line 125
Gives hope again that well-born men may shine ;
The meanest in your nature, mild and good,
The noble rest secured in your blood.

Oft have we wondered how you hid in peace
A mind[3] proportioned to such things as these ; 130
How such a ruling spirit you could restrain,
And practise first over yourself to reign.

Your private life did a just pattern give,
How fathers, husbands, pious sons should live ;
Born to command, your princely virtues slept, 135
Like humble David's, while the flock he kept.

But when your troubled country called you forth,
Your flaming courage, and your matchless worth,
Dazzling the eyes of all that did pretend,
To fierce contention gave a prosperous end. 140

1.—Quarto, *this nation.*   2.—Quarto, *piety.*
3.—Quarto, *Amid.*

Still as you rise, the state, exalted too,
Finds no distemper while 'tis changed by you ;
Changed like the world's great scene ! when, without
    noise,
The rising sun night's vulgar lights destroys.

Had you, some ages past, this race of glory   145
Run, with amazement we should read your story ;
But living virtue, all achievements past,
Meets envy still, to grapple with at last.

This Cæsar found ; and that ungrateful age,
With losing him fell[1] back to blood and rage ;   150
Mistaken Brutus thought to break their yoke,
But cut the bond of union with that stroke.

That sun once set, a thousand meaner stars
Gave a dim light to violence, and wars,
To such a tempest as now threatens all,   155
Did not your mighty arm prevent the fall.

If Rome's great senate could not wield that sword,
Which of the conquered world had made them lord,
What hope had ours, while yet their power was new,
To rule victorious armies, but by you ?   160

You ! that had taught them to subdue their foes,
Could order teach, and their high spirits compose ;
To every duty could their minds engage,
Provoke their courage, and command their rage.

1.—Quarto, *went.*

So when a lion shakes his dreadful mane,   165
And angry grows, if he that first took pain
To tame his youth approach the haughty beast,
He bends to him, but frights away the rest.

As the vexed world, to find repose, at last
Itself into Augustus' arms did cast ;   170
So England now does, with like toil oppressed,
Her weary head upon your bosom rest.

Then let the Muses, with such notes as these,
Instruct us what belongs unto our peace ;
Your battles they hereafter shall indite,   175
And draw the image of our Mars in fight ;

Tell of towns stormed, of armies overrun,[1]
And[2] mighty kingdoms by your conduct won ;
How, while you thundered, clouds of dust did choke
Contending troops, and seas lay hid in smoke.   180

Illustrious acts high raptures do infuse,
And every conqueror creates a muse.
Here, in low strains, your milder deeds we sing ;
But there, my lord ; we'll bays and olive bring

To crown your head ; while you in triumph ride 185
O'er vanquished nations, and the sea beside ;
While all your neighbour-princes unto you,
Like Joseph's sheaves, pay reverence, and bow.

1.—Quarto, *overcome.*   2.—Quarto, *Of.*

L

TO MY WORTHY FRIEND, MR. WASE.

THE TRANSLATOR OF GRATIUS.

THUS, by the music, we may know
When noble wits a-hunting go,
Through groves that on Parnassus grow.

The Muses all the chase adorn ;
My friend on Pegasus is borne ;　　　　5
And young Apollo winds the horn.

Having old Gratius in the wind,
No pack of critics e'er could find,
Or he know more of his own mind.

Here huntsmen with delight may read　　10
How to choose dogs for scent or speed,
And how to change or[1] mend the breed ;

What arms to use, or nets to frame,
Wild beasts to combat or to tame ;
With all the mysteries of that game.　　15

1.—1654, *and.*

But, worthy friend ! the face of war
In ancient times doth differ far
From what our fiery battles are.

Nor is it like, since powder known,
That man, so cruel to his own,   20
Should spare the race of beasts alone

No quarter now, but with the gun
Men wait in trees from sun to sun,
And all is in a moment done.

And therefore we expect your next   25
Should be no comment, but a text
To tell how modern beasts are vexed.

Thus would I further yet engage
Your gentle Muse to court the age
With somewhat of your proper rage ;   30

Since none does more to Phœbus owe,
Or in more languages can show
Those arts which you so early know.

AD COMITEM MONUMETENSEM DE

BENTIVOGLIO SUO.

FLORIBUS Angligenis non hanc tibi necto corollam,
Cum satis indigenis te probet ipse Liber :
Per me Roma sciet tibi se debere, quod Anglo
Romanus didicit cultius ore loqui.
Ultima quæ tellus Aquilas duce Cæsare vidit,   5
Candida Romulidum te duce scripta videt.
Consilio ut quondam Patriam nil juveris, esto !
Sed studio cives ingenioque juvas.
Namque dolis liber hic instructus, et arte Batava,
A Belga nobis ut caveamus, ait.   10
Horremus per te civilis dira furoris
Vulnera ; discordes Flandria quassa monet.
Hic discat miles pugnare, orare senator ;
Qui regnant, leni sceptra tenere manu.
Macte, Comes ! virtute novâ, vestri ordinis ingens 15
Ornamentum, ævi deliciæque tui !
Dum stertunt alii somno vinoque sepulti,
Nobilis antiquo stemmate digna facis.

TO HIS WORTHY FRIEND,
MASTER EVELYN,

UPON HIS TRANSLATION OF LUCRETIUS.

THAT chance and atoms make this all
In order democratical,
Where bodies freely run their course,
Without design, or fate, or force,
In English verse Lucretius sings,   5
As if with Pegasean wings,
He soared beyond our utmost sphere
And other worlds discovered there ;
His boundless and unruly wit,
To Nature does no bounds permit ;   10
But boldly has removed those bars
Of heaven and earth and seas and stars,
By which she was before supposed,
By moderate wits, to be enclosed,
Till his free muse threw down the pale,   15
And did at once dispark them all.
   So vast this argument did seem,
That the wise author did esteem
The Roman language (which was spread
O'er the whole world, in triumph led)   20

Too weak, too narrow to unfold
The wonders which he would have told.
This speaks thy glory, noble friend !
And British language does commend ;
For here Lucretius whole we find,   25
His words, his music, and his mind.
Thy art has to our country brought
All that he writ, and all he thought.
Ovid translated, Virgil too,
Showed long since what our tongues could do ;   30
Nor Lucan we, nor Horace spared ;
Only Lucretius was too hard.
Lucretius, like a fort, did stand   ·
Untouched, till your victorious hand
Did from his head this garland bear,   35
Which now upon your own you wear ;
A garland ! made of such new bays,
And sought in such untrodden ways,
As no man's temples e'er did crown,
Save this great author's, and your own !   40

OF A WAR WITH SPAIN, AND A FIGHT AT SEA.

Now, for some ages, had the pride of Spain
Made the sun shine on half the world in vain ;
While she bid war to all that durst supply
The place of those her cruelty made die.
Of nature's bounty men forebore to taste,   5
And the best portion of the earth lay waste,
From the new world her silver and her gold
Came, like a tempest, to confound the old ;
Feeding with these the bribed Electors' hopes,
Alone she gave us emperors and popes ;[1]   10
With these accomplishing her vast designs,[2]
Europe was shaken with her Indian mines.
    When Britain, looking with a just disdain[3]
Upon this gilded majesty of Spain,
And knowing well that empire must decline,   15
Whose chief support and sinews are of coin,
Our nation's solid virtue[4] did oppose
To the rich troublers of the world's repose.
    And now some months, encamping on the main,

1.—*She made at pleasure Emperors and Popes.* MS. in a copy of the edition of 1664 that belonged to Col. Cunningham. (See *Notes and Queries,* 3rd series, ix. **192.**) This and the preceding line do not occur in the folio.

2.—*With these advancing her unjust designs.* Col. Cunningham's copy.

3.—*When our Protector looking with disdain.* Ibid.

4.—*Her native force and virtue,* folio.

Our naval army had besieged Spain;   20
They that the whole world's monarchy designed,
Are to their ports by our bold fleet confined;
From whence our Red Cross they triumphant see,
Riding without a rival on the sea.

    Others may use the ocean as their road,   25
Only the English make it their abode,
Whose ready sails with every wind can fly,
And make a covenant with the inconstant sky;[1]
Our oaks secure, as if they there took root,
We tread on billows with a steady foot.   30

    Meanwhile the Spaniards in America,
Near to the line the sun approaching saw,
And hoped their European coasts to find
Cleared from our ships by the autumnal wind;
Their huge capacious galleons stuffed with plate,   35
The labouring winds drive slowly towards their fate.
Before St. Lucar they their guns discharge,
To tell their joy, or to invite[2] a barge;
This heard some ships of ours, (though out of view)
And, swift as eagles, to the quarry flew;   40
So heedless lambs, which for their mothers bleat,
Wake hungry lions, and become their meat.

    Arrived, they soon begin that tragic play,
And with their smoky cannons banish day;
Night, horror, slaughter, with confusion meets,   45
And in their sable arms embrace the fleets.

   1.—This and the preceding line do not occur in the folio.
   2.—Folio, *call forth.*

Through yielding planks the angry bullets fly,
And, of one wound, hundreds together die ;
Born under different stars one fate they have,
The ship their coffin, and the sea their grave !   50
Bold were the men which[1] on the ocean first
Spread their new sails, when shipwreck was the
    worst ;
More danger now from man alone we find
Than from the rocks, the billows, or the wind.
They that had sailed from near the Antarctic Pole, 55
Their treasure safe, and all their vessels whole,
In sight of their dear country ruined be,
Without the guilt of either rock or sea !
What they would spare, our fiercer art destroys,
Surpassing storms in terror and in noise.   60
Once Jove from Ida did both hosts survey,
And, when he pleased to thunder, part the fray ;
Here, heaven[2] in vain that kind retreat should sound,
The louder cannon had the thunder drowned.
Some, we made prize ; while others, burned and
    rent,   65
With their rich lading to the bottom went ;
Down sinks at once (so Fortune with us sports !)
The pay of armies, and the pride of courts.
Vain man ! whose rage buries as low that store,
As avarice had digged for it before ;   70
What earth, in her dark bowels, could not keep

1.—Folio, *who.*   2.—Folio, *Heaven here.*

From greedy hands, lies safer in the deep,
Where Thetis kindly does from mortals hide
Those seeds of luxury, debate, and pride.

And now, into her lap the richest prize   75
Fell, with the noblest of our enemies ;
The Marquis (glad to see the fire destroy
Wealth that prevailing foes were to enjoy)
Out from his flaming ship his children sent,
To perish in a milder element ;   80
Then laid him by his burning lady's side,
And, since he could not save her, with her died.
Spices and gums about them melting fry,
And, phœnix-like, in that rich nest they die ;[1]
Alive, in flames of equal love they burned,   85
And now together are to ashes turned ;
Ashes ! more worth than all their funeral cost,
Than the huge treasure which was with them lost.[2]

1.—In Col. Cunningham's copy, after this line, the following
passage occurs :—

> *Death bitter is for what we leave behind,*
> *But taking with us all we have is kind.*
> *What could he more than hold for term of life,*
> *His Indian treasures and more precious wife ?*
> *Alive, &c. . . . . lost.*
> *Fair Venus wept, her tender hands she wrung,*
> *That love should perish whence herself was sprung.*
> *Her son endeavouring their lives to save,*
> *Drenched all his feathered arrows in the wave :*
> *Since when so slow, and so unsure they move,*
> *That never more we may expect such love.*

2.—The poem ends with this line in the folio.

These dying lovers, and their floating sons,
Suspend the fight, and silence all our guns ;   90
Beauty and youth about to perish, finds
Such noble pity in brave English minds,
That (the rich spoil forgot, their valour's prize)
All labour now to save their enemies.
How frail our passions ! how soon changed are   95
Our wrath and fury to a friendly care !
They that but now for honour, and for plate,
Made the sea blush with blood, resign their hate ;
And, their young foes endeavouring to retrieve,
With greater hazard than they fought, they dive.[1] 100

    With these, returns victorious Montague,
With laurels in his hand, and half Peru.
Let the brave generals divide that bough,
Our great Protector hath such wreaths enow ;
His conquering head has no more room for bays ; 105
Then let it be as the glad nation prays ;
Let the rich ore forthwith be melted down,
And the state fixed by making him a crown ;
With ermine clad, and purple, let him hold
A royal sceptre, made of Spanish gold.   110

1.—The poem, as reprinted in the editions of his poems published during Waller's life, ends with this line ; the remaining
lines appeared in Bennet's edition of "The Second Part,"
headed, *Some Verses belonging to a Copy in the First Part of
his Poems, entitled Upon a War with Spain, and a Fight at
Sea. The close of it was originally thus.*——They were again
omitted in the edition of 1705.

TO HIS WORTHY FRIEND,
SIR THOS. HIGGONS,

UPON THE TRANSLATION OF "THE VENETIAN TRIUMPH."

THE winged lion's not so fierce in fight,
As Liberi's hand presents him to our sight ;
Nor would his pencil make him half so fierce,
Or roar so loud, as Businello's verse ;
But your translation does all three excel,   5
The fight, the piece, and lofty Businel.
As their small galleys may not hold compare
With our tall ships, whose sails employ more air ;
So does the Italian to your genius vail,
Moved with a fuller and a nobler gale.   10
Thus, while your muse spreads the Venetian story,
You make all Europe emulate her glory ;
You make them blush weak Venice should defend
The cause of Heaven, while they for words contend ;
Shed Christian blood, and populous cities raze,   15
Because they're taught to use some different phrase.
If, listening to your charms, we could our jars
Compose, and on the Turk discharge these wars,
Our British arms the sacred tomb might wrest
From Pagan hands, and triumph o'er the East ;   20
And then you might our own high deeds recite,
And with great Tasso celebrate the fight.

PART OF THE FOURTH BOOK OF VIRGIL, TRANSLATED.

Beginning

. . . . Talesque miserrima fletus
Fertque refertque soror. . . . . .

And ending with

Adnixi torquent spumas, et cærula verrunt.

ALL this her weeping sister does repeat
To the stern man, whom nothing could entreat ;
Lost were her prayers, and fruitless were her tears !
Fate, and great Jove, had stopped his gentle ears.
As when loud winds a well-grown oak would rend   5
Up by the roots, this way and that they bend
His reeling trunk ; and with a boisterous sound
Scatter his leaves, and strew them on the ground ;
He fixed stands ; as deep his root doth lie
Down to the centre, as his top is high ;   10
No less on every side the hero pressed,
Feels love and pity shake his noble breast,
And down his cheeks though fruitless tears do roll,
Unmoved remains the purpose of his soul.
Then Dido, urged with approaching fate,   15
Begins the light of cruel Heaven to hate ;
Her resolution to dispatch and die,
Confirmed by many a horrid prodigy !
The water, consecrate for sacrifice,
Appears all black to her amazed eyes ;   20

The wine to putrid blood converted flows,
Which from her none, not her own sister, knows.
Besides, there stood, as sacred to her lord,
A marble temple which she much adored,
With snowy fleeces and fresh garlands crowned ;   25
Hence every night proceeds a dreadful sound ;
Her husband's voice invites her to his tomb,
And dismal owls presage the ills to come.
Besides, the prophecies of wizards old
Increased her terror and her fall foretold ;   30
Scorned, and deserted, to herself she seems,
And finds Æneas cruel in her dreams.
   So to mad Pentheus, double Thebes appears,
And furies howl in his distempered ears ;
Orestes so, with like distraction tossed,   35
Is made to fly his mother's angry ghost.
   Now grief and fury at their height arrive ;
Death she decrees, and thus does it contrive.
Her grieved sister, with a cheerful grace,
(Hope well dissembled shining in her face)   40
She thus deceives.   "Dear sister ! let us prove
The cure I have invented for my love.
Beyond the land of Ethiopia lies
The place where Atlas does support the skies,
Hence came an old magician, that did keep   45
The Hesperian fruit, and made the dragon sleep ;
Her potent charms do troubled souls relieve,
And, where she lists, make calmest minds to grieve :
The course of rivers, or of heaven, can stop,

And call trees down from the airy mountain's top. 50
Witness, ye Gods ! and thou, my dearest part !
How loath I am to tempt this guilty art.
Erect a pile, and on it let us place
That bed where I my ruin did embrace ;
With all the reliques of our impious guest,   55
Arms, spoils, and presents, let the pile be dressed ;
(The knowing woman thus prescribes) that we
May rase the man out of our memory."
    Thus speaks the Queen, but hides the fatal end
For which she doth those sacred rites pretend.   60
Nor worse effects of grief her sister thought
Would follow, than Sichæus' murder wrought ;
Therefore obeys her ; and now, heaped high,
The cloven oaks and lofty pines do lie ;
Hung all with wreaths and flowery garlands round, 65
So by herself was her own funeral crowned !
Upon the top the Trojan's image lies,
And his sharp sword, wherewith anon she dies.
They by the altar stand, while with loose hair
The magic prophetess begins her prayer :   70
On Chaos, Erebus, and all the gods,
Which in the infernal shades have their abodes,
She loudly calls, besprinkling all the room
With drops, supposed from Lethe's lake to come.
She seeks the knot which on the forehead grows   75
Of new-foaled colts, and herbs by moonlight mows.
A cake of leaven in her pious hands
Holds the devoted Queen, and barefoot stands ;

One tender foot was bare, the other shod.
Her robe ungirt, invoking every god,   80
And every power, if any be above,
Which takes regard of ill-requited love!
　Now was the time when weary mortals steep
Their careful temples in the dew of sleep;
On seas, on earth, and all that in them dwell,   85
A death-like quiet, and deep silence fell;
But not on Dido! whose untamed mind
Refused to be by sacred night confined;
A double passion in her breast does move,
Love, and fierce anger for neglected love.   90
Thus she afflicts her soul: "What shall I do?
With fate inverted, shall I humbly woo?
And some proud prince, in wild Numidia born,
Pray to accept me, and forget my scorn?
Or shall I with the ungrateful Trojan go,   95
Quit all my state, and wait upon my foe?
Is not enough, by sad experience! known
The perjured race of false Laomedon?
With my Sidonians shall I give them chase,
Bands hardly forced from their native place?   100
No;—die! and let this sword thy fury tame;
Nought but thy blood can quench this[1] guilty flame.
Ah, sister! vanquished with my passion, thou
Betray'dst me first, dispensing with my vow.
Had I been constant to Sichæus still,   105
And single-lived, I had not known this ill!"

　　　1.—1658, *thy.*

Such thoughts torment the Queen's enraged breast,
While the Dardanian does securely rest
In his tall ship, for sudden flight prepared ;
To whom once more the son of Jove appeared ;   110
Thus seems[1] to speak the youthful deity,
Voice, hair, and colour, all like Mercury.
    " Fair Venus' seed ! canst thou indulge thy sleep,
Nor better guard in such great danger keep ?
Mad, by neglect to lose so fair a wind !   115
If here thy ships the purple morning find,
Thou shalt behold this hostile harbour shine
With a new fleet, and fire, to ruin thine ;
She meditates revenge, resolved to die ;   120
Weigh anchor quickly, and her fury fly."
    This said, the god in shades of night retired.
Amazed Æneas, with the warning fired,
Shakes off dull sleep, and, rousing up his men,
" Behold ! the gods command our flight again
Fall to your oars, and all your canvas spread ;   125
What god soe'er that thus vouchsaf'st to lead,
We follow gladly, and thy will obey ;
Assist us still, smoothing our happy way,
And make the rest propitious ! "—With that word
He cuts the cable with his shining sword ;   130
Through all the navy doth like ardour reign,
They quit the shore, and rush into the main ;
Placed on their banks, the lusty Trojans sweep
Neptune's smooth face, and cleave the yielding deep.

1.—1658, *seem'd.*

M

UPON THE LATE STORM, AND OF THE DEATH OF HIS HIGHNESS ENSUING THE SAME.

WE must resign !   Heaven his great soul does claim
In storms, as loud as his immortal fame ;
His dying groans, his last breath, shakes our isle,
And trees uncut fall for his funeral pile ;
About his palace their broad roots are tossed   5
Into the air.—So Romulus was lost !
New Rome in such a tempest missed her king,
And from obeying fell to worshipping.
On Œta's top thus Hercules lay dead,
With ruined oaks and pines about him spread ;   10
The poplar, too, whose bough he wont to wear
On his victorious head, lay prostrate there ;[1]
Those his last fury from the mountain rent :
Our dying hero from the continent
Ravished whole towns ; and forts from Spaniards reft,
As his last legacy to Britain left.   [15
The ocean, which so long our hopes confined,
Could give no limits to his vaster mind ;

1.—This and the preceding line do not occur in the broadside, or in Wither's *Salt upon Salt* (1659), where Waller's lines are quoted "according to the Author's printed copy."

Our bounds' enlargement was his latest toil,
Nor hath he left us prisoners to our isle ;   20
Under the tropic is our language spoke,
And part of Flanders hath received our yoke.
From civil broils he did us disengage,
Found nobler objects for our martial rage ;
And, with wise conduct, to his country showed   25
Their ancient way of conquering abroad.
Ungrateful then ! if we no tears allow
To him, that gave us peace and empire too.
Princes, that feared him, grieve, concerned to see
No pitch of glory from the grave is free.   30
Nature herself took notice of his death,
And, sighing, swelled the sea with such a breath,
That, to remotest shores her billows rolled,
The approaching fate of her great ruler told.

TO THE KING,

UPON HIS MAJESTY'S HAPPY RETURN.

THE rising sun complies with our weak sight,
First gilds the clouds, then shows his globe of light
At such a distance from our eyes, as though
He knew what harm his hasty beams would do.
  But your full majesty at once breaks forth   5
In the meridian of your reign.   Your worth,
Your youth, and all the splendour of your state,

M 2

(Wrapped up, till now, in clouds of adverse fate!)
With such a flood of light invade our eyes,
And our spread hearts with so great joy surprise,　　10
That if your grace incline that we should live,
You must not, sir! too hastily forgive.
Our guilt preserves us from the excess of joy,
Which scatters spirits, and would life destroy.
All are obnoxious! and this faulty land,　　15
Like fainting Esther, does before you stand,
Watching your sceptre. The revolted sea
Trembles to think she did your foes obey.

　Great Britain, like blind Polypheme, of late,
In a wild rage, became the scorn and hate　　20
Of her proud neighbours, who began to think
She, with the weight of her own force, would sink.
But you are come, and all their hopes are vain;
This giant isle has got her eye again.
Now she might spare the ocean, and oppose　　25
Your conduct to the fiercest of her foes.
Naked, the Graces guarded you from all
Dangers abroad; and now your thunder shall.
Princes that saw you, different passions prove,
For now they dread the object of their love;　　30
Nor without envy can behold his height,
Whose conversation was their late delight.
So Semele, contented with the rape
Of Jove disguised in a mortal shape,
When she beheld his hands with lightning filled,　　35
And his bright rays, was with amazement killed.

And though it be our sorrow, and our crime,
To have accepted life so long a time
Without you here, yet does this absence gain
No small advantage to your present reign ;   40
For, having viewed the persons and the things,
The councils, state, and strength of Europe's kings,
You know your work ; ambition to restrain,
And set them bounds, as Heaven does to the main.
We have you now with ruling wisdom fraught,   45
Not such as books, but such as practice, taught.
So the lost sun, while least by us enjoyed,
Is the whole night for our concern employed ;
He ripens spices, fruits, and precious gums,
Which from remotest regions hither comes.   50

    This seat of yours (from the other world removed)
Had Archimedes known, he might have proved
His engine's force fixed here. Your power and skill
Make the world's motion wait upon your will.

    Much suffering monarch ! the first English born   55
That has the crown of these three nations worn !
How has your patience, with the barbarous rage
Of your own soil, contended half an age ?
Till (your tried virtue, and your sacred word,
At last preventing your unwilling sword)   60
Armies and fleets which kept you out so long,
Owned their great sovereign, and redressed his wrong.
When straight the people, by no force compelled,
Nor longer from their inclination held,
Break forth at once, like powder set on fire,   65

And, with a noble rage, their King require ;
So the injured sea, which from her wonted course,
To gain some acres, avarice did force,
If the new banks, neglected once, decay,
No longer will from her old channel stay ;   70
Raging, the late got land she overflows,
And all that's built upon't, to ruin goes.
　　Offenders now, the chiefest, do begin
To strive for grace, and expiate their sin.
All winds blow fair, that did the world embroil ;   75
Your vipers treacle yield, and scorpions oil.
　　If then such praise the Macedonian got,
For having rudely cut the Gordian knot,
What glory's due to him that could divide
Such ravelled interests ; has the knot untied,   80
And without stroke so smooth a passage made,
Where craft and malice such impeachments laid ?
　　But while we praise you, you ascribe it all
To His high hand, which threw the untouched wall
Of self-demolished Jericho so low ;   85
His angel 'twas that did before you go,
Tamed savage hearts, and made affections yield,
Like ears of corn when wind salutes the field.
　　Thus patience crowned, like Job's, your trouble ends,
Having your foes to pardon, and your friends ;   90
For, though your courage were so firm a rock,
What private virtue could endure the shock ?
Like your Great Master, you the storm withstood,
And pitied those who love with frailty showed.
　　Rude Indians, torturing all the royal race,   95

Him with the throne and dear-bought sceptre grace
That suffers best.   What region could be found,
Where your heroic head had not been crowned?
  The next experience of your mighty mind
Is how you combat fortune, now she's kind.   100
And this way, too, you are victorious found ;
She flatters with the same success she frowned.
While to yourself severe, to others kind,
With power unbounded, and a will confined,
Of this vast empire you possess the care,   105
The softer part falls to the people's share.
Safety, and equal government, are things
Which subjects make as happy as their kings.
  Faith, law, and piety, (that banished train !)
Justice and truth, with you return again.   110
The city's trade, and country's easy life,
Once more shall flourish without fraud or strife.
Your reign no less assures the ploughman's peace,
Than the warm sun advances his increase ;
And does the shepherds as securely keep   115
From all their fears, as they preserve their sheep.
  But, above all, the Muse-inspired train
Triumph, and raise their drooping heads again !
Kind Heaven at once has, in your person, sent
Their sacred judge, their guard, and argument.   120

  Nec magis expressi vultus per aenea signa,
  Quam per vatis opus mores, animique, virorum
  Clarorum apparent [1] .   .   .   .

1.—This quotation (Horace, Ep. II. i. 248) was added when
the poem was reprinted in the edition of 1664.

ON ST. JAMES'S PARK,

AS LATELY IMPROVED BY HIS MAJESTY.

OF the first Paradise there's nothing found ;
Plants set by Heaven are vanished, and the ground ;
Yet the description lasts ; who knows the fate
Of lines that shall this paradise relate ?
   Instead of rivers rolling by the side   5
Of Eden's garden, here flows in the tide ;
The sea, which always served his empire, now
Pays tribute to our Prince's pleasure too.
Of famous cities we the founders know ;
But rivers, old as seas, to which they go,   10
Are nature's bounty ; 'tis of more renown
To make a river, than to build a town.
   For future shade, young trees upon the banks
Of the new stream appear in even ranks ;
The voice of Orpheus, or Amphion's hand,   15
In better order could not make them stand ;
May they increase as fast, and spread their boughs,
As the high fame of their great owner grows !
May he live long enough to see them all
Dark shadows cast, and as his palace tall !   20
Methinks I see the love that shall be made,
The lovers walking in that amorous shade ;
The gallants dancing by the river's side ;
They bathe in summer, and in winter slide.
Methinks I hear the music in the boats,   25
And the loud echo which returns the notes ;

While overhead a flock of new-sprung fowl
Hangs in the air, and does the sun control,
Darkening the sky ;[1] they hover o'er, and shroud
The wanton sailors with a feathered cloud.   30
Beneath, a shoal of silver fishes glides,
And plays about the gilded barges' sides ;
The ladies, angling in the crystal lake,
Feast on the waters[3] with the prey they take ;
At once victorious with their lines, and eyes,   35
They make the fishes, and the men, their prize.
A thousand Cupids on the billows ride,
And sea-nymphs enter with the swelling tide ;
From Thetis sent as spies, to make report,
And tell the wonders of her sovereign's court.   40
All that can, living, feed the greedy eye,
Or dead, the palate, here you may descry ;
The choicest things that furnished Noah's ark,
Or Peter's sheet, inhabiting this park ;
All with a border of rich fruit-trees crowned,   45
Whose loaded branches hide the lofty mound.
Such various ways the spacious alleys lead,
My doubtful Muse knows not what path to tread.
Yonder, the harvest of cold months laid up,
Gives a fresh coolness to the royal cup ;   50
There ice, like crystal firm, and never lost,

1.—Folio, *aire*. 1664 and subsequent editions, *Darkening
the sky they hover o're.*
2.—This and the preceding line do not occur in the folio.
3.—Folio, *water.*

Tempers hot July with December's frost ;
Winter's dark prison, whence he cannot fly,
Though the warm spring, his enemy, draws[1] nigh.
Strange ! that extremes should thus preserve the snow,
High on the Alps, or in deep caves below.   [55

Here, a well-polished Mall gives us the joy
To see our Prince his matchless force employ ;
His manly posture, and his graceful mien,
Vigour and youth, in all his motions seen ;   60
His shape so lovely,[2] and his limbs so strong,
Confirm our hopes we shall obey him long.
No sooner has he touched the flying ball,
But 'tis already more than half the Mall ;
And such a fury from his arm[3] has got,   65
As from a smoking culverin 'twere shot.

Near this my Muse, what most delights her, sees
A living gallery of aged trees ;
Bold sons of earth, that thrust their arms so high,
As if once more they would invade the sky.   70
In such green palaces the first kings reigned,
Slept in their shades, and angels entertained ;
With such old counsellors they did advise,
And, by frequenting sacred groves, grew wise.
Free from the impediments of light and noise,   75
Man, thus retired, his nobler thoughts employs.
Here Charles contrives the ordering of his states,
Here he resolves his neighbouring princes' fates ;

1. Folio, *grows.*   2.—Folio, *comely.*   3.—1664, *aim.*

What nation shall have peace, where war be made,
Determined is in this oraculous shade ;   80
The world, from India to the frozen north,
Concerned in what this solitude brings forth.
His fancy, objects from his view receives ;
The prospect, thought and contemplation gives.
That seat of empire here salutes his eye,   85
To which three kingdoms do themselves apply ;
The structure by a prelate raised, Whitehall,
Built with the fortune of Rome's capitol ;
Both, disproportioned to the present state
Of their proud founders, were approved by Fate.[1] 90
From hence he does that antique pile behold,
Where royal heads receive the sacred gold ;
It gives them crowns, and does their ashes keep ;
There made like gods, like mortals there they sleep ;
Making the circle of their reign complete,   95
Those suns of empire ! where they rise, they set.[2]
When others fell, this, standing, did presage
The crown should triumph over popular rage ;
Hard by that house, where all our ills were shaped,
The auspicious temple stood, and yet escaped.   100
So snow on Ætna does unmelted lie,
Whence rolling flames and scattered cinders fly ;
The distant country in the ruin shares ;
What falls from heaven the burning mountain spares.

1.—Folio, *states* and *Fates.*
2.—This and the preceding line are not in the folio.

Next, that capacious hall he sees, the room   105
Where the whole nation does for justice come ;
Under whose large roof flourishes the gown,
And judges grave, on high tribunals, frown.
Here, like the people's pastor he does go,[1]
His flock subjected to his view below ;   110
On which reflecting in his mighty mind,
No private passion does indulgence find ;
The pleasures of his youth suspended are,
And made a sacrifice to public care.
Here, free from court compliances, he walks,   115
And with himself, his best adviser, talks ;
How peaceful olive may his temples shade,
For mending laws, and for restoring trade ;
Or, how his brows may be with laurel charged,
For nations conquered, and our bounds enlarged. 120
Of ancient prudence here he ruminates,[2]
Of rising kingdoms, and of falling states ;
What ruling arts gave great Augustus fame,
And how Alcides purchased such a name.
His eyes, upon his native palace bent,   125
Close by, suggest a greater argument.
His thoughts rise higher, when he does reflect
On what the world may from that star expect
Which at his birth appeared, to let us see
Day, for his sake, could with the night agree ;   130

1.--Folio, *Here he does like the people's pastor go.*
2.—Folio, *meditates.*

A prince, on whom such different lights did smile,
Born the divided world to reconcile !
Whatever Heaven, or high extracted blood
Could promise, or foretell, he will make good ;
Reform these nations, and improve them more,　135
Than this fair park, from what it was before.

TO THE QUEEN, UPON HER ·MAJESTY'S BIRTHDAY,

AFTER HER HAPPY RECOVERY FROM A DANGEROUS SICKNESS.

FAREWELL the year ! which threatened so
The fairest light the world can show.
Welcome the new ! whose every day,
Restoring what was snatched away
By pining sickness from the fair,　　　5
That matchless beauty does repair
So fast, that the approaching spring,
(Which does to flowery meadows bring
What the rude winter from them tore)
Shall give her all she had before.　　　10
　　But we recover not so fast
The sense of such a danger past ;
We that esteemed you sent from heaven,
A pattern to this island given,
To show us what the blessed do there　　15

And what alive they practised here,
When that which we immortal thought,
We saw so near destruction brought,
Felt all which you did then endure,
And tremble yet, as not secure.   20
So though the sun victorious be,
And from a dark eclipse set free,
The influence, which we fondly fear,
Afflicts our thoughts the following year.
　　But that which may relieve our care   25
Is, that you have a help so near
For all the evil you can prove,
The kindness of your royal love ;
He that was never known to mourn,
So many kingdoms from him torn,   30
His tears reserved for you, more dear,
More prized, than all those kingdoms were !
For when no healing art prevailed,
When cordials and elixirs failed,
On your pale cheek he dropped the shower,   35
Revived you like a dying flower.

Nunc itaque et versus et cætera ludicra pono,
Quid verum, *atque decens, curo et rogo, et omnis in hoc sum.* [1]

1.—Horace, Ep. I. i. 10.

TO A FAIR LADY, PLAYING WITH A SNAKE.

STRANGE ! that such horror and such grace
Should dwell together in one place ;
A fury's arm, an angel's face !

'Tis innocence, and youth, which makes
In Chloris' fancy such mistakes, 5
To start at love, and play with snakes.

By this and by her coldness barred,
Her servants have a task too hard ;
The tyrant has a double guard !

Thrice happy snake ! that in her sleeve 10
May boldly creep ; we dare not give
Our thoughts so unconfined a leave.

Contented in that nest of snow
He lies, as he his bliss did know,
And to the wood no more would go. 15

Take heed, fair Eve ! you do not make
Another tempter of this snake ;
A marble one so warmed would speak.

INSTRUCTIONS TO A PAINTER,

FOR THE DRAWING OF THE POSTURE AND PRO-
GRESS OF HIS MAJESTY'S FORCES AT SEA, UNDER
THE COMMAND OF HIS HIGHNESS-ROYAL; TO-
GETHER WITH THE BATTLE AND VICTORY
OBTAINED OVER THE DUTCH, JUNE 3, 1665.

FIRST draw the sea, that portion which between
The greater world and this of ours is seen ;
Here place the British, there the Holland fleet,
Vast floating armies! both prepared to meet.
Draw the whole world, expecting who should[1] reign,
After this combat, o'er the conquered main.   [5
Make Heaven concerned, and an unusual star
Declare the importance of the approaching war.
Make the sea shine with gallantry, and all
The English youth flock to their Admiral,   10
The valiant Duke ! whose early deeds abroad,
Such rage in fight, and art in conduct showed.
His bright sword now a dearer interest draws,
His brother's glory, and his country's cause.
   Let thy bold pencil hope and courage spread   15
Through the whole navy, by that hero led ;

1.—Folio, *shall.*

Make all appear, where such a Prince is by,
Resolved to conquer, or resolved to die.
With his extraction, and his glorious mind,
Make the proud sails swell more than with the wind;
Preventing cannon, make his louder fame [20
Check the Batavians, and their fury tame.
So hungry wolves, though greedy of their prey,
Stop when they find a lion in their way.
Make him bestride the ocean, and mankind 25
Ask his consent to use the sea and wind.
While his tall ships in the barred channel stand,
He grasps the Indies in his armed hand.
    Paint an east wind, and make it blow away
The excuse of Holland for their navy's stay; 30
Make them look pale, and, the bold Prince to shun,
Through the cold north and rocky regions run.
To find the coast where morning first appears,
By the dark pole the wary Belgian steers;
Confessing now he dreads the English more 35
Than all the dangers of a frozen shore;
While from our arms, security to find,
They fly so far, they leave the day behind.
Describe their fleet abandoning the sea,
And all their merchants left a wealthy prey; 40
Our first success in war make Bacchus crown,
And half the vintage of the year our own.
The Dutch their wine, and all their brandy lose,
Disarmed of that from which their courage grows;
While the glad English, to relieve their toil, 45

N

In healths to their great leader drink the spoil.

His high command to Afric's coast extend,
And make the Moors before the English bend ;
Those barbarous pirates willingly receive
Conditions, such as we are pleased to give.   50
Deserted by the Dutch, let nations know
We can our own and their great business do ;
False friends chastise, and common foes restrain,
Which, worse than tempests, did infest the main.
Within those Straits, make Holland's Smyrna fleet 55
With a small squadron of the English meet ;
Like falcons these, those like a numerous flock
Of fowl, which scatter to avoid the shock.[1]
There paint confusion in a various shape ;
Some sink, some yield ; and, flying, some escape. 60
Europe and Africa, from either shore,
Spectators are, and hear our cannon roar ;
While the divided world in this agree,
Men that fight so, deserve to rule the sea.

But, nearer home, thy pencil use once more,   65
And place our navy by the Holland shore ;
The world they compassed, while they fought with
   Spain,
But here already they resign the main ;
Those greedy mariners, out of whose way
Diffusive Nature could no region lay,   70

1.—*Of scatter'd Fowl, which would avoid the shock.*—Col.
Cunningham's copy.

At home, preserved from rocks and tempests, lie,
Compelled, like others, in their beds to die.
Their single towns, the Iberian armies pressed;
We all their provinces at once invest;
And, in a month, ruin their traffic more   75
Than that long war could in an age before.
　But who can always on the billows lie?
The watery wilderness yields no supply.
Spreading our sails, to Harwich we resort,
And meet the beauties of the British court.   80
The illustrious Duchess, and her glorious train,
(Like Thetis with her nymphs) adorn the main.
The gazing sea-gods, since the Paphian Queen
Sprung from among them, no such sight had seen.
Charmed with the graces of a troop so fair,   85
Those deathless powers for us themselves declare,
Resolved the aid of Neptune's court to bring,
And help the nation where such beauties spring;
The soldier here his wasted store supplies,
And takes new valour from the ladies' eyes.   90
　Meanwhile, like bees, when stormy winter's gone,
The Dutch (as if the sea were all their own)
Desert their ports, and, falling in their way,
Our Hamburg merchants are become their prey.
Thus flourish they, before the approaching fight;   95
As dying tapers give a blazing light.
　To check their pride, our fleet half-victualled goes,
Enough to serve us till we reach our foes;
Who now appear so numerous and bold,

The action worthy of our arms we hold.   100
A greater force than that which here we find,
Ne'er pressed the ocean, nor employed the wind.
Restrained a while by the unwelcome night,
The impatient English scarce attend the light.
But now the morning (heaven severely clear !)   105
To the fierce work indulgent does appear ;
And Phœbus lifts above the waves his light,
That he might see, and thus record, the fight.
     As when loud winds from different quarters rush,
Vast clouds encountering one another crush ;   110
With swelling sails so, from their several coasts,
Join the Batavian and the British hosts.
For a less prize, with less concern and rage,
The Roman fleets at Actium did engage ;
They, for the empire of the world they knew,   115
These, for the Old contend, and for the New.
At the first shock, with blood and powder stained,
Nor heaven, nor sea, their former face retained ;
Fury and art produce effects so strange,
They trouble Nature, and her visage change.   120
Where burning ships the banished sun supply,
And no light shines but that by which men die,
There York appears ! so prodigal is he
Of royal blood, as ancient as the sea !
Which down to him, so many ages told,   125
Has through the veins of mighty monarchs rolled !
The great Achilles marched not to the field
Till Vulcan that impenetrable shield,

And arms, had wrought; yet there no bullets flew,
But shafts and darts which the weak Phrygians
    threw.   130
Our bolder hero on the deck does stand
Exposed, the bulwark of his native land;
Defensive arms laid by as useless here,
Where massy balls the neighbouring rocks do tear.
Some power unseen those princes does protect,   135
Who for their country thus themselves neglect.
    Against him first Opdam his squadron leads,
Proud of his late success against the Swedes;
Made by that action, and his high command,
Worthy to perish by a prince's hand.   140
The tall Batavian in a vast ship rides,
Bearing an army in her hollow sides;
Yet, not inclined the English ship to board,
More on his guns relies, than on his sword;
From whence a fatal volley we received;   145
It missed the Duke, but his great heart it grieved;
Three worthy persons from his side it tore,
And dyed his garment with their scattered gore.
Happy! to whom this glorious death arrives,
More to be valued than a thousand lives!   150
On such a theatre as this to die,
For such a cause, and such a witness by!
Who would not thus a sacrifice be made,
To have his blood on such an altar laid?
The rest about him struck with horror stood,   155
To see their leader covered o'er with blood.

So trembled Jacob, when he thought the stains
Of his son's coat had issued from his veins.
He feels no wound but in his troubled thought ;
Before, for honour, now, revenge he fought ;   160
His friends in pieces torn, (the bitter news
Not brought by Fame) with his own eyes he views.
His mind at once reflecting on their youth,
Their worth, their love, their valour, and their truth,
The joys of court, their mothers, and their wives, 165
To follow him, abandoned,—and their lives !
He storms and shoots, but flying bullets now,
To execute his rage, appear too slow ;
They miss, or sweep but common souls away ;
For such a loss Opdam his life must pay.   170
Encouraging his men, he gives the word,
With fierce intent that hated ship to board,
And make the guilty Dutch, with his own arm,
Wait on his friends, while yet their blood is warm.
His winged vessel like an eagle shows,   175
When through the clouds to truss a swan she goes ;
The Belgian ship unmoved, like some huge rock
Inhabiting the sea, expects the shock.
From both the fleets men's eyes are bent this way,
Neglecting all the business of the day ;   180
Bullets their flight, and guns their noise suspend ;
The silent ocean does the event attend,
Which leader shall the doubtful victory bless,
And give an earnest of the war's success ;
When Heaven itself, for England to declare,   185

Turns ship, and men, and tackle, into air.
   Their new commander from his charge is tossed,
Which that young prince had so unjustly lost,
Whose great progenitors, with better fate,
And better conduct, swayed their infant state.   190
His flight towards heaven the aspiring Belgian took,
But fell, like Phaëton, with thunder strook ;
From vaster hopes than his he seemed to fall,
That durst attempt the British Admiral ;
From her broad sides a ruder flame is thrown   195
Than from the fiery chariot of the sun ;
That, bears the radiant ensign of the day,
And she, the flag that governs in the sea.
   The Duke, (ill pleased that fire should thus prevent
The work which for his brighter sword he meant) 200
Anger still burning in his valiant breast,
Goes to complete revenge upon the rest,
So on the guardless herd, their keeper slain,
Rushes a tiger in the Libyan plain.
The Dutch, accustomed to the raging sea,   205
And in black storms the frowns of heaven to see,
Never met tempest which more urged their fears,
Than that which in the Prince's look appears.
Fierce, goodly, young ! Mars he resembles, when
Jove sends him down to scourge perfidious men ; 210
Such as with foul ingratitude have paid,
Both those that led, and those that gave them aid.
Where he gives on, disposing of their fates,
Terror and death on his loud cannon waits,

With which he pleads his brother's cause so well, 215
He shakes the throne to which he does appeal.
The sea with spoils his angry bullets strow,
Widows and orphans making as they go;
Before his ship fragments of vessels torn,
Flags, arms, and Belgian carcasses are borne ; 220
And his despairing foes, to flight inclined,
Spread all their canvas to invite the wind.
So the rude Boreas, where he lists to blow,
Makes clouds above, and billows fly below,
Beating the shore ; and, with a boisterous rage, 225
Does heaven at once, and earth, and sea engage.
   The Dutch, elsewhere, did through the watery field
Perform enough to have made others yield ;
But English courage, growing as they fight,
In danger, noise, and slaughter, takes delight ; 230
Their bloody task, unwearied still, they ply,
Only restrained by death, or victory.
Iron and lead, from earth's dark entrails torn,
Like showers of hail from either side are borne ;
So high the rage of wretched mortals goes, 235
Hurling their mother's bowels at their foes !
Ingenious to their ruin, every age
Improves the arts and instruments of rage.
Death-hastening ills Nature enough has sent,
And yet men still a thousand more invent ! 240
   But Bacchus now, which led the Belgians on,
So fierce at first, to favour us begun ;
Brandy and wine, (their wonted friends) at length

Render them useless, and betray their strength.
So corn in fields, and in the garden, flowers, 245
Revive and raise themselves with moderate showers;
But overcharged with never-ceasing rain,
Become too moist, and bend their heads again.
Their reeling ships on one another fall,
Without a foe, enough to ruin all. 250
Of this disorder, and the favouring wind,
The watchful English such advantage find,
Ships fraught with fire among the heap they throw,
And up the so-entangled Belgians blow.
The flame invades the powder-rooms, and then, 255
Their guns shoot bullets, and their vessels men.
The scorched Batavians on the billows float,
Sent from their own, to pass in Charon's boat.
 And now, our royal Admiral success
(With all the marks of victory) does bless; 260
The burning ships, the taken, and the slain,
Proclaim his triumph o'er the conquered main.
Nearer to Holland, as their hasty flight
Carries the noise and tumult of the fight,
His cannons' roar, forerunner of his fame, 265
Makes their Hague tremble, and their Amsterdam;
The British thunder does their houses rock,
And the Duke seems at every door to knock.
His dreadful streamer (like a comet's hair,
Threatening destruction) hastens their despair: 270
Makes them deplore their scattered fleet as lost,
And fear our present landing on their coast.

The trembling Dutch the approaching Prince be-
    hold,
As sheep a lion leaping towards their fold ;
Those piles, which serve them to repel the main, 275
They think too weak his fury to restrain.
" What wonders may not English valour work,
Led by the example of victorious York ?
Or, what defence against him can they make,
Who, at such distance, does their country shake ? 280
His fatal hand their bulwarks will o'erthrow,
And let in both the ocean, and the foe ; "
Thus cry the people ;—and, their land to keep,
Allow our title to command the deep ;
Blaming their States' ill conduct, to provoke   285
Those arms, which freed them from the Spanish yoke.
    Painter ! excuse me, if I have awhile
Forgot thy art, and used another style ;
For, though you draw armed heroes as they sit,
The task in battle does the Muses fit ;   290
They, in the dark confusion of a fight,
Discover all, instruct us how to write ;
And light and honour to brave actions yield,
Hid in the smoke and tumult of the field,
Ages to come shall know that leader's toil,   295
And his great name, on whom the Muses smile ;
Their dictates here let thy famed pencil trace,
And this relation with thy colours grace.
    Then draw the parliament, the nobles met,
And our great monarch high above them set ;   300

Like young Augustus let his image be,
Triumphing for that victory at sea,
Where Egypt's Queen, and Eastern Kings o'erthrown,
Made the possession of the world his own.
Last draw the Commons at his royal feet,   305
Pouring out treasure to supply his fleet ;
They vow with lives and fortunes to maintain
Their King's eternal title to the main ;
And with a present to the Duke, approve
His valour, conduct, and his country's love.   310

TO THE KING.

GREAT Sir ! disdain not in this piece to stand,
Supreme commander both of sea and land.
Those which inhabit the celestial bower,
Painters express with emblems of their power ;
His club Alcides, Phœbus has his bow,   315
Jove has his thunder, and your navy you.
But your great providence no colours here
Can represent ; nor pencil draw that care,
Which keeps you waking to secure our peace,
The nation's glory, and our trade's increase ;   320
You, for these ends, whole days in council sit,
And the diversions of your youth forget.
Small were the worth of valour and of force,
If your high wisdom governed not their course ;
You as the soul, as the first mover you,   325
Vigour and life on every part bestow ;

How to build ships, and dreadful ordnance cast,
Instruct the artists, and reward their haste.
  So Jove himself, when Typhon heaven does brave,
Descends to visit Vulcan's smoky cave,   330
Teaching the brawny Cyclops how to frame
His thunder, mixed with terror, wrath, and flame.
Had the old Greeks discovered your abode,
Crete had not been the cradle of their god ;
On that small island they had looked with scorn, 335
And in Great Britain thought the thunderer born.

UPON HER MAJESTY'S NEW BUILDINGS
AT SOMERSET HOUSE

GREAT Queen! that does our island bless
With princes and with palaces;
Treated so ill, chased from your throne,
Returning, you adorn the town;
And, with a brave revenge, do show   5
Their glory went and came with you.
   While Peace from hence, and you were gone,
Your houses in that storm o'erthrown,
Those wounds which civil rage did give,
At once you pardon, and relieve.   10
   Constant to England in your love,
As birds are to their wonted grove,
Though by rude hands their nests are spoiled,
There the next spring again they build.
   Accusing some malignant star,   15
Not Britain, for that fatal war,
Your kindness banishes your fear,
Resolved to fix for ever here.
But what new mine this work supplies?
Can such a pile from ruin rise?   20
This, like the first creation, shows
As if at your command it rose

Frugality and bounty too,
(Those differing virtues) meet in you ;
From a confined, well-managed store,   25
You both employ and feed the poor.[1]
   Let foreign princes vainly boast
The rude effects of pride and cost ;
Of vaster fabrics, to which they
Contribute nothing but the pay ;   30
This, by the Queen herself designed,
Gives us a pattern of her mind ;
The state and order does proclaim
The genius of that royal dame.
Each part with just proportion graced,   35
And all to such advantage placed,
That the fair view her window yields,
The town, the river, and the fields,
Entering, beneath us we descry,
And wonder how we came so high.   40
   She needs no weary steps ascend ;
All seems before her feet to bend ;
And here, as she was born, she lies ;
High, without taking pains to rise.

1.—After this line,
    Like him which once desir'd to know
    For what good deed men us'd him so.
           Col. Cunningham's copy.

EPITAPH TO BE WRITTEN UNDER THE LATIN INSCRIPTION

UPON THE TOMB OF THE ONLY SON OF THE LORD ANDOVER.

'Tis fit the English reader should be told,
In our own language, what this tomb does hold.
'Tis not a noble corpse alone does lie
Under this stone, but a whole family.
His parents' pious care, their name, their joy,   5
And all their hope, lies buried with this boy ;
This lovely youth ! for whom we all made moan,
That knew his worth, as he had been our own.
   Had there been space and years enough allowed,
His courage, wit, and breeding to have showed,   10
We had not found, in all the numerous roll
Of his famed ancestors, a greater soul ;
His early virtues to that ancient stock
Gave as much honour, as from thence he took.
   Like buds appearing ere the frosts are passed,   15
To become man he made such fatal haste,
And to perfection laboured so to climb,
Preventing slow experience and time,
That 'tis no wonder Death our hopes beguiled ;
He's seldom old that will not be a child.   20

TO MR. KILLIGREW,

UPON HIS ALTERING HIS PLAY, " PANDORA," FROM A
TRAGEDY INTO A COMEDY, BECAUSE NOT APPROVED
ON THE STAGE.

SIR, you should rather teach our age the way
Of judging well, than thus have changed your play;
You had obliged us by employing wit,
Not to reform Pandora, but the pit;
For as the nightingale, without the throng   5
Of other birds, alone attends her song,
While the loud daw, his throat displaying, draws
The whole assembly of his fellow-daws;
So must the writer, whose productions should
Take with the vulgar, be of vulgar mould;   10
Whilst nobler fancies make a flight too high
For common view, and lessen as they fly.

EPIGRAM UPON THE GOLDEN MEDAL.

OUR guard upon the royal side !
On the reverse our beauty's pride !
Here we discern the frown and smile,
The force and glory of our isle.
In the rich medal, both so like   5
Immortals stand, it seems antique ;
Carved by some master, when the bold
Greeks made their Jove descend in gold,
And Danae wondering at that shower,
Which falling, stormed her brazen tower.   10
Britannia there, the fort in vain
Had battered been with golden rain ;
Thunder itself had failed to pass ;
Virtue's a stronger guard than brass.

THE NIGHT-PIECE ;

OR, A PICTURE DRAWN IN THE DARK.

DARKNESS, which fairest nymphs disarms,
Defends us ill from Mira's charms ;
Mira can lay her beauty by,
Take no advantage of the eye,
Quit all that Lely's art can take,   5
And yet a thousand captives make.
    Her speech is graced with sweeter sound
Than in another's song is found ;
And all her well-placed words are darts,
Which need no light to reach our hearts.   10
    As the bright stars, and Milky Way,

O

Showed by the night, are hid by day ;
So we, in that accomplished mind,
Helped by the night, new graces find,
Which, by the splendour of her view,   15
Dazzled before, we never knew.

    While we converse with her, we mark
No want of day, nor think it dark ;
Her shining image is a light
Fixed in our hearts, and conquers night.   20

    Like jewels to advantage set,
Her beauty by the shade does get ;
There blushes, frowns, and cold disdain,
All that our passion might restrain,
Is hid, and our indulgent mind   25
Presents the fair idea kind.

    Yet, friended by the night, we dare
Only in whispers tell our care ;
He that on her his bold hand lays,
With Cupid's pointed arrows plays ;   30
They with a touch, (they are so keen !)
Wound us unshot, and she unseen.

    All near approaches threaten death ;
We may be shipwrecked by her breath ;
Love, favoured once with that sweet gale,   35
Doubles his haste, and fills his sail,
Till he arrive where she must prove
The haven, or the rock, of love.

    So we the Arabian coast do know
At distance, when the spices blow ;   40
By the rich odour taught to steer,
Though neither day nor stars appear

ON THE PICTURE OF A FAIR YOUTH,

TAKEN AFTER HE WAS DEAD.

As gathered flowers, while their wounds are new,
Look gay and fresh, as on the stalk they grew ;
Torn from the root that nourished them, awhile
(Not taking notice of their fate) they smile,
And, in the hand which rudely plucked them, show 5
Fairer than those that to their autumn grow ;
So love and beauty still that visage grace ;
Death cannot fright them from their wonted place.
Alive, the hand of crooked Age had marred
Those lovely features, which cold death has spared.
No wonder then he sped in love so well,   [10
When his high passion he had breath to tell ;
When that accomplished soul, in this fair frame,
No business had but to persuade that dame,
Whose mutual love advanced the youth so high,   15
That, but to heaven, he could no higher fly.

OF A TREE CUT IN PAPER.

FAIR hand ! that can on virgin paper write,
Yet from the stain of ink preserve it white ;
Whose travel o'er that silver field does show
Like track of leverets in morning snow.
Love's image thus in purest minds is wrought,   5
Without a spot or blemish to the thought.
Strange that your fingers should the pencil foil,
Without the help of colours or of oil !
For though a painter boughs and leaves can make,
'Tis you alone can make them bend and shake ;   10
Whose breath salutes your new-created grove,
Like southern winds, and makes it gently move.
Orpheus could make the forest dance ; but you
Can make the motion and the forest too.
A poet's fancy when he paints a wood,   15
By his own nation only understood,
Is as in language so in fame confined ;
Not like to yours, acknowledged by mankind.
All that know Nature and the trees that grow,
Must praise the foliage expressed by you,   20
Whose hand is read wherever there are men :
So far the scissor goes beyond the pen.

TO A LADY,

FROM WHOM HE RECEIVED THE FOREGOING COPY WHICH FOR MANY YEARS HAD BEEN LOST.

NOTHING lies hid from radiant eyes;
All they subdue become their spies.
Secrets, as choicest jewels, are
Presented to oblige the fair;
No wonder, then, that a lost thought   5
Should there be found, where souls are caught.
   The picture of fair Venus (that
For which men say the goddess sat)
Was lost, till Lely from your look
Again that glorious image took.   10
   If Virtue's self were lost, we might
From your fair mind new copies write.
All things but one you can restore;
The heart you get returns no more.

OF ENGLISH VERSE.

POETS may boast, as safely vain,
Their works shall with the world remain;
Both, bound together, live or die,
The verses and the prophecy.

But who can hope his lines should long   5
Last in a daily changing tongue?
While they are new, envy prevails;
And as that dies, our language fails.

When architects have done their part,
The matter may betray their art ;   10
Time, if we use ill-chosen stone,
Soon brings a well-built palace down.

Poets that lasting marble seek,
Must carve in Latin, or in Greek ;
We write in sand, our language grows,   15
And, like the tide, our work o'erflows.

Chaucer his sense can only boast ;
The glory of his numbers lost !
Years have defaced his matchless strain ;
And yet he did not sing in vain.   20

The beauties which adorned that age,
The shining subjects of his rage,
Hoping they should immortal prove,
Rewarded with success his love.

This was the generous poet's scope ;   25
And all an English pen can hope,
To make the fair approve his flame,
That can so far extend their fame.

Verse, thus designed, has no ill fate,
If it arrive but at the date   30
Of fading beauty ; if it prove
But as long-lived as present love.

TO THE DUCHESS,

WHEN HE PRESENTED THIS BOOK TO HER ROYAL
HIGHNESS.

MADAM ! I here present you with the rage,
And with the beauties, of a former age ;
Wishing you may with as great pleasure view
This, as we take in gazing upon you.
Thus we writ then : your brighter eyes inspire   5
A nobler flame, and raise our genius higher.
While we your wit and early knowledge fear,
To our productions we become severe ;
Your matchless beauty gives our fancy wing,
Your judgment makes us careful how we sing.   10
Lines not composed, as heretofore, in haste,
Polished like marble, shall like marble last,
And make you through as many ages shine,
As Tasso has the heroes of your line.

    Though other names our wary writers use,   15
You are the subject of the British muse ;
Dilating mischief to yourself unknown,
Men write, and die, of wounds they dare not own.
So the bright sun burns all our grass away,
While it means nothing but to give us day.   20

TO THE DUCHESS OF ORLEANS,

WHEN SHE WAS TAKING LEAVE OF THE COURT AT DOVER.

THAT sun of beauty did among us rise ;
England first saw the light of your fair eyes ;
In English, too, your early wit was shown ;
Favour that language, which was then your own,
When, though a child, through guards you made
    your way ;   5
What fleet or army could an angel stay ?
Thrice happy Britain ! if she could retain
Whom she first bred within her ambient main.
Our late burned London, in apparel new,
Shook off her ashes to have treated you ;   10
But we must see our glory snatched away,
And with warm tears increase the guilty sea ;
No wind can favour us ; howe'er it blows,
We must be wrecked, and our dear treasure lose !
Sighs will not let us half our sorrows tell,—   15
Fair, lovely, great, and best of nymphs, farewell !

TO A FRIEND OF THE AUTHOR,

A PERSON OF HONOUR, WHO LATELY WRIT A
RELIGIOUS BOOK, ENTITLED, " HISTORICAL
APPLICATIONS, AND OCCASIONAL MEDITA-
TIONS, UPON SEVERAL SUBJECTS."

BOLD is the man that dares engage
For piety in such an age !
Who can presume to find a guard
From scorn, when Heaven's so little spared ?
Divines are pardoned; they defend   5
Altars on which their lives depend ;
But the profane impatient are,
When nobler pens make this their care ;
For why should these let in a beam
Of divine light to trouble them,   10
And call in doubt their pleasing thought,
That none believes what we are taught ?
High birth, and fortune, warrant give
That such men write what they believe ;
And, feeling first what they indite,   15
New credit give to ancient light.
Amongst these few, our author brings
His well-known pedigree from kings.
This book, the image of his mind,
Will make his name not hard to find ;   20
I wish the throng of *Great* and *Good*
Made it less easily understood !

OF HER ROYAL HIGHNESS, MOTHER TO THE PRINCE OF ORANGE;

AND OF HER PORTRAIT, WRITTEN BY THE LATE DUCHESS OF YORK WHILE SHE LIVED WITH HER.

HEROIC nymph ! in tempests the support,
In peace the glory of the British court !
Into whose arms the church, the state, and all
That precious is, or sacred here, did fall.
Ages to come, that shall your bounty hear,   5
Will think you mistress of the Indies were ;
Though straiter bounds your fortunes did confine,
In your large heart was found a wealthy mine ;
Like the blest oil, the widow's lasting feast,
Your treasure, as you poured it out, increased.   10
While some your beauty, some your bounty sing,
Your native isle does with your praises ring ;
But, above all, a nymph of your own train
Gives us your character in such a strain,
As none but she, who in that court did dwell,   15
Could know such worth, or worth describe so well.
So while we mortals here at heaven do guess,
And more our weakness, than the place, express,
Some angel, a domestic there, comes down,
And tells the wonders he hath seen and known.   20

ON THE STATUE OF KING CHARLES I.

AT CHARING CROSS.

THAT the First Charles does here in triumph ride,
See his son reign where he a martyr died,
And people pay that reverence as they pass,
(Which then he wanted !) to the sacred brass,
Is not the effect of gratitude alone,   5
To which we owe the statue and the stone ;
But Heaven this lasting monument has wrought,
That mortals may eternally be taught
Rebellion, though successful, is but vain,
And kings so killed rise conquerers again.   10
This truth the royal image does proclaim,
Loud as the trumpet of surviving Fame.

EPITAPH ON COLONEL CHARLES CAVENDISH.

HERE lies Charles Ca'ndish : let the marble stone,
That hides his ashes, make his virtue known.
Beauty and valour did his short life grace,
The grief and glory of his noble race !
Early abroad he did the world survey,   5
As if he knew he had not long to stay ;
Saw what great Alexander in the East,
And mighty Julius conquered in the West ;

Then, with a mind as great as theirs, he came
To find at home occasion for his fame ;   10
Where dark confusion did the nations hide,
And where the juster was the weaker side.
Two loyal brothers took their sovereign's part,
Employed their wealth, their courage, and their art ;
The elder did whole regiments afford ;   15
The younger brought his conduct and his sword.
Born to command, a leader he begun,
And on the rebels lasting honour won.
The horse, instructed by their general's worth,
Still made the King victorious in the north.   20
Where Ca'ndish fought, the Royalists prevailed ;
Neither his courage, nor his judgment, failed.
The current of his victories found no stop,
Till Cromwell came, his party's chiefest prop.
Equal success had set these champions high,   25
And both resolved to conquer or to die.
Virtue with rage, fury with valour strove ;
But that must fall which is decreed above !
Cromwell, with odds of number and of fate,
Removed this bulwark of the church and state ;   30
Which the sad issue of the war declared,
And made his task, to ruin both, less hard.
So when the bank, neglected, is o'erthrown,
The boundless torrent does the country drown.
Thus fell the young, the lovely, and the brave ;   35
Strew bays and flowers on his honoured grave !

THE TRIPLE COMBAT.

WHEN through the world fair Mazarin had run,
Bright as her fellow-traveller, the sun,
Hither at length the Roman eagle flies,
As the last triumph of her conquering eyes.
As heir to Julius, she may pretend   5
A second time to make this nation[1] bend ;
But Portsmouth, springing from the ancient race
Of Britons, which the Saxon here did chase,
As they great Cæsar did oppose, makes head,
And does against this new invader lead.   10
That goodly nymph, the taller of the two,
Careless and fearless to the field does go.
Becoming blushes on the other wait,
And her young look excuses want of height.
Beauty gives courage ; for she knows the day   15
Must not be won the Amazonian way.
Nor does her grace the better title want ;
Our law's indulgent to the occupant.[2]
Legions of Beauties[3] to the battle come,
For Little Britain these, and those for Rome.   20

1.—Tonson, *island*.
2.—This couplet is not in Tonson's edition.
3.—Tonson, *Cupids*.

Dressed to advantage, this illustrious pair
Arrived, for combat in the list appear.
What may the Fates design ! for never yet
From distant regions two such beauties met.
Venus had been an equal friend to both,　　　　25
And victory to declare herself seems loth ;
Over the camp, with doubtful wings, she flies,
Till Chloris shining in the field she spies.
The lovely Chloris well-attended came,
A thousand Graces waited on the dame ;　　　　30
Her matchless form made all the English glad,
And foreign beauties less assurance had ;
Yet, like the Three on Ida's top, they all
Pretend alike, contesting for the ball ;
Which to determine, Love himself declined,　　　35
Lest the neglected should become less kind.
Such killing looks ! so thick the arrows fly !
That 'tis unsafe to be a stander-by.
Poets, approaching to describe the fight,
Are by their wounds instructed how to write.　　40
They with less hazard might look on, and draw
The ruder combats in Alsatia ;
And, with that foil of violence and rage,
Set off the splendour of our golden age ;[1]
Where Love gives law, Beauty the sceptre sways,　45
And, uncompelled, the happy world obeys.

1.—Bennet, *the Golden Age.*

UPON OUR LATE LOSS OF THE DUKE OF CAMBRIDGE.

THE failing blossoms which a young plant bears,
Engage our hope for the succeeding years;
And hope is all which art or nature brings,
At the first trial, to accomplish things.
Mankind was first created an essay;   5
That ruder draught the deluge washed away.
How many ages passed, what blood and toil,
Before we made one kingdom of this isle !
How long in vain had nature striven to frame
A perfect princess, ere her Highness came !   10
For joys so great we must with patience wait ;
'Tis the set price of happiness complete.
As a first fruit, Heaven claimed that lovely boy ;
The next shall live, and be the nation's joy.

OF THE LADY MARY, &c.

As once the lion honey gave,
Out of the strong such sweetness came ;
A royal hero, no less brave,
Produced this sweet, this lovely dame.

To her the prince, that did oppose   5
Such mighty armies in the field,
And Holland from prevailing foes
Could so well free, himself does yield.

Not Belgia's fleet (his high command)
Which triumphs where the sun does rise,   10
Nor all the force he leads by land,
Could guard him from her conquering eyes.

Orange, with youth, experience has ;
In action young, in council old ;
Orange is, what Augustus was,   15
Brave, wary, provident, and bold.

On that fair tree which bears his name,
Blossoms and fruit at once are found ;
In him we all admire the same,
His flowery youth with wisdom crowned !   20

Empire and freedom reconciled
In Holland are by great Nassau ;
Like those he sprung from, just and mild,
To willing people he gives law.

Thrice happy pair ! so near allied   25
In royal blood, and virtue too !
Now love has you together tied,
May none this triple knot undo !

The church shall be the happy place
Where streams, which from the same source run,
Though divers lands awhile they grace,   [30
Unite again, and are made one.

A thousand thanks the nation owes
To him that does protect us all ;
For while he thus his niece bestows,   35
About our isle he builds a wall ;

A wall ! like that which Athens had,
By the oracle's advice, of wood ;
Had theirs been such as Charles has made,
That mighty state till now had stood.   40

P

TO THE PRINCE OF ORANGE, 1677.

WELCOME, great Prince, unto this land,
　　Skilled in the arts of war and peace ;
Your birth does call you to command,
　　Your nature does incline to peace.

When Holland, by her foes oppressed　　　5
　　No longer could sustain their weight ;
To a native prince they thought it best
　　To recommend their dying state.

Your very name did France expel ;
　　Those conquered towns which lately cost　　10
So little blood, unto you fell
　　With the same ease they once were lost.

'Twas not your force did them defeat ;
　　They neither felt your sword nor fire ;
But seemed willing to retreat,　　　　　15
　　And to your greatness did conspire.

Nor have you since ungrateful been,
　　When at Seneff you did expose,
And at Mount Cassal, your own men,
　　Whereby you might secure your foes.　　20

Let Maestricht's siege enlarge your name,
　　And your retreat at Charleroy ;
Warriors by flying may gain fame,
　　And Parthian-like their foes destroy.

Thus Fabius gained repute of old,   25
    When Roman glory gasping lay ;
In council slow, in action cold,
    His country saved, running away.

What better method could you take ?
    When you by beauty's charms must move,   30
And must at once a progress make,
    I' th' stratagems of war and love.

He that a princess' heart would gain,
    Must learn submissively to yield ;
The stubborn ne'er their ends obtain ;   35
    The vanquished masters are o' the field.

Go on, brave Prince, with like success,
    Still to increase your hoped renown,
Till to your conduct and address,
    Not to your birth, you owe a crown.   40

Proud Alva with the power of Spain
    Could not the noble Dutch enslave ;
And wiser Parma strove in vain
    For to reduce a race so brave.

They now those very armies pay,   45
    By which they were forced to yield to you ;
Their ancient birthright they betray,
    By their own votes you them subdue.

Who can then liberty maintain
    When by such arts it is withstood ?   50
Freedom to princes is a chain,
    To all that spring from royal blood.

ON THE DUKE OF MONMOUTH'S
EXPEDITION

INTO SCOTLAND IN THE SUMMER SOLSTICE, 1678.

SWIFT as Jove's messenger, the winged god,
With sword as potent as his charming rod,
He flew to execute the King's command,
And in a moment reached that northern land,
Where day contending with approaching night,　　5
Assists the hero with continued light.
On foes surprised, and by no night concealed,
He might have rushed ; but noble pity held
His hand a while, and to their choice gave space,
Which they would prove, his valour or his grace.　10
This not well heard, his cannon louder spoke,
And then, like lightning, through that cloud he broke.
His fame, his conduct, and that martial look,
The guilty Scotch with such a terror strook,
That to his courage they resign the field,　　15
Who to his bounty had refused to yield.
Glad that so little loyal blood it cost,
He grieves so many Britons should be lost ;
Taking more pains, when he beheld them yield,
To save the flyers, than to win the field ;　　20
And at the Court his interest does[1] employ,

1.—Bennet, *did*.

That none, who 'scaped his fatal sword, should die.
   And now, these rash bold men their error find,
Not trusting one beyond his promise kind ;
One ! whose great mind, so bountiful and brave,   25
Had learned the arts to conquer and to save.
   In vulgar breasts no royal virtues dwell ;
Such deeds as these his high extraction tell,
And give a secret joy to him who reigns,
To see his blood triumph in Monmouth's veins ;   30
To see a leader whom he got and chose,
Firm to his friends, and fatal to his foes.
   But seeing envy, like the sun, does beat,
With scorching rays, on all that's high and great,
This, ill-requited Monmouth ! is the bough   35
The Muses send to shade thy conquering brow.
Lampoons, like squibs, may make a present blaze ;
But time and thunder pay respect to bays.
Achilles' arms dazzle our present view,
Kept by the Muse as radiant and as new   40
As from the forge of Vulcan first they came ;
Thousands of years are past, and they the same ;
Such care she takes to pay desert with fame !
Than which no monarch, for his crown's defence,
Knows how to give a nobler recompense.   45
Covered with dust at one another thrown,
How can the lustre of their wit be shown ?
What Hector got for well defending Troy,
The Greeks did with the ruined town destroy.

UPON THE EARL OF ROSCOMMON'S TRANSLATION OF HORACE,

"DE ARTE POETICA;" AND OF THE USE OF POETRY.

ROME was not better by her Horace taught,
Than we are here to comprehend his thought;
The poet writ to noble Piso there;
A noble Piso does instruct us here,
Gives us a pattern in his flowing style,   5
And with rich precepts does oblige our isle:
Britain ! whose genius is in verse expressed,
Bold and sublime, but negligently dressed.
    Horace will our superfluous branches prune,
Give us new rules, and set our harps in tune;   10
Direct us how to back the winged horse,
Favour his flight, and moderate his force.
    Though poets may of inspiration boast,
Their rage, ill-governed, in the clouds is lost.
He that proportioned wonders can disclose,   15
At once his fancy and his judgment shows.
Chaste moral writing we may learn from hence,
Neglect of which no wit can recompense.

The fountain which from Helicon proceeds,
That **sacred stream !** should never water weeds,   20
Nor make the crop of therns and thistles **grow**,
Which envy or perverted nature sow.
   Well-sounding verses are the charm **we use**,
Heroic thoughts and **virtue to** infuse ;
Things of deep sense **we may** in prose unfold,   25
But they **move** more in lofty numbers told.
By the loud trumpet, which **our** courage aids,
We learn that sound, as **well** as sense, persuades.
   The Muses' friend, **unto** himself severe,
With silent pity looks on all that **err ;**   30
But where a brave, a public action shines,
That he rewards with his immortal lines.
Whether it be in council or in fight,
His country's honour is his chief delight ;
Praise of great acts he scatters as a seed,   35
Which may the like in coming ages breed.
   Here taught the fate of verses (always prized
With admiration, or as much despised),
Men will be less indulgent to their faults,
And patience have to cultivate their thoughts.   40
Poets lose half the praise they should have got,
Could it be known what they discreetly blot ;
Finding new words, that to the ravished ear
May like the language of the gods appear,
Such as, of old, wise bards employed to make   45
Unpolished men their wild retreats forsake ;
Law-giving heroes, famed for taming brutes,

And raising cities with their charming lutes ;
For rudest minds with harmony were caught,
And civil life was by the Muses taught.   50
So wandering bees would perish in the air,
Did not a sound, proportioned to their ear,
Appease their rage, invite them to the hive,
Unite their force, and teach them how to thrive,
To rob the flowers, and to forbear the spoil,   55
Preserved in winter by their summer's toil ;
They give us food, which may with nectar vie,
And wax, that does the absent sun supply.

THESE VERSES WERE WRIT IN THE TASSO OF HER ROYAL HIGHNESS.

TASSO knew how the fairer sex to grace,
But in no one durst all perfection place.
In her alone that owns this book is seen
Clorinda's spirit, and her lofty mien,
Sophronia's piety, Erminia's truth,   5
Armida's charms, her beauty, and her youth.
  Our princess here, as in a glass, does dress
Her well-taught mind, and every grace express.
More to our wonder than Rinaldo fought,
The hero's race excels the poet's thought.   10

OF AN ELEGY MADE BY MRS. WHARTON ON THE EARL OF ROCHESTER.

THUS mourn the Muses ! on the hearse
Not strewing tears, but lasting verse,
Which so preserve the hero's name,
They make him live again in fame.
Chloris, in lines so like his own,   5
Gives him so just and high renown,
That she the afflicted world relieves,
And shows that still in her he lives ;
Her wit as graceful, great, and good ;
Allied in genius, as in blood.   10
His loss supplied, now all our fears
Are, that the nymph should melt in tears.
Then, fairest Chloris ! comfort take,
For his, your own, and for our sake,
Lest his fair soul, that lives in you,   15
Should from the world for ever go.

TO MR. CREECH,

ON HIS TRANSLATION OF "LUCRETIUS."

WHAT all men wished, though few could hope to see,
We are now blessed with, and obliged by thee.
Thou, from the ancient, learned Latin store,
Giv'st us one author, and we hope for more.
May they enjoy thy thoughts !—Let not the stage   5
The idlest moment of thy hours engage ;
Each year that place some wondrous monster breeds,
And the wit's garden is o'errun with weeds.
There, Farce is Comedy ; bombast called strong ;
Soft words, with nothing in them, make a song.   10
'Tis hard to say they steal them now-a-days ;
For sure the ancients never wrote such plays.
These scribbling insects have what they deserve,
Not plenty, nor the glory for to starve.
That Spenser knew, that Tasso felt before ;   15
And death found surly Ben exceeding poor.
Heaven turn the omen from their image here !
May he with joy the well-placed laurel wear !
Great Virgil's happier fortune may he find,
And be our Cæsar, like Augustus, kind !   20

But let not this disturb thy tuneful head ;
Thou writ'st for thy delight, and not for bread ;
Thou art not cursed to write thy verse with care ;
But art above what other poets fear.
What may we not expect from such a hand,   25
That has, with books, himself at free command ?
Thou know'st in youth, what age has sought in vain ;
And bring'st forth sons without a mother's pain.
So easy is thy sense, thy verse so sweet,
Thy words so proper, and thy phrase so fit,   30
We read, and read again ; and still admire
Whence came this youth, and whence this wondrous
    fire !
  Pardon this rapture, sir ! but who can be
Cold, and unmoved, yet have his thoughts on thee ?
Thy goodness may my several faults forgive,   35
And by your help these wretched lines may live.
But if, when viewed by your severer sight,
They seem unworthy to behold the light,
Let them with speed in deserved flames be thrown !
They'll send no sighs, nor murmur out a groan ;   40
But, dying silently, your justice own.

SUNG BY MRS. KNIGHT, TO HER MAJESTY, ON HER BIRTHDAY.

THIS happy day two lights are seen,
A glorious saint, a matchless queen ;
Both named alike, both crowned appear,
The saint above, the Infanta here.
May all those years which Catherine   5
The martyr did for heaven resign,
Be added to the line
Of your blessed life among us here !
For all the pains that she did feel,
And all the torments of her wheel,   10
May you as many pleasures share !
May Heaven itself content
With Catherine the Saint !
Without appearing old,
An hundred times may you,   15
With eyes as bright as now,
This welcome day behold !

WRITTEN ON A CARD THAT HER MAJESTY TORE AT OMBRE.

THE cards you tear in value rise ;
So do the wounded by your eyes.
Who to celestial things aspire,
Are by that passion raised the higher.

TRANSLATED OUT OF SPANISH.

THOUGH we may seem importunate,
While your compassion we implore ;
They whom you make too fortunate,
May with presumption vex you more.

OF HER MAJESTY, ON NEW-YEAR'S DAY,
1683.

WHAT revolutions in the world have been,
How are we changed since we first saw the Queen !
She, like the sun, does still the same appear,
Bright as she was at her arrival here !
Time has commission mortals to impair,   5
But things celestial is obliged to spare.

   May every new year find her still the same
In health and beauty as she hither came !
When Lords and Commons, with united voice,
The Infanta named, approved the royal choice ;   10
First of our queens whom not the King alone,
But the whole nation, lifted to the throne.

   With like consent, and like desert, was crowned
The glorious Prince that does the Turk confound.
Victorious both ! his conduct wins the day,   15
And her example chases vice away ;
Though louder fame attend the martial rage,
'Tis greater glory to reform the age.

OF TEA, COMMENDED BY HER MAJESTY.

VENUS her myrtle, Phœbus has his bays ;
Tea both excels, which she vouchsafes to praise.
The best of queens, and best of herbs, we owe
To that bold nation which the way did show
To the fair region where the sun does rise,   5
Whose rich productions we so justly prize.
The Muse's friend, tea does our fancy aid,
Repress those vapours which the head invade,
And keeps that palace of the soul serene,
Fit on her birth-day to salute the Queen.   10

PROLOGUE FOR THE LADY-ACTORS:

SPOKEN BEFORE KING CHARLES II.

AMAZE us not with that majestic frown,
But lay aside the greatness of your crown !
For your diversion here we act in jest,
But when we act ourselves we do our best.
You have a look which does your people awe,   5
When in your throne and robes you give them law,
Lay it by here, and use a gentler smile !
Such as we see great Jove's in picture, while
He listens to Apollo's charming lyre,
Or judges of the songs he does inspire.   10
Comedians on the stage show all their skill,
And after do as Love and Fortune will.
We are less careful, hid in this disguise ;
In our own clothes more serious and more wise.
Modest at home, upon the stage more bold,   15
We seem warm lovers, though our breasts be cold ;
A fault committed here deserves no scorn,
If we act well the parts to which we're born.

PROLOGUE TO THE "MAID'S TRAGEDY."

SCARCE should we have the boldness to pretend
So long renowned a tragedy to mend,
Had not already some deserved your praise
With like attempt.   Of all our elder plays
This and Philaster have the loudest fame ;   5
Great are their faults, and glorious is their flame.
In both our English genius is expressed ;
Lofty and bold, but negligently dressed.
     Above our neighbours our conceptions are ;
But faultless writing is the effect of care.   10
Our lines reformed, and not composed in haste,
Polished like marble, would like marble last.
But as the present, so the last age writ ;
In both we find like negligence and wit.
Were we but less indulgent to our faults,   15
And patience had to cultivate our thoughts,
Our Muse would flourish, and a nobler rage
Would honour this than did the Grecian stage.
     Thus says our author, not content to see
That others write as carelessly as he ;   20
Though he pretends not to make things complete,
Yet, to please you, he'd have the poets sweat.

In this old play, what's new we have expressed
In rhyming verse, distinguished from the rest ;
That as the Rhone his hasty way does make   25
(Not mingling waters) through Geneva's lake,
So having here the different styles in view,
You may compare the former with the new.
   If we less rudely shall the knot untie,
Soften the rigour of the tragedy,   30
And yet preserve each person's character,
Then to the other this you may prefer.
'Tis left to you : the boxes, and the pit,
Are sovereign judges of this sort of wit.
In other things the knowing artist may   35
Judge better than the people ; but a play,
(Made for delight, and for no other use)
If you approve it not, has no excuse.

Q

EPILOGUE TO THE "MAID'S TRAGEDY."

SPOKEN BY THE KING.

THE fierce Melantius was content, you see,
The king should live ; be not more fierce than he ;
Too long indulgent to so rude a time,
When love was held so capital a crime,
That a crowned head could no compassion find,　　5
But died—because the killer had been kind !
Nor is't less strange, such mighty wits as those
Should use a style in tragedy like prose.
Well-sounding verse, where princes tread the stage,
Should speak their virtue, or describe their rage.　　10
By the loud trumpet, which our courage aids,
We learn that sound, as well as sense, persuades ;
And verses are the potent charms we use,
Heroic thoughts and virtue to infuse.
　　When next we act this tragedy again,　　15
Unless you like the change, we shall be slain.
The innocent Aspasia's life or death,
Amintor's too, depends upon your breath.
Excess of love was heretofore the cause ;
Now if we die, 'tis want of your applause.　　20

EPILOGUE TO THE "MAID'S TRAGEDY."

DESIGNED UPON THE FIRST ALTERATION OF THE
PLAY, WHEN THE KING ONLY WAS LEFT ALIVE.

ASPASIA bleeding on the stage does lie,
To show you still 'tis the *Maid's Tragedy*.
The fierce Melantius was content, you see,
The king should live ; be not more fierce than he ;
Too long indulgent to so rude a time,   5
When love was held so capital a crime,
That a crowned head could no compassion find,
But died—because the killer had been kind !
This better-natured poet had reprieved
Gentle Amintor too, had he believed   10
The fairer sex his pardon could approve,
Who to ambition sacrificed his love.
Aspasia he has spared ; but for her wound
(Neglected love !) there could no salve be found.
   When next we act this tragedy again,   15
Unless you like the change, I must be slain.
Excess of love was heretofore the cause ;
Now if I die, 'tis want of your applause.

OF THE INVASION AND DEFEAT OF THE
TURKS, IN THE YEAR 1683.

THE modern Nimrod, with a safe delight
Pursuing beasts, that save themselves by flight,
Grown proud, and weary of his wonted game,
Would Christians chase, and sacrifice to fame.
 A prince with eunuchs and the softer sex   5
Shut up so long, would warlike nations vex,
Provoke the German, and, neglecting heaven,
Forget the truce for which his oath was given.
 His Grand Vizier, presuming to invest
The chief imperial city of the west,   10
With the first charge compelled in haste to rise,
His treasure, tents, and cannon, left a prize ;
The standard lost, and janizaries slain,
Render the hopes he gave his master vain.
The flying Turks, that bring these tidings home,   15
Renew the memory of his father's doom ;
And his guard murmurs, that so often brings
Down from the throne their unsuccessful kings.
 The trembling Sultan's forced to expiate
His own ill-conduct by another's fate.   20
The Grand Vizier, a tyrant, though a slave,

A fair example to his master gave ;
He Bassa's head, to save his own, made fly,
And now, the Sultan to preserve, must die.

    The fatal bowstring was not in his thought,   25
When, breaking truce, he so unjustly fought ;
Made the world tremble with a numerous host,
And of undoubted victory did boast.
Strangled he lies ! yet seems to cry aloud,
To warn the mighty, and instruct the proud,   30
That of the great, neglecting to be just,
Heaven in a moment makes an heap of dust.

    The Turks so low, why should the Christians lose
Such an advantage of their barbarous foes ?
Neglect their present ruin to complete,   35
Before another Solyman they get ?
Too late they would with shame, repenting, dread
That numerous herd, by such a lion led ;
He Rhodes and Buda from the Christians tore,
Which timely union might again restore.   40

    But, sparing Turks, as if with rage possessed,
The Christians perish, by themselves oppressed ;
Cities and provinces so dearly won,
That the victorious people are undone !

    What angel shall descend to reconcile   45
The Christian states, and end their guilty toil ?
A prince more fit from heaven we cannot ask
Than Britain's king, for such a glorious task ;
His dreadful navy, and his lovely mind,
Give him the fear and favour of mankind ;   50

His warrant does the Christian faith defend ;
On that relying, all their quarrels end.
The peace is signed, and Britain does obtain
What Rome had sought from her fierce sons in vain.

    In battles won Fortune a part doth claim,   55
And soldiers have their portion in the fame ;
In this successful union we find
Only the triumph of a worthy mind.
'Tis all accomplished by his royal word,
Without unsheathing the destructive sword ;   60
Without a tax upon his subjects laid,
Their peace disturbed, their plenty, or their trade.
And what can they to such a prince deny,
With whose desires the greatest kings comply ?

    The arts of peace are not to him unknown ;   65
This happy way he marched into the throne ;
And we owe more to heaven than to the sword,
The wished return of so benign a lord.

    Charles ! by old Greece with a new freedom graced,
Above her antique heroes shall be placed.   70
What Theseus did, or Theban Hercules,
Holds no compare with this victorious peace,
Which on the Turks shall greater honour gain,
Than all their giants and their monsters slain :
Those are bold tales, in fabulous ages told ;   75
This glorious act the living do behold.

A PRESAGE OF THE RUIN OF THE TURKISH EMPIRE.

PRESENTED TO HIS MAJESTY ON HIS BIRTHDAY.

SINCE James the Second graced the British throne,
Truce, well observed, has been infringed by none;
Christians to him their present union owe,
And late success against the common foe;
While neighbouring princes, loth to urge their fate, 5
Court his assistance, and suspend their hate.
So angry bulls the combat do forbear,
When from the wood a lion does appear.
This happy day peace to our island sent,
As now he gives it to the continent.   10
A prince more fit for such a glorious task,
Than England's king, from Heaven we cannot ask;
He, great and good! proportioned to the work,
Their ill-drawn swords shall turn against the Turk.
Such kings, like stars with influence unconfined, 15
Shine with aspect propitious to mankind;
Favour the innocent, repress the bold,
And, while they flourish, make an age of gold.
Bred in the camp, famed for his valour young;
At sea successful, vigorous, and strong;   20

His fleet, his army, and his mighty mind,
Esteem and reverence through the world do find.
A prince with such advantages as these,
Where he persuades not, may command a peace.
Britain declaring for the juster side,   25
The most ambitious will forget their pride ;
They that complain will their endeavours cease,
Advised by him, inclined to present peace,
Join to the Turk's destruction, and then bring
All their pretences to so just a king.   30
   If the successful troublers of mankind,
With laurel crowned, so great applause do find,
Shall the vexed world less honour yield to those
That stop their progress, and their rage oppose?
Next to that power which does the ocean awe,   35
Is to set bounds, and give ambition law.
   The British monarch shall the glory have,
That famous Greece remains no longer slave ;
That source of art and cultivated thought !
Which they to Rome, and Romans hither brought. 40
   The banished Muses shall no longer mourn,
But may with liberty to Greece return ;   .
Though slaves, (like birds that sing not in a cage)
They lost their genius, and poetic rage ;
Homers again, and Pindars, may be found,   45
And his great actions with their numbers crowned.
   The Turk's vast empire does united stand ;
Christians, divided under the command
Of jarring princes, would be soon undone,

Did not this hero make their interest one ;   50
Peace to embrace, ruin the common foe,
Exalt the Cross, and lay the Crescent low.
   Thus may the Gospel to the rising sun
Be spread, and flourish where it first begun ;
And this great day, (so justly honoured here !)   55
Known to the East, and celebrated there.

    Hæc ego longævus cecini tibi, maxime regum !
    Ausus et ipse manu juvenum tentare laborem.—VIRG.

TO HIS MAJESTY,

BUDA and Rhodes proud Solyman had torn
From those, whom discord made the Pagan scorn :
Vienna too besieged, had been his prize,
Had not the approach of winter made him rise :
This motto practised, you have turned the scale,   5
Christians united by your help prevail.
Thus you enlarge the bounds of Christendom,
Though public interest keep you still at home.
The Gallic Prince his glory did increase,
When among subjects he made duels cease :   10
But sure the Britain merits more renown,
That has made sovereigns lay their weapons down.
So peaceful ! and so valiant ! are extremes,
Not to be found, but in our matchless James.
The well-defended Buda, with the spoil   15
Was bravely got, but with much blood and toil :
Your nobler art of making peace destroys
The barbarous foe, without expense or noise.
So Heaven with silence favours our increase,
Preventing blasts and making tempests cease.   20

The world from Chaos was to Order brought,
By making peace among the parts that fought :
From like confusion you have Europe freed,
And with like concord made their arms succeed.
Victorious Peace, with this well-chosen word,   25
To Turks more fatal than the Imperial sword,
Has for reward to your high merit given,
A title to be called the Son of Heaven.

—For they shall be called the Children of God.—MATT. v. 9.

EPITAPH ON SIR GEORGE SPEKE.

UNDER this stone lies virtue, youth,
Unblemished probity and truth ;
Just unto all relations known,
A worthy patriot, pious son ;
Whom neighbouring towns so often sent,   5
To give their sense in parliament ;
With lives and fortunes trusting one
Who so discreetly used his own.
Sober he was, wise, temperate,
Contented with an old estate,   10
Which no foul avarice did increase,
Nor wanton luxury make less.
While yet but young his father died,
And left him to a happy guide ;

Not Lemuel's mother with more care   15
Did counsel or instruct her heir,
Or teach with more success her son
The vices of the time to shun.
An heiress she ; while yet alive,
All that was hers to him did give ;   20
And he just gratitude did show
To one that had obliged him so ;
Nothing too much for her he thought,
By whom he was so bred and taught.
So (early made that path to tread,   25
Which did his youth to honour lead)
His short life did a pattern give
How neighbours, husbands, friends, should live.
    The virtues of a private life
Exceed the glorious noise and strife   30
Of battles won ; in those we find
The solid interest of mankind.
    Approved by all, and loved so well,
Though young, like fruit that's ripe, he fell.

EPITAPH ON HENRY DUNCH, ESQ.,

IN NEWINGTON CHURCH, IN OXFORDSHIRE, 1686.

HERE lies the prop and glory of his race,
Who, that no time his memory may deface,
His grateful wife, under this speaking stone
His ashes hid, to make his merit known.
Sprung from an opulent and worthy line,   5
Whose well-used fortune made their virtues shine,
A rich example his fair life did give,
How others should with their relations live.
A pious son, a husband, and a friend,
To neighbours too his bounty did extend   10
So far, that they lamented when he died,
As if all to him had been near allied.
His curious youth would men and manners know,
Which made him to the southern nations go.
Nearer the Sun, though they more civil seem,   15
Revenge and luxury have their esteem ;
Which well observing he returned with more
Value for England, than he had before ;
Her true religion, and her statutes too,
He practised not less than seeked to know ;   20
And the whole country grieved for their ill fate,
To lose so good, so just a magistrate.
To shed a tear may readers be inclined,
And pray for one he only left behind,
Till she, who does inherit his estate,   25
May virtue love like him, and vices hate.

SONG.

CHLORIS! farewell.   I now must go ;
For if with thee I longer stay,
Thy eyes prevail upon me so,
I shall prove blind, and lose my way.

Fame of thy beauty, and thy youth,   5
Among the rest, me hither brought ;
Finding this fame fall short of truth,
Made me stay longer than I thought.

For I'm engaged by word and oath,
A servant to another's will ;   10
Yet, for thy love, I'd forfeit both,
Could I be sure to keep it still.

But what assurance can I take,
When thou, foreknowing this abuse,
For some more worthy lover's sake,   15
Mayst leave me with so just excuse ?

For thou mayst say, 'twas not thy fault
That thou didst thus inconstant prove ;
Being by my example taught
To break thy oath, to mend thy love.   20

No, Chloris ! no : I will return,
And raise thy story to that height,
That strangers shall at distance burn,
And she distrust me reprobate.

Then shall my love this doubt displace,   25
And gain such trust, that I may come
And banquet sometimes on thy face,
But make my constant meals at home.

TO MR. GRANVILLE (NOW LORD LANSDOWNE),

ON HIS VERSES TO KING JAMES II.

AN early plant ! which such a blossom bears,
And shows a genius so beyond his years ;
A judgment ! that could make so fair a choice ;
So high a subject to employ his voice ;
Still as it grows, how sweetly will he sing   5
The growing greatness of our matchless King !

LONG AND SHORT LIFE.

CIRCLES are praised, not that abound
In largeness, but the exactly round :
So life we praise that does excel
Not in much time, but acting well.

TRANSLATED OUT OF FRENCH.

FADE, flowers ! fade, Nature will have it so ;
'Tis but what we must in our autumn do !
And as your leaves lie quiet on the ground,
The loss alone by those that loved them found.
So in the grave shall we as quiet lie,   5
Missed by some few that loved our company ;
But some so like to thorns and nettles live,
That none for them can, when they perish, grieve.

SOME VERSES OF AN IMPERFECT COPY,

DESIGNED FOR A FRIEND, ON HIS TRANSLATION OF OVID'S "FASTI."

ROME'S holy-days you tell, as if a guest
With the old Romans you were wont to feast.
Numa's religion, by themselves believed,
Excels the true, only in show received.
They made the nations round about them bow,   5
With their dictators taken from the plough ;
Such power has justice, faith, and honesty !
The world was conquered by morality.
Seeming devotion does but gild a knave,
That's neither faithful, honest, just, nor brave ;   10
But where religion does with virtue join,
It makes a hero like an angel shine.

    *   *   *   *   *

PRIDE.[1]

NOT the brave Macedonian youth alone,
But base Caligula, when on the throne,
Boundless in power, would make himself a god,
As if the world depended on his nod.
The Syrian King to beasts was headlong thrown,   5
Ere to himself he could be mortal known.
The meanest wretch, if Heaven should give him line,
Would never stop till he were thought divine.
All might within discern the serpent's pride,
If from ourselves nothing ourselves did hide.   10
Let the proud peacock his gay feathers spread,
And woo the female to his painted bed ;
Let winds and seas together rage and swell;
This Nature teaches, and becomes them well.
"Pride was not made for men :" a conscious sense 15
Of guilt, and folly, and their consequence,
Destroys the claim, and to beholders tells,
Here nothing but the shape of manhood dwells.

EPITAPH ON THE LADY SEDLEY.

HERE lies the learned Savil's heir ;
So early wise, and lasting fair,
That none, except her years they told,
Thought her a child, or thought her old.
All that her father knew or got,   5

1.—Tonson, Reflection on these words—*Pride was not made for man.*

His art, his wealth, fell to her lot ;
And she so well improved that stock,
Both of his knowledge and his flock,
That wit and fortune, reconciled
In her, upon each other smiled.   10
While she, to every well-taught mind,
Was so propitiously inclined,
And gave such title to her store,
That none, but the ignorant, were poor.
The Muses daily found supplies,   15
Both from her hands and from her eyes.
Her bounty did at once engage,
And matchless beauty warm, their rage.
Such was this dame in calmer days,
Her nation's ornament and praise !   20
But when a storm disturbed our rest,
The port and refuge of the oppressed.
This made her fortune understood,
And looked on as some public good.
So that (her person and her state,   25
Exempted from the common fate)
In all our civil fury she
Stood, like a sacred temple, free.
May here her monument stand so,
To credit this rude age ! and show   30
To future times, that even we
Some patterns did of virtue see ;
And one sublime example had
Of good, among so many bad.

EPITAPH UNFINISHED.

GREAT soul ! for whom Death will no longer stay,
But sends in haste to snatch our bliss away.
O cruel Death ! to those you take more kind,
Than to the wretched mortals left behind !
Here beauty, youth, and noble virtue shined,   5
Free from the clouds of pride that shade the mind.
Inspired verse may on this marble live,
But can no honour to thy ashes give————

      *   *   *   *   *

UPON A LADY'S FISHING WITH AN ANGLE.

SEE where the fair Clorinda sits, and seems
Like new-born Venus risen from the streams ;
In vain the beauties of the neighbouring field,
    In vain the painted flowers' pride
    With their faint colours strive to hide   5
That flower to which Flora herself would yield.
    Each object's pleasant to the sight,
    The streams, the meadows yield delight,
But nothing fair as her you can espy
Unless i' th' brook (her looking-glass) you chance to
    cast your eye.   10

See how she makes the trembling angle shake,
Touched by those hands that would make all men
    quake.
See how the numerous fishes of the brook

(**For now** the armour of their scales
Nothing against **her charms prevails**)   15
Willingly hang themselves **u pon her hook ;**
   See how they crowd and **thronging wait**
   Greedy **to catch the** proffered **bait ;**
In her more bright and smoother hands content
Rather to die, than live in their own watery element. 20

With how **composed a look** and cheerful **air,**
(Calm as the stream and as the season **fair)**
With careful eyes she views the dancing float,
   Longing to have it disappear,
   That she its head may higher rear,   25
And make it swim i' th' air above the moat ;
   She sits as silent as the fish,
   Seems burdened with no other wish,
So well she's masked under this fair pretence,
An infidel would swear she's made of perfect inno-
   cence.   30

But ah ! Clorinda's is a cruel game,
As she with water sports, she sports with flame,
She innocently angles here, but then
   Thousands of charming baits she lays,
   A thousand other several ways ;   35
Her beauteous eyes ensnare whole shoals of men,
   Each golden hair's a fishing line,
   Able to catch such hearts as mine,
And he that once views her bewitching eyes,
To her victorious charms (like me) must ever be a
   prize.   40

ON MRS. HIGGONS.

INGENIOUS Higgons never sought
To hide the candour of her thought ;
And now her clothes are lost, we find
The nymph as naked as her mind :
Like Eve while yet she was untaught   5
To hide herself or know a fault.
For a snatched ribbon she would frown,
But cares too little for her gown ;
It makes her laugh, and all her grief
Is lest it should undo the thief.   10
Already she begins to stretch
Her wit, to save the guilty wretch,
And says she was of goods bereft
By her own bounty, not by theft.
She thought not fit to keep her clothes   15
Till they were eaten up with moths,
But made a nobler use of store,
To clothe the naked and the poor.
Should all that do approve the fair
Her loss contribute to repair,   20
Of London she would have the fate,
And rise (undone) in greater state,
In points, and hoods, and Indian gown,
As glorious as the new-built town.

DIVINE POEMS.

OF DIVINE LOVE.

SIX CANTOS.

I. Asserting the authority of the Scripture, in which this love
is revealed.—II. The preference and love of God to man in the
creation.—III. The same love more amply declared in our
redemption.—IV. How necessary this love is to reform mankind, and how excellent in itself.—V. Showing how happy the
world would be, if this love were universally embraced.—VI.
Of preserving this love in our memory, and how useful the contemplation thereof is.

CANTO I.

The Grecian muse has all their gods survived,
Nor Jove at us, nor Phœbus is arrived;
Frail deities! which first the poets made,
And then invoked, to give their fancies aid.
Yet if they still divert us with their rage,   5
What may be hoped for in a better age,
When not from Helicon's imagined spring,
But Sacred Writ, we borrow what we sing?
This with the fabric of the world begun,
Elder than light, and shall outlast the sun.   10

Before this oracle, like Dagon, all
The false pretenders, Delphos, Ammon, fall ;
Long since despised and silent, they afford
Honour and triumph to the eternal Word.

As late philosophy our globe has graced,   15
And rolling earth among the planets placed,
So has this Book entitled us to heaven,
And rules to guide us to that mansion given ;
Tells the conditions how our peace was made,
And is our pledge for the great Author's aid.   20
His power in Nature's ample book we find,
But the less volume does express His mind.

This light unknown, bold Epicurus taught
That his blessed gods vouchsafe us not a thought,
But unconcerned let all below them slide,   25
As fortune does, or human wisdom, guide.
Religion thus removed, the sacred yoke,
And band of all society, is broke.
What use of oaths, of promise, or of test,
Where men regard no God but interest ?   30
What endless war would jealous nations tear,
If none above did witness what they swear ?
Sad fate of unbelievers, and yet just,
Among themselves to find so little trust !
Were Scripture silent, Nature would proclaim,   35
Without a God, our falsehood and our shame.
To know our thoughts the object of his eyes,
Is the first step towards being good or wise ;
For though with judgment we on things reflect,

Our will determines, not our intellect. 40
Slaves to their passion, reason men employ
Only to compass what they would enjoy.
His fear to guard us from ourselves we need,
And Sacred Writ our reason does exceed ;
For though heaven shows the glory of the Lord, 45
Yet something shines more glorious in his Word ;
His mercy this (which all his work excels !)
His tender kindness and compassion tells ;
While we, informed by that celestial Book,
Into the bowels of our Maker look. 50
Love there revealed (which never shall have end,
Nor had beginning) shall our song commend ;
Describe itself, and warm us with that flame
Which first from heaven, to make us happy, came.

CANTO II.

THE fear of hell, or aiming to be blessed,
Savours too much of private interest.
This moved not Moses, nor the zealous Paul,
Who for their friends abandoned soul and all ;
A greater yet from heaven to hell descends, 5
To save, and make his enemies his friends.
What line of praise can fathom such a love,
Which reached the lowest bottom from above ?
The royal prophet, that extended grace
From heaven to earth, measured but half that space.
The law was regnant, and confined his thought ; [10

Hell was not conquered when that poet wrote ;
Heaven was scarce heard of until he came down,
To make the region where love triumphs known.
    That early love of creatures yet unmade,   15
To frame the world the Almighty did persuade ;
For love it was that first created light,
Moved on the waters, chased away the night
From the rude Chaos, and bestowed new grace
On things disposed of to their proper place ;   20
Some to rest here, and some to shine above ;
Earth, sea, and heaven, were all the effects of love.
And love would be returned ; but there was none
That to themselves or others yet were known ;
The world a palace was without a guest,   25
Till one appears that must excel the rest ;
One ! like the Author, whose capacious mind
Might, by the glorious work, the Maker find ;
Might measure heaven, and give each star a name ;
With art and courage the rough ocean tame ;   30
Over the globe with swelling sails might go,
And that 'tis round by his experience know ;
Make strongest beasts obedient to his will,
And serve his use the fertile earth to till.
When, by his Word, God had accomplished all,   35
Man to create he did a council call ;
Employed his hand, to give the dust he took
A graceful figure, and majestic look ;
With his own breath conveyed into his breast
Life, and a soul fit to command the rest ;   40

Worthy alone to celebrate his name
For such a gift, and tell from whence it **came.**
Birds sing his praises in a wilder note,
But not with lasting numbers and with thought,
Man's great prerogative ! but above all   44
His grace abounds in his new favourite's fall.

    If he create, it is a world he makes ;
If he be angry, the creation shakes ;
From his just wrath our guilty parents fled ;
He cursed the earth, but bruised the serpent's head.
Amidst the storm his bounty did exceed,   [50
In the rich promise of the Virgin's seed ;
Though justice death, as satisfaction, craves,
Love finds a way to pluck us from our graves.

CANTO III.

NOT willing terror should his image move ;
He gives a pattern of eternal love ;
His Son descends to treat a peace with those
Which were, and must have ever been, his foes.
Poor he became, and left his glorious seat   5
To make us humble, and to make us great ;
His business here was happiness to give
To those whose malice could not let him live.

    Legions of angels, which he might have used,
(For us resolved to perish) he refused ;   10
While they stood ready to prevent his loss,
Love took him up, and nailed him to the cross.

Immortal love ! which in his bowels reigned,
That we might be by such a love constrained
To make return of love.   Upon this pole   15
Our duty does, and our religion, roll.
To love is to believe, to hope, to know ;
'Tis an essay, a taste of heaven below !

He to proud potentates would not be known ;
Of those that loved him he was hid from none.   20
Till love appear we live in anxious doubt ;
But smoke will vanish when that flame breaks out ;
This is the fire that would consume our dross,
Refine, and make us richer by the loss.

Could we forbear dispute, and practise love,   25
We should agree as angels do above.
Where love presides, not vice alone does find
No entrance there, but virtues stay behind ;
Both faith, and hope, and all the meaner train
Of moral virtues, at the door remain.   30
Love only enters as a native there,
For, born in heaven, it does but sojourn here.

He that alone would wise and mighty be,
Commands that others love as well as he.
Love as he loved !—How can we soar so high ?—   35
He can add wings, when he commands to fly.
Nor should we be with this command dismayed ;
He that examples gives, will give his aid ;
For he took flesh, that where his precepts fail,
His practice, as a pattern, may prevail.   40
His love, at once, and dread, instruct our thought ;

As man he suffered, and as God he taught.
Will for the deed he takes ; we may with ease
Obedient be, for if we love we please.
Weak though we are, to love is no hard task,   45
And love for love is all that Heaven does ask.
Love ! that would all men just and temperate make,
Kind to themselves, and others, for his sake.

   'Tis with our minds as with a fertile ground,
Wanting this love they must with weeds abound,   50
(Unruly passions) whose effects are worse
Than thorns and thistles springing from the curse.

CANTO IV.

To glory man, or misery, is born,
Of his proud foe the envy, or the scorn ;
Wretched he is, or happy, in extreme ;
Base in himself, but great in Heaven's esteem ;
With love, of all created things the best ;   5
Without it, more pernicious than the rest ;
For greedy wolves unguarded sheep devour
But while their hunger lasts, and then give o'er ;
Man's boundless avarice his want exceeds,
And on his neighbours round about him feeds.   10

   His pride and vain ambition are so vast,
That, deluge-like, they lay whole nations waste.
Debauches and excess (though with less noise)
As great a portion of mankind destroys.
The beasts and monsters Hercules oppressed   15

Might in that age some provinces infest ;
These more destructive monsters are the bane
Of every age, and in all nations reign ;
But soon would vanish, if the world were blessed
With sacred love, by which they are repressed.   20
 Impendent death, and guilt that threatens hell,
Are dreadful guests, which here with mortals
  dwell ;
And a vexed conscience, mingling with their joy
Thoughts of despair, does their whole life annoy ;
But love appearing, all those terrors fly ;   25
We live contented, and contented die.
They in whose breast this sacred love has place,
Death, as a passage to their joy, embrace.
Clouds and thick vapours, which obscure the day,
The sun's victorious beams may chase away ;   30
Those which our life corrupt and darken, love
(The nobler star !) must from the soul remove.
Spots are observed in that which bounds the year ;
This brighter sun moves in a boundless sphere ;
Of heaven the joy, the glory, and the light,   35
Shines among angels, and admits no night.

CANTO V.

THIS Iron Age (so fraudulent and bold !)
Touched with this love, would be an Age of Gold ;
Not, as they feigned, that oaks should honey drop,
Or land neglected bear an unsown crop ;

Love would make all things easy, safe, and cheap; 5
None for himself would either sow or reap;
Our ready help, and mutual love, would yield
A nobler harvest than the richest field.
Famine and death, confined to certain parts,
Extended are by barrenness of hearts. 10
Some pine for want where others surfeit now;
But then we should the use of plenty know.
Love would betwixt the rich and needy stand,
And spread Heaven's bounty with an equal hand;
At once the givers and receivers bless, 15
Increase their joy, and make their suffering less.
Who for himself no miracle would make,
Dispensed with Nature for the people's sake;
He that, long fasting, would no wonder show,
Made loaves and fishes, as they ate them, grow, 20
Of all his power, which boundless was above,
Here he used none but to express his love;
And such a love would make our joy exceed,
Not when our own, but other mouths we feed.

    Laws would be useless which rude nature awe; 25
Love, changing nature, would prevent the law;
Tigers and lions into dens we thrust,
But milder creatures with their freedom trust.
Devils are chained, and tremble; but the Spouse
No force but love, nor bond but bounty, knows. 30
Men (whom we now so fierce and dangerous see)
Would guardian angels to each other be;
Such wonders can this mighty love perform,

Vultures to doves, wolves into lambs transform !
Love what Isaiah prophesied can do,　　　　　35
Exalt the valleys, lay the mountains low,
Humble the lofty, the dejected raise,
Smooth and make straight our rough and crooked
　　　ways.
Love, strong as death, and like it, levels all ;
With that possessed, the great in title fall ;　　40
Themselves esteem but equal to the least,
Whom Heaven with that high character has blessed.
This love, the centre of our union, can
Alone bestow complete repose on man ;
Tame his wild appetite, make inward peace,　　45
And foreign strife among the nations cease.
No martial trumpet should disturb our rest,
Nor princes arm, though to subdue the East ;
Where for the tomb so many heroes (taught
By those that guided their devotion) fought.　　50
Thrice happy we, could we like ardour have
To gain his love, as they to win his grave !
Love as he loved ! A love so unconfined,
With arms extended, would embrace mankind.
Self-love would cease, or be dilated, when　　55
We should behold as many selfs as men ;
All of one family, in blood allied,
His precious blood, that for our ransom died.

CANTO VI.

THOUGH the creation (so divinely taught !)
Prints such a lively image in our thought,
That the first spark of new-created light,
From Chaos struck, affects our present sight ;
Yet the first Christians did esteem more blessed   5
The day of rising, than the day of rest,
That every week might new occasion give,
To make his triumph in their memory live.
Then let our Muse compose a sacred charm,
To keep his blood among us ever warm,   10
And singing as the blessed do above,
With our last breath dilate this flame of love.
But on so vast a subject who can find
Words that may reach the ideas of his mind ?
Our language fails; or, if it could supply,   15
What mortal thought can raise itself so high ?
Despairing here, we might abandon art,
And only hope to have it in our heart.
But though we find this sacred task too hard,
Yet the design, the endeavour, brings reward.   20
The contemplation does suspend our woe,
And makes a truce with all the ills we know.
As Saul's afflicted spirit, from the sound
Of David's harp, a present solace found ;
So on this theme while we our Muse engage,   25
No wounds are felt, of fortune or of age.
On divine love to meditate is peace,

S

And makes all care of meaner things to cease.
　　Amazed at once, and comforted, to find
A boundless power so infinitely kind,　　　　　　　30
The soul contending to that light to flee
From her dark cell, we practise how to die ;
Employing thus the poet's winged art,
To reach this love, and grave it in our heart.
Joy so complete, so solid, and severe,　　　　　　35
Would leave no place for meaner pleasures there ;
Pale they would look, as stars that must be gone,
When from the East the rising sun comes on.

> Floriferis ut Apes in saltibus omnia libant,
> Sic nos Scripturæ depascimur aurea dicta ;
> Aurea perpetuâ semper dignissima vitâ.
> Nam Divinus Amor, cum cœpit vociferari,
> Diffugiunt Animi terrores.—LUCR.
>
> Exul eram, requiesque mihi, non Fama petita est,
> Mens intenta suis ne foret usque malis.
> Namque ubi mota calent Sacrâ mea Pectora Musâ,
> Altior humano Spiritus ille malo est.—*De Trist.*

OF DIVINE POESY.

TWO CANTOS.

Occasioned upon sight of the 53rd chapter of Isaiah turned into verse by Mrs. Wharton.

CANTO I.

POETS we prize, when in their verse we find
Some great employment of a worthy mind.
Angels have been inquisitive to know
The secret which this oracle does show.
What was to come, Isaiah did declare,   5
Which she describes as if she had been there ;
Had seen the wounds, which, to the reader's view,
She draws so lively that they bleed anew.
As ivy thrives which on the oak takes hold,
So with the prophet's may her lines grow old !   10
If they should die, who can the world forgive,
(Such pious lines !) when wanton Sappho's live ?
Who with his breath his image did inspire,
Expects it should foment a nobler fire ;
Not love which brutes as well as men may know,   15
But love like his, to whom that breath we owe.
Verse so designed, on that high subject wrote,
Is the perfection of an ardent thought ;
The smoke which we from burning incense raise,
When we complete the sacrifice of praise.   20
In boundless verse the fancy soars too high
For any object but the Deity,
What mortal can with Heaven pretend to share

In the superlatives of wise and fair?
A meaner subject when with these we grace,   25
A giant's habit on a dwarf we place.
Sacred should be the product of our Muse,
Like that sweet oil, above all private use,
On pain of death forbidden to be made,
But when it should be on the altar laid.   30
Verse shows a rich inestimable vein,
When, dropped from heaven, 'tis thither sent again.
    Of bounty 'tis that he admits our praise,
Which does not him, but us that yield it, raise;
For as that angel up to heaven did rise,   35
Borne on the flame of Manoah's sacrifice,
So, winged with praise, we penetrate the sky;
Teach clouds and stars to praise him as we fly;
The whole creation, (by our fall made groan!)
His praise to echo, and suspend their moan.   40
For that he reigns, all creatures should rejoice,
And we with songs supply their want of voice.
The church triumphant, and the church below,
In songs of praise their[1] present union show;
Their joys are full; our expectation long;   45
In life we differ, but we join in song.
Angels and we, assisted by this art,
May sing together, though we dwell apart.
Thus we reach heaven, while vainer poems must
No higher rise than winds may lift the dust.   50

1.—Divine Poems, 1685, a.

From that they spring; this from his breath that
    gave,
To the first dust, the immortal soul we have;
His praise well sung, (our great endeavour here)
Shakes off the dust, and makes that breath appear.

CANTO II.

He that did first this way of writing grace,
Conversed with the Almighty face to face;
Wonders he did in sacred verse unfold,
When he had more than eighty winters told.
The writer feels no dire effect of age,   5
Nor verse, that flows from so divine a rage.
Eldest of Poets, he beheld the light,
When first it triumphed o'er eternal night;
Chaos he saw, and could distinctly tell
How that confusion into order fell.   10
As if consulted with, he has expressed
The work of the Creator, and his rest;
How the flood drowned the first offending race,
Which might the figure of our globe deface.
For new-made earth, so even and so fair,   15
Less equal now, uncertain makes the air;
Surprised with heat and unexpected cold,
Early distempers make our youth look old;
Our days so evil, and so few, may tell
That on the ruins of that world we dwell.   20
Strong as the oaks that nourished them, and
    high,

That long-lived race did on their force rely,
Neglecting Heaven ; but we, of shorter date !
Should be more mindful of impendent fate.
To worms, that crawl upon this rubbish here,   25
This span of life may yet too long appear ;
Enough to humble, and to make us great,
If it prepare us for a nobler seat.
Which well observing, he, in numerous lines,
Taught wretched man how fast his life declines ;   30
In whom he dwelt before the world was made,
And may again retire when that shall fade.
The lasting Iliads have not lived so long
As his and Deborah's triumphant song.
Delphos unknown, no Muse could them inspire,   35
But that which governs the celestial choir.
Heaven to the pious did this art reveal,
And from their store succeeding poets steal.
Homer's Scamander for the Trojans fought,
And swelled so high, by her old Kishon taught.   40
His river scarce could fierce Achilles stay ;
Hers, more successful, swept her foes away.
The host of Heaven, his Phœbus and his Mars,
He arms, instructed by her fighting stars.
She led them all against the common foe ;   45
But he (misled by what he saw below !)
The powers above, like wretched men, divides,
And breaks their union into different sides.
The noblest parts which in his heroes shine,
May be but copies of that heroine.   50

Homer himself, and Agamemnon, she
The writer could, and the commander, be.
Truth she relates in a sublimer strain,
Than all the tales the boldest Greeks could feign ;
For what she sung that Spirit did indite, 55
Which gave her courage, and success, in fight.
A double garland crowns the matchless dame ;
From Heaven her poem, and her conquest, came.
    Though of the Jews she merit most esteem,
Yet here the Christian has the greater theme ; 60
Her martial song describes how Sisera fell ;
This sings our triumph over death and hell.
The rising light employed the sacred breath
Of the blest Virgin and Elizabeth.
In songs of joy the angels sung his birth ; 65
Here how he treated was upon the earth
Trembling we read! the affliction and the scorn,
Which for our guilt so patiently was borne !
Conception, birth, and suffering, all belong
(Though various parts) to one celestial song ; 70
And she, well using so divine an art,
Has in this concert sung the tragic part.
    As Hannah's seed was vowed to sacred use,
So here this lady consecrates her Muse.
With like reward may Heaven her bed adorn, 75
With fruit as fair as by her Muse is born !

OF THE PARAPHRASE ON THE LORD'S
PRAYER,

WRITTEN BY MRS. WHARTON.

SILENCE, you winds ! listen, ethereal lights !
While our Urania sings what Heaven indites ;
The numbers are the nymph's ; but from above
Descends the pledge of that eternal love.
Here wretched mortals have not leave alone,　　　5
But are instructed, to approach his throne ;
And how can he to miserable men
Deny requests which his own hand did pen ?
　In the Evangelists we find the prose
Which, paraphrased by her, a poem grows ;　　　10
A devout rapture ! so divine a hymn,
It may become the highest seraphim !
For they, like her, in that celestial choir,
Sing only what the Spirit does inspire.
Taught by our Lord, and theirs, with us they may 15
For all but pardon for offences pray.

SOME REFLECTIONS OF HIS UPON THE SEVERAL PETITIONS IN THE SAME PRAYER.

1.

His sacred name with reverence profound
Should mentioned be, and trembling at the sound
It was Jehovah; 'tis Our Father now;
So low to us does Heaven vouchsafe to bow! Ps. xviii. 9.
He brought it down, that taught us how to pray; 5
And did so dearly for our ransom pay.[1]

2.

His kingdom come.   For this we pray in vain,
Unless he does in our affections reign.
Absurd it were to wish for such a King,
And not obedience to his sceptre bring,   10
Whose yoke is easy, and his burthen light,
His service freedom, and his judgments right.[2]

3.

His will be done.   In fact 'tis always done;
But, as in Heaven, it must be made our own.
His will should all our inclinations sway,   15
Whom Nature, and the universe, obey

1.—1685, *Brethren to him that taught us how to pray,*
     And did so dearly for our Ransom pay.

2.—This couplet does not occur in the edition of 1685.

Happy the man ! whose wishes are confined
To what has been eternally designed ;
Referring all to his paternal care,
To whom more dear than to ourselves we are.[1]　　20

4.

It is not what our avarice hoards up ;
'Tis he that feeds us, and that fills our cup ;
Like new-born babes depending on the breast,
From day to day we on his bounty feast ;
Nor should the soul expect above a day　　25
To dwell in her frail tenement of clay ;
The setting sun should seem to bound our race,
And the new day a gift of special grace.

5.

That he should all our trespasses forgive,
While we in hatred with our neighbours live ;　　30
Though so to pray may seem an easy task,
We curse ourselves when thus inclined we ask.
This prayer to use, we ought with equal care
Our souls, as to the sacrament prepare.
The noblest worship of the Power above,　　35
Is to extol, and imitate his love ;
Not to forgive our enemies alone,
But use our bounty that they may be won.

1.—This and three preceding lines are not in the edition of
1685.

6.

Guard us from all temptations of the foe,
And those we may in several stations know ;　　40
The rich and poor in slippery places stand.
Give us enough ! but with a sparing hand !
Not ill-persuading want, nor wanton wealth,
But what proportioned is to life and health.
For not the dead, but living, sing thy praise,　　45
Exalt thy kingdom, and thy glory raise.

> Favete linguis ! . . . . .
> Virginibus puerisque canto.—HORAT.

ON THE FEAR OF GOD.

IN TWO CANTOS.

CANTO I.

THE fear of God is freedom, joy, and peace,
And makes all ills that vex us here to cease.
Though the word fear some men may ill endure,
'Tis such a fear as only makes secure.
Ask of no angel to reveal thy fate ;　　5
Look in thy heart, the mirror of thy state.
He that invites will not the invited mock,
Opening to all that do in earnest knock.
Our hopes are all well-grounded on this fear
All our assurance rolls upon that sphere.　　10

This fear, that drives all other fears away,
Shall be my song, the morning of our day !
Where that fear is, there's nothing to be feared ;
It brings from Heaven an angel for our guard.
Tranquillity and peace this fear does give ;   15
Hell gapes for those that do without it live.
It is a beam, which he on man lets fall,
Of light, by which he made and governs all.
'Tis God alone should not offended be ;
But we please others, as more great than he.   20
For a good cause, the sufferings of man
May well be borne ; 'tis more than angels can.
Man, since his fall, in no mean station rests,
Equal to angels, or below the beasts.
He with true joy their hearts alone does fill,   25
That thirst and hunger to perform his will.
Others, though rich, shall in this world be vexed,
And sadly live in terror of the next.
The world's great conqueror would his point pursue,
And wept because he could not find a new ;   30
Which had he done, yet still he would have cried,
To make him work until a third he spied.
Ambition, avarice, will nothing owe
To Heaven itself, unless it make them grow.
Though richly fed, man's care does still exceed ;   35
Has but one mouth, but would a thousand feed.
In wealth and honour, by such men possessed,
If it increase not, there is found no rest.
All their delight is while their wish comes in ;

Sad when it stops, as there had nothing been.   40
'Tis strange men should neglect their present store,
And take no joy but in pursuing more ;
No ! though arrived at all the world can aim ;
This is the mark and glory of our frame.
A soul capacious of the Deity,   45
Nothing but he that made can satisfy.
A thousand worlds, if we with him compare
Less than so many drops of water are.
Men take no pleasure but in new designs ;
And what they hope for, what they have outshines.   50
Our sheep and oxen seem no more to crave,
With full content feeding on what they have ;
Vex not themselves for an increase of store,
But think to-morrow we shall give them more.
What we from day to day receive from Heaven,   55
They do from us expect it should be given.
We made them not, yet they on us rely,
More than vain men upon the Deity ;
More beasts than they ! who will not understand
That we are fed from his immediate hand.   60
Man, that in him has being, moves, and lives,
What can he have, or use, but what he gives ?
So that no bread can nourishment afford,
Or useful be, without his Sacred Word.

CANTO II.

EARTH praises conquerors for shedding blood,
Heaven those that love their foes, and do them good.
It is terrestrial honour to be crowned
For strowing men, like rushes, on the ground.
True glory 'tis to rise above them all,   5
Without advantage taken by their fall.
He that in fight diminishes mankind,
Does no addition to his stature find ;
But he that does a noble nature show,
Obliging others, still does higher grow ;   10
For virtue practised, such a habit gives,
That among men he like an angel lives ;
Humbly he doth, and without envy, dwell,
Loved and admired by those he does excel.
Fools anger show, which politicians hide ;   15
Blessed with this fear, men let it not abide.
The humble man, when he receives a wrong,
Refers revenge to whom it doth belong :
Nor sees he reason why he should engage,
Or vex his spirit for another's rage.   20
Placed on a rock, vain men he pities, tossed
On raging waves, and in the tempest lost.
The rolling planets, and the glorious sun,
Still keep that order which they first begun ;
They their first lesson constantly repeat,   25
Which their Creator as a law did set.
Above, below, exactly all obey ;

But wretched men have found another way ;
Knowledge of good and evil, as at first,
(That vain persuasion !) keeps them still accursed ! 30
The Sacred Word refusing as a guide,
Slaves they become to luxury and pride.
As clocks, remaining in the skilful hand
Of some great master, at the figure stand,
But when abroad, neglected they do go, 35
At random strike, and the false hour show ;
So from our Maker wandering, we stray,
Like birds that know not to their nests the way.
In him we dwelt before our exile here,
And may, returning, find contentment there, 40
True joy may find, perfection of delight,
Behold his face, and shun eternal night.

   Silence, my Muse ! make not these jewels cheap,
Exposing to the world too large a heap.
Of all we read, the Sacred Writ is best, 45
Where great truths are in fewest words expressed.
   Wrestling with death, these lines I did indite ;
No other theme could give my soul delight.
O that my youth had thus employed my pen !
Or that I now could write as well as then ! 50
But 'tis of grace, if sickness, age, and pain,
Are felt as throes, when we are born again ;
Timely they come to wean us from this earth,
As pangs that wait upon a second birth.

OF THE LAST VERSES IN THE BOOK.

WHEN we for age could neither read nor write,
The subject made us able to indite ;
The soul, with nobler resolutions decked,
The body stooping, does herself erect.
No mortal parts are requisite to raise   5
Her that, unbodied, can her Maker praise.
    The seas are quiet when the winds give o'er ;
So, calm are we when passions are no more !
For then we know how vain it was to boast
Of fleeting things, so certain to be lost.   10
Clouds of affection from our younger eyes
Conceal that emptiness which age descries.
    The soul's dark cottage, battered and decayed,
Lets in new light through chinks that time has made ;
Stronger by weakness, wiser men become,   15
As they draw near to their eternal home.
Leaving the old, both worlds at once they view,
That stand upon the threshold of the new.

. . . . Miratur limen Olympi.—VIRG.

NOTES.

NOTES.

TO THE QUEENE, &c.

This dedication to Henrietta Maria is here printed for the first time, exactly as it stands in a small folio volume, the property of Edmund Waller, Esquire, of Farmington Lodge, Northleach, which contains a transcript, corrected in another hand, of most of the poems which appeared in the editions of 1645— neither the transcript nor the corrections are in the handwriting of the poet, and the book came into Mr. Waller's possession by purchase.

TO MY LADY SOPHIA.

This address is headed as above in Mr. Waller's transcript, with a note by the corrector which informs us that the lady was Lady Sophia Bertie, a daughter of that Earl of Lindsey, who afterwards fell in the King's service at Edgehill: she married Sir Richard Chaworth, and died in 1689, aged 72.

the former Pope.

The transcript has *the present Pope*, which fixes its date as earlier than that of any edition of the poems. Maffeo Barberini, (Urban VIII.), the Pope alluded to, having died July 29, 1644.

T 2

AN ADVERTISEMENT TO THE READER.

There are three editions of Waller's poems dated 1645.

(i) The | Workes | of | Edmond Waller | Esquire, | Lately a Member of the Ho | nourable House of | Commons, | in this Present Parliament. | London. | Printed for Thomas Walkley. | 1645. Title—and B—H in eights.

Some copies of this edition have on the title-page Imprimatur | Na. Brent. Decem. 30. 1644.

(ii) Poems, &c. | Written By | Mr. Ed. Waller | of Beckonsfield, Esquire ; Lately a | Member of the Honourable | House of Commons, | And Printed by a Copy of | his own hand-writing. | All the Lyrick Poems in this Booke | were set by Mr. Henry Lawes, Gent. | of the Kings Chappell and one of his Ma- | jesties Private Musick. | Printed and Published according to Order. | London, | Printed by I. N. for Hu. Mosley, at the Princes | Armes in Pauls Church-yard, | 1645. A (4 leaves)—N 4 in eights. O—P 2 in eights.

(iii) Poems, &c. | Written By | Mr. Ed. Waller | of Beckonsfield, Esquire ; lately a | Member of the Honourable | House of Commons, | All the Lyrick Poems in this Booke | were set by Mr. Henry Lawes Gent. | of the Kings Chappell, and one of his | Majesties Private Musick, | Printed and Published according to Order. | London, | Printed by T. W. for Humphrey Mosley, at the | Princes Armes in Pauls Church- | yard, 1645. B—I 2 in eights. It appears from a comparison of Mr. Hazlitt's collation of this edition with that of other copies which **I** have seen, that the signatures vary, but the contents are the same.

It has been customary to describe now one, now another **of these** three **as the** *genuine first edition*, but **there is** nothing **to show that any** one of them **had the** countenance **of the author, in** fact, in the edition **of 1664** the contrary **is distinctly** stated, **and Waller had,** almost certainly, left England **before Dec. 30,** 1644, **the date** upon which **the** earliest **of** them **was** licensed ; **this edition, (i), the text of which I have not thought it** necessary **to collate, is full of** misprints, **and is** denounced **in this** advertisement which appears **in** both **(ii) and (iii) as** "surruptitious," **though, as a** matter of **fact, (iii) consists** simply **of the** sheets **of** (i) bound **up with a fresh title and the addition of the last seven poems** contained **in (ii). The** advertisement **was probably written by Mosley, who in a somewhat** similar **address prefixed to his** edition **of Milton's poems, of this year,** congratulates himself **on the** success **which had attended his** publication **of** Waller.

THE PRINTER **TO THE** READER.

Fenton expresses **a** belief **that** this preface **was** either **written by** Waller, **or** by his immediate direction, **and was** designed **"for a** modest memorial **"** prepara- **tory to** his standing candidate for **the Provostship of** Eton College. **But it is improbable** that the poet had **this special post, if indeed he had any at** all, in view **at** the date of **the** publication **of** this edition of his

poems, as Dr. John Meredith, whom he was anxious
to succeed at Eton, did not die till the following
year.   In Fenton's edition (1729) the signature
Albinovanus, the exact applicability of which to
Waller is not obvious, was for the first time appended
to this address.

POSTSCRIPT.   *Nova carmina pango.*

I have been unable to trace these words—they do
not occur in Virgil : possibly the writer was thinking
of Ecl. iii. 86.   " Pollio et ipse facit nova carmina."

PREFACE TO THE SECOND PART OF MR. WALLER'S POEMS.

In 1690 appeared " The Second Part of Mr.
Waller's Poems containing his alteration of the
Maid's Tragedy, And whatever of his is yet un-
printed : Together with some other Poems, Speeches,
&c., that were printed Severally and never put into the
First Collection of his Poems.   London, Printed for
Tho. Bennet.   MDCXC."   8º.   There seems no
reason to doubt that this preface, which appeared in
this edition, was written, as has always been supposed,
by Francis Atterbury—a correspondent writing in
Notes and Queries [7th S. xi. p. 266] has been kind
enough to mention, for my benefit, a copy of " The
Maid's Tragedy Altered.   With some other Pieces.
By Edmund Waller, Esq ; not before Printed in the
several Editions of his Poems.   London, Printed for
Jacob Tonson.   1690," in which there is a MS.
addition, signed " Jacob Tonson, Senr.," to the note

printed at the beginning of the book : the note run thus—" *Most of the following Pieces, being unfinish'd, were never intended to be publish'd ; but that a Person, who had borrowed a Manuscript Copy of them, took upon him to print them.*" After the words " *a Person,*" Tonson has written " Dr. Atterbury borrow'd them of Dr. Birch." Atterbury is further connected with Bennet by the fact that on Aug. 30, 1706, he preached his funeral sermon in St. Paul's, in which he speaks of having known him for twenty years.

OF THE DANGER HIS MAJESTY ESCAPED IN THE ROAD AT ST. ANDREWS.

The events which form the subject of this poem occurred in September, 1623, upon the arrival of the Prince at St. Andere (now Santander) on his return to England from Madrid. He reached the coast on St. Matthew's Day, attended by a train of Spanish noblemen, and having dined in the neighbourhood of the port, was in the afternoon informed of the arrival of the English fleet under the command of the Earl of Rutland. I quote what follows from a contemporary pamphlet, " The Joyfull Returne Of The Most Illustrious Prince Charles, Prince of Great Britaine, from the Court of Spaine. . . . 1623," which purports to be written " from the report of some of his Highnesse traine that attended in the voyage." One is almost inclined to think, from a comparison of its language with that of the poem, that Waller must have seen it. " How soone are joyes turned into sorrowes ? safetie into dangers, a shining forenoone into a gloomy euening ? His Highnesse, after all that feasting and

triumphing in Saint Andera, being desirous to go
aboord that goodly ship, (the Admirall of his Fleet)
called the Prince (a title due to it for the brauery and
Princely building of it) spent so much time that the
euening drew on apace, and with the euening a more
threatning enemy : for not onely the tyde resisted his
coming backe (his Highnesse being then in his own
Barge, and his owne Watermen rowing in it) but a
storme began to arise, and the billows to swel high,
before the Watermen had gottē halfe way frō the ships
to the towne, the distance between the shore and the
ships being at least a Spanish league. The Watermen
were strong, cunning, and couragious, but the furious
waues taught their Oares another mañer of practise
than euer they were put to upon the Thames. To the
town they could not possibly get, against a winde
and tyde so raging, or if they had ventured, it had
been dangerous, in regard a huge Barke (to saue her
selfe) lay very neer to the mouth of the Harbour : to
the shore they were as fearefull to put, it being full of
rocks ; to the ships back againe to flie for succour,
night (a darke night) being spred over that Horizon,
denied that comfort, for if they should misse the
ships, they were in doubt to be carried into the maine,
the channell where the Fleet was anchored, running
with an impetuous and irresistible torrent. In this
full-Sea of Horrors the Prince resolued to turn back
towards the ships, and to fall in upon the first they
could fasten, rather than trust to the mercy of the
rockes, upon euery one of which sat ineuitable destruction. What could Hope trust to here, where neither
the watermens skill nor strength could incourage

them to bring safety to **their** Master? The clouds
opened, and discharged their artillery of raine, lightning and thunder : elements of contrary nature, war-
ring **one** upon another, whilst the waters (which were
called up to decide the controuersie) quarrelling **with**
the winds, made the uproare more horrid and **tempestuous.** And so much greater was the danger, by how
much the night (by reason of the storme) grew darker
and darker : yet at last that omnipotent Arme, which
can tear up rocks from their center, and that voyce which
can call in the winds, and still them with the mouing
of his finger, sent a Doue with an Oliue branch in her
bill as an assurance of comfort. **For by** casting **out a**
rope from a ship called **the** Defiance (which with
much hazard of his life one of **the** Prince's watermen
catched hold off), by spying a light in **the same** ship,
his Highnesse and all in the Barge with him, (praise be
given **to** the Almighty **Pilot** that **stood at Helme)**
were with unspeakable joy **receiued into** that shippe,
and there tooke **up** his lodging **till** the next morning :
nothing **at all** daunted at these terrors, sithence dangers
to noble minds **are but the** triumphs of their constant
sufferings."

P. 1, *ll.* 13-32.—Edward **IV.** employed the Earl
of Warwick to negotiate on his behalf with the Duke
of Savoy for **the** hand **of** his daughter, the Lady Bona,
sister-**in-law to Louis XI. :** the Earl's proposals were
accepted, but before the treaty could be ratified, Edward
had met and fallen **in love with** Elizabeth Woodville,
his future Queen. **His** subsequent neglect of Warwick
caused him to transfer his allegiance to Henry VI., and
led to a renewal of **the civil** war. "Nothing," says

Fenton, "could have been more happily imagin'd than the subject which Mr. Waller has selected to insinuate the Prince's resolution to forsake the Infanta." It has been suggested that this poem was re-cast and elaborated in accordance with subsequent events, but though the marriage treaty between Charles and Henrietta was not actually signed till Nov. 10, 1624, there is nothing in the verses inconsistent with their having been written, as Fenton supposes, in 1623, or at any rate in the beginning of 1624. Waller has of course exaggerated, or even imagined the effect produced upon Charles by what Sir Henry Wotton calls his "ambulatory view" of Henrietta, but while Buckingham was still at Madrid he had been approached by one Grey, an English friar, with the suggestion that Mary de Medicis might be induced to offer her youngest daughter as a substitute for the Infanta. Grey subsequently proceeded to England, and though Buckingham and Mary denied all knowledge of the intrigue, James I. consented to allow Lord Kensington to be sent to Paris to sound the disposition of the French Court upon the subject. Lord Kensington arrived in Paris on Feb. 15, 1624, and on March 15 Buckingham disclosed to the Houses the project of a French alliance for the Prince of Wales.

P. 2, *ll.* 41-2.—L. 42 is repeated, p. 161, l. 134, as a translation of Æn. iv. 583, "Annixi torquent spumas, et cœrula verrunt." Cf. Fairfax, "Godfrey of Bulloigne," xv. 12—

> . . . . "Some with strong Oars sweep
> The Waters smooth, and brush the buxom Wave,
> Their Breasts in sunder cleave the yielding deep."

P. 3, *l.* 45.—Sort = *company* or *crowd*.

P. 3, *l.* 54.—Imitated from Cæsar's answer to the boatman—"Quid times? Cæsarem vehis." Cf. **Mrs.** Philips. "**To** his Majesty (Charles II.) **at his passage** into England "—

> "**Charles and** his mighty hopes you bear :
> A greater now than Cæsar's here."

P. 3, *l.* 66.—Cf. p. 9, ll. 21-2.

P. 4, *l.* 76.—Impeach = *obstruct.* Cf. p. 31, l. 12, p. 166, l. 82, and "Godfrey of Bulloigne," xi. 52—

> "And there it seems the mighty Prince intends
> *Godfredo's* hoped Entrance to impeach."

P. 4, *ll.* 85-93.—Cf. Æn. I. 81-101.

P. 5, *ll.* 117-18.—Fenton refers these lines to Claudian, *De nupt. Honor. et Mar.*, 247-50.

> Ceu geminæ Prestana rosæ per jugera regnant,
> Hæc largo matura die, saturataque vernis
> Roribus, indulget spatio ; latet altera nodo,
> Nec teneris audet foliis admittere soles."

P. 6, *l.* 135.—This line is repeated p. 13, l. 1.

P. 7, *ll.* 163-64.—Ovid, Ex Ponto, iv. 3. 35. "Omnia sunt hominum tenui pendentia filo."

P. 7, *l.* 163.—Fenton refers this line to Iliad viii. 19-20—

> Σειρὴν χρυσείην ἐξ οὐρανόθεν κρεμάσαντες
> Πάντες δ' ἐξάπτεσθε θεοὶ πᾶσαί τε θέαιναι.

TO THE QUEEN.

Fenton supposes this poem to have been addressed to the Queen shortly after her arrival in England, and the language of it would seem to support his view.

He printed a glowing account of the attractions of
Henrietta from a letter of Lord Kensington to
Charles, who himself appears to have regarded the
alliance with much less enthusiasm : writing (Aug.
13, 1624) to the Earl of Carlisle, who was then in
Paris, he says : " Yet use what industry you can to
reduce them to reason, for I respect the person of the
lady as being a worthy creature, fit to be my wife ; and
as ye love me put it to a quick issue one way or
other."

P. 9, *ll.* 45-46.—Cf. Fairfax, "Godfrey of Bulloigne,"
vi. 70—

> " For in the secret of her troubled Thought,
> A doubtful Combat, Love and Honour fought."

P. 9, *ll.* 49-52.—"At Paris the Prince spent one
whole day to give his mind some contentment
in viewing of a famous City and Court, which
was a neighbour to his future estates, But for the
better Veiling of their visages, his Highnesse and
the Marquesse (*afterwards Duke, of Buckingham, his
Achates*) bought each of them a Perriwigge somewhat
to overshaddow their foreheads. . . . Towards Evening, by a meere chance, in appearance, though under-
lined with providence, they had a full sight of the
Queene Infanta, and of the princesse Henriettæ Marie
with other great Ladyes at the practise of a Masquing
Daunce, which was then in preparation." (Wotton,
Short View of the Life and Death of Buckingham,
1642.)

P. 10, *ll.* 57-58.—This idea is repeated p. 57,
ll. 11-12.

OF HIS MAJESTY'S RECEIVING THE NEWS OF THE
DUKE OF BUCKINGHAM'S DEATH.

The news of the assassination of the Duke of
Buckingham (Aug. 23, 1628) was brought to the
King by Sir John Hippesly, while he was at prayers at
Southwick, the seat of Sir Daniel Norton, about five
miles from Portsmouth. According to Clarendon,
" His Majesty continued unmoved and without the
least change in his countenance till prayers were
ended : " Another account (*Court and Times of
Charles I.*, vol. 1, 390) says, " when this news was
brought by one Charles Price, the twenty-first chapter
of Acts was reading, where observe the twenty-eighth
verse, &c."

P. 11, *l.* 8.—The Earl of Lindsey was immediately
appointed to succeed Buckingham in the command of
the fleet for the relief of Rochelle, which sailed Sept. 4.

P. 11, *l.* 15.—John Felton was a member of an old
Suffolk family, and of the blood of the Earl of Arundel,
who, together with his wife and son, Lord Maltravers,
visited him in prison on the day before his execution.
Waller is probably thinking of the " ten-penny knife "
which the assassin purchased at a cutler's on Tower
Hill.

P. 11, *ll.* 17-20.—The allusion is to the picture by
Timanthes of the sacrifice of Iphigenia, wherein the
painter having expressed various degrees of grief in
the faces of Calchas, Odysseus, Ajax, and Menelaus,
represented Agamemnon, the father of the victim,
with his face buried in the folds of his drapery.

P. 12, *ll.* 31-32.—" Some that observe the passages
in Court, say the King seems as much affected to the

duke's memory as he was to his person, minding nothing so much for the present as the advancement of his friends and followers." (Mead to Stuteville, Sept. 20, 1628.)

"The news we received on Saturday was as followeth : . . . That the duchess (*of Buckingham*) hath confirmed unto her, for her own and her son's life, Roper's office, in the King's Bench, worth £4,000 a-year : and that some talked (but mine author would not believe it) as though the profits of the Admiralty here, and the customs of Ireland also, should for twenty-one years to come be applied to the duchess and her children." (The same to the same, Oct. 11, 1628.)

" Sir Henry Hungate, the duke's bosom friend, is sworn gentleman of the Privy Chamber in Sir William Crofte's place, who hath stood suspended there from any time these three years, ever since he spoke against the duke in parliament ; as likewise was Sir Ralph Clare, in whose place young Ashburnham, the duke's nephew, is sworn."

"Two of the duke's footmen are sworn the king's footmen, and the rest of the duke's servants are to attend the Marquis of Hamilton." (The same to the same, Nov. 1, 1628.)

TO THE KING ON HIS RETURN FROM SCOTLAND.

These lines, the first, as far as I can discover, of Waller's that were printed, appeared in " Rex Redux," 1633, a collection of verses written by members of the University of Cambridge and addressed to Charles I. upon his return to England after his coronation at Edinburgh.

OF SALLE.

During the early years of the reign of Charles I., the ravages committed by the Salle rovers formed a constant subject of complaint in the House of Commons.   In July, 1625, Sir Walter Erle mentioned to the House that, during the last few weeks, English vessels had been captured by them off the Scilly Islands, and on Aug. 11 of the same year a letter from one William Legg, a prisoner to the Moorish pirates at Salle, was read in the House, and witnesses, who had escaped, were in attendance to speak of the barbarous cruelty of their captors.   Spoil, it was said, had been committed upon the English coasts to such an extent that vessels scarce dare venture from port. Subsequently squadrons had been sent out, one under the command of Sir Francis Steward, and another under Sir Samuel Argall, to clear the English seas of pirates, but they both returned without having effected anything.   At last on Feb. 26, 1637, a fleet of six ships, subsequently joined by two others, carrying in all 990 men sailed from England, and on March 24 anchored in Salle roads.   Salle apparently consisted of two parts, Old and New Salle, and at this time the governor of New Salle was in a state of revolt against the authority of the King of Morocco.   It was only by occupying Old Salle with the consent of the governor and joining in a civil war that the English were able to effect their object.   On Sept. 19, the Moorish ambassador came on board the fleet, which set sail and landed 339 rescued captives at Torbay on Oct. 6. *(A True Journall of the Sally Fleet, &c.   Published by John Dunton, London 1637.)*

P. 13, *ll.* 13-15.—1 Samuel, xv. 33.

TO THE KING ON HIS NAVY.

In all the editions from 1664 to 1712 this poem was
printed first, and in that of 1711 a date, 1626, was for
the first time assigned to it, the writer of the " Life "
prefixed to the book being of opinion that the lines
were occasioned by the expedition against Spain,
under Lord Wimbledon, which sailed in that year.
Rymer (*Short View of Tragedy*, 1693, p. 79) dates it
1632, without giving any reason for his view. Fenton
rejects the first of these dates because in the same
edition (1711) the poem *Of the danger his Majesty
escaped*, *&c.*, was clearly assigned to a wrong year
(1621), and the second, because there was not in
1632 any naval armament considerable enough to form
the subject of the poem : he himself decides in favour
of 1636, because the Dutch, having concluded a
league with France against Spain, had, by thei
encroachments on the English fisheries in 1635 made
it necessary for Charles to assert his sovereignty over
the narrow seas, by fitting out a fleet, of which
Waller's friend, the Earl of Northumberland, was next
year appointed Admiral. The preparation of this fleet,
being regarded as " only an artifice of State to draw
money from the subject," was the occasion of much
public dissatisfaction, and Fenton thinks this was a
happy opportunity for Waller to make his court to the
King, by " proclaiming his navy to be, as in truth it
was, the glory and defence of the Nation." Bell (1854)
rejected Fenton's date on account of the absence of
any special allusion to the circumstances detailed

above, but he follows him and other editors in finding
in the third and fourth lines a reference to a war between
France and Spain. It seems to me that these lines
ought to be assigned to the year 1627, when Buckingham was busily engaged in the preparation of the
fleet, which, numbering 100 sail and having on board
7,000 soldiers, eventually left Stokes Bay on June
27. I see in lines 3 and 4 a reference, not to a war
between France and Spain, but to an agreement
between the two countries, which was ratified at Paris
in April, 1627, and, though of short duration, was, as
far as I am aware, the only occasion, about this time,
upon which they can be said to have forgotten their
hatred.

P. 15, *l.* 1.—Cf. Fairfax, "Godfrey of Bulloigne,"
xv. 32.

> " Thy Ship (Columbus) shall her Canvass wing
>   Spread o'er that World."

P. 15, *ll.* 5-6.—Cf. p. 153, ll. 61-2.

P. 15, *ll.* 7-8.—Fenton quotes from Varro,
"Qui potis plus urget ; ut pisces minutos magnus
comest."

P. 15, *ll.* 19-24.—Johnson (Life of Waller) says,
" In the poem on the Navy those lines are very noble
which suppose the King's power secure against a second
deluge; so noble, that it were almost criminal to remark
the mistake of 'centre' for 'surface,' or to say that the
empire of the sea would be worth little if it were not
that the waters terminate in land."

U

UPON HIS MAJESTY'S REPAIRING OF PAUL'S.

Cf. "Cooper's Hill," 19-24.

> " Paul's the late theme of such a Muse, whose flight
> Has bravely reach'd and soar'd above thy height ;
> Now shalt thou stand, tho' sword, or time, or fire,
> Or zeal, more fierce than they, thy fall conspire,
> Secure, whilst thee the best of poets sings,
> Preserv'd from ruin by the best of Kings."

In the first edition of his poem (1642) Denham appended as a side-note to these lines the words *Master Waller*, which became *M. W.* in later editions.

Cf. also Dryden, "Annus Mirabilis" st. 275—

> " Nor could thy fabric, Paul's, defend thee long,
>   Though thou wert sacred to thy Maker's praise,
> Though made immortal by a poet's song,
>   And poets' songs the Theban walls could raise."

P. 16, *l.* 2.— I am unaware of any authority for this accentuation of Melita.

P. 16, *l.* 3.—The cathedral had suffered from fire in 1561, and though the repairs had been vigorously proceeded with up to 1566, in that year they were abandoned and nothing was done for more than fifty years. In the interval the building had, according to Dugdale, been much damaged by "the corroding quality of the coal smoke" in the neighbourhood, and had been permitted generally to go to decay.

P. 16, *ll.* 5-18.—On Nov. 16, 1620, James I. had issued a commission upon the subject of the repair of St. Paul's, and for a short time this was acted upon, but we soon hear that the Duke of Buckingham had " borrowed " some of the stone collected about the Cathedral and employed it in the repair of the water-gate at York House, and the work was again abandoned. In 1631 Charles, at the instigation of Laud, visited the Cathedral, and on April 10 issued a commission under the Great Seal which recited that the building was then in a state of decay. Commissioners were appointed to collect money for its repair, but, at first at least, his subjects' hearts did not respond at all freely to the King's touch, and only £5,400 were subscribed in two years. The work was finally interrupted by the troubles of the Civil War, and some of the materials which had been collected were handed over by the Parliament to the parishioners of St. Gregory's for the repair of their church.

P. 17, *ll.* 20-21.—Houses appear to have been actually built up against the walls of the Cathedral upon land belonging to the Church : these, in spite of the protests of their owners, were, by order of the Privy Council, all removed before the end of 1632.

P. 17, *l.* 35.—"Reduce "= bring back : *reducere.*

P. 18, *ll.* 51-4.—The repairs were begun in April, 1633, and Fenton, supposing that two years might *reasonably be allowed* for the completion of the Choir, has dated this poem 1635. I have been unable to discover when the Choir was actually finished, but the repairs were continued for nine years, and Denham's allusion, in 1642, to St. Paul's as *the late theme* of Waller, would seem to suggest a later date for the poem.

P. 18, *l.* 54.—Charles subscribed out of the ecclesiastical fines the sum of £10,295 5s. 6d., which was applied to the erection of a Portico, designed by Inigo Jones, and intended as "an ambulatory for such as

usually walking in the body of the Church disturb'd
the solemn service in the Choir."

TO MR. HENRY LAWES, &c.

These lines first appeared among Waller's poems in
the edition of 1668. I have retained the date then
assigned to them, although the reference to Noy (l. 15)
as still pleading, creates a difficulty.

Henry Lawes, whose musical connection with
"Comus" and so much of the lyric poetry of the
reign of Charles I. is well known, was born in 1600,
probably at Salisbury, where his father was vicar-
choral. He was a pupil of Coperario, and in 1625
was appointed one of the Gentlemen of the Chapel
Royal and Clerk of the Cheque to Charles I. He
lived to compose the anthem for the Coronation of
Charles II., and, dying in 1662, was buried in
Westminster Abbey.

P. 19, *l.* 15.—William Noy, notorious as the
inventor of ship-money, was born at St. Burian,
in Cornwall, in 1577. After three years spent
at Exeter College he entered at Lincoln's Inn,
and, according to Anthony à Wood, applied himself with great diligence to the study of the
law. He sat in the Parliaments of 1621, 1624,
1625, and 1628, in all of which he opposed the King,
at length in 1631 he was prevailed upon to accept the
post of Attorney-General, and in that office "grew
the most hateful man that ever lived." (Weldon, *The
Court of K. Charles continued.*) Clarendon says of
him that he thought "he could not give a clearer
testimony that his knowledge in the Law was greater

than all other men's, than by making **That, Law,**
which all other men believed *Not* to be so." He
died at Tunbridge Wells, Aug. 9, 1634; and though
Fenton's suggestion that this poem may originally
have been dated 1625 is â poor solution of the
difficulty referred to above, I am unable to find a
better.

A reference to Noy in Collop's *Poesis Rediviva,*
1656, p. 79, seems inconsistent with the account of
his early years given in the *Athenæ Oxonienses*—

> " To prove wild youth makes good man th' proverb take,
> See how the wilder Colts best horses make !
> Who *Noy* in Law, *Butler* in's art excels ?
> Who *Julius* or *Severus* parallels ?"

P. 20, *ll.* 27-28.—Lawes, to ridicule the practice of
singing songs the words of which neither the singer
nor the audience understood, set to music a succession of titles of Italian airs as they appeared in
an index, and was successful in passing them off as
a veritable Italian song. He published this composition in *Ayres and Dialogues,* 1653.

THE COUNTRY TO MY LADY OF CARLISLE.

This lady was the famous **Lucy Percy,** daughter of
Henry, Earl of Northumberland, and aunt of
Sacharissa. Her political intrigues have occupied
the attention of the historians of our time, as her
beauty did that of the poets of her own, and it may be
said that the former have united in clearing her
character from the scandalous aspersions cast upon it
by Sir Philip Warwick. Lady Carlisle died suddenly,
on Nov. 5, 1660, and was buried at Petworth.

P. 21, l. 2.—Comply = please : *complaire.*

P. 21, ll. 7-10.—Cf. the address " To the Queene,"
*yet if your Matie please to listen what Echo the country
returnes to so loud a praise.*

THE COUNTESS OF CARLISLE IN MOURNING.

This poem was addressed to the Countess of
Carlisle upon the death of her husband, who died at
Whitehall, April 5, 1636. James Hay, first Earl of
Carlisle, was the son of Sir James Hay of Kingask,
educated partly in France, he had, in early life, served
in the Scotch Guards at Paris. Handsome, accomplished, and of fascinating manners, he soon found his
way into the good graces of James I., who showered
wealth and honours upon him : he was created Gentleman of the King's Bedchamber, Comptroller of
Scotland, 1608, Lord Bewlie, 1609, Viscount Don-
caster and Earl of Carlisle, K.G. He was Master of
the Great Wardrobe from 1616 to 1636. He married
firstly Honora, daughter and heiress of Lord Denny,
and on the death of that lady, the Countess of Northumberland hoped, by a marriage between him and
her daughter, to effect the release of her husband, who
was confined in the Tower for supposed complicity in
the Gunpowder Plot. Northumberland, however,
declared that he would rather die in prison than owe
his release to a Scottish adventurer at the price of his
daughter's hand, and when Lady Lucy visited him, he
attempted to detain her in the Tower, saying that he
was a Percy, and could not endure that his daughter
should dance any Scotch jigs; he also offered her
£20,000 if she would consent to be ruled by him.

His efforts were unavailing, and on Nov. 5, **1617**, Chamberlain writes to Dudley Carleton, "On Thursday the Lord **Hay** married his mistress the Lady Lucy **Percy**, and that night **the King** and Princess honoured the wedding supper with **their presence at** the Wardrobe."

Cf. Herrick **(ed.** Pollard, **I. 78), "Upon a black twist rounding the arm of the** Countess of Carlisle."

P. 23, *ll.* 26-30.—Carlisle had been employed **by** James I. upon various embassies, **notably to** mediate between the Emperor **and the States of** Bohemia, **and between Louis** XIII. **and the French** Protestants, **but Waller has greatly exaggerated "the power of his enchanting tongue."**

P. 23, *ll.* 33-36.—Shortly **before his marriage to** Lady **Lucy Percy** the Earl **of** Carlisle entertained **her at a** masque and supper, which occupied the workmanship and **invention of thirty cooks for twelve** days, and **cost more than** £2,200. **Sir Anthony Weldon states that he (Carlisle) "imported live sturgeon** from **the Black Sea, which were served whole at** his banquets, **and that his suppers consisted of a rapid succession of the most costly dishes, the greater part** of which passed **untouched to his servants, one of whom** was seen **devouring a pie, composed of** ambergris, magisterial **of pearl and musk, which cost** £10." During his courtship **he lived in Richmond Park,** where he made **"solemn feasts twice a** week at least **with** that cost **and expense that the Lady of** Northumberland dares **not so much as once invite him** by reason of his **curiosity." (Chamberlain to** Dudley Carleton, Aug. 9, 1617.)

P. 23, *ll.* 37-43.—The Earl of Carlisle set out May 17, 1624, to join Lord Kensington in Paris in negotiating the marriage contract between Charles and Henrietta.   On May 1, 1625, the marriage was celebrated by proxy, on a stage erected opposite the west-end of Notre Dame, and the Princess was surrendered into the hands of the two lords by her brother, Louis XIII.

P. 23, *ll.* 46-48.—Fenton compares Claudian, *in Rufin,* I. 165-7—

> . . . "novi quo Thessala cantu
> Eripiat lunare jubar" . . .

IN ANSWER TO ONE WHO WRIT AGAINST A FAIR LADY.

P. 24, *ll.* 13-18.—These lines, now first included among Waller's poems, were printed by Neve (*Cursory Remarks on English Poets,* 1789, p. 71) from a manuscript of the middle of the reign of Charles I., in which they concluded the poem.

P. 25, *l.* 19.—Cf. Spenser, *Fairy Queen,* Book I, cant. 7, st. 33.

OF HER CHAMBER.

"Her (Lady Carlisle's) *chamber,* as it was called, was unlike any other reception-room in England at that time, and seems to have partaken rather of the character of the *salons* of brilliant Frenchwomen a century later." (De Fonblanque, *Annals of the House of Percy,* p. 399.)

TO PHYLLIS.

In Mr. Waller's transcript is written, as a note to the heading of this poem, *the lady Carlile,* but she is obviously not the lady addressed, and I am afraid the identity of Phyllis is undiscoverable.

P. 27, *ll.* 19-22.—Fenton compares with these lines the following from **Sir John** Suckling's *Brennoralt*, act iii. sc. 1.

> " Tempests of wind thus (as my storms of grief
>   Carry my tears which should relieve my heart,)
>   Have hurry'd to the thankless ocean clouds,
>   And show'rs, that needed not the courtesy;
>   **When the poor** plains have languished **for he want,**
>   **And almost** burnt asunder."

TO MR. GEORGE SANDYS, &c.

These lines were prefixed to Sandys' *Paraphrase upon the Divine* **Poems,** 1638, *folio.*

UPON BEN. JONSON.

These lines, headed **Upon Ben :** *Johnson, the most excellent* **of comick Poets,** first appeared in *Jonsonus Virbius,* 1638, *quarto,* a collection of poems in memory of Jonson, who died in the preceding year, edited by Bp. Duppa. Waller told Aubrey that he was not acquainted with Ben Jonson.

TO MY LORD OF NORTHUMBERLAND, UPON THE DEATH OF HIS LADY.

Algernon Percy, tenth Earl of Northumberland (born Sept. 29, 1602, died Oct. 13, 1668), married in 1629 Lady Anne Cecil, daughter of the Earl of Salisbury, receiving with her a marriage portion of £11,000. Like his sister, Lady Lucy, he was not successful in obtaining for his marriage the approbation of his father, who said that " the blood of Percy would not mix with the blood of Cecil if you poured them into a dish." The Countess died Dec. 6, 1637. The following extract from a letter from Garrard to Lord Wentworth, Dec. 16, 1637, announcing her death, is the best possible commentary on this poem—" She was a virtuous and religious young lady, so apt and fitted for him which by his wisdom he had wrought her to, that hardly he will find the like. At the time of her sickness I was witness of his love and care of her. Never out of her chamber, seldom from her bed-side, not parting from her till all the visible signs of death were on her, about an hour and a half before she expired : he took her death most heavily : passion hath the least outward power of him of any man I know ; yet in this it had got on him a great mastery. My Lord Conway and I never left him—bad com-forters both, for *he* held his peace, and *I* could not tell what to say. In these things time doth all ; yet I brake silence first, being sent of some messages betwixt his Lordship and the other sad family at Salisbury House. He intended a solemn funeral and a costly one, which would have been a fortnight in preparing : but my Lord of Salisbury made it his earnest suit to him to do it with all speed and privacy, especially since she died of that disease [*the small pox*], and that two of his daughters were sick of the same disease in the House ; which was yielded unto. So she was embalmed, sent in a barge to Syon, from whence his servants attended to Petworth, where she is interred. I never knew a more general lamentation for the death of any this long time. My Lord of Northumberland is come to his sister Carlisle's house, part of Salisbury House. Some little time he intends to spend at Syon, and then he will return to Court and to his place and begin the world anew again."

P. 31, *ll.* 7-9.—Fenton quotes from the letter of Sulpicius to Cicero on the death of his daughter Tullia: "Nullus dolor est quem non longinquitas temporis minuat ac molliat ; hoc te expectare tempus tibi turpe est, ac non ei rei sapientia tua te occurrere."

P. 31, *ll.* 17-24.—Æmilius, having destroyed the empire of Macedon, lost his two sons, one five days before, the other three days after his triumph.

His speech appears in Valerius Maximus, **V. 10. 2,** "Precatus sum, ut si adversi quid Populo Romano immineret, totum in meam domum converteretur.'

TO MY LORD ADMIRAL, &c.

Mr. John Bruce writing to *Notes and Queries*, 4th Series, iii. **222,** was, I believe, the first to point out that Fenton was wrong in referring this poem to the time when the Earl of Northumberland was appointed General of the English Army against the Scots, and to a sickness feigned by him to relieve himself of his command. The Earl was nominated Lord Admiral, March 18, 1638 (his appointment is dated April **13),** and the following extracts from the Strafford Corre-spondence leave no doubt as to the date and the reality of the illness to which Waller alludes. Garrard writing to Lord Wentworth (May **10,** 1638), after describing the nature of the Earl's complaint and the remedies applied by Mayerne and Baskerville, his physicians, says, "these last two nights he rested very well, so that the lookers-on as well as the physicians begin to conceive good hopes of his recovery, which I beseech

God to grant, since he is one of the noblest and
bravest gentlemen this age hath bred ; the King, the
kingdom, all his friends would have an unspeakable
loss of him, he is infinitely lamented by all sorts of
men."

Writing again, on July 3 of the same year, to Lord
Wentworth, Garrard announces the Earl's recovery
and says, "He is a well-beloved man here in England,
I never knew greater lamentations made for any man's
recovery. I never had so long a time of sorrow ; for
seven weeks I did nothing heartily but pray, not sleep
nor eat, in all that time I never bowled ; I hope now
we shall have days of mirth, if the Scots will give us
leave."

This poem appeared in the second (1642) and
third (1651) editions of Carew's poems.

P. 33, *l.* 10.—The second wife of the Earl of Northumberland was Elizabeth, daughter of Theophilus,
second Earl of Suffolk, through whom he became
possessed of Northumberland House in the Strand.

P. 33, *l.* 12.—Cf. p. 42, ll. 45-56, and Pope,
Autumn, ll. 15-16.

"When tuneful Hylas with melodious moan,
　　Taught rocks to weep and made the mountains groan."

P. 33, *ll.* 17-20.—Laud, writing to Lord Wentworth, May 14, 1638, says, "My Lord of Northumberland was at the last made Lord Admiral till the
Duke of York come of age. . . . but now, (which I
am heartily sorry to write) all the hopes of his service
are in danger, for he hath been in a high fever now
these three weeks ; and though the physicians speak
of out of danger, yet for my part, out of my love to

him and his worth, **am very** fearful. **I pray God**
comfort **and** repair him, **for his loss will** be great in
these times."

P. 34, *l.* **28.**—A reference to the Countess **of Car
lisle**, the Earl's sister : **the** illness of his brother, Henry
Percy (*The next support, fair hope of your great name*),
appears to be referred to in l. 30. Garrard, writing to
Lord Wentworth, **May 10, 1638** (the letter quoted
from above), **says, "his** brother Percy hath **also** been
desperately sick **of a** burning fever, stark **mad** with it,
but mends somewhat, though slowly. I thought **last
week we should have lost both** the brothers together."

P. 34, *ll.* **33-34.**—Cf. *Samson* Agonistes, 727-8—

> "**but now with head** declin'd
> **Like a fair flower surcharg'd** with dew she weeps."

TO THE QUEEN MOTHER OF FRANCE, &c.

After **her exile from France, Marie de Medicis had
lived at Brussels and Avênes in Hainault ;** in Aug.,
**1638, she announced her intention of visiting England,
and** in **spite of the remonstrances of Charles I.,** con-
veyed through Boswell, his agent at the Hague, **she
started on Sept. 25 : on Sept. 30 her servant** Mon-
sigot announced to Charles that she was on the way,
and in **deference to the** pleadings of Henrietta Maria,
he ordered that she should be honourably received **on
her arrival. She landed at Harwich** on Oct. 19.
Her welcome appears to have been of **a** very mixed
character, and after living in St. James's Palace for
three years, as a pensioner of the King, she was in
Aug., 1641, on the petition of Parliament, removed
from the kingdom.

P. 35, *ll.* 9-11.—Echard, quoted by Fenton, says she arrived at the time of such extreme wet and windy weather, that the water-men distinguished it by the name of *Queen-Mother weather.* In a masque presented at York House, Nov. 5, 1626, Marie de Medicis had been "represented as enthroned in the midst of the celestial deities upon the sea which separated England and France, welcoming the Elector and Electress as well as her three daughters with their husbands, the Kings of England and Spain and the Prince of Piedmont." (Gardiner, *England under Buckingham and Charles I.*, ii. 100.)

P. 36, *ll.* 13-16.—Cf. Æn. vi. 785-8—

> " qualis Berecyntia mater
> Invehitur curru Phrygias *turrita* per urbes,
> Læta deum partu centum complexa nepotes,
> Omnes cœlicolas, omnes supera alta tenentes."

P. 36, *l.* 30.—Marie de Medicis was daughter of the Grand Duke of Tuscany: the references in the preceding lines are to Tasso, with whom Waller was familiar through the medium of Fairfax's translation.

UPON THE DEATH OF MY LADY RICH.

Lady Anne Cavendish, only daughter of William, Earl of Devonshire, married to Lord Rich, heir of the Earl of Warwick, died in her 27th year, on Aug. 24, 1638, at Lees, and was buried at Felstead, in Essex. Dr. John Gauden composed a long Latin inscription upon her, in prose, and Sidney Godolphin wrote some verses to her memory, which were first printed with Gauden's Funeral Sermon on her son, Lord

Robert Rich, 1658, and included by Fenton in his
edition of Waller.

P. 37, *l.* 4.—Cf. Pope, *Windsor Forest*, 45-56—

> " To savage beasts and savage laws a prey,
>   And Kings more furious and severe than they."

P. 37, *ll.* 21-24.—Cf. Oldham, *To Madam L.E.,
upon her Recovery*—

> " The Queen of Love (we're told) once let us see
>   That Goddesses from wounds could not be free."

P. 38, *l.* 26.—Her mother was Christian (so called
from having been born on Christmas Day), daughter
of Edward, Lord Bruce of Kinloss, who claimed descent
from Robert Bruce (cf. l. 32). This lady, one of the
most intelligent and distinguished women of her time,
after having contributed to the Restoration by secret
intrigues with Monk, died Jan. 16, 1675.

P. 38, *ll.* 41-42.—Fenton says these lines are imitated from Aurelius Victor's character of Fabricius, *qui
difficilius ab honestate quam sol a suo cursu averti
posset.*

P. 39, *ll.* 57-58.—Cf. the poem on p. 60, *Tell me,
lovely, loving pair !*

P. 39, *ll.* 61-62.—Cf. Sidney Godolphin's lines—

> " The largest mind, and which did most extend
>   To all the laws of daughter, wife, and friend."

P. 39, *ll.* 75-76.—Cf. p. 127, ll. 10-12.

P. 40, *ll.* 86-89.—Cf. Oldham, *On the Death of
Mrs. Katherine Kingscourt*—

> " 'Twas sure some noble Being left the Sphere,
>   Which deign'd a little to inhabit here,
>   And can't be said to die but disappear."

And Flatman, *On the Death of Charles II.* —

> " But Princes, (like the wondrous Enoch) should be free
> 　From **Death's** unbounded Tyranny,
> 　And when their Godlike Race is run,
> 　And nothing glorious left undone,
> Never submit to Fate, but only disappear."

Browning, in a private letter, expressed admiration for this idea, but assigned the credit of it to Flatman.

THRYSIS, GALATEA.

The lady, whose death is lamented in this poem, was Lady Mary Feilding, eldest daughter of William, first Earl of Denbigh, and Mary, daughter of Sir George Villiers, and sister of George, first Duke of Buckingham. She was married in 1620 to James, first Duke of Hamilton (then Earl of Arran), and died May 10, 1638.

P. 41, *l.* 16.—Fenton quotes from Florus, Proœm 2, "ad constituendum ejus imperium contendisse virtus et fortuna videantur."

P. 41, *ll.* 19-20.—The Duke of Hamilton traced his descent from a sister of King James III. of Scotland, and the right of his family to succeed to the crown, upon failure of the Stuart line, was recognized by Parliament. Lady Hamilton was Lady of the Bedchamber to Henrietta Maria, and was, according to Burnet, admitted by her " into an entire confidence and friendship."

P. 41, *ll.* 29-34.—Cf. Cicero, *de Senect.* xix. 30. "Quasi poma ex arboribus, cruda si sint, vi avelluntur; si matura et cocta, decidunt: sic vitam adolescentibus vis aufert; senibus maturitas.

ON MY LADY DOROTHY SIDNEY'S PICTURE.

Anthony Vandyck arrived in England about the end of March, or the beginning of April, 1632, having previously paid a short visit to this country in 1630, There are at least three portraits of Sacharissa painted by him, to one of which this poem doubtless alludes. The Earl of Leicester sat to him in 1632, but the language of the lines "To Vandyck," and the apparent age of Lady Dorothy in her portraits, seem to point to a later date, when he had painted a series of English pictures. Sir William Temple had a portrait of her, probably a copy of one of Vandyck's ; writing to him, Dorothy Osborne says : " I have sent you my picture because you wished for it : but pray let it not presume to disturb my lady Sunderland's."

P. 43, *l.* 1.—The reference is to the *Arcadia* of Sir Philip Sidney, the great-uncle of Lady Dorothy, in which **Pyrocles** and Musidorus, seeing the portraits of Philoclea and Pamela (*Musidorus' flame*) hanging in the house of Calander, fall in love with them and ultimately marry the originals. Dorus was the name assumed by Musidorus when he disguised himself as a shepherd and obtained entrance into the house of Dametas, the guardian of Pamela.

P. 43, *ll.* 4-5.—Cf. p. 216, l. 2.

TO VANDYCK.

P. 45, *ll.* 49-50.—Cf. p. 28, ll. 17-18.

AT PENSHURST.

P. 46, *ll.* 17-20.—Cf. p. 16, ll. 11-15.

P. 47, *ll.* 25-27.—Cf. Ben Jonson, *To Penshurst.* 13-16—

> "That taller Tree, which of a Nut was set,
> At his great Birth, where all the Muses met.
> There in the writhed Bark, are cut the Names
> Of many a Sylvane, taken with his flames."

TO MY LORD OF LEICESTER.

P. 47, *l.* 12.—The Earl of Leicester started from Rye, to act as ambassador at the Court of France, May 17, 1636, and took his leave of the French King, upon his return to England, March 14, 1639.

OF THE MISREPORT OF HER BEING PAINTED.

P. 50, *l.* 17.—Cf. Spenser, *Muipotmos,* st. 21, ll. 3-4.
" There lavish Nature in her best attire,
    Powres forth sweete odors and alluring sights."

P. 50, *l.* 22.—Thaumantias, *i.e.,* Iris, the daughter of Thaumas.

OF HER PASSING THROUGH A CROWD OF PEOPLE.

P. 51, *l.* 8.—*admiral,* the leading ship of a squadron.
P. 51, *l.* 13.—*insults* = exults.

FABULA PHŒBI ET DAPHNES.

There is a tradition that these lines were written by Sir John Suckling, and by him sent to Waller.

SONG—*Say, Lovely Dream!*

This poem was printed in Beaumont's Poems, 1653 : it was probably conveyed straight from the edition of 1645 of Waller, as a misprint, *Shales* for *Shades,* occurs in both.

TO THE SERVANT OF A FAIR LADY.

P. 55, *l.* 1.—Dorothy Osborne, writing to Sir William Temple, frequently speaks of her maid, Jane Wright, as his " fellow-servant."

TO A VERY YOUNG LADY.

This lady, a younger sister of Sacharissa, was married to John, eldest son of Sir Thomas Pelham, Jan. 20, 1647.

TO AMORET.

Fenton says that he had heard the Duke of Buckingham say that the person whom Waller celebrated under the title of Amoret was Lady Sophia Murray. This lady, the daughter of the Earl of Annandale, was certainly an acquaintance of Waller, she was implicated in his plot, but it seems to me more likely that Amoret stands for Lady Anne Cavendish, afterwards Lady Rich. In the edition of 1645 the poem which immediately follows this is headed : *On the Friendship betwixt Sacharissa and Amoret,* and the note to it in Mr. Waller's transcript is *Lady Dor. Sidnie & Lady Anne Candish wife to my Lord Rich :* what is said there of the friendship between the two agrees with the lines on the death of Lady Rich, p. 37.

ON HER COMING TO LONDON.

These lines are here for the first time included in Waller's poems ; they occur among the State Papers, Dom. Charles I. CCCCXIV. 19, and were sent to *Notes and Queries,* 4th series, iii. 1, by Mr. John Bruce. In places, the paper upon which they are written is worn, and the words in brackets are conjectural. At the end of the poem is written, *Intended to her Lap at her coming to London, March the* 2, 1638. The figure "8" has apparently been written over a "7."

AT PENSHURST.

P. 64, *ll.* 21-23.—An allusion to Mount Sion, a hill from the foot of which the mineral waters at Tunbridge Wells issue.

THE BATTLE OF THE SUMMER ISLANDS.

The Bermudas derived their name of Summer Islands from the fact that Sir George Somers was wrecked upon them in 1609 while on his way to Virginia. James I. granted a charter to certain merchant-adventurers for the colonization and government of the islands, and the rules and regulations of the Company were published in 1621—"Orders and Constitutions, Partly collected out of his Majestie's Letters Patents ; and partly by authority and in vertue of the said Letters Patents." Waller, in speaking of them as " late-discovered isles," appears to have been ignorant of, or to have purposely ignored, the visit which Juan Bermudez, a Spaniard, is said to have paid to them in 1522. Historians of the Bermudas have delighted to point out inaccuracies in Waller's description, and have even declared that the event which this poem celebrates is geographically impossible. There is no evidence, beyond a vague tradition, that the poet ever visited the islands, and when he says, " Bermudas walled with rocks, who does not know ? " he is only crediting his audience with the same kind of familiarity with the place as he had himself, such as could be derived from the accounts of others. Waller certainly did not invent this story of the Whales, and it is possible that Marvell may have had this particular incident in his mind when he wrote of the Bermudas—

> " Where He the huge sea-monsters wracks,
> That lift the deep upon their backs."
>
> *Marvell*, vol. i. p. 39 (ed. Aitken).

The whole of Marvell's poem, Fairfax, " Godfrey of

Bulloigne," **xv.** 35-36, **xvi. 11,** and Spenser, "Faeric Queene," iii. 6. 42, should be compared with **Waller's** description of the islands.

P. 66, *l.* 12.—No. 200 of the "Orders" above mentioned is a curious commentary on this line— "No kind of Timber-wood growing in the said Ilands shall be used for firewood." It appears that the orange-crop had suffered severely from the loss of the protection from the wind which the cedars had afforded.

P. 67, *ll.* 46-47.—Cf. Oldham, "Verses. Presenting a Book to Cosmelia"—

> " Sure Heaven preserv'd her by the Fall uncurst,
> To tell how good the Sex was made at first."

P. 70, *ll.* 29-30.—Cf. Horace, Odes i. 3. 9-12.

P. 70, *l.* 49.—Robert Rich, Earl of Warwick, was one of the principal proprietors of the Bermudas (a parish there still bears his name); he had been mainly instrumental in settling the colony there and else-where in the West Indies. He disposed of twenty of his shares in the Bermuda Company to one Trott for £600, a sale which involved his family in liti-gation after his death.

P. 71, *l.* 11.—Spenser, "Faerie Queene," v. 1. 12.

P. 73, *l.* 64.—Æn. 11, 749. *Repeat* = seek again, Latin *repeto.* Cf. Dryden, "Annus Mirabilis," 257—

> " And while through burning labyrinths they retire,
> With loathing eyes repeat what they would shun."

WHEN HE WAS AT SEA.

These lines were first printed by Neve (*Cursory Remarks on English Poets*, 1789,) and afterwards, from another MS., in the "Tixall Poetry," 1813.

TO MY LORD OF FALKLAND.

[Cf. Cowley, *To the Lord Falkland. For his safe Return from the* Northern Expedition *against the* SCOTS.]

This poem was occasioned by the miserable expedition against the Scots which was organized in Feb., 1639. The General-in-Chief was the Earl of Arundel, and, in spite of his protests, the Earl of Holland, "the most incompetent of men," was forced upon him as his General of Horse. Holland, celebrated for the courtliness of his manners and his handsome person, owed his appointment solely to the favour of the Queen, and his conduct was said to have led to the failure of the Expedition, though Professor Gardiner (*Fall of the Monarchy of Charles I.*, vol. i. pp. 230-1) acquits him of the treachery with which he has been charged.

P. 76, *ll.* 26-28.—Cf. Oldham, "To the Memory of Mr. Atwood"—

> " Like the fair teeming Hebrew, she
> Did travail with a wrangling progeny,
> And harbour'd in her bowels feuds and civil wars."

Cf. Fairfax, "Godfrey of Bulloigne," xx. 114—

> " And as a Lyon strikes him with his train,
> His Native Wrath to quicken and to move ;
> So he awak'd his fury and disdain "—

and xv. 50.

Cowley, "On his Majesties Return out of Scotland "—

> " How justly would our Neighbours smile
> At these mad quarrels of our Isle
> Sweld with proud hopes to snatch the whole away,"—

*   *   *   *   *   *

" This noise at home was but Fates policie
To raise our Spirits more high.
So a bold Lyon ere he seeks his prey,
Lashes his sides, and roars, and then away "

Dryden, " Astræa Redux," 115-18—

" Tremble, ye nations, **who** secure before,
Laughed at those arms that 'gainst ourselves we bore
Roused by the lash **of his** own stubborn tail,
Our Lion now will foreign foes assail."

OF THE QUEEN.

The opening of this poem has been imitated by
Leigh Hunt in his address to Queen Victoria.

" The lark dwells lowly, Madam,—on the ground,—
And yet his Song within the heavens is found," &c.

THE APOLOGY OF SLEEP, &C.

Mr. Gosse (*Shakespeare to Pope*, p. 69), followed
by Mrs. Ady (*Sacharissa*, Julia Cartwright, p. 34),
has treated this poem as addressed to Sacharissa—
"The Lady who can do anything but Sleep when she
pleaseth " is, of course, the Queen.

PUERPERIUM.

Fenton supposes that this poem was written shortly
before the Queen was delivered of her fourth son,
Henry, Duke of Gloucester (born at Oatlands, July
20, 1640), in the midst of the Scotch troubles.

P. 82, *ll.* 5-12.—Cf. Lucretius, I. 29-40.

P. 82, *l.* 16.—Fenton has remarked upon Waller's
accentuation of " halcýon," " in which he has never
been, nor deserves to be imitated by others "; he

quotes Sandys, *Translation of the Metamorphoses,*
Bk. xi.—

> "Seven winter days with peaceful calms possest,
> Alcyon sits upon her floating nest."

TO AMORET.

P. 83, *ll.* 1-2.—Cf. Suckling, Brenroralt—

> "Her face is like the milky way i' th' sky,
> A meeting of gentle lights without a name."

P. 83, *ll.* 6-11.—These lines are printed, with
some variations, as part of a poem, a patchwork of
several of Waller's, in *Wits' Recreations,* 1640. I have
not thought it necessary to note the variations which
appear in such of Waller's poems as are contained
in the above collection, they are obviously the result
of faulty copying or imperfect recollection.

TO PHYLLIS.

This appears in *W. R.,* as "The cunning Cur-
tezan," and is followed by "The Fall" (p. 96),
which is headed "The Reply."

À LA MALADE.

P. 85, *ll.* 19-20.—"I mention them not upon
account of that couplet, but one that follows; which
ends with the very same rhymes and words (*appear*
and *clear*) that the couplet but one after that does;
and therefore in my Waller there is a various reading
of the first of these couplets; for there it runs thus—

> "'So lightnings in a stormy air,
> Scorch more than when the sky is fair.'"
> *Bp. of Rochester to Pope, Sept.* 27, 1721.

P. 86, *ll.* 22-24.—Cf. Oldham, "To Madam
L. E."—

> "By every breach in that fair lodging made,
> Its blest Inhabitant is more display'd,"

and p. 272, ll. 13-14.

FOR DRINKING OF HEALTHS.

In Mr. Waller's transcript, from which the first six and last ten lines of this poem are here for the first time printed, this piece is headed, "An answeare to on that writ against Healths." It may have been directed against Prynne, who in 1628 published *Healthes : Sicknesse. Or A Compendious And briefe Discourse ; prouing the drinking and pledging of Healthes, to be Sinfull, and utterly Unlawfull unto Christians.*

Cf. Fuller, "David's Heinous Sin," st. 27—

" My prayers for friends' prosperity and wealth
Shall ne'er be wanting ; but if I refuse
To hurt myself by drinking others' health,
O, let ingenuous natures me excuse.
  If men bad manners this esteem, then I
  Desire to be esteem'd unmannerly,
  That to live well will suffer wine to die."

OF MY LADY ISABELLA, &C.

This lady was Lady Isabella Rich, daughter of the Earl of Holland, afterwards married to Sir James Thynne of Longleat. She was the subject of much scandal in her day, and Dorothy Osborne, writing to Sir W. Temple, says, "But my Lady Isabella, that speaks, and looks and sings and plays and all so prettily, why cannot I say that she is free from faults as her sister believes her ?"

OF MRS. ARDEN.

Fenton suggests that this lady may have been a Maid of Honour or a Gentlewoman of the Bed-chamber to Henrietta Maria, and the same who is mentioned as having taken part in Montague's *Shepherd's Paradise.*   Cf. Marvell, "The Fair Singer."

OF THE MARRIAGE OF THE DWARFS.

This poem, which appears in *W. R.* 1640, headed "On the two Dwarfs that were marryed at Court, not long before Shrovetide," celebrates the marriage of Richard Gibson and Anne Shepherd, each of whom was three feet ten inches high.   Charles I. and his Queen were present at the wedding, and the latter appears to have promised the bride a diamond ring, which, however, she never received.   Richard Gibson was page to the King.   Under Franz Cleyn he attained considerable success in painting, and taught Queen Anne and her sister.   He died July 23, 1690, in the 75th year of his age ; his widow survived till 1709, when she was 89 years old.

THE FALL.

P 96, *ll.* 15-16.—Cf. Oldham, "The Dream"—
" So heretofore were the first Lovers laid
On the same Turf of which themselves were made."

P. 96, *ll.* 23-4.—Cf. Ayres, "On the Death of Cynthia's Horse"—
" A Heaven of Beauty overpressed thy Back,
This might have made Alcides shoulders crack,
And Atlas truckled under such a weight."

OF SYLVIA.

P. 97, *l.* 1. Cf.—Horace, Odes iv. 13. 1.—
" Audivere, Lyce, Di mea vota."

THE BUD.

Printed in *W. R.*, 1640, and *Ayres and Dialogues,* 1653.

P. 98, *l.* 8.—D'Israeli omitted to notice this line in discussing the meaning and use of *purpureus* and *purple* in the *Curiosities of Literature,* q. **v.**

P. 98, *l.* 14.—The text of this line is unsatisfactory. In *W. R.* the passage runs—

> " And if loose **breath** so much can do,
> **It may as** well inform of love."

The verb "inform" is used **by** Waller (see p. **77,** l. **11, and p. 78, l. 24), and** Hammond (*Poems, By W. H.,* **1655)** has

> " For lamely **would** the Will's bright Chariot move,
> If not inform'd by friendly heat of **Love.**"

One would **have preferred** *inform'd,* **if** it had **not** been corrected in **the Errata** of the edition **of 1682 :** " in forms of **love,"** *i.e.,* constrained into the language of love, affords **perhaps some** contrast **to "our** *loose* breath."

ON THE DISCOVERY OF A LADY'S PAINTING.

In *W. R.,* 1640, " On a patch'd up Madam."

OF LOVING AT FIRST SIGHT.

Printed in *W. R.,* 1640, **where it** immediately **follows the preceding poem, and is** headed " The Reply **on the Contrary** "; **it also** appears in Francis **Beaumont's Poems, 1653,** signed **Tho.** Batt.

P. 100, *ll.* 3-4.—In *W. R.*—

> " **I now no** painted colours find,
> But settled stand **upon** the shore."

"**Snatched from myself,**" from Horace, Odes iv. 13. **20.**—"**Quæ me surpuerat** mihi."

THE SELF-BANISHED.

W. R., 1640, "The Melancholy **Lover**:" it forms the beginning of the patchwork poem referred to in the note on p. 83, ll. 6-11: also printed in *Ayres and Dialogues,* 1653.

TO A FRIEND, &C.

W. R., 1640, "The Variable Lover; or a Reply to the Melancholy Lover." Robert Keck says this poem is addressed to "Mr. Alexander Hambden, a cousin of the Author." Keck appears to have contemplated an edition of Waller, and has left behind him a copy of the edition of 1705 with MS. notes, which is now in the Dyce Collection at South Kensington.

TO ZELINDA.

In the edition of 1645 this poem is headed "Palamede to Zelinde. Ariana, lib. 6"; it had appeared in *W. R.*, 1640, as "The Ladyes Slave to his Mistresse." In one of the tales added in the 1639 edition of the "Ariane" of Des Marets, Zelinde, in answer to Palamede, expresses her determination to wed none but a Prince.

TO A LADY SINGING A SONG OF HIS COMPOSING.

Ayres and Dialogues, "To the same Lady singing the former Song," *i.e.*, "While I listen," &c.

P. 105, *ll.* 5-8.—It is impossible to arrive at the origin of this figure; it occurs in a fragment of "The Myrmidons" of Æschylus, where it is introduced by the words, "Ὣs δ'ἐστὶ μύθων τῶν Λιβυστικῶν λόγος," and Porson, in his edition of the " Medea," has collected instances of its use by other classical authors. This is, I believe, its first appearance in English poetry, though probably few who have admired Byron's well-known lines are aware of it.

Cf. K. Philips, " On Controversies in Religion"—

> " And meets that Eagle's destiny, whose breast
> Felt the same shaft which his own feathers drest."

TO THE MUTABLE FAIR.

In *IV. R.*, 1640, this follows "Fairest piece," &c., and is headed "The Reply"; it was also printed in Francis Beaumont's Poems, 1653.

P. 108, *ll.* 55-56.—Cf. p. 104, ll. 39-40. "Camoens, speaking of the voyages of the Argonauts and of Ulysses, says that the undertakings of the Portuguese shall give credit to all those fables in surpassing them."—Bayle, iv. 84.

TO CHLORIS.

In the edition of 1645 these verses were headed " To Chloris uppon a favour receaved." Fenton had seen a copy of an old edition in which there was a note that Mr. Waller said this poem was " supposititious "; he was unable to reject it, and could only suppose that the poet " wrote it when he was young, and afterwards was too delicate to own it under the title which it bears in the first impression "; it appears in *Ayres and Dialogues*, vol. ii., 1655, headed " To a Lady, more affable since the war began " !

CHLORIS AND HYLAS.

In *W. R.*, 1640, "On the approaching Spring."
P. 114, *ll.* 1-2.—Cf. Pope, "Spring," 25-26.

> " Why sit we mute, when early linnets sing,
> When warbling Philomel salutes the spring?"

IN ANSWER OF SIR JOHN SUCKLING'S VERSES.

P. 117, *l.* 28.—Cf. Oldham, "A fragment of Petronius paraphras'd "—

> " I hate Fruition, now 'tis past,
> 'Tis all but nastiness at best ;
> The homeliest thing that man can do."

ON A BREDE OF DIVERS COLOURS.

In *W. R.*, 1640, "On a brede of divers colours, woven by four Maids of Honour, and presented to the Queen on New Year's Day last."
P. 121, *ll.* 5-6.—Cf. p. 242, ll. 11-12.

TO CHLORIS.

These lines, after appearing in the edition of 1645, were, for some reason, omitted from all the other editions published during Waller's life.

BEHOLD THE BRAND OF BEAUTY TOSSED!

Printed in Francis Beaumont's Poems, 1653.

WHILE I LISTEN TO THY VOICE.

Ayres and Dialogues, 1653.

GO, LOVELY ROSE !

W. R., 1640, "On the Rose." *Ayres and Dialogues,* vol. ii., 1655.

Cf. **Pope,** " Spring," 61 *et seq.* in the original MS.—

> " Go flow'ry wreath, and let my Sylvia know,
>   Compared to thine how bright her beauties show ;
>   Then die ; and dying, teach the lovely maid
>   How soon the brightest beauties **are** decayed."

The above seem **to be** a direct imitation of Waller's lines, but as **has been** pointed out (*Notes and Queries,* 5th series, **xi.** 275), the **simile** was so common in the sixteenth and seventeenth centuries "**that** it would be almost **impossible to say who did** not use it. Among the **best** known **are Spenser,** *Faerie Queene,* Bk. **ii. 12. 74-75.** **Fairfax,** *Tasso,* **xvi. 14-15.** Giles **Fletcher,** *Christ's Victorie.* **Fanshawe's transl.** *Pastor Fido,* and again in *Additional Poems.* **Samuel** Daniel, *Description of Beauty translated out of Marino,* and again in *Sonnet* **to Delia.** Stanley, *Time Recovered.* **Harrington,** *Orlando Furioso,* Bk. **i. 42-43.** It is used by Erasmus **in his** Colloquies **more than** once, and **is to be found** in Ausonius, Catullus, (**both** quoted **by** Burton in his *Anatomy*) and the *Book of Wisdom.* **It is also more or** less closely **followed** by Chaucer, Drummond, **Cleveland,** Prior, **&c."** To the above may **be added, Robert** Chester, and, **perhaps best** known **of all, Herrick.**

Kirke White added—

> " **Yet,** though **thou fade,**
>   **From thy dead** leaves let fragrance rise ;
>   **And teach the maid**
>   **That goodness Time's** rude hand defies,
>   **That Virtue lives** when Beauty dies."

Lines, **which, in** Southey's opinion, Waller might **have written if he had** pursued the subject in this **vein.**

UNDER A LADY'S PICTURE.

W. R., 1640, " To be ingraven under the Queen's Picture." Lines 1-2 are here printed for the first time from a common-place book of Edmund Waller, the son of the poet, now in the possession of Mr. Waller; there the heading is, "This was written under my Lady Speke's Picture."

WRITTEN IN MY LADY SPEKE'S SINGING-BOOK.

These lines, printed here for the first time, are taken from the common-place book mentioned above. See note on " Epitaph on Sir George Speke. "

TO ONE MARRIED TO AN OLD MAN.

W. R., 1640, " To the wife being marryed to that old man" (referring to another epigram which precedes).

AN EPIGRAM ON A PAINTED LADY, &c.

This appeared in the edition of 1645, and was not reprinted during Waller's life.

P. 131, *ll.* 1-2.—Cf. Vaughan, *Upon Mr. Fletcher's Playes.*

> " For thou hast drain'd Invention, and he
> That writes hereafter, doth but pillage thee."

P. 132, *l.* 8 *and l.* 12.—Melantius and Aspasia are characters in "The Maid's Tragedy," which Waller "altered." While all the critics agree in regarding "The Maid's Tragedy" as the joint production of the two dramatists, some have ascribed more than three-fourths of it to Beaumont.

VERSES TO DR. GEORGE ROGERS, &C.

These lines first appeared with the *Oratio In Gymnasio Patavino Habita Prid. Cal. Maii An.* 1646, &c., *a Georgio Rogers Anglo, Docturæ gradu suscepto,* in what the bookseller calls *Auctarium sive superpondium hoc poeticum,* given him by Dr. Downes, F.C.P.L. There are several other copies of verses, all but Waller's, in Latin, among them one signed *Ioan. Euelinus Anglus.* Dr. Rogers was incorporated in the University of Oxford, April 14, 1647, and afterwards became President of the College of Physicians.

TO MY LADY MORTON, &C.

This poem first appeared as a broadside, *London, Printed for Henry Herringman on the Lower walk of the New Exchange.* 1661. It was doubtless written, as it purports to have been, in France, and was printed by Waller when the prophecy contained in ll. 45-46 had been fulfilled. I suppose it is in connection with this poem that Robert Wild speaks of Waller as "Great Poet and true Prophet too." Ann, Countess of Morton, was the daughter of Sir Edward Villiers, half-brother of George, first Duke of Buckingham. She married Robert Douglas, Lord Dalkeith, who, on the death of his father, became Earl of Morton. The story of her flight, disguised as a French servant, from Oatlands to France, in 1646, with the Princess Henrietta, is well known. She died in December, 1654.

P. 135, *ll.* 31-32.—Cf. p. 200, l. 5.

Y

TO SIR WILLIAM DAVENANT, &C.

These lines first appeared in a little 12mo book published in Paris in 1650, *A Discourse upon Gondibert. An Heroick Poem Written by Sir William D'Avenant With an Answer to it by Mr. Hobbs*, they were reprinted with both the editions of "Gondibert" published in 1651. The heading at first was, "To Sir William D'Avenant, Upon his two first books of Gondibert, finished before his Voyage to America"—the words "Written in France," were substituted for the last six of this title, in the "1664" and other editions of Waller's Poems. Sir William Davenant (1606-1668), his "Gondibert," his misfortunes, and the sport he made for the wits of his time are all too well known to need particular mention here. He had been in trouble in connection with the Army Plot in 1641, and had fled to France, but afterwards returned to England, and was, on March 8, 1644, accused by the Parliament of High Treason. He formed the design of conveying a party of artificers, chiefly weavers, from France to Virginia, but the vessel in which he had embarked having been captured by one of the ships in the service of the English Parliament, he was confined in Cowes Castle, and afterwards in the Tower.

A PANEGYRIC TO MY LORD PROTECTOR, &C.

There were two editions of this poem in 1655—

(i) A | Panegyrick | To | My Lord Protector, | Of | The present Greatness and joynt Inn | terest of His Highness, and this Nation. | By E. W. Esq. | London, | Printed for Richard Lowndes at the White Lyon in | S. Pauls Church-yard, neer the little Northdore. | **1655.** Quarto. A 3 (p. 1) to B 3. Title and five leaves, blank leaf besides at each end.

(ii) **A** | Panegyrick | **To** My | Lord Protector, | **By A** | Gentleman | That | **Loves the** Peace, Union, and Prosperity | **Of The** | English Nation. | Claudian : &c. | Gaudet enim virtus testes sibi jungere Musas, | Carmen amat quisquis Carmine digna gerit. | London, | Printed **by** Thomas Newcomb, in Thames-street | **over** against Baynards-Castle, **1655. Small** folio. Title and three leaves.

In spite **of the** hint which **is given as to** the authorship, which **one** would **rather have** expected to find in **a** second impression, the **text leaves no** doubt that **(i) is the first,** possibly pirated, edition. I only know **of** the existence of **two** copies **of (ii),** one in the Bodleian, and **one in the library of** Mr. **Buxton** Forman, which he very **kindly allowed me to** collate. I have adopted the text **of this edition.** The " Panegyric " was not reprinted until **1690, by Bennet and by Tonson, whose editors appear to have** used **MS.** copies, **as there are** variations, verbal **and** unimportant, **from the texts of the Quarto and Folio in** both their editions.

No one probably **would see these lines** sooner than **the person to** whom **they** were addressed, **and the letter from Cromwell to Waller** (June 13, **1655) which I have printed in the** Introduction would seem **to show that they had not been written or** circulated **in MS. long** before **the date of** their publication,— (" May **31 "** MS. note **on** the copy of (i) in the British Museum),—**but I am inclined to** think **that** part at least **of the poem was in** circulation nearly two years

before, for in 1653 appeared "The Incomparable
Poem Gondibert Vindicated," &c., where these lines
occur—

> "You think they feign, that is they lie,
>   That spake of *Gondibert* so high.
>   If that their Verses were much taller
>   *Waller* hath since out-Gondid *Waller*."

The reference can hardly be to anything but
the "Panegyric," (I know of nothing written by
Waller between this and the preceding poem),—
which is introduced, not as Mr. Gosse supposes, on
account of its "pompous rhetoric," but the unworthi-
ness of its subject.   It is possible that Waller re-cast
and made additions to the poem, as he appears to
have done to "Instructions to a Painter," and that it
was not sent to Cromwell till it was printed.

P. 138, *ll.* 9-10.—Cf. Fairfax, "Godfrey of
Bulloigne," iii. 52—

> " Above the Waves as Neptune lift his Eyes,
>   To chide the Winds that Trojan Ships oppressed."

P. 139, *ll.* 39-40.—Cf. Marvell, "An Horatian
Ode," &c., 97-98—

> " What may not then our Isle presume,
>   While Victory his crest does plume ?"

P. 142, *l.* 100.—Cf. Pope, "Windsor Forest," 400—

> " And seas but join the regions they divide."

P. 142, *l.* 105.—The last great sea-fight between
Blake and Tromp, in which the latter was killed,
July 29, 1653.

P. **145,** *ll.* 165-68.—Cf. Fairfax, "Godfrey of Bulloigne," viii. 83—

> " So, when a lion shakes his dreadful mane,
>   And beats his tail, with courage proud, and wroth,
>   If his commander come, who first took pain
>   To tame his youth, his lofty crest down go'th."

P. **145,** *l.* 175.—Dorothy Osborne, writing to Sir William Temple in 1653, says : "My Lord Saye, I am told, has writ a romance since his retirement in the Isle of Lundy, and Mr. Waller, they say, is making one of our wars, which, if he does not mingle with a great deal of pleasing fiction, cannot be very diverting, sure the subject is so sad." It is possible this may only refer to the present poem, there is no trace of any poem by Waller on the Civil War.

TO MY WORTHY FRIEND MR. WASE.

These lines first appeared with Wase's translation of the *Cynegeticon* of Gratius Faliscus, 1654. At the end of the "Preface to the Reader," one Mr. Robert Creswel, addressing Wase, and speaking of Gratius, says :

> " One who has all the right that man can doe,
>   You set forth him, and noble Waller you."

Christopher Wase, Fellow of King's College, Cambridge, was the author of a translation of the *Electra* and several other works. He dedicated his translation of Gratius to Lord Herbert, son of the Earl of Pembroke, to whom he was tutor. The following letter from Waller to an unknown correspondent was

printed by Mr. Hazlitt in his *Collections and Notes:*—
"April 1652. S^r my noble frend the Earle of
Deuenshire being now about to the send the younge
Lord his sonn into the world hath asked my aduise
concerning a gouerner for him, wch occasion I tooke
to comend our good frend Mr Wase, speaking so well
(that is so deseruedly) of him, that my Lord hath a
great desire to see and conferr wth him, & to that
end will beare his charges to Latimers in Buckinghamshire, where his Ldp now is. Truly (S^r) if
Mr Wase be not prouided of some other very good
imployment, he can not come into a nobler family in
England, nor fynde better entertainment any where.
This is the opinion of, S^r, y^r obedient Seruant,
"Waller."

AD COMITEM MONUMETENSEM, &C.

These lines were first printed with the Earl of
Monmouth's translation of Cardinal Bentivoglio's
History of the Wars of Flanders, published in 1654.
Henry Carey, Earl of Monmouth, was born about
1595, and died June 13, 1661 : he was the author of
several translations from the French and Italian,
upon which he was complimented by Sir John
Suckling, Sir William Davenant, and other poets of
his day.

TO HIS WORTHY FRIEND, MASTER EVELYN.

These lines are here printed as they appear in the
"1664," and other editions of Waller's Poems : they
were first printed in *An Essay on the first book of T.*

Lucretius Carus, &c.   Interpreted and made English
Verse by J. Evelyn, Esq : · · · London : **1656.**, in a
slightly different form—

> " *Lucretius* with a stork-like fate,
>   **Born and** translated in a state,
>   Comes to proclaim in English Verse
>   **No Monarch Rules the** Universe ;
>   **But chance and Atomes make** *this All*
>   **In Order Democratical,**
>   **Where Bodies freely run** their course,
>   Without design, **or** Fate, or Force.
>   **And this** in such a strain he **sings,**
>   **As if his** Muse **with Angels wings**
>   **Had soar'd beyond our utmost sphere**
>   **And other Worlds discover'd there ;**
>   **For his immortal boundless wit**
>   **To Nature does no bounds permit ;**
>   **But boldly,"** &c.

There are also the following minor variations—l.
13, *they were* for *she was,* l. 14 *narrow* for *moderate,*
l. 21, *A Tongue too narrow* for *Too weak, too
narrow.*

P. 149, *ll.* 17-22.—Cf. Lucretius, i. 135-38.
P. 150, *l.* 38.—Cf. Lucretius, iv. 1-2.

OF A WAR WITH SPAIN, AND A FIGHT AT SEA.

This poem was, as far as I can discover, first
printed, in folio, with the poem on St. James's Park,
(*q.v.*) where it is headed, "Of our late War with
Spaine and first Victory at sea near St. Lugar."
Spain having declared war against England, **Feb. 16,
1656,** a fleet was sent to the Mediterranean under the
command of Blake and Montague : **several** projects

for its employment were formed and abandoned, and it remained for some months inactive, before Cadiz. On September 8, Captain Richard Stayner in the *Speaker*, going with two other vessels to a neighbouring bay to take in water, fell in with eight galleons, all of which he either captured or destroyed. His exploit forms the subject of Waller's lines.

P. 153, *l.* 49.—Fenton refers this to Cicero, *de Divinat. II.*—"Omnesne qui Cannensi pugnâ ceciderunt, uno astro fuerint? Exitus quidem omnium unus et idem fuit."

P. 154, *l.* 77.—The Marquis of Badajos, Viceroy of Mexico.

P. 154, *l.* 82.—Cf. Fairfax, "Godfrey of Bulloigne," xx. st. 98—

"And, for he could not save her, with her dy'd."

P. 155, *l.* 89.—The Marquis, with his wife and eldest daughter, perished in the flames; his two sons and two younger daughters, together with about a hundred of the crews of the galleons, were rescued by the English.

P. 155, *ll.* 95-96.—Cf. "The Maid's Tragedy Altered"—

"How frail is Man! how quickly changed are
Our wrath and fury to a loyal care."

P. 155, *l.* 101.—In the edition of 1711, this poem, faced by a portrait of "Generall Mountague, since Earle of Sandwich," is headed, "Of a War with Spain, and Fight at Sea, by General Montague. In the year 1656." As a matter of fact, Montague was not even present at the engagement, though he was, upon his arrival at Portsmouth, entrusted with the care of the prisoners and treasure, and afterwards conducted them to London, where he received the thanks of the House of Commons. Stayner, the real hero, for his share in this, and in Blake's victory off Santa Cruz (April 20, 1657), was knighted by Cromwell. Cf. Marvell, "On the Victory obtained by Blake," &c., ll. 117-18—

> " Bold Stayner leads ; this fleet's designed by fate
> To give him laurel, as the last did plate."

TO HIS WORTHY FRIEND SIR THOMAS HIGGONS, &C.

Sir Thomas Higgons was born at Westbury, in Shropshire, in 1624 ; he married (1st) Elizabeth, widow of Robert Devereux, 3rd Earl of Essex (he delivered an oration at her funeral, Sept. 16, 1656), and (2nd) in 1661, Bridget, daughter of Sir Bevil Grenville. He was knighted June 17, 1663, and after having been employed in various diplomatic missions, he died of apoplexy, Nov. 24, 1691, and was buried in Winchester Cathedral. He published, besides "The Venetian Triumph," a "Panegyric to the King on his Restoration," 1660, and a "History of Isuf Bassa," 1684. Waller's lines were printed with "A Prospective of the Naval Triumph of the Venetians over the Turk. To Signor Pietro Liberi That Renowned and famous Painter. By Gio. Francesco Busenello. London, &c. 1658"; they did not appear among his poems till 1682.

P. 156, *l.* 1.—"The winged lion," the arms of Venice.

PART OF THE FOURTH BOOK OF VIRGIL, TRANSLATED.

"The Passion of Dido for Aeneas as it is incomparably exprest in the fourth book of Virgil, translated by Edmund Waller and Sidney Godolphin, Esqrs." 1658. Reprinted 1679. Waller's portion was first included among his poems in the "1664" edition. John Boys, in the preface to his "Aeneas His Descent into Hell," 1661, says, "The fourth (whose subject is the passion of Dido for Aeneas) hath been equally blest, as having been made speak English by the united Studies of two Gentlemen no less eminent than the former [Sandys]. I wish that the whole Aeneis had learn'd our modern dialect from such excellent masters."

P. 160, *l.* 86.—Cf. Pope, "Eloisa to Abelard," 166—

"A death-like silence, and a dread repose."

UPON THE DEATH OF THE LORD PROTECTOR.

These lines were first printed as a small-folio broad-side, [*Upon the late* | *Storme,* | *and of the death* | *of his* | *Highnesse* | *Ensuing the same,* | *By Mr. Waller. London Printed for H.H.*] and afterwards with Dryden's and Sprat's poems on the same occasion —[*Three Poems* | *Upon the Death of his late | Highnesse | Oliver | Lord Protector | Of | England, Scotland and | Ireland. Written |*

By { *Mr. Edm. Waller.*
{ *Mr. Jo. Dryden.*
{ *Mr. Sprat,* of Oxford.

London, | Printed by William Wilson, and are to be sold in | Well-yard neer Little St. Bartholomew's | Hospitall. **1659.** Title, and B—F 2 in fours. Reprinted in **1682,** *Three Poems Upon the Death of the Late Usurper Oliver Cromwell &c.*]

P. 162, *ll.* 9-12.—Fenton quotes from *Hercules Œtæus,* 1638-42—

> " Aggeritur omnis silva, et alternæ trabes
> In astra tollunt Herculi angustum rogum :
> Rapit alta flammis pinus, et robur tenax,
> Et brevior ilex silva : contexit pyram
> Populea silva, **frondis** Herculeæ nemus."

P. 162, *ll.* 14-16.—Dunkirk was ceded to England as a result of the victory of the combined armies of England and France over the Spaniards, June 17, 1658.

TO THE KING, UPON HIS MAJESTY'S HAPPY RETURN.

First edition—*To the | King, | Upon | His Majesty's | Happy Return.* | **After** the last line of the poem, **By Ed. Waller Esq.** | **Printed** *for Richard Marriot, in St. Dunstans Church-yard, Fleetstreet.* Title, and three leaves, small folio. MS. note on the title of the copy in the British Museum, *June 9th.*

P. 164, *ll.* 13-14.—Fenton sees in these lines a reference to the death of William Oughtred, Rector of Aldbury, the great mathematician, who, being upwards of eighty years of age, expired in a transport of joy upon hearing of the Restoration.

P. 165, *ll.* 41-42.—Cf. Dryden, "Astræa Redux," 76-77—

> "He made all countries where he came his own,
>   And, viewing monarchs' secret arts of sway,"—

P. 165, *ll.* 55-56.—Upon the medal struck in honour of the birth of Charles II. was inscribed HACTENUS . ANGLORUM . NULLI . round the four shields of (i) France and England, (ii) Scotland, (iii) France, and (iv) Ireland, he being the first Prince, born in Enland, entitled to bear these arms.

P. 166, *ll.* 83-84.—Two medals were struck at the Restoration, one inscribed "Sicut Argentum Probasti Me," and on the reverse, "Magna Opera Domini"; the other, "Carolus II. Rex.," and on the reverse, "Magnalia Dei."

P. 166, *ll.* 87-88.—Cf. Beaumont and Fletcher, "Philaster," act iii. sc. i.

> "The People
> Against their nature are all bent before him :
> And, like a field of standing corn that's mov'd
> With a stiff gale, their heads bow all one way."

P. 166, *ll.* 95-98.—Cf. Oldham, "To the Memory o Mr. C. Morwent"—

> "Those Indians who their Kings by Tortures choose,
>   Subjecting all the Royal Issue to that Test,
>   Could ne'er thy Sway refuse."

P. 167, *ll.* 107-108.—Cf. "The Maid's Tragedy Altered"—

> "Justice and Bounty in a Prince are things
>   That Subjects make as happy as their Kings."

A | Poem | on | St. James's | Park | As lately improved by his | Majesty. | Written by Edmund Waller, Esq ; | London, | Printed for Gabriel Bedel and Thomas Collins | at the Middle-Temple-Gate. 1661. Title and seven leaves, small folio. On p. 11 begins, "Of our late war with Spain," &c. ; at the end, "The Reader is desired to take notice that a false Copy of these verses on St. James's Park was surreptitiously and very imperfectly printed in one sheet, without the Author's knowledge and consent, several lines being there left out." I have not met with any traces of this surreptitious copy.

P. 168, *ll.* 1-3.—Cf. Pope, "Windsor Forest," 7, 8—

> " The groves of Eden vanished now so long,
> Live in description."

P. 168, *l.* 6.—Among the improvements was the introduction into the Park of a stream of water from the Thames.

P. 170, *ll.* 57-66.—The reference is to the game of "paille-maille," a favourite diversion of Charles II.

P. 171, *l.* 87.—Cardinal Wolsey.

P. 171, *l.* 95.—Cf. Addison, " The Campaign "—

> " To make the series of his toils complete."

P. 171, *ll.* 101-104.—Cf. Cowley, " Ode to Mr. Hobbes "—

> " So contraries on Ætna's top conspire ;
> Here hoary frosts ; and by them breaks out fire :
> A secure peace the faithful neighbours keep ;
> Th' embolden'd snow next to the flame does sleep,"

and Claudian, " Raptus Proserp." I. 164-68.

P. 172, *ll.* 109-10.—At the Coronation of Charles II. a medal was struck, upon the reverse of which the King was represented as a shepherd tending his sheep; the inscription was " Dixi . Custodiam . xxiii . April . 1661 . ", and on the edge, " Coronato . Pastore . Ovat . Ovile ."

P. 172, *ll.* 128-30.—This star, the references to which are numerous, was observed about noon, when Charles I. was returning from St. Paul's after having given thanks for the birth of his son.

TO THE QUEEN, UPON HER MAJESTY'S BIRTHDAY.

Catherine of Braganza was born Nov. 14, 1638, but her birthday was observed in England upon the 25th. These lines were written in 1663. " Orinda " (Mrs. Philips), who had herself written a poem on the same occasion, characterizes them as the worst verses that ever fell from Waller's pen.

P. 174, *ll.* 33-36.—Cf. Fairfax, " Godfrey of Bulloigne," xx. 129—

> " And her fair face, fair bosom, he bedews
> With tears ; tears of remorse, of ruth, of sorrow :
> As the pale rose her colour lost renews,
> With the fresh drops fall'n from the silver morrow :
> So, she revives ; and cheeks empurpled shows,
> Moist with their own tears, and with tears they borrow."

P. 174, *Nunc itaque,* &c.—This quotation concluded the edition of 1664.

TO A FAIR LADY PLAYING WITH A SNAKE.

Keck says, " 'Twas formerly not unusual among our English ladies for coolness in y⁰ hot weather to carry a snake in their sleeve."

INSTRUCTIONS TO A PAINTER.

In the original edition of this poem, after the title as given in the text, "Ut, qui vos Imperatores vestros, & Anglorum Res gestas semper ornavit, Humanitate vestrâ levatus, potius quam acerbitate violatus esse videatur. Cicero pro Arch. Poet. By Edm. Waller Esq; London, Printed for Henry Herringman, at the Anchor on the Lower Walk of the New Exchange. 1666." Small folio, title and eight leaves, A 2—E.

Waller, no doubt, derived the idea of this form of composition from the poem of Businello (see p. 156), and he himself was imitated by Denham, Marvell, and others, to such an extent that, in 1680, the writer of a broadside was provoked to revolt against the practice—

> " Each puny brother of the rhyming trade
> At every turn implores the Painter's aid,
> And fondly enamour'd of his own foul brat,
> Cries in an ecstacy, Paint this, Draw that!"

For the events celebrated in this poem, cf. Dryden, "Annus Mirabilis."

P. 176, *l.* 7.—The star appeared Dec. 24, 1664.

P. 177, *l.* 34.—Alluding to the orders sent to de Ruyter to return with the Smyrna and East India ships by the coasts of Norway and Denmark.

P. 177, *ll.* 39-41.—The Dutch Bordeaux fleet, together with other merchant-ships, to the number of more than a hundred and thirty, was captured and condemned by the English in Nov., 1664, before the declaration of war, while Opdam was lying at Goree.

P. 178, *ll.* 49-50.—In Oct., 1664, Sir Thomas Allen concluded a peace with the Algerines.

P. 178, *l.* 64.—The MS. in the copy which belonged to Col. Cunningham, to which I have before alluded, ends with this line.

P. 179, *l.* 94.—The English Hamburg fleet, missing a vessel which had been sent to warn them of the departure of the Duke of York for the coast of England, set sail, and was nearly all captured by the Dutch.

P. 181, *l.* 138.—Opdam commanded the combined fleets of Holland and Denmark and defeated the Swedes in the Sound, in 1658.

P. 181, *l.* 141.—Cf. Dryden, "Annus Mirabilis," st. 59—

> "On high-raised decks the haughty Belgians ride."

P. 181, *l.* 147.—The Earl of Falmouth, Lord Muskerry, and Mr. Boyle, second son of the Earl of Burlington.

P. 183, *l.* 213.—Cf. Dryden, "Annus Mirabilis," st. 280—"And eager flames give on to storm the rest," and "Indian Emperor," act ii., sc. 3, "The enemy gives on, by fury led."

P. 184, *ll.* 237-40.—Cf. Fuller, "David's Heinous Sin," st. 39—

> "Were there not used, in the days of yore,
>   Enough men-murdering engines, but our age
> Witty in wickedness, must make them more,
>   By new-found plots, man's malice to enrage?
>   So that fire-spitting cannons to the cost
>   Of Christian blood, all valour have engross'd,
>   Whose finding makes that many a life is lost."

UPON HER MAJESTY'S NEW BUILDINGS AT
SOMERSET HOUSE.

Henrietta Maria returned to England in December,
1660, and took up her residence at Somerset House,
which she enlarged and beautified.

Waller's lines first appeared as a **folio** broadside in
1665.

Cf. Cowley's poem on the same subject, and "**The**
Speech of Her Majesty the Queen Mother's Palace,
Upon the Reparation **and** Enlargement of it by Her
Majesty," **1665**.

EPITAPH ON THE ONLY SON **OF LORD** ANDOVER.

The son **of Viscount** Andover (eldest son **of the**
Earl of Berkshire), **for whom** this epitaph was in-
tended, died in **1641, and** was buried **in** New-Elm
Church, Oxfordshire.

TO MR. KILLIGREW, &C.

These lines, headed "**Of** Pandoras **not** being
approved **upon the** stage as a Tragedy," were published
in 1665, **with "Three** Playes Written by Sir William
Killigrew, Vice-Chamberlain **to** Her Majesty the
Queen Consort." Sir William Killigrew, the eldest
of the five sons of Sir Robert Killigrew, was born at
Hanworth in 1605; he was governor of Pendennis
Castle, and **commanded** two troops of the King's
Guard throughout the **Civil War ;** at the Restoration
he became Gentleman-Usher **to** the King, and later,
Vice-Chamberlain **to** the Queen Consort. **He** died
in **1693**.

z

EPIGRAM UPON THE GOLDEN MEDAL.

Frances Theresa, daughter of William Stuart, third son of the first Lord Blantyre, sat to Roettier, the medallist, as a model for Britannia. Pepys says (Feb. 25, 1667), "At my goldsmiths did observe the King's new medal, where in little there is Mrs. Stewart's face as well done as ever I saw anything in my whole life I think; and a pretty thing it is that he should choose her face to represent Britannia by."

Cf. Marvell, " Last Instructions to a Painter," 714, "And female Stewart there rules the four seas," alluding to the inscription "Quatuor Maria Vindico," which surrounded the figure of Britannia.

OF A TREE CUT IN PAPER.

Lines 15-20 of this poem are supplied from a transcript in Mr. Waller's possession, in which the title is, "On the Lady Isabella [Thynne's] cutting Trees in Paper.' (See p. 90.) There is a note at the end of the poem, " I had these verses from my Lady Long in 1656. Her LaP had several other copies of Mr. Waller's verses (of which Mr. Waller had not duplicats) which she lent to the Dutches of Beaufort, and were never return'd. Their friendship is now broken : but I hope her Grace will be so kind as to grant transcripts of them upon ye reprinting of ye book." The poem first appeared in the "1668 " edition.

TO A LADY FROM WHOM HE RECEIVED THE FOREGOING COPY, &c.

In the late Col. Cunningham's copy this was headed, "To Mrs. Steward who brought him the verses he had lost, and **was** then sitting to Mr. **Lilly** for her picture."

TO THE DUCHESS, WHEN HE PRESENTED **THIS** BOOK TO HER **ROYAL** HIGHNESS.

These lines, headed **"This** Booke, never Dedicated **to** any before humbly desires the Patronage of hir **R.** Highness," are inscribed **in a** copy of the edition of 1668, **now in** the British **Museum.** Mary of Modena **arrived in** England **Nov. 21, 1673,** but as this volume has also inscribed **in it the** lines on **the** Death of **the** Duke of Cambridge, it **was** probably not presented **to** her **till after the event which they** commemorate.

TO THE DUCHESS **OF ORLEANS.**

The Duchess **of Orleans, "la** belle **Henriette,"** took leave of the **Court at Dover, June 2, 1670,** returned to St. **Cloud, and died on the 30th** of the **same** month.

TO A FRIEND OF THE AUTHOR, **&C.**

George, first Earl of Berkeley (1628-1698), published **"Historical Applications** and Occasional Meditations **Upon** Several Subjects, Written **by a Person of Honour,"** in 1666. Waller's **lines** were **prefixed to a French** translation of this work published **in the** following year.

OF HER ROYAL HIGHNESS, **MOTHER TO** THE PRINCE **OF** ORANGE.

These lines did not appear among Waller's poems **till 1686, when no** doubt the title was added to them.

Mary, Princess of Orange (born Nov. 4, 1631), died
Dec. 24, 1660, and Ann, Duchess of York, in 1671.

ON THE STATUE OF KING CHARLES I.

This statue was cast, about 1630, by Hubert Le
Sœur for the Lord Treasurer Weston, who intended
to set it up in his gardens at Roehampton. Before it
could be removed from the place, near the church in
Covent Garden, where it was cast, the Civil War
began, and the Parliament sold it to John Rivett, a
brazier, with strict orders to break it up. Rivett is
said to have disposed of hundreds of knives, the
handles of which, he said, were made from the
bronze of the statue, but on May 16, 1660, the Earl
of Portland, the son of the Lord Treasurer, informed
the House of Lords that he had discovered where the
statue was hid, and as he supposed it was his, he
asked that the Sheriff might serve a replevin, there
being no court of law to which he could resort ; as,
however, Rivett subsequently presented it to the
King, it may be inferred that his right was recognized.
It was set up in its present position in 1674.

EPITAPH ON COLONEL CHARLES CAVENDISH.

Charles Cavendish, second son of William, second
Earl of Devonshire, was born in London, May 20,
1620. After spending some time in travelling, and
in gaining military experience in Holland, he returned
to England in 1642, and at once began to distinguish
himself in the Civil War. He was slain in an
engagement at Gainsborough, July 28, 1643, and
was buried at Newark ; his remains were removed
and laid by those of his mother at Derby, in 1675,
when this epitaph was probably written.

THE TRIPLE COMBAT.

The Duchess of Mazarin arrived in England in 1675 : she and the Duchess of Portsmouth are sufficiently well known, but I am unable to identify Chloris, the third combatant : possibly the Duchess of Cleveland may be meant. Evelyn speaks of seeing "the King sitting and toying with his concubines, Portsmouth, Cleveland, and Mazarin."

P. 205, *l.* 20.—The Duchess of Portsmouth was born in Lower Bretagne, which was known as "Little Britain."

F. 206, *l.* 42.—Alluding to the ravages committed by the French under Turenne in Alsace.

UPON OUR LATE LOSS OF THE DUKE OF CAMBRIDGE.

Charles, Duke of Cambridge, the first son of the Duke of York by Mary of Modena, was born Nov. 7, 1677, and died when he was about a month old.

OF THE LADA MARY, &C.

The Prince of Orange landed at Harwich, Oct. 9, 1677, and was married to Princess Mary on Nov. 4, following.

TO THE PRINCE OF ORANGE.

This poem was first printed by Chalmers in his edition of the British Poets, 1810.

ON THE DUKE OF MONMOUTH'S EXPEDITION.

The expedition was rendered necessary by a rebellion following on the murder of Archbishop Sharp, May 3, 1679. The Duke gained a decisive victory over the Covenanters at Bothwell-bridge, June 22, 1679.

P. 213, *ll.* 46 *ad fin.*—These lines are supplied from the common-place book of the poet's son.

UPON THE EARL OF ROSCOMMON'S TRANSLATION OF HORACE.

These lines were published in 1680 with a translation of the "Ars Poetica" by Wentworth Dillon, fourth Earl of Roscommon. Lord Roscommon (1633?-1685) was also the author of "An Essay upon Translated Verse," and is distinguished as the first critic who publicly praised "Paradise Lost."

P. 214, *ll.* 7-8.—Cf. p. 224, ll. 7-8.

P. 214, *ll.* 11-12.—Cf. Pope, "Essay on Criticism," 86-7.

> " The winged courser, like a gen'rous horse,
> Shows most true mettle when you check his course."

P. 215, *ll.* 23-8.—Cf. p. 226, ll. 9-14.

OF AN ELEGY MADE BY MRS. WHARTON, &C.

Mrs. Wharton, the wife of Thomas, eldest son of Philip, Lord Wharton, was daughter and co-heiress with the Countess of Abingdon, of Sir Henry Lee of Ditchley in Oxfordshire: her great-aunt was the Earl of Rochester's mother.

TO MR. CREECH, &C.

Fenton says that this poem is not Waller's, but in the Epistle Dedicatory to George Pitt, Esq. (2nd edition of the translation of Lucretius), Creech says, "But it would be improper to be my own trumpet, and Mr. Waller, Mr. Evelyn, and a Thousand more beside the publick approbation have freed me from all the little disturbances of Cavils." Thomas Creech, (born 1659), Fellow of Wadham College, Oxford, was the author of translations of portions of Ovid, Juvenal, Horace, &c; he took orders in 1699, and was presented by his college to the living of Welwyn, in Hertfordshire, **but** committed suicide in the following year.

SUNG BY MRS. KNIGHT, &C.

The Queen was born **on** St. Catherine's **Day,** and was frequently painted **in** the character of **that** Saint. Mrs. Knight is frequently mentioned by Pepys and Evelyn, **and** " Orinda " **tells** " Poliarchus " she would be **more proud to have** one assurance from him, than to **have her verses " composed by** Will. **Lawes, were he still alive, and sung by Mrs.** Knight."

OF TEA, COMMENDED **BY HER** MAJESTY.

This is, as far as **I have been** able to discover, the first poem in English written **in** praise of tea, which was in Waller's time an article of luxury. **It became** a fashionable beverage at Court, owing to the example of the Queen, **who had been** accustomed to **it in** Portugal, and **the treatise of** Bontekoe, **a** Dutch physician, published **in 1678,** setting forth its medicinal **virtues, led to its general use in** many parts **of Europe.**

P. **222,** *l.* 1.—Cf. Virgil, Ecl. vii. 62, " Formosæ **myrtus Veneri, sua** laurea **Phœbo."**

OF THE INVASION AND **DEFEAT OF** THE **TURKS.**

The Turks, **under the** Grand Vizier, **Cara** Mustapha, **laid** siege **to** Vienna in July, 1683, **but on Sept. 10 they were** driven from the walls in great **disorder by John Sobieski,** king of Poland. To shield **himself from the** obloquy of this defeat, the

Sultan was compelled to sacrifice his favourite, the Grand Vizier, who was strangled at Belgrade, Dec. 25, 1683.

P. 228, *l.* 16.—Ibrahim, the father of the Sultan Mahomet, had been deposed and strangled in 1649.

P. 229, *l.* 23.—The Grand Vizier had ordered the execution of the Bassa of Buda, on the pretended ground that he had failed in performing his duty in an engagement with the Imperialists before Vienna.

P. 229, *ll.* 39-40.—Cf. p. 234, ll. 1-2.

A PRESAGE OF THE RUIN OF THE TURKISH EMPIRE.

P. 233. "Ausus et ipse," &c. Virgil. Æn. v. 499.

TO HIS MAJESTY, UPON HIS MOTTO, &C.

This poem, reprinted here for the first time, is found in some copies of the edition of 1686, on a separate leaf inserted after the Table of Contents. Buda fell September 2, 1686, so it was probably written while the book was going through the press.

EPITAPH ON SIR GEORGE SPEKE.

Sir George Speke, second Baronet, was the son of Hugh Speke of Hasilbury, who died July 15, 1661. Sir George represented Bath and Chippenham in several Parliaments, and died Jan. 14, 1682. His mother (born Mayney) was Waller's niece.

EPITAPH ON HENRY DUNCH, ESQ.

This gentleman was a member of the family of Dunch, settled at Newington, a branch of the family of the same name of Little Wittenham, in Berkshire: they were connected by marriage with both Cromwell and Waller.

TO MR. GRANVILLE.

George Granville, or Grenville, second son of
Bernard Granville, was born in 1667 ; he was entered
at Trinity College, Cambridge, in 1677, and before
he was twelve years old recited verses of his own to
the Duchess of York when she visited the University.
He was created Lord Lansdowne, Dec. 30, 1711,
and died Jan. 30, 1735. Johnson says of him, "he
had no ambition above the imitation of Waller, of
whom he has copied the faults and very little more."

EPITAPH ON THE LADY SEDLEY.

Lady Sedley, mother of the poet, was the daughter
of Sir Henry Savil, the learned Provost of Eton.

P. **243,** *ll.* 27-8.—Cf. Walpole, *Account of Lord
Somers,* "one of those divine men, who, like a chapel
in a palace, remain unprofaned, while all the rest is
Tyranny, Corruption, and Folly."

UPON A LADY'S FISHING.

Printed here for the first time from a MS. in the
Library of the Royal Society.

ON MRS. HIGGONS.

These lines were first printed by Chalmers, in 1810.

DIVINE POEMS.

Waller's "Divine Poems" were, with the exception
of the lines on "The Fear of God," collected and
published in 1685. I only know of the existence of
one copy of the book, that in the library of Mr.
H. Buxton Forman, who has very kindly allowed me
to collate it.

Divine | Poems. | By Edmond Waller Esq; |

Licensed, | Octob. 3. 1685 | Rob. Midgley. | In the
Savoy : | Printed for Henry Herringman ; and are
to | be sold by Jos. Knight and Fran. Saun- | ders, at
the Sign of the Anchor in the | Lower Walk of the
New-Exchange in the | Strand. 1685. A 2—C 2 in
eights.

P. 255, *l.* 18.—This line was correctly printed in
the editions of 1682 and 1686, but in that of 1694,
by some accident, the word " Nature " dropped out ;
the editor of the next edition substituted " several,"
which has since appeared in the text, and destroyed
the sense.

P. 258.—The Latin lines are adapted from
Lucretius iii. 11-16, omitting l. 15—

> " Floriferis ut apes in saltibus omnia libant,
>   Omnia nos itidem depascimur **aurea dicta,**
>   Aurea perpetua semper dignissima vita,
>   **Nam** simul ac ratio tua cœpit vociferari.
>   .   .   .   .
>   Diffugiunt animi terrores "—

and Ovid, De Trist, iv. 1. 2-3, and 43-44—

> " Sic ubi **mota** calent viridi mea pectora thyrso
>   Altior," &c.

OF THE LAST VERSES IN THE BOOK.

Mr. Waller has a transcript of these lines, headed,
" The last verses my dear ffather made."

P. 272, *ll.* 12-13.—Fuller says that Monica, the
mother of Augustine, " saw a glimpse of happiness
through the chinks of her sickness-broken body."

Cf. Pope, " Dunciad," iv. 125-26—

> " And you, my Critics, in the chequer'd shade,
>   Admire new light thro' holes yourselves have made."

INDEX TO FIRST LINES.

THE END.